MIDNIGHT VISIT

A shot exploded outside our door. Then a man called out Pa's name.

"We want to know whether you're for or against us."

As the man talked, I slipped to the window and peeked out a corner just as a couple of riders lit torches. I could make out a dozen men on horseback, their faces covered with bandannas, lined up in front of our porch so close I could see the hatred in their eyes.

At the sight of the flames Pa screamed, "Don't fire the place! There's women and children in here!"

I aimed my gun at the nearest rider holding a torch. A mite smaller than the others, he had a nervous look about him, and his eyes blinked constantly.

Little did I know I had a bead on Jesse James. . . .

The Memoirs of H. H. Lomax:

THE DEMISE OF BILLY THE KID
THE REDEMPTION OF JESSE JAMES

THE REDEMPTION
OF
JESSE JAMES

Preston Lewis

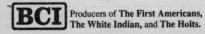

BCI Producers of **The First Americans,**
The White Indian, and **The Holts.**

Book Creations Inc., Canaan, NY • Lyle Kenyon Engel, Founder

BANTAM BOOKS
NEW YORK • TORONTO • LONDON • SYDNEY • AUCKLAND

THE REDEMPTION OF JESSE JAMES

*A Bantam Book / published by arrangement with
Book Creations Inc.*

Bantam edition / September 1995

*Produced by Book Creations Inc.
Lyle Kenyon Engel, Founder*

ISBN 0-553-56542-7

Published simultaneously in the United States and Canada

*Bantam Books are published by Bantam Books, a division of Bantam
Doubleday Dell Publishing Group, Inc. Its trademark, consisting of
the words "Bantam Books" and the portrayal of a rooster, is
Registered in U.S. Patent and Trademark Office and in other
countries. Marca Registrada. Bantam Books, 1540 Broadway, New
York, New York 10036.*

PRINTED IN THE UNITED STATES OF AMERICA

RAD   0 9 8 7 6 5 4 3 2 1

For Scott and Melissa,
who have brought so much joy
to my life.

Introduction

History is made up of little people whose names are usually forgotten with the passage of time. Henry Harrison Lomax was such a person. Those who have read *The Demise of Billy the Kid*, the initial volume in THE MEMOIRS OF H. H. LOMAX, will remember that I first came upon this vagabond's writings while conducting research at the Southwest Collection on the campus of Texas Tech University.

I was delighted to have the opportunity to study those papers. This is the second manuscript to result from that work. Though others had seen the Lomax collection, I was the first to find it worth extensive study, primarily because Lomax was an insignificant character. Historians are more interested in the lawmakers, the generals, and the politicians. Those were the types of people Henry Harrison Lomax despised, likely because they had succeeded in life whereas his own story was largely a succession of failures.

Lomax seems to have been well traveled and well acquainted—though not always on the best of terms—with some of the biggest names in the history of the Old West. Seeking wealth and adventure, he left home in the aftermath of the Civil War. He found more adventure than wealth. If his stories are to be believed—and I find

1

they generally stand up to historical scrutiny—he came within an eyelash of great wealth several times, only to be denied those riches by circumstance or unscrupulous characters. When he grew too infirm to continue his travels, he went to live with his youngest sister, Harriet Lomax Scott. He was in his seventies or eighties when he started writing his memoirs, primarily to spite his sister, who apparently grew tired of his constant ramblings about his western adventures and told him to write his stories down so she wouldn't have to listen to him. The memoirs became the passion of his final years, for he wrote about twenty-two thousand pages and filled two trunks with them.

From his writings in his later years Lomax emerges as an irascible man, perhaps slightly embittered by his life's failures, whether at finding wealth or a wife. The best I can tell, he was never married, though he tried several times. He apparently had no children and certainly no legitimate ones. His legacy was simply his writings, however flawed they might be.

But his writings were no more flawed than the man himself. That has been the appeal of his memoirs to me. He wrote about himself and others with an unblinking eye. By today's enlightened standards he would be considered a racist, a chauvinist, or several of the other "ists" the proponents of political correctness brand those they consider offensive. I have tried to tone down Lomax's language where it might be considered objectionable, without, however, emasculating his writing or his sentiment. After all, he was writing about a different era of our history. Had he been as enlightened as many of these self-same proponents of political correctness, his prose would have been as colorless as theirs. As it is, his writings give an unvarnished view of life in the Ozarks, in the mining camps, on the cattle drives, with the railroads, and beside the buffalo hunters.

The Redemption of Jesse James covers the Civil War years, when Arkansas teetered between the Union and the

Confederacy and Lomax teetered between childhood and adulthood. Henry Harrison Lomax was born January 9, 1850, the next to youngest of the nine children of George Washington Lomax and his wife, the former Abigail Dawson. About 1839 the couple were married in Floyd County, Kentucky, when he was twenty-seven and she was eighteen. From there they moved to Arkansas, where all their children were born.

The 1860 census for Cane Hill, Washington County, Arkansas, records the nine children of George Washington and Abigail Lomax:

Thomas Jefferson Lomax, born 1840
Constance Louise Lomax, 1841
John Adams Lomax, 1842
James Monroe Lomax, 1844
Andrew Jackson Lomax, 1845
Van Buren Lomax, also 1845
Melissa Irene Lomax, 1847
Henry Harrison Lomax, 1850
Harriet Lomax, 1853

Except for Constance Louise Lomax, all H. H. Lomax's brothers and sisters are mentioned in his account of the Civil War years. To date—and I've read just over half of Lomax's papers—I have been unable to determine what happened to Constance during those troubled years.

Other Cane Hill area residents listed in the 1860 census and pertinent to *The Redemption of Jesse James* include the Burke and Fudge families.

Gordon Burke and his wife, SincereAnne, both born in 1826, were married about 1842 in Alabama and came to Arkansas two years later. Their offspring were:

DeeAnne Burke, born 1843
RuthAnne Burke, 1845
LouAnne Burke, 1849
Joseph Donald Burke, 1851

Beryl Fudge and his wife, Corrine, were married about 1845, apparently in Missouri, where they may have had two children, both of whom died shortly after birth. They moved to Arkansas about 1848 and had one more child, Amanda Beth Fudge, in 1849. Amanda seems to have been the first girl Lomax ever took a shine to. The outcome of that relationship may well explain why he never took a wife. That, though, is mere speculation.

In 1993 I visited Washington County with Bantam Editor Tom Dupree. We saw what was left of Cane Hill, once the biggest town in Washington County but today a sleepy community that time and the major highways have passed by. The Lomax place was south of Cane Hill near where the abandoned mill is today on State Highway 45. The hills are thick with trees and brush, and the farms are still worked as they were more than a century ago.

Though H. H. Lomax throughout his memoirs refers to his home as Cane Hill, it was variously known as Steam Mill and Boonsboro or Boonsborough during his family's life there. But Cane Hill was the community's first and last name. Cane Hill has the distinction of being the site of one of the first colleges west of the Mississippi. When the war broke out, Cane Hill College closed its doors, and the entire faculty and student body marched off to war. Locals say the unit was the first company west of the Mississippi formed to serve the Confederacy.

Dupree and I also walked the Prairie Grove Battlefield, a well-kept park about seven miles northeast of Cane Hill. Though the battle was nothing on the scale of those fought back east or even in Tennessee, it was the largest fought in Washington County during the Civil War. The 34th Arkansas Infantry, a Washington County regiment that included three of Henry Lomax's brothers, fought on home soil at Prairie Grove. Though today few outside of Arkansas have heard of the battle, it was pivotal for Cane Hill because it assured Union control of Washington County. The Confederates fought back the only way they could—guerrilla warfare. Ultimately this internecine warfare pitted neighbor against neighbor and, surprisingly, often turned allies against each other. The motives of the guerrillas, bushwhackers, or partisans, as they often were called, ranged from greed to lust, but most often they were merely a matter of survival.

Before I encountered the memoirs of H. H. Lomax, I had given little thought to pioneer and Civil War life in Arkansas; the state seemed almost too eastern to have been involved in the winning of the West. I've since discovered its rich and colorful pioneer history and have developed a particular fondness for Washington County. It's a good place for your ancestors to have lived.

—PRESTON LEWIS
Lubbock, Texas
January 1995

Chapter One

I never much cared for Jesse James. He was about as likable as a rabid mongrel, but sorry though he may have been, he was downright lovable compared to his momma. Now there was a cur of a woman. She was rough as a cob and twice as ugly, which is a bad thing to say about a man's momma, even if it's true.

I never took to her and she never took to me, though she did take out after me a couple times, once with a shotgun and once with a frying pan. Some said Jesse James finally ran me out of the Ozarks, but that just wasn't true. My conscience and his momma are what sent me packing west.

The truth of the matter is I might never have met any of the James family had it not been for Abraham Lincoln. Old Abe—not some cannonball over Fort Sumter and not slavery—brought on the War Between the States, and the war brought out the meanness of folks in the Ozarks.

Up until then the Ozarks was as near to heaven as a young boy could find, short of getting into some girl's sack drawers. There were streams to fish, woods to hunt, rocks to throw, trees to climb, and places to hide. Of course, my folks didn't see it that way. To them there were fields to plow, cows to milk, hogs to feed, wood to chop, water to tote, and other innumerable chores to do.

We lived on 228 acres of land bordering Jordan Creek about a mile south of Cane Hill, Arkansas. Things weren't so bad the year the war started, since most of the fighting took place up in Missouri. That spring we planted corn, Irish potatoes, wheat, and vegetables on the thirty-four acres of land Pa and his sons, myself included, had cleared of trees and stumps over the years. Unlike some families around Cane Hill, we didn't have any slaves, unless that's what you consider us kids—and at times that's what I figured Pa and Momma thought of us. Some days when Pa was riding me about sloshing milk from the pail or chopping more crop than weeds when I hoed the fields, I decided war would be a fine change from my personal bondage. I couldn't figure why Old Abe was more concerned about freeing the slaves than about freeing me from the yoke my parents had placed on my skinny shoulders.

The way I saw it, if Pa and Momma had brought me into the world, they should've made my life easier rather than putting me to doing chores. Almost from the day I was born, I was ready to run away from home. Pa was in the goldfields of California, trying to get rich, when I was birthed on January 9, 1850. Momma named me Henry Harrison Lomax because all my brothers had been named after presidents, like my father, George Washington Lomax. She told folks my initials but not my name, insisting that Pa would be the first one she would tell, me being his offspring. I guess no one would have ever known my full name had something happened to Pa in California. Around Cane Hill folks took to calling me Hurry Home Lomax since no one knew my real name. Even after Pa returned in 1851, some folks still called me Hurry Home.

Momma said I was born with the worst case of wanderlust she had ever seen. If Thomas Jefferson Lomax, my oldest brother, hadn't barred the door and fought me off, I would've crawled away from Cane Hill the day after

I was born, she said. Now, I never knew Momma to
stretch the truth, so I figure that was the gospel. If I
hadn't felt the urge to move before my pa returned from
California, I sure did after he got back. He spoke of
places—all with romantic names like the Sierra Nevadas,
the Pacific Ocean, and the Golden Gate—he had seen in
California. When he told of his adventures, my feet'd start
to moving and my mind'd go to wandering. I knew one
day I'd see those things for myself.

Pa didn't come back rich from California. In fact, he
had lost or traded everything he took with him, save a
cracked ambrotype of Momma and the clothes on his
back. The only things he returned with that he didn't have
when he left were a crippled leg and an American flag
that had flown over Sutter's Mill itself. That limp kept
him out of the war, but the flag got him—and me—into
trouble.

Through the end of 1861 we figured our out-of-the-
way place was going to avoid the war, even though my
two oldest brothers had already enlisted by then. Early
on it seemed the Union and the Confederacy had both
forgotten about our corner of Arkansas. We got in our
crops that fall and felt about as smug as a hog in the corn
crib.

That all changed in 1862. War has a way of spreading
like a bloodstain, and it began to drip over the border into
Arkansas. If the damn Missourians had seceded from the
Union like they should have, we might've never had to
worry about hiding our valuables and hoarding our food,
but they didn't have the guts God gave a worm, so they
stuck with the Union.

In February of 1862 we began hearing of trouble in
Arkansas: a little fight at Potts Hill, then a tiff over at
Sugar Creek, and finally a skirmish at Bentonville in Benton County just to the north of us. When March came
around there was a run-in at Berryville and finally a hell
of a fight at Elkhorn Tavern in Benton County. Elkhorn
Tavern claimed a thousand or more Confederate casual-

ties and probably half again as many Yankee dead and wounded. Fact was, Confederate soldiers blindfolded could outshoot Yankees in daylight *and* in dark, but there were just so damn many of them bluebellies down south that we couldn't make ammunition fast enough to wipe them out. It was like attacking a plague of locusts with a folded newspaper—you knew you had to be killing plenty but there were thousands more crawling at your feet. Since the Yankees couldn't outshoot us, they damn sure tried their best to outloot us. They'd swipe an acorn from a crippled squirrel, and there were times us home folk couldn't take a leak without a Yankee trying to steal it.

At the start of the war my two oldest brothers, Thomas Jefferson and John Adams, enlisted in Fayetteville. They wound up in the 3rd Arkansas Infantry and were sent east to fight. We all went to Fayetteville to see them off. Momma insisted on getting an ambrotype made of the family, and it became her treasure because it showed all her sons together.

Me and my other brothers—James Monroe, Andrew Jackson, and Van Buren—wanted to enlist, too, because war seemed such a grand and noble thing, what with the bands playing, the girls swooning, and the soldiers marching in step with good rifles on their shoulders. Momma, though, dashed our Confederate patriotism, saying two sons were enough to send off to war, and Pa said the Southern boys'd whip those Yankees faster than a banker'd steal you blind.

Me and my brothers, of course, were mightily disappointed that we couldn't go east with Tom and John to assist with the spanking. I mostly wanted to see some new territory, even if it was east rather than west. And if I had to fight Yankees to do it, that was okay with me. Jim, Andy, and Van were interested in whipping Yankees, too, but they were of courting age and figured a uniform was a good way to impress the ladies. Either way, it was embarrassing that we couldn't stand up to our momma and do what a man—or boy—felt like doing.

Now, not everybody in northwest Arkansas rallied round the Confederacy. Some up and joined the Yankee army. A good number more, likely of inferior intelligence and breeding, felt sorry for the Yankees, them being so far from home and their mommas, but not sorry enough to join them and not men enough to stand up to the rest of us. These fellows took to the hills, hiding out and avoiding us of saner Southern mind. To my way of thinking, those fellows should've just moved north into Missouri among their own kind.

Some men just disappeared, and you didn't know what happened to them for years. Gordon Burke was one of those. His place bordered ours across Jordan Creek. He was so dumb he didn't know ground beans from coffee—and he was the smart one of his brood. His wife, SincereAnne, was plainer than a log cabin and wouldn't have had a man look at her, much less marry her, if it weren't for her eyes. They were crossed.

Gordon and SincereAnne Burke had three girls—DeeAnne, RuthAnne, and LouAnne—before they got it right and had a boy. They named him Joe Don, though for the life of me I can't understand why it wasn't Joe-Anne. Most folks around Cane Hill, though, came to call him Pooty Burke because he had this talent all us other boys admired. He could stink up a hollow quicker than a polecat.

I always figured the aroma of his pipe music was what turned his mother's eyes ajar. And I suspect the noise was what made a coward of his father—it sounded too much like artillery. When the war started, Gordon Burke didn't say much. Everyone figured he was just too dumb to understand politics, though most knew he resented slavery, likely because he didn't have any slaves of his own.

After the battle of Elkhorn Tavern, the Confederate government sent General T. C. Hindman to Arkansas to raise the soldiers necessary to drive the Yankees back up to Missouri where they belonged. The appointment of

General Hindman taught me there was one thing more powerful than Momma, and that was the damned government. Hindman declared martial law and began to enforce the conscription act against every able-bodied man in the region. It wasn't enough that two of my brothers had volunteered to fight Yankees; the damned government decided it would volunteer the rest of them. Just a few months before, us four remaining Lomax boys had been willing to sign up for the glorious adventure, and then the damned government came along and didn't give us a choice. Not only that, they were taking our horses, mules, food, and fodder for the cause. We were fortunate to hold on to two broken-down old mules. What the Confederate army didn't take, the damn Yankees tried to loot. It got where your friends were no better than your enemies.

Jim, Andy, and Van marched off to war as part of the 34th Arkansas Infantry. Pa was dismissed for service, since his crippled leg made him unfit for what infantry do the most—march. The army deemed me too young for soldiering, calling me seed corn for the South. Pooty's pa was considered able-bodied—there being no requirement for an able mind—and was ordered to join the Confederate Army just like my brothers. That's when Gordon Burke decided he couldn't fight to preserve slavery, no matter that he would've been fighting to protect his home and family as well. So, like a lot of other Union sympathizers, he left his family and took to the hills.

That summer General Hindman issued an order permitting small groups of Southern men to operate behind enemy lines as irregular troops. We came to call them bushwhackers. So not only did we have legitimate Confederate and Union troops wandering the hills trying to kill each other, we had secesh and Union irregulars ambushing each other and plaguing every household in Arkansas. Anytime you met folks you had to be careful what you said, because you never knew for certain whose side they were on. If you insulted the President, it had better be the right one—Abe Lincoln or Jeff Davis—or it was

treason on the spot and you could get shot, hung, or
knifed. On top of that, many bushwhackers became little
more than common outlaws, using the breakdown of es-
tablished law as an excuse to settle personal grudges, steal
from defenseless women and children, and burn homes
and crops.

I couldn't decide if Gordon Burke was a bushwhacker or just a coward. I just know the day the Confederates came back to collect the so-called volunteers, he
had retreated into the hills. So we found ourselves neigh-
boring a known—but cowardly—Union sympathizer.
Though I think Pa leaned toward the Union, he had five
sons fighting for the Confederacy, so we were considered
secesh.

For a while our lives didn't change much, though
having but two broken-down mules instead of the other
six strong ones cut into our farming. Other than that
everything remained the same. I still thought Pooty was
dumb, and I knew for a fact his sisters were so ugly flies
wouldn't land on them.

Pooty and I got in rock fights and went about making
each other's lives as miserable as we could, but we had
been doing that before the war broke out. Pooty didn't
have much of a sense of humor and always held grudges—
like the time we took our hounds coon hunting. We treed
a big old coon, and one of us had to climb up and knock
him out of the tree so the hounds could tear him apart. I
grabbed a stout branch and climbed halfway to the moon
before I was within reach of that snarling, overgrown ro-
dent. I shook the limb, but he held on, so I jabbed him
lightly and saw I could knock him off when the time was
right. The old hound dogs just howled and barked, anxious for their supper.

"I can't budge him!" I shouted down. "Throw some
rocks at him."

After I explained to Pooty what a rock was, he found
a couple and chunked them, but his aim was as bad as a
Yankee soldier's. I yelled to him to move closer in where
he had a better chance of hitting the raccoon. When he

was within range, I hauled off and swatted that coon off the limb. I never saw a coon fly, but that one never quit trying until he landed right at Pooty's feet. All of a sudden Pooty disappeared in a ball of growling fur. When he reappeared from amidst the hounds and the coon, he was cursing and threatening me.

"You did that on purpose," he yelled, "trying to knock that coon on my feet."

"That's a damn lie," I answered truthfully. I'd been aiming for his head.

Pooty couldn't take a joke. Take the time I found a momma and her kittens under a rock pile. I convinced Pooty it'd be fun to catch and kill them, and I told him if he'd poke them out with a stick, I'd grab them so he wouldn't get scratched. He thought that was a good idea. He found a dead limb and got down on his hands and knees, then hesitated and studied me real hard.

"This ain't a bobcat den, is it?"

"Nope."

"Promise?"

"Cross my heart and hope to die."

He nodded confidently and shoved the limb into the den.

"It's a polecat den," I said.

Pooty jumped back, but it was too late. Momma skunk sprayed him in the face. I'd never seen anyone turn green before, but Pooty did and took to puking. He ran away screaming and jumped in Jordan Creek, but skunk vapors don't wash off that easily. If he hadn't smelled so bad, I would've helped.

He ran to SincereAnne, and I could've sworn the odor straightened her eyes for a minute. She got some vinegar and tried to wash the stink off, but for all her scrubbing and all Pooty's yelling and puking, it only cut the aroma slightly. Usually when vinegar failed to remove the stink from clothes, we would bury them. I suggested we do that with Pooty, but no one saw the humor in it, especially not SincereAnne.

I got in some trouble over this. Pa thrashed my behind but good with his razor strop. In fact, I don't remember a harder spanking, save maybe the time my sister Melissa annoyed me and I hauled off and slapped her. Pa spanked me but good, teaching me a lesson I never forgot: Never slap a female when he was around. Anyway, Momma gave SincereAnne all her vinegar and then commenced to lecturing me about what the Good Book said about loving thy neighbor as thyself. Of course, the Good Lord never had Pooty Burke and his ugly sisters for neighbors, either, or there might have been one less commandment.

For all our differences, the War Between the States finally brought me and Pooty together, much to our mutual disgust. Come late summer of 1862, after most of the able-bodied men had been conscripted and the rest had taken to the hills, cavalry from both armies roamed about looking for each other. In addition to that, the bushwhackers on both sides became predators, at first tormenting the households of those unsympathetic to their cause and then, as the war wore on, tormenting everybody who was weaker than them. After several farms around Cane Hill had been hit by one side or the other, Pa sat down at the supper table one night and announced that SincereAnne and her kids were coming to live with us.

I about spat out the corn bread and cane syrup I was eating. "Why? They ain't orphans," I said, looking to Momma for support.

"Times are mean," Pa answered, "especially for a woman and children alone."

My sister Melissa, who was three years older than me, crossed her arms and shook her head, giving Pa a stare that would've melted wax. "No beaus'll come calling me if those ugly Burke girls move in." I admired Lissa's way with words and regretted I'd ever slapped her.

Momma, though, wasn't as appreciative. "There won't be many beaus, period, coming around until this war is over. And that's not a nice thing to say about those girls."

I couldn't help but come to Lissa's aid. "You always told us to tell the truth, Momma."

"They can't help it," she started, "if they're ug—homely."

"Sure they can," I shot back. "They can wear sacks over their heads."

"Henry Harrison Lomax," Pa said, his voice rising like a bad wind, "the decision has been made for their safety and ours."

"Ours?" I couldn't believe what Pa had said.

"Between the soldiers and the bushwhackers, things aren't safe for anybody, so folks are pairing off, Union families with Confederate families."

Lissa cocked her head at Pa. "Are you for the South or not? You don't believe in slavery, and neither does old man Burke."

Nobody had ever asked Pa that before. "My boys are fighting for the South. I'm for my boys."

"You didn't answer my question, Pa," she shot back.

"Girl, I gave you all the answer you're gonna get."

"I ain't a girl, Pa."

"You ain't a woman, either."

Lissa bowed up her back and pouted her lips until she looked like a perch. Pa's face reddened, and he pointed his fork at me, then at Lissa, Momma, and meek little Harriet, my baby sister. "There'll be no back talk to me at the table or anytime after the Burkes move in. I ain't gonna put up with it in front of others."

Nothing else was said at the supper table. Once Pa had made up his mind, he was harder to budge than a fat lady on an anvil.

I went to bed that night lower than a mole's belly and prayed all the skunk perfume had faded from Pooty's face. The idea of losing the war didn't seem nearly as upsetting as the idea of Pooty moving in with us. It wasn't fair, what with his sisters being so damn ugly. At least with Lissa and Harriet, who were damn pretty—though I didn't care for them knowing I thought that—Pooty was going to have some decent scenery to look at. Me, I was just going to have to pray I never saw his sisters in the altogether or it might turn me into a gelding.

Almost as bad as the thought of the Burke girls was the fact that I was going to have to share my loft bed with Pooty. Our house had a kitchen and separate eating room on one end and two bedrooms on the other end. You couldn't go from the kitchen to the bedrooms without going outside and across the dogtrot or climbing into the loft that ran the length of the house and opened into the kitchen and Ma and Pa's bedroom. The loft was where my sisters and I slept.

Before I climbed into bed, I hid my prized belongings. I wedged my bag of marbles behind a loose brick in the chimney and slipped the dog-eared deck of playing cards Momma didn't know I had between a rafter and a loose shingle. I made sure my pocketknife stayed in my pocket. The only other thing I had was the American flag Pa had brought back from California. There wasn't any place big enough to hide it, so I put it on a broken milk stool I propped against the angled roof where it met the loft floor.

For all my brothers, the war had already begun. For me it began the next day when Pooty Burke came to stay with us. Had he stayed where he belonged, I would never have had the pleasure of meeting Jesse James or kissing Amanda Fudge.

Chapter Two

Come midmorning that awful next day, Pa hitched up our two broken-down mules to the farm wagon and ordered me to go with him to the Burke place. Though our homes weren't two hundred yards from each other, we had to go upstream a quarter-mile to the nearest wagon crossing, then back down to the Burke place. I wasn't too pleased to learn that we would be carrying their furniture and belongings back to our house. As far as I was concerned, Pooty could tote them across Jordan Creek himself, but Pa had a different idea about being neighborly than I did.

SincereAnne Burke was standing on the porch, arms crossed, foot tapping on the wooden plank, as we approached. The Burke hounds took to yapping and howling. When Pa halted the team beside the porch, SincereAnne greeted him. "It's about time you showed up."

Pa released a deep breath and rattled the reins. The confused mules hesitated, then jerked the wagon forward. "Good day, Mrs. Burke," Pa said as he circled the wagon around and started back for the crossing. My smile grew wider than a crescent moon. Pa wasn't going to take any sass from the Burkes either.

SincereAnne looked like she had been slapped with

a piece of raw liver, her eyes moving in opposite directions. She took to running after the wagon. "George, George, please," she cried.

I waved good-bye, then stuck out my tongue when I saw Pooty and his sisters run out onto the porch. Pa jerked the wagon to a halt just then and almost made me bite my tongue off.

SincereAnne had this sour expression on her face like she'd been sucking on green persimmons. Before she could say a thing, Pa pointed his finger at her nose. "I ain't your husband, and I won't be spoken down to. I'll be neighborly and watch out for you and your girls until all the meanness is through, but don't call me George again. It's Mr. Lomax to you and your brood."

SincereAnne began to eat humble pie, apologizing for her rudeness, begging for one more chance and promising she'd do better. I figured that was like promising to take the stubborn out of a mule.

Pa nodded and aimed the wagon back toward the Burke cabin, which was maybe a third the size of ours, Gordon Burke not having enough sons to add on to the place. Once again he stopped the wagon beside the porch, then tied the reins and jumped down. "Come on, Henry," he said, "let's load up their belongings and get home."

No sooner had I touched shoe to ground than SincereAnne was there, just as courteous as a Sunday School teacher. "Whatever you want us to do to help, Mr. Lomax," she offered, "you just let us know. Girls."

I about gagged when the three Burke sisters stepped off the porch. They were dressed in their best gingham dresses and matching bonnets. They were uglier than weeds in a field but at least had the good sense to wear their bonnets so you only saw their faces from the front. As they marched by me, LouAnne, the youngest, hauled off and slapped me across the cheek.

"It's not nice to stick our your tongue." She smiled.

I spun around to see if Pa'd seen what she'd done, but he was talking to SincereAnne. I was tempted to slap

LouAnne back but decided that wasn't smart, not within Pa's sight.

"Point out what you want loaded," Pa said, leading me into the cabin, "and have Pooty give us a hand."

"You mean Joe Don?"

I giggled as I passed Pooty, but he stuck out his foot and tripped me. I stumbled into Pa, who turned around to slap me.

"Pooty tripped me."

"His name is Joe Don," SincereAnne reminded me.

"Whatever his name is, he tripped me," I *reminded* her.

"He did not."

Pooty laughed.

"Give us a hand, JoeAnne," I called, and the laughing stopped.

It took us a half hour to load two beds, a couple rocking chairs, three trunks of clothes and keepsakes, and all the food she had in the house, including the store-bought and everything she had canned. Then we cleared out the smokehouse and took from the barn what tools Pa thought we would need.

Finally Pooty brought out the shotgun, the only weapon Gordon Burke had left his family before fleeing.

"I'll take that," Pa said, grabbing it from him. "Is it loaded?"

"Nope," Pooty replied.

"Where's the powder and shot?" Pa asked.

"Ain't none."

"Hard to hunt or defend yourself without powder and shot."

"He can always club them to death," I suggested.

Pa put the gun in the wagon and told the girls to climb aboard. I averted my eyes so I wouldn't be blinded. "I figure on walking back," I announced, not caring to be seen with a wagonload of ugly.

Pa's eyes narrowed. I could tell he was no more excited about the prospect of riding with those women than I was, but before he could order me otherwise, he was

distracted by a commotion barreling out of the woods. A
black stallion burst out of the trees and charged our way.

"Wait!" called the rider in a soft, feminine voice.

Everyone tensed for a moment until Pooty announced, "It's Amanda." He licked his lips.

I'd never seen a girl ride like that, but here she came,
heels flailing against the stallion's flank. The galloping
horse unnerved our mules. They stamped and tossed their
heads. I wondered how come the army had stolen our
mules yet missed such a fine steed.

Amanda charged to the very corner of the cabin, then
reined the horse up hard and jumped off as it stopped.
She landed on the ground as gracefully as a panther, and
I was amazed to see she had been riding bareback. I was
even more impressed when I studied her. She had hair
the color of fresh straw and eyes as green as new grass.
She was just beginning to fill out her dress, which meant
she was about my age or a little older. Unlike the skinny
Burke sisters, she had some plump flesh on her bones.

Amanda was everything the Burke sisters were not,
and I was immediately taken by her.

"I came to say good-bye," she announced.

"We're just moving across the creek," Pooty said.

"I'm not supposed to cross the creek, but Father
won't know, as long as I don't tarry." She winked at Pooty.

"It's not far," I announced. "I can show you."

Amanda looked my way. "Who are you?"

"I'm Henry Lomax, and this is my father. The
Burkes'll be living at our place."

"Amanda Fudge is my name," she said.

Pa climbed onto the wagon seat. "Time we were going," he said. SincereAnne shook her head as she looked
at her house a final time, then joined Pa in the wagon.

I had heard of the Fudges, but they pretty much kept
to themselves, Amanda being their only child and them
sheltering her as much as they could, though there was
gossip of her momma slipping out of her husband's traces
once in a while.

"Pa," I volunteered, "I can ride with Amanda across the creek here and show her our place so she won't have to stay long."

Pa nodded. I was happy as a duck in water until Pooty spoke up.

"I'll ride, too."

"The horse won't carry three," I objected.

Amanda gave me the cutest smile ever sent my direction. "Sure it will."

Though I had just met her, I thought I saw a glint of mischief in the twinkle of her green eyes and the curve of her lips.

"Then everybody get moving," Pa said as he rattled the reins and turned the wagon toward the crossing.

Amanda vaulted up on the horse's back in the blink of an eye, then pointed at me. "You next." She edged the stallion toward me and I jumped up, swinging my leg over the animal's back, then slid behind her and slipped my arms around her waist.

"You ready, JoeAnne?" I asked Pooty. To my delight Amanda giggled.

Pooty growled and made a leap for the horse, but just then Amanda flicked the reins, and the stallion stepped away from him. Pooty splattered against his side and fell to the ground.

Amanda whispered over her shoulder, "Push him off in the creek."

I laughed. Pooty thought I was laughing at him and took to grumbling.

"I'm sorry," Amanda purred. "The stallion's frisky."

Pooty bounced up from the ground, took a running start, then stopped to make sure the stallion wasn't going to flinch again. The animal stood like a rock. Pooty clambered aboard and put his arms around my waist.

"Get your hands off me," I ordered.

"You got your arms around Amanda."

"I won't ride fast, boys," Amanda announced as she

put her hand on mine and pulled my arms from her waist.
I tingled at the touch of her fingers.

Pooty settled his crease on the stallion's back, then
whistled to his hounds.

"You boys ready?" Amanda asked.

"I am," I said.

"No tricks," Pooty said.

Amanda turned the horse toward the creek and
started at a walk, with Pooty's hounds trailing us. Pooty
took to whistling a little ditty, and Amanda took to giggling. When we reached the stream, she let her stallion
blow and water for a moment. Then, halfway across, she
yelled, "Now!"

I jerked my elbows forward, then backward, ram-
ming them into Pooty's gut. He stopped whistling and
gasped for air.

Amanda shook the stallion's reins, and the animal
bolted forward. I grabbed her waist. Pooty screamed, flailing to grab my arm or shirt. The stallion charged across
the creek, and Pooty tumbled backward into the water.

I looked back in time to see him splash.

The stallion emerged from the stream, then hit the
bank, quickly climbing the steep slope to the plain, where
our home and fields awaited. Amanda and I were whooping and hollering at our trick. When we reached the
house, I jumped down, took the reins, and tied the stallion
to a porch post. Amanda slid off the animal, both of us
still laughing.

"That was fun," she said, then leaned over and kissed
me on the cheek. It *had* been fun, but not near as much
fun as the touch of her lips.

It was a bit embarrassing, though, when I realized
my little sister Harriet was sitting on the porch. "A girl
kissed Henry, Momma, a girl kissed Henry!" she yelled.

Momma came out on the porch, accompanied by
Lissa. They all stared, and I knew they were about to ask
a lot of questions, but Pooty never gave them a chance.
He came barreling up the creek embankment, straight for

me. I stepped away from Amanda, doubled my fists, and stood there in my best prizefighter pose, trying to impress Amanda even more.

With the look of a wild animal in his eyes, Pooty screamed wildly and charged headlong into me. As I swung for him, he dove for my waist, driving me into the ground and knocking my breath away for a moment. We rolled around in the dirt, swinging and clawing for each other but mostly missing. Pooty was soaked. My clothes got wet and stained with mud, grass, and fresh horse apples deposited by Amanda's stallion. I was embarrassed that Pooty had knocked me down in front of her.

We both managed to get to our feet and take several more wild swings at each other.

"Stop it!" Momma yelled. "Stop it!"

When we didn't, she waded into the battle, jerked me by the arm, and flung me toward the porch. She screamed at Pooty to stop as well.

"We have to live together for a spell," she kept repeating.

Pooty and I were heaving for breath, madder than wet cats. Momma was yelling. Harriet and Lissa were screaming. And Amanda was giggling like she enjoyed it all.

Momma pointed us each to a different end of the porch, then turned to Amanda. "What happened, young lady?"

Amanda smiled like an angel. "I gave them a ride from the Burke place. Pooty fell in the river and—"

"They pushed me!" Pooty cried.

"—he blamed Henry and me for knocking him off."

Now, I knew that was a lie, but it didn't seem so bad coming from lips as sweet as hers.

Momma couldn't settle it, so she shook her head. "When your pa gets home, we'll get this straightened out."

Amanda smiled. "I need to get home or my father'll be angry."

Momma nodded. "See that you do."

Amanda tossed me a quick grin, then untied the stallion and jumped atop the animal. I caught a flash of pale leg and decided it was worth it, no matter what punishment I received.

About five minutes later Pa arrived with the wagonload of ugly. Momma was waiting on the porch, her arms crossed, her foot tapping.

SincereAnne saw Pooty and jumped out of the wagon, running to see what had happened. Pooty explained his side of things, which was nearer the truth than my side, but Amanda had plowed a good furrow for me to spread a little manure in, and I embellished her account.

Pa shook his head. "I don't know who's telling the truth."

"I do," SincereAnne interrupted. "Joe Don doesn't lie."

Pa shrugged. "Maybe so, maybe not. This reminds me of a couple hardheaded oxen I had one time. They wouldn't take to a plow or each other. Both were all piss and vinegar. You know what I did?"

"Shot the one named Pooty?" I volunteered.

Pa growled. "I yoked them together for a month. They turned out to be the best-mannered oxen I ever worked."

"You ain't yoking me," Pooty said. For once we agreed on something.

"No, sir, I'm not, but you two boys'll do all your chores together, you'll sit together at meals, you'll clean up together, and you'll make your bed together until you can learn to behave like civilized people instead of Indians."

My only consolation was that I hadn't been fighting one of Pooty's ugly sisters. We were yoked about three weeks, each of us wary of the other and disgusted with our punishment. The worst by far was having to sleep in the same bed in the loft. I swore I could still smell the skunk on him.

And then one night about three weeks later, our punishment didn't seem so harsh and our personal vendetta didn't seem near as important as we had thought.

That was when the night riders first visited our place.

Chapter Three

It was Pooty's fault the bushwhackers showed up.

While I was attending to some business in the outhouse one afternoon, Pooty was snooping around the loft. I must admit I was lingering at the outhouse, not because the seat was comfortable or the aroma that good but because it was about the only place I could go to get away from Pooty and his sisters. When I stepped out, I was shocked to see an American flag flying from a pole on the roof.

My first fear was that the damn Yankees had taken over the farm while I was taking a dump. I was so mad I could've whipped a brigade of the best Union troops, especially since they were no better fighters than a gang of schoolboys. But my exit from the outhouse must've scared them all off, because there wasn't a one around to be seen. I figured they were preparing a surprise attack against me. Of course, I still had a secret weapon I could unleash upon them—the Burke sisters. Those girls were ugly enough to turn back a regiment apiece. The only thing I didn't know was whether more Yankees would die from terror or laughter at the sight.

But whether or not the Burke sisters were ready to help, I was ready to fight. I doubled up my fists and marched toward the house, expecting the Yankee hordes to come charging from behind the creek embankment. "Come out, you Yankee cowards!" I yelled.

That's when Pooty Burke stepped around the corner, his hands knotted into fists as well. Then it began to sink in. I glanced up at the roof again and saw that the flag was hanging from a cane fishing pole, not a flagstaff. That wasn't some Yankee's flag; that was the flag Pa had brought back from Sutter's Mill and given me. I looked again to be sure and recognized the water stains and a tattered corner.

Pooty grinned like he had won the war single-handed. I decided to teach him some manners.

"That's my flag!" I yelled.

"Not anymore. That flag shouldn't belong to a traitor."

"I ain't a traitor."

"Are too."

I spat and charged Pooty. He screamed and charged me. We met beneath the flag and tore into each other like a hound against a coon. I socked him in the jaw. He answered with a fist to my stomach, doubling me over. While I was gasping for breath, he had the bad manners to punch me in the ear. I screamed and charged again, grabbing him just below the hips and lifting him from his feet, then driving him hard into the ground.

"Aaaahh!" he cried. I thought I had him whipped, but like the eel he was he slipped free.

We grabbed each other and took to wrestling and punching. His hounds and mine gathered around us, howling and barking and creating such a commotion that Pa came barreling out of the house with his rifle in his hands and a scowl on his face. Momma and SincereAnne followed like his shadow.

"Stop it!" Pa yelled.

I hesitated a moment, and Pooty took the opportunity to punch me in the nose. I started spewing blood and curse words.

Pa handed his rifle to Momma, then grabbed me and

Pooty by the hair, calming us down in his own way. Pooty and I looked like we'd been sorting wildcats.

"What's this about?" he demanded.

I wiped blood and snot off my nose, then flung it toward Pooty. With my bloodied finger I pointed to the roof. "He stole my flag."

Pooty growled. "He shouldn't have a Union flag."

"Shut up, boy, unless I tell you to speak," Pa ordered. "Now, which one of you hung this flag?"

I shook my head. Pa turned to Pooty, who said nothing. "Answer me, boy."

"You didn't tell me to speak," Pooty replied, acting like he was smarter than a college professor in a library.

Pa raised his hand to slap Pooty, but SincereAnne gasped and he remembered the boy wasn't his. "Answer me, boy," he repeated.

Pooty lifted his bruised chin and thrust out his chest. "I found the flag and hung it."

Shaking with anger, Pa turned to Pooty's mother. "SincereAnne, I'm going to wallop your boy and mine with a razor strop. If we're gonna live together for our own protection, we can't let politics keep getting in the way."

"You'll not whip him, Mr. Lomax," she answered back. "He didn't mean no harm."

Pa was mad enough to eat splinters. He wasn't used to back talk from a woman. His voice shook with rage when he spoke. "Mischief begets trouble, SincereAnne."

She lifted her hand to make a point, but a shout from the porch interrupted her.

"Pa," cried Melissa.

"Hush up, Lissa, this is no concern of yours."

Glancing at the porch, I saw Lissa holding Harriet's hand. Behind them stood DeeAnne, RuthAnne, and Lou-Anne, all pointing to the creek.

"Pa," Lissa said, "by the creek."

When we turned, we saw three riders sitting on their horses and staring at us. My stomach suddenly felt queasy.

I was uncertain whether it was from the fight or from the three strangers eyeing us.

Momma handed Pa his rifle as he stepped away from us boys.

"Hello," he called.

The three riders sat motionless. They made no threatening moves, and that made them all the more frightening.

"Get that damn flag down," Pa whispered over his shoulder. When he didn't hear movement, he growled a single word. *"Now."*

"Where's the ladder?" I asked Pooty.

"Behind the cabin."

We both ran to retrieve it, then propped it against the wall. I scurried up the rungs and jerked the cane pole from between the shingles where Pooty had wedged it.

"Hand it to me," Pooty ordered.

I wanted to hand it to him right up 'side the face, but I didn't figure that would help the situation any, not with Pa all keyed up and those three riders watching us like a mountain lion considers its prey. After untying the flag, I tossed the pole at Pooty's feet and quickly folded the flag, shoving it beneath my shirt as I climbed down the ladder.

The three men watched a moment longer, then turned their horses upstream and rode toward Cane Hill. They seemed all the more evil by their silence and their unhurried retreat.

Wordless threats weigh heavier on the mind than threats spoken. While the rest of us nervously stood around, SincereAnne disappeared inside the house and returned with Pa's razor strop. "Do what you think's best. Mischief begets trouble."

I couldn't believe she was going to let my pa whip her son. If Pooty got a whipping, I knew I was going to get one, too. I was so mad I wanted to knock SincereAnne cross-eyed, but since someone had already done that, I grumbled my disappointment to myself.

Handing his rifle to Momma and taking the razor strop, Pa nodded to me and Pooty. "Boys, let's visit the barn."

Pooty and I bit our lips and followed Pa. There we got a beating like none I'd ever received before. Pa not only warmed our behinds, he heated them so that we couldn't sit down until supper for fear of catching a chair on fire. He beat us until I cursed the cow that gave its hide for the razor strop. When he was through, it seemed like me and Pooty didn't have that many things to disagree about. There was one thing, though, we definitely agreed upon: When bedtime came, we were sleeping on our stomachs.

We waited until suppertime to leave the barn and return to the house, taking small steps because big ones hurt too much. Before sitting down at the table, we both climbed up to the loft. I returned the flag to its place; then we fetched our feather pillows, eased back down the ladder to the kitchen, and fluffed those pillows on our chairs. We held our breath as we settled down, soft as hens atop their first eggs.

Momma had fried bacon and warmed creamed corn that she had canned. SincereAnne had made the biscuits. Like just about everything else, SincereAnne had a different philosophy about biscuits than Momma. Rather than light and fluffy, SincereAnne preferred them hard enough to chip a tooth and heavy enough to break your foot if you dropped one. It was a damn shame she was a Union woman rather than a Rebel sympathizer. Her biscuits could've doubled the output of cannonball and grapeshot for the Confederate states west of the Mississippi River.

Pa said the blessing, giving thanks for our food—though not mentioning the biscuits by name—and asking God's protection over us. I said a silent prayer myself, asking only for those things I truly needed: a thicker hide on my butt, a new set of teeth once I was done eating biscuits, and fourteen kegs of gunpowder so I could blow Pooty's behind all the way to Missouri.

We all passed our plates to Pa, who divided the food as evenly as possible among the ten of us. Though I was hungrier than a bear after a winter hibernation, I didn't make any sudden moves for fear my behind would reignite.

"Boys," Pa started, "I hope you've learned a lesson. Mischief can be dangerous. I don't know what those three men were up to today, but I don't like it."

I wasn't about to argue. All I was going to do was nod—though not too vigorously—at everything Pa said.

"You boys need to find something you can do that's fun," SincereAnne interjected, "and quit tormenting each other."

I turned to look at her, then decided against it, not knowing which eye to stare at. Her eyes were so crossed I was certain she could see around corners.

"Henry," she asked, "Joe Don enjoys playing marbles. Do you play marbles?"

Fact was, I was a good marble player. However, if Pooty would steal my flag, he'd steal my marbles, too, if he ever found them behind the loose brick in the chimney. "I don't play well, ma'am."

Out of the corner of my eye I saw Pooty lick his lips. He must've figured he could beat me.

I knew better.

"Maybe tomorrow you two can play marbles after your chores are done." SincereAnne looked at Pa. "If that's okay with Mr. Lomax?"

Pa nodded. "As long as there's no mischief."

After supper the women did the dishes, and me and Pooty joined Pa on the front porch. He sat in a rocking chair while Pooty and I leaned against the wall to air out our smoldering bottoms.

"I know you boys got some friskiness in you, but these are dangerous times. What you did today, Pooty, could bring a passel of troubles for us."

It was the type of lecture I had heard dozens of times before, but I guess fathers always feel obligated to pound some sense into their offspring. The problem with fathers is they don't want you to have any more fun than they have, which is none, excepting of course when they squeak the bed with their wives. But I guess if I'd paid more attention to his lectures I wouldn't have gotten kicked by mules, stung by hornets, and injured a dozen other ways.

Pooty and I didn't say a word, just waited for Pa to finish his lecturing. When he changed the subject, he told us about the chores he had planned for us, which made me wish he was lecturing us again.

The women joined us before the light faded away, and we sat silently for a bit. Then little Harriet began to sing a hymn. We all joined in. I was more of a hummer than a singer, my voice being scratchier than a kitten's claws, but it was a peaceful moment, the last we would have for years.

After good dark we all retired to bed, feeling pretty good for the most part, except those of us with fried bottoms. Still wary of each other, me and Pooty undressed and crawled into bed, then lowered ourselves onto our stomachs.

We didn't say much at first. Then Pooty made an admission I was glad to hear.

"My behind's too sore to poot."

"Your pa ever whip you like that?"

"Nope. I don't remember the last time he took a switch to me."

I could only shake my head. I'd been swatted for about every wrong a kid could do, and I'd learned some good lessons—like don't slap your sister, don't spit in the house, don't talk back to your father, don't tell a lie that you can't cover with another one, and don't fight over someone borrowing your flag.

"Pa never liked a switch," I said. "Says it's not wide enough. He always wanted a little more to show for his effort than a thin welt." I figured Pooty's pa had failed him miserably by not giving him more backside lessons. Maybe that was why Pooty was so dumb and I was so smart.

It might have been midnight before we dozed off, but we didn't sleep long. Abruptly we heard our hounds howling, then gunshots, and finally the cries of the women.

I jumped out of bed, pulled on my pants, and scurried down the ladder into Pa and Momma's bedroom. The Burke women came in from the other bedroom, and I heard Pooty behind me as I ran.

In the darkness I could just make out Pa by the window, holding his rifle. "You women, get on the floor," he whispered. "Stay low, and don't get in front of any windows."

"Pa," I said, "what do you want me to do?"

"Come here and take my pistol."

I slipped over to the door and took the weapon, hoping Pa wouldn't see that my hand was trembling.

"Don't shoot unless I say so."

The weapon felt cold in my hand. I was nervous as a yearling at cutting time. It didn't help when I stepped away from Pa and bumped into Pooty. "Aaah," I called out, swinging the pistol around to face the imagined threat. Pooty dropped to the floor, trembling.

Another shot exploded outside our door. Then a man called out Pa's name.

"George Lomax?"

"What do you want?" Pa yelled.

"Want you to come out and visit."

"I don't visit after dark. What do you want?"

"We want to know whether you're for or against us."

As the man talked, I slipped to the window and peeked out a corner just as a couple riders lit torches. I could make out a dozen men on horseback, their faces covered with bandannas, lined up in front of our porch so close I could see the hatred in their eyes.

At the sight of the flames Pa screamed, "Don't fire the place! There's women and children in here!"

I aimed my gun at the nearest rider holding a torch. A mite smaller than the others, he had a nervous look about him, and his eyes blinked constantly. Those eyelids were flapping so much I figured he might just come right out of his saddle and take to flight. I was hoping he would so I could plug him and watch him fall.

Little did I know I had a bead on Jesse James.

"You for or against us, Lomax?"

Pa faced a decision as tough as picking one of the Burke sisters to marry. He had to be for whoever was outside the house. But were they Union or Confederate? "I'm for you," he called out.

"Wise choice, Lomax, but you don't know who we are. Are you for states' rights or federal rights?"

"I've got five sons fighting for the Confederacy. That makes me Southern."

"Then why you flying a Union flag over your house?"

"Damn you, Pooty," Pa growled under his breath, "see what you did?" He cleared his throat. "The Burke boy did it, not knowing any better. The Burkes are staying with us until Gordon comes home."

"He doesn't have a home to come back to," the bush-whacker yelled. "We just took care of that."

SincereAnne screamed, and her daughters took to sobbing. I was glad it was dark so I couldn't see them cry. I felt sorry for them. Pooty groaned.

"You best turn the Burkes out," the bushwhacker yelled, "before someone decides to burn down your home, too."

"They don't have any place to go," Pa answered.

"They can go to hell," came the bushwhacker's reply. "If that flag ever appears here again, we'll burn you out no matter what."

"It won't," Pa answered.

"Let's burn 'em out now," cried the rider I named Blinky.

The man who seemed to be in charge turned to him. "You do as I say—and I say no," he grated.

Blinky snorted. The leader, astride a black horse, shook his head. "You better remember who's in charge, you damn fool kid."

When Blinky didn't answer, the leader raised his rifle above his head and yelled. The riders circled the house, whooping and shooting their guns in the air. Figuring I could knock one out of the saddle, I lifted the gun level with the window.

"Don't shoot," Pa growled, "or they'll fire the house."

"Yes, sir." Gritting my teeth, I watched the riders. The leader's black horse seemed mighty familiar.

The women were all sobbing, except Lissa, who crawled to me and lifted her head to look outside. "Get down, Lissa," I said.

"I want to see the cowards."

"Hush up, girl," Pa said, "and get with the women."

Lissa grumbled, then crawled back across the room.

Finally the riders peeled away from the house, tossed their torches to the ground, and rode off in the darkness. Pa must've waited half an hour before he opened the door and slipped onto the dogtrot.

"Pooty, you keep the women inside," he commanded. "Henry, you come with me."

I slid out the door. It was an eerie feeling, thinking some coward might be hiding in the darkness to shoot me down. I took a deep breath and followed Pa around the house. There was a flickering light out back, and when we reached the corner we saw the night riders had torched the outhouse.

"It could've been worse," Pa said. "The house, the barn, and the smokehouse are still standing. We didn't lose anything we can't rebuild."

Pa was right . . . though that outhouse was my refuge from Pooty.

As we circled back around the house, we lowered

our guns, then lifted them again at the sounds from the
front porch. It was the women, still weeping.

"I told you women to stay inside."

SincereAnne sobbed, "My home, they've burned it."

I looked across Jordan Creek and through the trees
could make out the orange glow that had been their
house.

"See what you done, Pooty?" I asked, but Pa slapped
me.

"Henry, you just remember that mischief begets
trouble."

Chapter Four

We were all a little shaky the next day, especially when we saw they had shot all but four of our hounds. After we buried them, Pa set us to cutting gunports in the loft at each end of the house while he built heavy plank shutters to hang inside the windows so we could close them in an attack. Momma was disappointed because she had to remove the curtains she had sewn.

After a meager lunch of SincereAnne's leftover brick biscuits and boiled potatoes, Pa brought four empty barrels from the barn and placed one in the kitchen, one in his bedroom, and one at each end of the loft to hold water for drinking or fighting fire if the night riders tried to burn us out.

Pooty and I must've toted a thousand pails of water from Jordan Creek to fill those barrels. Pooty wasn't cocky like before, but he wasn't any more likable, either, because he kept complaining about all the work Pa was putting us to.

It was midafternoon and we were still hauling water when we heard the sound of galloping horses approaching from the Burke place. We both flinched and ran to the top of the embankment, ready to dart home and alert Pa. Then I spotted a black stallion and a rider with golden hair bouncing behind her. It was Amanda Fudge. Strong though her stallion was, a barrel-chested bay gelding kept pace, its rider a boy not more than two or three years older than me.

Both riders charged their mounts headlong across the creek and up the embankment, then jerked the reins. Pooty grinned at the sight of Amanda. I guess he wasn't as dumb as I'd figured.

My smile wilted when I realized her companion was none other than Blinky, whose eyelids were flapping so much I was afraid he'd go floating away any moment. I figured it was his gun belt that kept him weighted down in the saddle.

I lowered my two pails to the ground, took off my hat, and ran my fingers through my hair. I decided to visit. So did Pooty.

"Hi, Henry. Hi, Pooty," she said. "I heard your place was attacked last night."

"Where'd you hear that?" I asked, eyeing Blinky. "Me and Pa held them gutless cowards off." Blinky gritted his teeth.

"I helped," Pooty added.

"I'm glad you weren't hurt."

Her concern made me feel pretty good, though I wasn't sure whether she was talking to me or Pooty.

"It true they burned your outhouse?"

I acknowledged it was and should've asked her why she didn't ask Blinky, him likely being the son of a bitch that torched it, but I didn't think about it at the time. Blinky just sat in his saddle like he couldn't talk and blink at the same time.

As Amanda lifted her leg over the back of her horse, I saw an expanse of pale white flesh that made me a bit uncomfortable beneath my britches. She slid off and landed nimbly, then looked at Pooty. "You still mad at me for winning your marbles?"

Pooty shrugged, a sly grin worming across his face.

"You beat him at marbles?" I asked, careful not to turn my back on Blinky.

She nodded. "I won 'em all, and I won't give 'em back."

I laughed. Maybe Pooty *was* as dumb as I thought, letting a girl beat him at marbles. "Maybe we can play. I'm better than Pooty."

"Okay." She cut me a smile that could've melted granite.

"She'll beat you, Henry. She has a way of rattling you."

I couldn't believe what she did next. She stepped over and kissed Pooty, then planted a kiss full upon my lips. I'd been thrown from a horse, beaten with a razor strop, and stung by hornets, but nothing compared to that. My knees went mushy, though another part of me took up the slack. I figured if there was ever a girl who could take the wanderlust out of me, it was Amanda Fudge. She had good looks, a devastating smile, a terrific kiss, and a talent for playing marbles. As long as her eyes didn't cross on her, her biscuits weren't as heavy as bricks, and she could break the habit of kissing Pooty, what more could a fellow want?

As taken as I was, I was tempted to grab her and give her a kiss of my own doing, but Pooty picked up his pails. "Your pa's staring."

I knew we best get moving, because Pa wanted those barrels filled by nightfall. As I grabbed my buckets, Amanda bounded up onto the stallion's back and started toward the house, reining him in so I could keep pace. Blinky followed, and I made certain to keep Amanda's horse between us. I just didn't trust those blinking eyeballs.

Pa was waiting on the porch for us, and I figured he planned to chew my bottom for lingering with Amanda. Instead he stared at Amanda's black stallion and Blinky's bay gelding as Pooty walked inside.

"Good-looking horses," I said, hoping he'd forget to scold me for dallying.

"Too good," he said.

I didn't know what he meant, but any horse must look good to a man who'd had all his work animals—save for two broken-down mules—taken by the government. Amanda reined up in front of the porch, but Blinky rode on around the house in the direction of the outhouse. I passed Pa on the porch and went inside.

Pooty disappeared up in the loft, leaving LouAnne the only one in the kitchen. She slapped me as I passed by. "You should stay away from Amanda."

I was tempted to knock LouAnne's head off with a bucket, but that'd just mean I'd have to make another trip to the creek, and I was getting tired of that. So I stuck out my tongue instead.

She slapped me again. "You ever heard of Jezebel from the Bible?"

Seems I had heard the name, but I couldn't place it for certain. If she was in the Bible, she couldn't be too bad, I figured.

"Amanda," said LouAnne, "is a Jezebel."

That was high praise, for LouAnne was no doubt jealous of Amanda's looks. Carefully I climbed up the ladder, emptied the two pails in the nearest barrel, and followed Pooty back down. LouAnne had moved out of reach, or I would've bounced a bucket off her head. Instead I went outside to admire Amanda, still atop her stallion.

At first I didn't see Pa because he was bent over inspecting the horseshoe on the stallion's right rear leg. "What are you looking at?" she asked.

Pa shook his head. "I thought he picked up a stone in his shoe."

I thought that was kind of Pa, but Amanda looked at him nervously, then glanced at me and Pooty.

"I better check all his legs," Pa said, "and you boys better head on and get more water."

We hesitated as Blinky rode around the opposite end

of the house. "Don't be letting him check the stallion," he cried out.

Pa looked up from the hoof he was holding and gave Blinky a hard-eyed stare that said he suffered no man's insolence. Me and Pooty decided it was time to head back to the creek. Blinky was nervously tapping the handle of his revolver with his fingers as we walked away.

Pooty didn't seem to realize that Blinky had been one of the night riders. If he was too dumb to figure that out, I sure wasn't going to tell him.

I *was* tempted to inform him that I'd looked up Amanda's dress a couple times. Of course, as dumb as Pooty was, I'm not sure he was certain what was up her dress. Much as I hate to admit it, I didn't know for certain myself, just that whatever it was left me standing at attention. "You don't know much about girls, Pooty."

"I got more sisters than you do."

"But you don't have none that look like Amanda."

"Neither do you," he said.

I thought about slugging him for insulting Lissa and Harriet. Then he finished his thought.

"Yours are prettier."

Now, I have to admit Harriet and Lissa were fine-looking girls, although they didn't have that golden hair, those green eyes, and those long, pale legs, but I was pleased that Pooty had spoken so highly of them. Then, the more I thought about it, the more I wondered if he was having thoughts about my sisters like I was having about Amanda. I fumed at the idea.

We reached the stream and filled our buckets, then started back to the house just as Amanda galloped up with Blinky beside her. My chest—and other parts—swelled with pride when she smiled at me.

Blinky, though, had meanness in his eyes. He looked at me and Pooty, then smirked. "What do you see in these two girls, Amanda?"

Amanda just giggled.

"A war's going on, and they're doing girl's work."

I was tempted to challenge Blinky to a fight, but he kept toying with the revolver at his side, and I wasn't stupid. But I wasn't smart, either, because I just had to say something. "May be girl's work," I said, "but it ain't coward's work like those sons of bitches did that burned our outhouse."

Had I known then what I knew later about Jesse James, I wouldn't have suggested he was a son of a bitch. He didn't take kindly to insults to his momma, her being so mean and ugly.

"You calling me a son of a bitch?"

"No, just those bushwhackers."

"Then I guess you ain't talking about me."

Of course, it was all the same thing, and both Blinky and I knew it. He might have jerked his pistol on me had he not glanced over his shoulder and seen Pa approaching, rifle in hand. "Come on, Amanda. Let's get back to your place."

He glared at me for a second before both turned and rode away. Pa watched them disappear into the trees, then went back to the house, leaving me and Pooty to keep toting water.

It was suppertime before we finished filling those barrels. I was as tired and hungry as I'd ever been. As we neared the house, I saw Pa inspecting the ground mighty closely. I figured he had lost his pocketknife and didn't give it another thought as I washed up and went inside.

Momma had baked a ham and picked some fresh green beans from the garden as well. She had made biscuits herself for fear SincereAnne's bricks would plug us up so bad Momma'd have to doctor us with sassafras tea to open up our innards. Since we hadn't had a chance to rebuild the outhouse, none of us wanted that.

When Pa came in and sat down, he said the blessing, then served the meal. As we dug in, he looked down the table at SincereAnne.

"The Fudges good friends with you?"

SincereAnne shrugged. "Neighbors like you. They stick to themselves pretty much."

"What's his politics?"

"Secesh," she said, frowning at the taste of Momma's biscuits. "Too much baking soda."

Momma cringed and bit her lip. I could've sworn she looked at the rolling pin on her pie cabinet. I would've been glad to hand it to her if she'd asked.

"You're mighty talkative and mighty curious about the Fudges, Mr. Lomax. Any particular reason?" Sincere-Anne asked.

Pa looked at her a moment, trying to decide which of her eyes he should stare down. "Just being neighborly. That's all."

I knew something was bothering Pa, but I couldn't figure it out. He hadn't been his normal self since Amanda had ridden up.

Lissa, though, identified the problem and wasn't shy about announcing it. "Amanda rides a fine horse, she does. Wonder why the government agents didn't take it like they did ours."

Pa gave Lissa a stare that said she should keep her thoughts to herself. "Luck, I reckon."

Momma picked up the platter of biscuits, offering them to everyone but SincereAnne. "I made some apple cobbler," she announced. "We could use a treat after last night."

After cobbler Pooty and I, both exhausted, climbed to the loft and fell in bed while the women washed dishes. We had a good night's sleep, and everyone woke up the next morning optimistic about our future.

We spent the next three days finishing up the shut-ters, rebuilding the outhouse, and tending to the crops in the field. Pooty and I got along tolerably well. If we could manage to live side by side, I didn't understand why the United States couldn't live alongside the Confederate States without all the killing. Only thing I could figure

was that Abe Lincoln was crazy and some men just liked
to fight.

As a reward for all our work fortifying the place, Pa
gave us a day of rest, and it couldn't have worked out any
better, because Amanda came over. This time, though, she
was riding not the black stallion but a mule as broken
down as our two in the barn. I could tell it affected her
because her smile was not as wide nor her eyes as bright
as on her last visit. She dismounted.

"What happened to the stallion?" I asked.

"Got stolen."

"Where's Blinky?"

She grimaced. "You mean Jesse?"

"I don't know. You never introduced us."

Amanda looked at Pa when she answered. "Jesse
didn't find your pa too neighborly, stalking him with a
rifle and all, so he went back to Missouri."

I should've known Blinky was a Missourian, coward
that he was.

Pa had overheard my questions and her answers. He
shook his head, rose from his rocking chair on the porch,
and retreated inside.

Amanda grinned at me. "I came to play marbles."

Well, if she was going to play with me, marbles
wouldn't have been my first choice, but it would do. I
ran into the house and scurried up the ladder to the loft,
where I strode to the chimney and carefully removed the
loose brick that hid my bag of marbles. As I replaced it,
I heard a noise behind me and twisted around in time to
see Pooty's head ducking for cover. He had been spying
on me and now knew of my hiding place.

Seeing the little Yankee spy angered me, but I was
anxious to play marbles with Amanda so I ignored him.

"Good luck," he called with a mocking laugh.

I gritted my teeth and went outside.

Amanda had pulled a sack of marbles from a bag she
carried on her arm. "These used to be Pooty's."

I laughed. No wonder Pooty was mad at her. She had

taken him for about twice as many marbles as I had ever owned. I escorted her out behind the barn, where we wouldn't be seen if she developed an urge to kiss me again.

Harriet trailed us a ways, but I picked up a rock and chunked it at her. She ran back to the house, screaming for Momma. When Amanda and I were alone, I found a level patch of soft ground and with a stick drew a large circle in it.

"I'm not real good," Amanda said. "I just got lucky with Pooty."

"Pooty's real bad," I answered.

Now, the bigger and heavier the marble, the greater the chance of hitting and knocking smaller marbles out of the ring. We each picked a shooter, me the biggest one and her a tiny one.

"We playing for keeps?" I asked.

Amanda smiled. "I guess so."

We emptied our marbles in the circle. Being the gentleman, I allowed her to go first. She bent down on her hands and knees, eyeing the marbles thoughtfully, then wedged her tiny marble in her index finger, cocked her thumb, and shot. Her shooter barely caused a ripple among the herd of marbles.

"Nice try," I said, knowing this was going to be as easy as fooling Pooty.

I crawled to the circle, loaded my heavy shooter, and slid my hand to the edge of the line in the dirt. When I fired my shooter, it sent the marbles to flying like drunks before a temperance woman. I must've knocked a dozen or so out of the circle on a single shot.

Amanda shook her head. "Told you I wasn't very good." She fired again, her dinky marble bouncing off a larger marble and rolling back outside the circle.

I toyed with her, knowing I could beat her quickly but not wanting to end it too soon, for I enjoyed being close to her. After a half hour I had won all but about a dozen marbles she had been lucky enough to knock out of the circle. She was crestfallen.

"Sorry," I murmured when I took the last marble.

I feared she was going to cry, but she smiled weakly. I couldn't take her marbles, I knew, but I couldn't just give them back, either.

She offered to skin a cat for me if I'd give her back the marbles she'd lost. I thought that was a dumb trade until I realized I might be able to see her drawers. "Okay," I said, licking my lips. "You can have your marbles back if you skin a cat three times."

She shrugged. "Okay."

Quickly I gathered my marbles and dropped them in my bag, then did the same with hers. We slipped into the woods behind the barn and found an oak tree with a low branch.

"You sure you'll give me back my marbles if I do this?"

I nodded vigorously.

She boosted herself into the tree, sat down, then slid out on the branch. With both hands she grasped the branch beneath her, then slowly leaned back until her head was aimed for the ground. Her skirt fell away with her, and I found myself staring at her undies, which were store-boughts, not the flour sacks I was expecting. She lingered like that a minute, then lowered her legs, too.

For one glorious moment her entire bottom was exposed to my view. It was an inspiring sight. Then her skirt dropped back in place, and she released her grip and landed gracefully on her feet. She repeated the process twice more. I stood there with my mouth agape each time.

When she landed the final time, she smiled shyly. "I hope that didn't embarrass you."

"I'll manage," I croaked. "Let's head back to the barn and divide up the marbles."

"We can wait just a minute," she said, moving to me and kissing me full on the lips.

I decided we could spend a little more time in the woods. No telling what might have happened, as ripe as

Amanda seemed to be that day, but the U.S. Cavalry in-
terfered. No sooner had I started kissing her back than
we heard a bugle and the sound of horses.

Amanda broke from me quicker than an eye blink.
"What's that?"

"Sounds like soldiers," I said.

We moved to the edge of the woods and saw a patrol
of Union cavalry crossing our field.

"I've got to go," Amanda said, her voice panicked.

"I'll see you to your mule."

"No, no," she cried. "I've got to go now."

Before I could get a further explanation, she disappeared into the woods.

I took the two bags of marbles and started for the
house, barely beating a Union captain who studied me
suspiciously. Seeing a Yankee up close gave me the
chance to see if they really did have horns like all the
rabid southerners said. This one didn't, but I couldn't rule
out the possibility he had been dehorned already by some
Confederate boy.

Pa appeared on the porch, Momma on his left,
SincereAnne on his right. "Good day, Captain," he said.

The captain took off his hat, and I still couldn't see
any horns. "You secesh or Union, sir?"

SincereAnne stepped forward. "Union. Rebel bushwhackers burned my house to the ground, and I'm staying
with these fine folks."

The captain turned to Pa. "Sir, why aren't you in the
army?"

Pa stepped off the porch so the captain could see his
limp.

"Never mind."

Pa nodded. "You boys just as well make yourselves
at home, seeing as how that's what you'll do anyway."

The captain nodded. "Thank you, good sir, we do
appreciate the hospitality." He stood in his stirrups and
turned around to face his men. "You heard him, boys,
make yourselves at home."

The soldiers didn't need a second command. They jumped from their horses, ran to the field, and stripped all the corn that was near ripe, then plundered the smokehouse until there was nothing left but our salt in the ground.

Chapter Five

I'd never seen such a smile on Pooty's face as when those Union cavalry looted our place. He didn't understand that the Yankees were taking food from Burke as well as Lomax mouths. They were such thieves I figured they must've all started out as politicians, because a politician would steal a chaw of tobacco from your mouth if you as much as yawned. But the thievery didn't bother Pooty none because he was sure those Yankees were there to reinforce him the next time he and I had a little difference.

Pooty was proudest when they raised an American flag. He marched around like he was Abe Lincoln himself. The Yankee captain sat in his saddle for a bit until he was sure his men had cleaned out our corn patch and smokehouse, then nodded to his adjutant. "See that I get a couple of those hams and plenty of corn for myself."

"Yes, sir." The adjutant saluted and rode away to steal the stolen hams.

The captain looked at Pa, then at Amanda's poor mule still tied to the front porch. "You got any more working stock?"

"Just two mules in the barn, both worse off than this one."

"We'll be taking them," the captain announced.

"I can let you have this one," Pa said, pointing to Amanda's mule, "but not the others."

I couldn't believe Pa was giving away Amanda's mule, and the captain couldn't believe Pa was planning on keeping the other two.

"And what's to stop me from taking them?"

Pa cocked his head. "Your men'll suffer for it."

I couldn't believe how brave Pa was, standing up to a couple hundred Yankees. I knew their aim wasn't any good, but still, out of a couple hundred rounds, Pa couldn't help but get hurt if they started firing. Of course, the rest of us were in the most danger, since Yankees seldom hit what they were aiming at.

Leaning forward in his saddle, the captain scowled. "How are my men gonna suffer?"

"If you take those two mules, I can't plant a new crop, and there won't be anything for your men to steal next time they come through."

The captain's lips curled into a grin. Laughing, he pointed to Amanda's mule and ordered one of his men to appropriate the animal. "Pass the word to leave the two in the barn alone."

"Yes, sir." The soldier saluted, but I swear his aim was so bad he missed his forehead.

As the soldiers dispersed, DeeAnne, RuthAnne, and LouAnne slipped out onto the porch. Harriet and Lissa followed, but Momma shooed them back inside, ordering them to look from behind the windows.

SincereAnne stepped with her girls off the front porch and marched among the soldiers. The Yankees didn't impress me any with their smarts, because they took to whooping and hollering like they were seeing beautiful women. I shuddered to think what Yankee women must look like if the Burke women could cause such a stir.

With the soldiers distracted, Pa limped over to me. "What you got in your hands?"

I rattled the two pouches. "Marbles. I won them

from Amanda." I didn't admit I'd relinquished my claim for the chance to look at her drawers.

"Where is she?"

"She ran away when she saw the Yankees. She was scared."

Pa spat. "She had reason to be."

"Why'd you give away her mule?"

"There's a reason for that, too, Henry, but not one I'm sharing." He moved toward the cabin just as Lissa and Harriet tried to slip out and gruffly ordered them to stay inside.

Though the two girls were a bit miffed by his command, I agreed with it. If those devil Yankees thought DeeAnne, RuthAnne, and LouAnne were beautiful, they didn't deserve to see Lissa and Harriet.

I went inside the house and climbed up to the loft to hide my marbles, then scrambled back down for supper. Although the soldiers had taken most of our meat, they hadn't bothered our root cellar, so there was still food for us. Pooty, his sisters, and SincereAnne ate with the soldiers, but we kept to ourselves. I was angering over the Burkes eating our smoked meat and corn with the Yankees around campfires burning our wood while we ate boiled potatoes and beans by the light of a single candle.

"The Burkes aren't at all grateful," I protested.

"That's why we took them in, Henry," Pa scolded.

"So they wouldn't thank us?"

"No! So when Yankee soldiers came they might look more favorably upon our place instead of burning it to the ground. Henry, in this war there ain't gonna be any fence that's horse-high, bull-strong, pig-tight, and gooseproof. You still got a home, Henry. The Burkes don't, and it wasn't Yankees that burned their place."

"We don't know who burned their place," I shot back.

Pa looked at me, his eyes narrowing. "I do, but you're not to mention it to no one, Henry. Not Pooty, not Amanda, not no one."

I knew by the growl in his voice that he was serious. "Don't you think I ought to ride over and tell Amanda that the Yankees took her mule?" I offered.

Pa shook his head. "She ought to know what happened to it when she left it behind."

"I'll just let her know for sure."

"No!" Pa shouted. The ferocity in his voice surprised me. I couldn't figure it out until Lissa spoke up.

"Pa thinks Amanda's pa burned the Burke place. And our outhouse."

Pa cut a hard glance at Lissa. "I didn't say no such thing to you, girl."

"I ain't a girl," Lissa called back. "I saw you out inspecting the shoes on Amanda's stallion, then looking for the bushwhackers' tracks."

"Hush up, Lissa," Pa ordered, then pointed his fork at each of our noses. "Not a word of this is to be said to anyone, or they could come back and burn our place."

"We'll fight them off," I said.

Pa shook his head. "We ain't got a chance. One rifle, a pistol, our shotgun, and Pooty's. That's it, and not enough ammunition to last. We best save our ammunition for food and keep our mouths shut so we don't have to defend our hides. Do you all understand me? Not a word about this!"

The kitchen door swung open and Pooty marched in, carrying a saber and wearing a cavalryman's hat and scarf. "Look what I got, Henry. A sword a soldier took from a dead secesh and a Union hat and scarf to boot. And you ain't got nothing."

"I won your marbles from Amanda," I announced, failing to mention that I had agreed to give them back.

Pooty scoffed and started for the ladder to the loft. "I beat her the first time I played her, but she tricked me and beat me the next time and wouldn't play me again. She'll do the same to you."

Pa cleared his throat. "Pooty, don't you be wearing that hat and scarf about this place."

"You ain't my pa, so you can't order me around."

"I'll get my razor strop if that's what it takes."

I volunteered to retrieve it for him.

"You're mad because it's Yankees rather than secesh, you are."

"Pooty," Pa said, "the people that burned your house just might shoot you if they see you wearing a Yankee hat and kerchief."

"I'm big enough to take care of myself."

Pa's voice rose. "If you were big enough for that, you wouldn't be living with my family."

"That's right," came a voice from the door. Everyone turned to see SincereAnne standing there, her arms crossed over her bosom.

"Your boy and I were having a little discussion," Pa said.

Pooty shook his head. "I won't take orders from secesh."

"This time you will, Joe Don, because Mr. Lomax is right."

Pooty's face fell as hard as one of his momma's biscuits.

"You can keep them, Joe Don, but you can't wear them outside of this house."

Pooty's shoulders sagged. "Yes, ma'am." He climbed up the ladder and stomped across the loft.

"Thank you, SincereAnne," Pa said. "Are your girls coming in?"

SincereAnne smiled. "They don't get many attentions," she said. "They can stay out a while. I can't keep my angels forever."

Even in the dim light I thought I saw tears in her crossed eyes, and for once I felt sorry for her and her daughters. It was sad they couldn't do any better for themselves than Yankees.

After supper I climbed up the ladder to bed, half expecting Pooty to attack me with his new sword. But he lay still. Though it was dark, I could feel his eyes boring into me.

"The Yankees are going to win, Henry. They told me so."

"Didn't your momma tell you not to believe everything you hear?"

"They got repeating rifles, Henry, all alike. You've seen secesh troops. They don't have uniform guns."

"Secesh aim better than Yankees."

"I ain't greening you, Henry. Yankees'll win this war, and not just because I want them to. They got better equipment."

"Equipment don't win wars, Pooty. Men do."

"No matter, Henry. You'll be seeing more blue uniforms than butternut around these parts until the war's over."

I didn't believe him. Why should I have? After all, he was just a kid. But it turned out he was right.

The Union cavalry left three days later, after they had burned all our firewood as well as some of the rail fences we had built. Pa put me and Pooty to chopping firewood while he repaired fences. Pooty and I switched off, alternately chopping and stacking wood behind the house.

After two days of that we had replenished the wood pile, and Pa let us take it easy for a day. I was sitting on one end of the porch, and Pooty was sitting in the new outhouse, breaking it in with his pipe music, when Amanda Fudge topped the creek embankment and waved at me. I whistled and waved back, pleased as punch to see her.

"Jezebel," LouAnne said from the dogtrot, then retreated inside.

I didn't announce Amanda's arrival, figuring to keep her away from Pooty so we could trade slobber again. She came up wearing a yellow dress and a smile that sent my sap to rising. As she came near, she fluttered her lashes over those wide doe eyes, and my knees turned mushy. No girl had ever made me feel that way before. Although it was a mite uncomfortable, at the same time it was darn pleasurable.

"I came to get my mule," she said.

"Why'd you run away?"

"They were Yankees, hundreds of them. Pa told me never to linger around Yankees. Where's my mule?"

"The Yankees took it."

"Bastards," she hissed. "I hate Yankees."

I had never heard such vile language cross such pretty lips.

Amanda's disposition, though, turned around quicker than a tornado. She smiled. "If my mule's gone, I guess I made this trip for nothing—unless you want to play marbles again."

The thought had entered my mind. "You got time?"

"Since I had to walk, Pa won't know the difference a few extra minutes'll make. It won't take you long to beat me, will it?" She fluttered her eyelashes.

"Get around behind the barn," I told her, "before Pooty sees you. I'll get the marbles." I darted inside and up the ladder, fetching the two pouches and scrambling back outside before any of the women could ask what I was up to.

I ran around the barn, then dashed into the woods where I saw a flash of her yellow dress.

She giggled when I approached. "I recall your offer to give my marbles back, but I don't remember if I skinned a cat for you."

Before I could answer, Amanda climbed up an oak tree and onto a branch about head high. With her back to me, she balanced on the branch a few seconds, then looked over her shoulder. "Rather than skin a cat, how about if I just hang by my legs for a bit?"

I shrugged, trying to contain my excitement. "That'll do."

She nodded, then flung herself backward, the hem of her skirt dropping past her waist and shrouding her head.

I dropped both pouches of marbles, and my jaw fell, too. She had forgotten her drawers. I stood staring at that vee of peach fuzz between her legs. My mouth went dry, my forehead broke out in a sweat, my knees went mushy, and my britches suddenly seemed tight.

"Do I get my marbles back now?" she called as she began to rock on the limb. Then she flipped off and landed gracefully, her skirt dropping the curtain on the best performance I'd ever seen.

I could only nod.

Amanda drew a circle in the dirt. My hands still trembling, I picked up both pouches of marbles and dumped them inside the circle.

"You're forgetting to pick a shooter," she said, grabbing the big marble I had used the previous time.

Letting loose a deep breath, I reached for her hand to take my shooter back, but she jerked it away. "I'm using it this game."

I had barely picked another shooter before she took aim and started firing. She must've knocked a half-dozen marbles out of the ring on her first shot.

Come my turn, my hand was so weak and my fingers were trembling so much I could barely squeeze off a shot. She cleaned me out quicker than a circuit preacher empties a collection plate. She batted her eyes at me. "I just got lucky," she cooed as she gathered up all the marbles that had once belonged to Pooty and, more recently, to me.

All in all, I felt like I had come out ahead. After all, I'd never seen a girl's rigging before, and I had to admit I kind of liked the view. "You wanna see who can hang by his legs the longest?"

Amanda shook her head. "Nope."

"When do I get a chance to win my marbles back?"

"You don't."

"How about a kiss?"

"Nope," she said. "That's what the Burke sisters are for."

I about gagged, deciding it was time to quit suggesting things. Without looking at me again, Amanda tied the mouths on the pouches and started hiking for home.

"Good-bye," I called.

She didn't so much as look my way.

"How about another look?"

"Bastard," she called.

That language fit Yankees better than me. I walked home all sheepish, hoping Pooty wouldn't see me slip in the house, but he was waiting on the porch.

"LouAnne said Amanda came by. She won all your marbles, didn't she?"

I nodded and walked inside, where Momma and SincereAnne were mending clothes. "Who's Jezebel?" I asked.

Momma looked at me all puzzled. "What brought that up?"

SincereAnne answered my question. "She was a wicked queen who turned men against each other."

LouAnne just smiled at me like she was so smart. I climbed up into the loft and contemplated women. Later, after supper, I went right to bed. Pooty joined me shortly.

"I told you she'd take your marbles. Did she show you her bottom like she did me? It kind of rattles a fellow's aim."

Pooty talked a little more, but I pretended I was asleep. I couldn't get Amanda out of my mind. She was pretty and even sweet sometimes, but she had a dark side to her that just didn't belong to a girl that cute.

I pondered her the rest of that summer and into the fall.

As the days grew shorter, we collected what we could from the field and garden, but most of it had been stripped by the Yankee and Confederate patrols wandering through the area. For the most part we were left unharmed and managed to hold on to our two mules. We slaughtered a couple hogs that roamed the woods and ate what pork we wanted, then salted down the rest and left it in the smokehouse, knowing we'd never eat it all before soldiers from either side came and took it from us.

Pooty and I managed okay, not discussing politics

and not getting in any big fights. I showed him my dog-eared deck of cards and taught him to play a few games that his momma wouldn't have approved of. Pooty's sisters kind of grew on me, not that they got any prettier; they were decent girls and, unlike Amanda, guileless.

But in spite of all the company I grew lonely. I'd never been this long without my brothers around, and I missed them. Though Momma wrote them regular letters, we got none in return from Thomas or John in Virginia, but we did occasionally receive one from Jim, Andy, and Van. A couple times I caught DeeAnne writing a letter to someone, but she hid it from me, so I never knew who it was she corresponded with. I figured it was a Yankee who probably couldn't read anyway, because DeeAnne never got any letters back.

We'd pretty much gotten accustomed to the regular patrols from both armies marching through our area. And there was a good side to it: As long as the regular troops were around, the bushwhackers generally stayed hidden.

Toward the end of November, though, the Union Army marched to Cane Hill. I'd never seen so many soldiers. There were eight to ten thousand of them, and it seemed like every last one was camped on our place. All we needed was for a few Confederates to show up and we'd have us a full-scale battle.

That was what happened the last week in November.

Chapter Six

It was late November. The days were brisk, the nights cold. There were Yankees all about. Yankees in the fields. Yankees in the trees. Yankees along the creek. Yankees chopping wood. Yankees hauling water. Yankees making water. Yankees dropping mud. Yankees stealing our belongings.

An army doesn't have to fire a single shot to make a mess, and the Yankees had done just that. They trampled down our field, scared all the game from our woods, stole our rail fences for firewood, cleaned out our cellar for food, and pretty much took over things. We were lucky, though; the soldiers left our house alone because the Burke sisters had been kind to the cavalry when they had stopped by earlier in the fall.

With so many Yankees around, Pooty must've thought he'd died and gone to heaven. Me, I got accustomed to the idea once I overlooked their funny accents, their habit of stealing everything they could eat or carry, and their fondness for Old Abe Lincoln. Pooty and I walked around their camps, admiring their equipment. They'd give us squares of hardtack that tasted like petrified poison. I was surprised I didn't up and die after eating my first one, but the taste helped me understand why they were stealing all our food.

I didn't cause any trouble with the bluebellies. After all, they outnumbered me five thousand to one. I had a hard time liking them, though, because these were the fellows trying to kill my brothers. But I couldn't just hate them. That's what politicians and lawyers were for. These Yankees weren't many years older than me, and they were just as anxious to get back home as I was to get rid of them.

If I learned anything during their occupation, it was to watch my step. With no better food than they had, the Yankees sure had to unfeed a lot. For the most part they didn't unload themselves in the fields where we could've used the manure; they'd go in among the trees for a little privacy, unlimber their artillery, and fire away. Pooty couldn't help but be jealous, the soldiers stealing all his thunder and such. Go for a walk in the woods and you'd think a battle was in progress for all the explosions and the moaning and groaning. Army food and stolen victuals just didn't go through their plumbing well.

One morning two days before the end of November, we saw a sudden commotion in the camp. Bugles blared assembly, infantrymen grabbed their rifles, artillerymen hitched their cannon—there must've been thirty of them—and officers shouted orders. I figured they'd either spotted Confederate soldiers or had run out of places to relieve themselves.

Pooty and I raced among them, trying to figure out what was happening. An officer grabbed us by the shoulders and told us to get back to our house and stay there, as a battle was about to commence. That got our blood to racing. Caught up in the excitement, we were ready to charge down the valley with the troops and watch the fighting up close. Then we came face to face with a threat worse than any battle—our mothers.

Momma and SincereAnne came rushing through the soldiers, crying our names, then bursting into tears when they found us.

"Hurry, Henry," Momma said. "Come home before the shooting starts. We'll hide in the cellar."

That was about as embarrassing a moment as I could recall in all my life. Of course, the soldiers were too busy thinking about their own hides to be concerned about mine, but the notion that one of them might see Momma hounding me left a savage wound in my pride.

Momma and SincereAnne flapped their arms like mother hens trying to get their chicks to shelter before a storm. We begged and pleaded to stay, but they would hear nothing of it. We were their baby boys, and they were going to protect us, even if it killed us.

"Get to the cellar," Momma commanded.

Pooty and I squawked. Then I saw Pa limping toward the barn. I knew he was checking on the mules to make sure the Yankees didn't steal them—or eat them—before they left.

"Pa needs our help," I yelled.

Pooty and I broke for the barn as Momma and SincereAnne headed toward the cellar. At the barn we found the mules edgy and wanting outside.

"If shooting starts," Pa cried, "they'll panic and bust themselves up."

"Let me and Pooty take them out. We'll get away from here."

After pondering a moment, Pa nodded. "Only as long as you don't follow the soldiers. I don't want you getting shot."

"Okay," I answered. Pooty nodded his agreement.

Pa grabbed a couple halters and put them on the mules. Pooty and I were so excited we were shaking.

"Grab some hobbles," Pa said. "Don't dismount without hobbling the mules. We can't risk them breaking the reins if they panic."

I raced to the corner of the barn and grabbed two sets of hobbles, tossing one to Pooty as I returned. Pa boosted each of us up on the bare back of a mule, then opened the stalls. The nervous mules backed out of their stalls, then turned for the door and trotted outside.

"If you boys get shot, your mommas'll skin and tan my hide."

Pooty and I aimed our mules toward the Burke place, quickly crossing the creek and riding over to the black-ened ruins of Pooty's home. We lingered a minute, look-ing over our shoulders to see if any soldiers—or either of our mommas—were following us. Nobody had taken up our trail.

From down the valley we heard occasional gunshots, and I knew that was the direction I wanted to go. I had never seen war and was anxious to see what it looked like. I thought I'd never get the chance, because I still believed our Southerners would whip the Yankees and end the war before Christmas, well before the Confederate govern-ment came back for this seed corn.

"I wanna see the fight," I said to Pooty.

"Me, too."

I pointed to the ridge that paralleled the valley. "We can ride up there, climb a tree, and watch."

"Let's go," Pooty answered.

We kicked those mules into a run and quickly made it up the ridge, then raced along it toward the sounds of battle. The gunfire grew louder and more frequent, the explosion of cannon reverberating through the air. At a small clearing we jumped off our mules, tied them to a couple oak trees, and hobbled them. Then we ran to a tree and climbed up for a better view.

The rifle fire was ferocious, exceeded only by the blasts of cannon. A haze of white smoke rose like a fog over the battlefield, clouding our view. When we *could* see, it always seemed those five thousand Yankees out-numbered the Confederates. The roar of weapons mingled with the screams and cries of men fighting for their lives, the din carrying well in the crisp morning air. We were close enough to see men falling, but not close enough to see blood. We watched a group of Confederates charge a cannon, then disappear in a cloud of smoke and canister, and I prayed my brothers were not among the attackers.

I wanted the Southern boys to win and knew Pooty favored the Yankees, but we were so transfixed by the sight of death, by the roar and the smell of war, that we said nothing. We must've watched an hour or more, never realizing that the Confederates were gradually being pushed back—in our direction.

The first sign of trouble was the sound of pounding hooves racing toward us. Five Confederate soldiers, their horses lathered to a froth, charged into the clearing, reined up, and turned their mounts toward the battleground. Then the lieutenant, spotting our hobbled mules, jerked his pistol from its scabbard and looked about.

He pointed the mules out to the others, who also withdrew their weapons. I looked at Pooty. He was pale. I knew *I* was shaking. I screwed up the courage to yell, "Here we are! In the tree!"

The lieutenant spotted us first, then waved us down. "Who you boys be for in this war?"

"Arkansas," I answered before Pooty could open his mouth.

"What are you doing up there? Spying?"

"No, sir," I answered, descending the tree. "Pa sent me up here to hide the mules so the Yankees don't take them."

The lieutenant eyed me suspiciously.

"I was hoping I might see my brothers." I jumped to the ground, Pooty falling down behind me.

The soldiers holstered their guns. "What's their regiment?"

"Thirty-fourth Arkansas. You heard of Jim, Andy, or Van Lomax?"

The lieutenant frowned. "Nope. This is Marmaduke's cavalry." A gunshot whizzed overhead. "You boys better get home quick. There may be a difficulty up here."

"Yes, sir," I said, and me and Pooty darted for the mules.

Another shot flew by, and then a third splatted into the ground not twenty feet from me. We unhobbled and untied those mules quickly. Pooty bounded onto one animal's back and charged for home. I was about to take out after him when the lieutenant called me. "Boy," he said, "I'll give you some news if you promise you won't tell anyone."

"Cross my heart and hope to die."

"The Thirty-fourth is moving up from Van Buren. Should be around Prairie Grove in a week."

His message brought a smile to my lips. "Thanks."

"Don't tell a soul," he said. "It could endanger your kin."

"Yes, sir," I answered, checking to make sure Pooty was out of hearing range. Apparently the sight of secesh in uniform had put a great fright in him. He was so far gone I couldn't have reached him with a telegraph.

"Get going, boy," the lieutenant said, "before trouble runs up these hills."

I slapped the old mule on the behind and angled down the hill toward home as a few Rebel cavalrymen raced up the hillside. They had a wild, ragged look about them. Their uniforms were not nearly as uniform as those of the Yankees; many were splotched with their own blood. I saw one man with a dangling arm and a shattered jaw. All were cursing the infernal Yankees.

One wild cavalryman spotted me and reined his horse in my direction. Whooping and hollering, he jerked his hat from his head and waved it at me. "Skedaddle, boy, the Yankees is coming for another dance."

I kicked my old mule, getting as much out of him as I could, which wasn't much more than if I'd gotten off and pushed him. The woods cracked with an occasional shot and the resulting scream, and the rumble from the valley inched up the hill. I raced my mule on, sticking to the ridge until I was well past Pooty's place, then circling wide and approaching our house from the stream.

Figuring the Yankees had abandoned our place to

chase the Southern boys, I was shocked when I came around a bend in the creek and up the embankment. There were fewer soldiers around but a lot more activity in front of the house. At first I didn't understand what was happening, and my mule was so winded I couldn't beat him into more than a slow walk.

In the distance the battle rumbled like low thunder, blocking out the cries, screams, and moans until I drew within fifty yards of the house. It had been turned into a hospital. On the front porch I saw a half-dozen men holding a screaming man down on what looked like our dinner table while a doctor—or a carpenter, for that matter—sawed off his leg. The wounded—a hundred or more—were laid out row upon row in front of the house. They cried out to the battlefield trinity of Mother, God, and water; they writhed on dirty blankets or bare ground; they thrashed their legs in pain; they flailed their arms in futility.

I tried to ride on, but my mule shied away. I didn't understand why until I caught the aroma of death and decay, mingled with the smell of burnt powder and heated metal. The mule kept balking, even when I slapped him up beside the head and grabbed his ugly ear. As I was trying to convince him to advance, I heard my name.

"Henry, Henry!" Momma cried, running from among the wounded and charging toward me like a hungry Yankee after an unguarded chicken. "You're alive!" She bolted up to the mule and jerked me down. "Pooty said you'd been captured, maybe killed by secesh."

Though I was a mite shaken by her display, my mule was too tired to move. He just stood there, swatting his tail and drooling, while Momma kissed me. I was thrashing and trying to get out of her grip, wishing she would kiss the mule instead of me in front of everybody.

"Thank God you're all right. It's so terrible, all the killing."

Finally I broke free of her. "I've got to get the mule

to the barn, Momma." I tugged on his reins and dragged him behind me.

Stretcher bearers raced by, carrying more wounded to the front of the house. I put up the mule in the stall beside the one Pooty had been riding. Pooty's mule kept shaking his head, and I saw a spot of blood on his ear. Looking a little closer, I noticed a hole where a bullet had gone through. Pooty had had a close call.

I checked my own mule for wounds and after finding none went back outside and on toward the house. At one end of the porch were a half-dozen bodies stacked atop one another like cordwood. I walked among the wounded, staring at them and wincing at their terrible injuries.

Feeling faint at the sight of so much blood and shattered bone, I staggered a moment, then felt a comforting arm around my shoulders. I looked up and saw RuthAnne Burke. Her hands and dress were splotched with blood, and her face was streaked with tears. "You okay, Henry?"

"A little light-headed," I admitted.

She wiped some of her tears away with her blood-stained sleeve. "Why don't you go to the creek and splash some cool water on your face. When you feel up to it, start toting some water back. For some men it'll be the last thing we can ever do for them."

Taking a deep breath, I nodded.

RuthAnne pointed to a couple buckets on the porch, then patted me on the back. "Thank you."

Almost in a trance I walked toward the buckets, not realizing when I'd drawn even with our dinner table. I seemed to block out all sound—except for a sudden scream right beside me. When I jerked my head around, I saw the doctor sawing on a man's arm. The sight sent me jumping backward, then tripping over something in my path. I looked down at a bloody pile of amputated arms and legs. Grabbing the two buckets, I made a dash for the creek and managed to get behind the embankment before I started gagging and heaving.

Pooty was by the water, filling a couple pails of his

own. He looked up at the sound of my sickness. "Glad you made it back."

I nodded, gasped, then stumbled down to the creek, filling both buckets and waiting a minute until my head cleared. Pooty had returned to the house by then. When my knees lost their mushiness, I started back, too.

SincereAnne saw me with the water and offered me a tin can. "I'm pleased you weren't hurt," she said. "Think you could give water to the wounded?"

I exchanged one of my pails for her tin can, went to the nearest man, and squatted down beside him. He lay still, his eyes staring somewhere beyond me. "Want a drink?" I asked, dipping the tin in the water with one hand and sliding the other under his neck.

"He's dead," said a soldier beside me.

Never having touched a dead man before, I jerked my hand free, and his head clunked to the ground.

"Sorry," I murmured, but I don't think he heard me.

"That's okay, lad," said the wounded soldier. "He never had a girl, but he died looking at an angel." The soldier pointed to RuthAnne as she scurried past. "That's her."

I lifted the fellow's head and gave him a drink, then put his hat beneath him for a pillow. As I did, I looked around and saw RuthAnne, LouAnne, and DeeAnne all tending soldiers. Then I saw my sisters helping as well, and Momma and SincereAnne. I even spotted Pa up on the porch helping hold another soldier down while the doctor cut the flesh to make a flap to cover the stump of his leg.

I moved from soldier to soldier, offering water and what encouragement I could, but I never did have a way with words, especially not when I was talking to dying men. Scattered among the Yankees were a dozen or more Confederates. Not a single one of them got any less attention than the Yankees. Before the firing had started, the men had been enemies, but once they were downed they became brothers in blood.

Until that moment war had seemed glorious to me and I had envied my brothers, but no longer. I still didn't like Yankees for what Old Abe Lincoln had made them do, but I tried to comfort as many of them as I could in case one of my brothers was ever downed in battle.

I don't know how many trips I made to the creek before dusk, but when darkness finally slipped over the hills, I realized that the sounds of battle had died in the distance. For fully nine hours, maybe more, the two armies had fought each other. The Yankees had forced the Confederates to retreat, but they couldn't drive them from the hills. A line of campfires stretched along the top of the ridges for as far as a man could see.

The Yankees built fires in front of our house to keep the wounded warm. In the darkness I helped chop wood to feed those fires. Some men were carried into our house for extra warmth, but our place was not large enough to hold them all. Some were placed in our beds, but most were packed so closely together on the floor that it was difficult to walk across the room without stepping on someone. A handful of men who could walk climbed into the loft, which was where my family and the Burkes now slept, if they slept at all.

It was a woeful night—men moaning, screaming, dying quietly. The Burke sisters worked until dawn, as did Lissa. Little Harriet couldn't help as much as the older girls, but she crawled among the wounded, singing hymns to them. They seemed to like that, and several asked her to kiss them on the forehead or cheek. When Harriet tired out, she crawled into the corner and fell asleep. Mother found her, carried her into the loft, and placed her on my bed.

By morning the Confederate cavalry had slipped away, and the area was left to the Yankees. They dragged themselves back to our place and reassembled. Cooks built great fires and made the best soup they could with what they had. The doctors made sure the wounded got what they could eat, but they also shared the food with us. It was a thin soup, the kind Momma would've been laughed out of the county for making, but we were so tired and hungry it tasted good.

The cost of war was laid out before us the next day, when gravediggers dug thirty-seven graves at the edge of our field. The chaplain came to the house and requested that little Harriet sing a hymn at the burial service that afternoon. He said several of the wounded had requested it, knowing how much comfort her songs had brought to their comrades in their final hours.

Harriet, who was only eight or nine at the time, was nervous as the chaplain said a few words of solace over the dead soldiers. There must've been two or three hundred soldiers standing there, whispering among themselves, fidgety that the next burial might be their own.

But when the chaplain asked Harriet to sing, the soldiers went as quiet as I'd ever heard it on the farm. There wasn't a man whispering, not a bird singing, not a leaf rustling, just Harriet's high voice singing "Rock of Ages."

I had never seen so many men cry.

Chapter Seven

Two days later, after supply wagons caught up with the Yankees, the Union Army pulled out of Cane Hill, moving southeast toward Reed's Mountain and hoping to catch the Confederates by surprise. Before they left, the Yankees did me one last favor: They burned the college at Cane Hill. Momma had wanted me to go to college and get a little education, but I figured I was smart enough as I was. With the college burned, Momma wouldn't bother me again.

Only problem with the Yankees firing the college was, they burned up the rest of town. We heard the place looked like chimneyville, because that was about all that was left standing. Our place was spared because Yankee wounded were still recovering there and the Burke sisters had made such an impression on those boys.

Rumors were the Southern army was moving up from Van Buren to finish what the cavalry had started at the battle of Cane Hill and then take Fayetteville. That squared with what the Rebel lieutenant had told me.

The news didn't matter to Pooty. He'd returned to his old ways, bragging about what fine soldiers the Yankees were and how they had driven the secesh away. He took to wearing his cavalry hat and scarf inside the house until he became such a pest I wanted to pound a little education into him, but there were still a dozen Union soldiers recuperating inside.

I got lonely for my brothers. From the day I was born I'd always had brothers, and now there were none. I wanted to find them and tell them to dodge Yankee bullets because I had seen what bullets could do.

Since the Yankees had cleaned us out of food, we didn't have much to eat. Momma had enough flour to make biscuits, and Pa would bring in rabbits or squirrels he killed out in the woods. We shared the meat with the soldiers. I kept hoping SincereAnne would make some of her biscuits for them. If they survived that, I suspect they would have changed their allegiance to the Southern cause.

At every meal I ate only half of what I was served, saving the rest so I would have something to nibble on when I ran away to find my brothers. Momma noticed once and grabbed me by the ear afterward, hauling me to the corner. "Why aren't you eating all your supper?"

"Saving it for later," I replied.

"Don't story me, Henry. You've got that runaway look in your eye. You're not planning on going to see Amanda Fudge, are you?"

I told the truth. "No."

"You stay away from that girl. You hear me?"

"Yes, ma'am."

I retreated up the ladder into the loft, where RuthAnne and DeeAnne were eating their supper with a couple wounded Yankees. The soldiers were talking all sweet-mouthed and low, like they had itchy britches. I looked to make sure the fellows hadn't received head wounds that impaired their judgment in women. They hadn't. Only thing I could figure was, the farther soldiers got away from home, the less they cared about what others thought of their choice in women. I tried to hear what they were saying, but LouAnne came over.

She sidled over to me all nice and innocent, smiling as sweetly as a homely girl could. I tried to back away, but she came within range, cocked her arm, and slapped me across the face.

I was tempted to knock her all the way across the loft, but I didn't figure Pa would take too kindly to that brand of hospitality. "What'd you do that for?" I howled, rubbing my cheek.

"You looked like you needed it."

I could either fight or retreat. Having seen the Southern army retreat, I saw no shame in withdrawing to my corner of the loft and forgetting LouAnne.

Pooty came up later and wanted to play cards.

"Not until you tell me something. Why's LouAnne slapping me all the time?"

"Either she likes you or she hates your guts," Pooty said.

I wished I'd never asked. I was even more stunned when Pooty spoke again.

"DeeAnne likes your brother Thomas and has even written him."

Then I knew Pooty was lying. Not one of my brothers was crazy enough to like a Burke girl. Anxious to change the subject, I dealt cards. I had taught Pooty a little poker, and even though I always beat him he seemed to be fascinated by the game. Of course, I was a better card player and changed the rules as I went along. On top of that the deck was so dog-eared and torn I could pretty much tell by its backside every card Pooty had. My cheating was harmless, us not having anything worthwhile to bet, not even marbles since Amanda had ruined both my aim and my respect for the innocence of girls.

I whipped him fair and square about the first three or four hands, and he was getting mighty frustrated. I knew it must be taxing his feeble mind to play with someone as smart as me. About the fourth or fifth hand I drew a pair of jacks on the deal and took three cards, getting a pair of fives. Pooty took two cards, and from the back of them I was certain what he had. I decided to see just how dumb he was.

Showing my cards, I announced, "Two pair, jacks over fives."

Pooty grinned like he'd finally figured out what his middle leg was really for. "Four of a kind." He flashed his nines triumphantly before me. "I win."

Shaking my head, I said, "What do you mean, four of a kind?"

He looked at his hand as if he'd made a gigantic mistake. His brain was working so fast I could hear it groaning like a waterwheel at the gristmill.

"Four of a kind, nines."

I sighed and shook my head like I couldn't believe he could be so stupid. "Nope," I said. "You got two pair."

"Huh? I ain't blind. I see four nines."

"Nope. You got a pair of red nines and a pair of black nines. My jacks over fives beat your nines over nines."

Pooty scratched his head. "Wait a second," he finally said. "Each of your pairs has a black and a red card in it."

"The red-and-black rule applies when you've got all four cards."

Confused, he stared at me. "I don't know about that."

I was insulted. "Okay, you just go ask your momma," I said, knowing SincereAnne had as low an opinion of gambling as my momma did.

Pooty glanced over his shoulder a moment, then bit his lip. Suddenly he bent over and grabbed the cards, then scurried over to the Yankees and his sisters. "Which of these hands wins?" he asked the soldiers.

They laughed. "Poker, right?" asked one.

Pooty nodded.

"Four of a kind," said the other.

"The red-and-black rule doesn't count?"

The soldiers shrugged. "Never heard of it."

I could sense another fistfight coming on when Pooty glared over his shoulder at me.

But LouAnne, bless her heart, prevented it. "Momma," she called, "Henry's teaching Joe Don to play poker."

Quicker than dumplings through a goose, Sincere-Anne bolted up that ladder. My momma was right on her heels.

Pooty collapsed his cards into a single stack, and I scrambled to pick up the deck and hide it as well. But my clammy fingers fumbled the cards and scattered them on the floor for all to see.

SincereAnne jerked the cards from Pooty's hand and grabbed him by the ear. "You know better than to be playing with cards, Joe Don. They're the devil's pastime."

Momma stood over me, arms folded. "Where'd you get the cards?"

I figured it was time to place blame where blame was due. None of this would've happened if the damn Union Army hadn't invaded Arkansas. "A Yankee soldier gave them to me."

"Did not," Pooty interrupted. "You had them hid between the rafters and shingles before the soldiers ever arrived."

Momma looked about as amused as a miser with a hole in his pocket. "You been teaching him poker?"

Now, I'd been taught never to lie, but it just didn't always seem wise to tell the truth. This time, though, there was no way out of it. "No, I haven't been teaching him poker." That was the honest truth. I'd been teaching him rules I made up as I went along, so you couldn't really call it poker.

"He has too!" shouted Pooty.

"Joe Don doesn't tell stories like Henry," Sincere-Anne said.

Momma shot SincereAnne a look to melt glass, then turned to me.

I shrugged. "Ask the Yankees if there's any red-and-black rule in poker."

The soldiers shook their heads.

"See, it ain't poker. It's just a game."

Momma looked at me. "Was anything bet? Was that why you saved your biscuit and fried squirrel?"

"Pooty wanted me to, but I said no, that it was wrong."

Of course, Pooty screamed, "He's lying!"

Unfortunately I'd stretched the truth a little too far. Momma grabbed my ear and twisted it until I squealed like a stuck pig.

"If you weren't playing poker, why'd betting come up, Henry?"

She had a point. I'd run out of luck. "Pick up those cards," she ordered.

I tried to, but I couldn't reach them until she let go my ear. SincereAnne handed Momma the cards Pooty had been holding. After I'd gathered the rest, Momma snatched them from my hands and ordered me down the ladder. She marched to the fireplace and tossed the cards in, and the flames took to them like hogs to slop.

Then Momma marched me over to Pa, who was un-hooking his razor strop from its peg on the wall. It was going to be another night of sleeping on my belly. When Pa was done, he checked the strop to make sure it was okay, then sent me to bed, commanding me never to tell a lie again.

I certainly hadn't intended to tell a lie, but the facts got away from me. And I knew I'd never tell another lie unless it couldn't be avoided. I climbed up the ladder and into the loft.

Pooty grinned. I could hear his brain creaking again, so I knew he was trying to come up with something smart to say, but a bear'd sooner develop table manners than Pooty'd say something intelligent.

With my tail between my legs I snuck over to bed, pulled off my brogans, and got under the covers, not even bothering to exchange my clothes for a nightshirt. Then, more than ever, I wanted to see my brothers. I made up my mind to run away before dawn.

I wanted a good night's sleep, but RuthAnne and

DeeAnne giggled with those Yankees until late. Pooty made every possible effort to bump my sore behind. Though there was some risk in it for me, I prayed for Pooty to cut a nose-knocker that would drive his sisters downstairs and those soldiers back to Yankeeland, but he failed me as he had done several times already since rooming with us. During his stay I'd lost my marbles and my deck of cards. The only thing I still had, other than my flag, was my pocketknife, and I patted my pocket just to be sure. I considered using the knife to carve my initials on Pooty's behind, but I figured he'd accuse me of trying to kill him, and SincereAnne would believe him.

For someone so worried about her son learning a little about poker, SincereAnne didn't seem to mind her daughters staying up late and unattended with those Yankee soldiers. Of course, I figured the soldiers liked their company better after dark when they couldn't see the girls' faces.

I finally managed to doze off and awoke before anyone else. I put on my brogans, took my coat and hat, then grabbed my biscuit and squirrel. With great pleasure I pulled the blanket off Pooty to take with me and slipped down the ladder into the kitchen. I eased outside, then marched to the barn under a sliver of a moon. Inside I felt my way to the stalls where the mules were tied. In the darkness I checked out the two mules, feeling their ears for the one grazed during the battle. He seemed the stronger of the two.

I folded the blanket and tossed it over the animal's back, then fumbled about the stall until I found a halter. I slipped it over his head and led him out of the barn and toward the creek, pulling my coat tight against the morning cold. At the embankment I mounted and crossed Jordan Creek, then hit the road. In the early dawn I slipped through Cane Hill, where I saw the ruins of the college and the chimneys from burned-out stores and houses. Some lonesome hounds took to barking at me, spooking my mule. I guess I should've known running away was

stupider than Pooty's poker playing, but I was tired of the
Burkes, even if their presence had likely saved our place,
and I wanted to see my brothers so bad.

Early on I heard riders coming hard down the road,
so I ran my mule off into the bushes. I dismounted and
held his head, trying to calm him so he wouldn't make a
sound as a dozen riders galloped by on lathered horses. I
couldn't tell much about them, the light being so dim,
though I could've sworn the one in the lead was riding
the black stallion Amanda had ridden previously.

I waited a good ten minutes before I eased back on
the road to continue my trip. As I was congratulating myself for slipping around the twelve men, my mule flicked
his ears up and jerked his head, missing a stride. I caught
my breath, looked over my shoulder, and almost irrigated
my pants.

A lone rider on a black stallion was coming toward me.

My mule couldn't outrun him, but I didn't know
what else to try. I nudged my heel against the animal's
side and got him to jogging, but it was mere foolishness—
he didn't have the speed God gave a tortoise. Except for
a pocketknife in my britches, all I had was my wits. If
this man was related to Pooty, I might stand a chance; if
he wasn't, I probably didn't.

Carbine drawn, he came up behind me. "Whoa," he
yelled, "or I'll shoot!"

My hand was trembling as I yanked on the reins. The
rider, wearing a dark hat with a feathered plume and a
mask over his face, was beside me instantly. "What are
you doing, boy?"

"Riding."

When he cocked his carbine, I noticed two brass
brads nailed into the stock. He waved the carbine under
my nostrils like he wanted to pick my nose. "A boy out
this time of day can't be up to any good."

I figured I was doing less harm to folks than this
fellow, but it was an opinion I kept to myself.

"What's your name?"

"I can't tell you."

"Why not? This gun tells me you will."

"If I tell you, you might tell my momma and my pa."

"What difference does that make?"

"I'm off to join the army, and they don't know."

"Which army?"

Now I was stumped. If I picked the wrong army, it might be the last mistake I ever made. "The one my brothers joined."

He let out a long breath and wiggled the carbine at me again. "Now, just which one would that be?"

"If I say, you might shoot me."

"If you don't, I will anyway."

It didn't take much poker experience to realize I had no chance if I kept my mouth shut. At least I had a fifty-fifty chance if I admitted my allegiance.

"My finger's getting itchy."

Taking a deep breath, I expected to be shot the moment I answered. "The Confederate Army."

The fellow nodded, then lowered his carbine. "Going to fight Yankees, are you?"

"Yes, sir."

"The bastards," he replied.

The blood about froze in my veins—not from the weather but from the way he said "bastards." The word seethed hate. I had heard it pronounced that way by one other person: Amanda. This had to be her pa. I studied him hard and realized I'd seen his profile the night the riders burned our outhouse.

Now I was more scared than I had been before. There was something evil about this man who skulked around in the night, who believed in a cause but would not put on the uniform of that cause and fight face-to-face with the enemy.

In the morning light I was just able to make out the green of his eyes, the same green he had passed to his daughter. For some strange reason I wondered if he was wearing drawers.

Beryl Fudge gave me a hard stare, then slid his carbine in its saddle boot. "You the Lomax boy, the one folks called Hurry Home?"

I nodded. "Who are you?"

"No matter, or that we even met. How you gonna find the army?"

"I figure they'll be heading for Fayetteville."

Fudge eyed me suspiciously. "Where'd you hear that?"

I licked my lips and decided on a lie that would settle a score for me. "I found out from a blinky-eyed boy who'd been salting his meat in a little blond girl. Blinky said she gabbed about overhearing her pa talk about it."

What I could see of Fudge's face turned red, and even through his mask I could tell his jaw was clenched. His rein hand tightened into a fist while his gun hand dropped to the revolver on his belt.

"You wouldn't tell a fellow this girl's name, would you?"

"No, sir, I wouldn't, because I wouldn't want to dishonor her name, though I hear Blinky's mule isn't the only one that's ever gotten in her stable." For a moment I thought I'd committed suicide for sure. I certainly was glad when the steam quit coming out of his ears. "Maybe I best be riding on to find the army."

Fudge just stared at me. "One thing, boy: When you ride off the road and hide in the bushes, take off your hat. I caught the hat's profile, and that's how I knew there was someone here."

"Thanks," I said, relieved he was concerned about my safety in spite of my remarks.

"Another thing," he added. "Next time you visit your folks, tell them they'd be a lot safer if they kicked out those bastard Yankee lovers that's staying with them."

"I'll do that." I nudged my mule forward, half expecting to be shot in the back by the skunk, but I heard him gallop away. As soon as he was out of sight, I turned my mule into the brush, jumped down, and made more water than a brigade of Yankees.

I mounted up and had ridden a couple miles down the road when I caught sight of a plume of smoke off in the woods. I thought it might be Confederate soldiers making breakfast, so I turned down a wagon trail that led toward the smoke.

Through the trees I saw that it wasn't a campfire but smoke from a house that had been burned to the ground. As I came into a clearing, I heard a scream and saw a woman jump up from the ground in front of the smoldering rubble that had been her home. A little girl not more than four of five clung to her momma's nightgown. I realized they had been kneeling over a body.

The woman stood there, her soot-stained faced lined with the tracks of her tears. "They killed him," she kept repeating. "They killed my husband."

"Who?"

"The riders."

"Why?"

"They demanded his valuables, wanted to know where we hid our money and our silver. We had none. They didn't believe us. I begged them not to kill him. They killed him over nothing because we had nothing except this house and each other. Now I've lost that."

"You've got me, Momma," said the girl, shivering in the cold.

The woman picked up her daughter and hugged her.

"Do you know who it was, any of the riders?"

The woman shook her head.

"Was one riding a black stallion?"

She nodded. "The one that shot my husband."

Chapter Eight

I helped the woman bury her husband. The ground was dry and hard, so the digging took me most of the day. I wanted to get the man planted and ride on before sundown. They say it's bad luck to leave a grave uncovered, and I figured I was running low on luck, my last bit having drained away when I insulted Amanda to her father's face.

The new widow wanted to bury her husband in something, but all her quilts and blankets had burned in the fire. She looked at the blanket on my mule.

"Your blanket'd make a fine shroud. I'd pay you for it if I had the money," she said, "but I lost everything except the clothes on my back and my girl."

I felt sorry for the woman, but it was December. I shook my head. "I need it to stay warm."

She started bawling, but I refrained from telling her my blanket and all the firewood in the Ozarks wouldn't warm her husband up.

I walked over to the modest barn and pulled open the door. "Maybe there's something in here," I said. I found a couple gunny sacks, but nothing more of use. Stepping back outside, I waved them at the woman. "These'll have to do."

She kept bawling, her daughter along with her, as I

knelt down beside the body. I slipped the sack over his head and past his neck, then snugged it down on his narrow shoulders as best I could. The other sack I used to cover his hands and arms as far as it would go. I don't know that that burial shroud satisfied the woman, but she didn't have many other choices.

Together she and I rolled him over to the grave, then shoved him inside. Like a log he fell into his final resting place, but he landed all contorted, so I slid down in the hole to turn him on his back and straighten him out. The grave being a bit short, I had to bend his knees to make him fit, wedging his gunny-sacked head against one end of the grave and his bare feet against the other.

The widow woman peered into the grave and gasped. "You can't bury him on his back."

"Why not?"

"He never could sleep on his back, only his side. Turn him on his side."

Well, I wrestled that corpse until he was lying on his side, knees bent, head hanging down against his shoulder. It seemed to me he would've been a hell of a lot more comfortable the way I had him to begin with, but I'd never slept with the man. I started to ask her if he'd taken a leak before we planted him, just to make sure he didn't get the urge during the night and flood himself out, but I held my tongue. When I climbed out of the grave, me and the woman just looked at one another, not knowing exactly what to do next.

"Don't you need to say some words?" I asked, knowing I wasn't eloquent enough to address God on such a somber occasion.

The woman nodded, sobbing a little before she shook her head and composed herself. She picked up her daughter, hugged her tight to her bosom, then bowed her head and began to pray. "Dear God, Eb was a good man who did right by me and his girl. Take his soul to heaven and send to hell the son of a bitch who killed him. Amen."

"Son a bitch," the little girl said.

To my way of thinking, no better prayer was ever spoken.

Though I was anxious to get away from there, I knew I had to stay and cover the grave, making sure that every last clod I had removed from the hole was returned. A gravedigger who didn't do that was marked for an early death, and I didn't want to take that chance, not with the Yankees, bushwhackers, and Beryl Fudge around.

I worked fast and hard, wanting to put a little distance between me and the place before darkness set in. When I finally mounded the dirt up, the low-slung clouds loosed a light drizzle. The woman took to sobbing again, but these were tears of joy.

"It's a sign," she said.

A sign I was going to freeze my butt off that night, I thought. "Of what?"

"That Eb's soul's gone to heaven. Hallelujah," she cried.

"Hallelujah," echoed the little girl.

"Hallelujah," I said with as much enthusiasm as I could muster.

Now, I never believed in superstitions—unless they worked—so I didn't know what to make of her claim that Eb's soul had found a heavenly home. I figured he might be so confused being on his side rather than his back that he would never find his way to the outhouse if nature called, much less upstairs to his heavenly mansion.

The widow smiled, her tears mingling with the light drizzle upon her cheeks. "Thank you," she said. "We'd never've made it without you."

I shrugged. "How'll you and your girl manage?"

"We'll stay the night in the barn," she said. "After that I don't know."

"You got any friends or neighbors?"

"Neighbors yes, friends no. Eb had a bad arm and wasn't fit for the army. Didn't help matters he was for the Union."

"Good luck," I said, "but I gotta get going." I turned

to walk away, but she grabbed me by the arm and kissed me on the forehead, then held her little girl up to kiss me on the cheek. I felt bad about leaving them, but I had to find my brothers.

The widow and her daughter followed me to my mount. I climbed aboard, aimed the mule for the road, and waved over my shoulder as I left. I followed the road a ways but heard horses coming and drove my mule into the woods, never stopping to check what was behind me. After my encounter with Beryl Fudge I wanted to avoid getting killed like the poor man back down the road. The horsemen galloped by. I figured they might be cavalry or more bushwhackers and decided to stick to the back trails and hope I didn't encounter anybody with a personal or political grudge.

Bushwhackers were like snakes—no telling when you might encounter one—and they were just as unpredictable. I didn't get far that first night, seeing as how I had lost so much time burying that fellow on his side. I ate cold biscuits and squirrel, slept, then continued on my way. By the next night I no longer knew how far I had traveled, except that I was likely east of Prairie Grove and headed toward Fayetteville. Though I was making slow time, I'd not been seen, much less pestered, by a single bushwhacker, Yankee, or Confederate. Of course, I'd spent plenty of time in the cold, my fires never lasting long enough to do more than remind me what warmth was about. My blanket was thinner than a thief's alibi, and my feet were colder than a bushwhacker's heart. If I didn't freeze first, I was still aiming to make Fayetteville.

My third day out I was following a back trail when I heard a noise that could only be soldiers approaching the trail from the north. I rode into the brush and caught a glimpse of a Yankee cavalryman cautiously riding out onto the trail up ahead. I took off my hat and dismounted, grabbing the halter of the mule and patting his head to keep him quiet and calm.

Other cavalrymen appeared, pulling their carbines

and motioning to the rest to take both sides of the trail. I figured somebody was about to be ambushed, and I kept hoping it was Beryl Fudge. Then, just as suddenly as they had appeared, they disappeared, but I knew they were still there, waiting to pepper somebody. I wondered if I'd been a few minutes earlier if they might have filled me with so much lead that I would've rattled when I walked.

The woods turned still, without so much as the sound of a bird chirping. I wanted to get the hell out of there, but it was so quiet I didn't feel I could slip away without being heard. Gradually I heard a low pounding and realized it was my heart, beating so hard I feared the Yankees would hear it.

Somehow, over my throbbing heart, I heard the noise of more riders approaching. I squinted down the trail and saw five men in butternut uniforms cautiously coming in my direction. As best I could tell, a sergeant was in the lead, followed by a corporal with a pack mule, then three privates. I prayed that none of them were my brothers. I replaced my hat on my head and, with one hand beneath the halter and the other wrapped in the reins, made certain the mule wouldn't bolt when the shooting started.

The Confederate patrol drew nearer. I saw the sergeant turn in his saddle and start to give an order. But the first word I heard came from the woods, not the trail.

"Fire!"

The woods erupted in sound, smoke, and panic.

"Ambush!" screamed the sergeant as he fell from his horse onto the trail.

My mule tried to jerk free, but I climbed atop him. The guns kept firing, which was what I wanted because it gave me a chance to escape toward Prairie Grove. I plunged through the woods, the echoing gunfire covering the sound of my mule's dash through the brush. My chest was pounding like a blacksmith on an anvil.

Certain I'd made my escape, I forgot one thing: The trail I was trying desperately to avoid curved in the direction I was heading. The gunfire had stopped, but I wasn't too worried—until I heard the sound of galloping hooves.

In a panic I followed the trail around a limestone cliff. As the approaching hoofbeats grew louder, I knew I was running out of time. I jumped off the mule, tied the reins around my hand, and took my hat off as I led the animal to a clump of trees. My knees were shaking like a bed on a groom's wedding night.

Two mounts barreled around the bend in the trail. I was relieved to see that one was a pack mule and the second a horse ridden by a man in butternut. The man's eyes were wild. He reined up at the foot of the cliff and twisted around in his saddle, cupping his hand to his ear. His gaze flicked back and forth between the trail behind him and the four bags hanging on the pack mule.

The soldier looked up and down the trail as if he didn't know what to do. Next he studied the cliff and reined his horse around, starting for me. I stood motionless, hoping my mule wouldn't give me away. The corporal jumped from the saddle, quickly tied his horse, and turned to the pack mule, which had a U.S. brand on its rump. He jerked the bags from the pack saddle and dropped them at his feet.

By the clink of the bags when they landed, I knew he was carrying coin. No matter how little money was in those bags, it was surely more than I had ever seen in all my life. I swallowed hard.

The soldier slapped the pack mule away, and the animal bolted down the trail and into the woods. Quickly the soldier picked up a bag in each hand and scurried to the cliff. Finding a narrow crevice, he shoved the bags in, then returned for the others and wedged them atop the first two.

I figured that once he left, I would become the richest twelve-year-old in all of Arkansas.

Standing at the base of the cliff, the soldier picked up rocks and tossed them into the crevice. Then he gathered limbs and shoved them in as well, all the time look-

ing back down the trail for the Yankees. Grabbing a
downed limb not fifteen feet from me, he used it to sweep
away the tracks leading to the crevice.

He sighed loudly, then said to his horse, "Let's get
out of here. We'll come back with cavalry for the payroll."

I was still holding my breath, waiting for him to
mount and ride on, when he flung the broken limb into
the clump of bushes where my mule and me were hiding.
I flinched when the limb hit the brush, but my mule
spooked and tried to bolt.

"Who is that?" yelled the soldier.

I was fighting my mule and couldn't answer. The
soldier jerked his revolver.

"Don't shoot," I cried, fighting both fear and my
mule.

"Come out or I will."

"I'm just a boy," I called out, clawing my way from
behind the bushes and jerking the mule with me.

When I emerged in the clearing, he cocked the hammer on his revolver. "You spying on me? You a Unionist?"

"I heard gunfire down the trail, and then horses. I
hid so I wouldn't get shot, what with soldiers and bushwhackers all about."

The corporal didn't seem satisfied. "Where do you
live?"

"Cane Hill."

"Why're you so far from home?"

"Looking for my brothers. They're in the army."

The corporal eyed me skeptically. "What regiment?"

"Thirty-fourth Arkansas."

He released the hammer on the gun. "That's a Washington County outfit."

I breathed easier. "I'll just be on my way."

"No, sir," he said. "You're coming with me."

"You can't conscript me." I crossed my hands over
my chest.

"I'm taking you prisoner."

"What?"

"If you ain't got brothers in the Thirty-fourth, I'll have you shot as a spy."

The corporal wasn't smiling, and I couldn't tell if he was bluffing or not. That's one of the problems with wartime. You can never be certain who's bluffing and who's not, whether it's two soldiers behind that fence or two thousand. But a scared man doesn't bluff as well, and by the quiver of the corporal's hand on the revolver still pointed at my head, I knew he was nervous.

"You mount up, boy." He waved the gun at my mule.

I nodded, pulled myself atop the animal, and studied the limestone cliff closely, trying to memorize it like I would the combination to a bank safe. I was already planning to become so rich I could hire hands to do my chores.

The corporal climbed into the saddle, then pointed down the trail toward Prairie Grove. "Ride, boy, and don't try to run away or I'll shoot you like those Yankees shot my men."

As we rode, I glanced over my shoulder occasionally to check the landmarks so I could find the payroll later. Every time I checked, I saw that the corporal was still pointing the gun at my back. I wondered if I was that serious a threat to the Southern army.

Just when I figured the corporal was the meanest soldier in the South, I heard a strange noise. I looked back and saw him wiping tears from his eyes. His lip was quivering. "I lost my best friend back there, boy. Why won't those damn Yankees just go back up north and leave us be?"

"Their women are too ugly," I answered.

He snickered and put his gun away. "I don't own no slaves, and this wouldn't be none of my affair if them Yankees hadn't come down. I got a wife and two girls that are having to fend for themselves down Little Rock way. A man shouldn't have to leave his family to kick those bastards out." He nudged his horse up beside my mule.

Digging into his haversack, he pulled out a square of white hardtack and handed it to me.

I was grateful, having long since eaten the squirrel and biscuit I'd left home with. But, though I was hungrier than a long -winded preacher's congregation come Sunday dinner, I knew hardtack wasn't the type of food you attacked head on. You had to slip up on it, soak a corner of it in your mouth, and then nibble around the edges. I've heard of soldiers dulling saws, breaking chisels, and ruining axes trying to break off a bite. Teeth just don't stand a chance unless you can afford to take casualties.

Hardtack wouldn't have been so bad if it was just as hard as a rock. After all, I had attacked SincereAnne's biscuits and survived. But hardtack also *tasted* like a rock. I began to think maybe I should've gnawed on that limestone cliff to fill my stomach as well as to mark the spot.

"What's your name?" the corporal asked.

"Henry Harrison Lomax. Yours?"

"Johnny Rankin. Do me a favor, Henry?"

I shrugged. What choice did I have? "What?"

"Don't tell anyone I was crying, would you?"

"Your secret's good with me."

"That's two secrets we've got, then."

"Huh?"

"We both know where the payroll is. Don't tell that to anyone."

"I won't tell a person," I assured him, though I didn't mention that I wanted all the money for myself.

"A lot of good fighting men have earned their pay."

He was right; I knew my brothers deserved theirs, and I planned to make sure they got it.

We talked for a bit, me trying to finish that hardtack without it finishing me. It was near dark when we approached Prairie Grove. I could see a dozen campfires where a hundred Rebel boys were waiting in a state of excitement.

Rankin reported to the captain, a narrow, clean-shaven man who was highly agitated at the interruption. "What do you want?"

"The payroll escort was ambushed. I'm the only survivor."

"What about the payroll?"

"I hid it," the corporal said.

"Who's that?" the captain asked, pointing to me.

"Henry Lomax. He saw me hide the money. I need men to go back for it so we can get it before anyone else finds it."

"Can't do, Corporal. The Yankees are close. General Hindman's bringing up the soldiers tonight. We could have battle tomorrow."

"But what if somebody else finds it?" Rankin wanted to know.

The captain pointed at me. "If he's the only other one to know, shoot him."

Something caught in my throat, and it wasn't hardtack.

"He's just a boy."

The captain laughed. "So are most of these men," he said with a sweep of his arm around the camp.

Rankin seemed as stunned as me by the captain's answer.

"Will the Thirty-fourth Arkansas be up tomorrow?"

"I think so. What difference does it make?"

"The boy has brothers in the Thirty-fourth, soldiers who can vouch for him."

"They won't need to if you'll shoot him like I told you to."

"Is that an order, sir?"

The captain smiled, stroking his chin. "It's a suggestion. Just don't let him get away until after we get the payroll."

"Yes, sir." Rankin reined his horse about and ordered me to follow.

"You gonna shoot me?"

"Not tonight."

I felt better, but only for a moment.

"Maybe in the morning, though."

It was a terrible thought that my last meal on earth was possibly the hardtack I had just eaten.

Chapter Nine

I had a fitful night's sleep. Corporal Rankin tied a rope from my foot to his so I'd still be there in the morning if he had to shoot me. Every time he turned he woke me, but I turned gently, hoping he had a good night's sleep and awoke in a good mood. Of course, my innards were so stiff from eating hardtack I figured the bullets might bounce off me. Even so, I didn't want to take the chance.

About sunrise, when the sky was lighting up and the woods were still dim, we were roused from our sleep by a sergeant who grabbed the rope and jerked it like it was his mother-in-law's neck.

"Get with your men," he said, then moved on to pester other souls who were trying to get a little sleep.

"I don't have a unit," Rankin said, stretching his arms and rubbing his eyes. He stood and untied the rope.

"Join the Thirty-fourth for the day," I suggested. "You could turn me over to my brothers."

"We gotta find the Thirty-fourth first."

The captain who had ordered my execution ran by fussing. "Hurry up. Look sharp. General Hindman's approaching with his army."

I spat in disgust. Hindman was the general who had conscripted my three brothers. I cursed his name, then reconsidered. If it hadn't been for the general pressing my brothers into service, I'd still be doing chores in Cane Hill. And because of him I was on the verge of becoming rich. I decided I owed him a hug.

Shortly the troops of Hindman's army appeared on the Cane Hill–Fayetteville road. Rankin mounted his horse and motioned for me to pick up my blanket and climb atop my mule. No sooner was I seated than twenty officers approached. The one in the lead wore a gray uniform with two gold stars on the collar. It was General Hindman, a dashing fellow, his hair long and dark, his mustache flowing into a well-trimmed beard that followed his determined jawline.

Rankin saluted. Not being a soldier I didn't and drew an immediate scolding from one of the officers.

"Salute, soldier, when an officer passes!" yelled some colonel with nothing better to do.

At times it's easier to do what you're ordered than to explain. I saluted as smartly as I could. General Hindman nodded and rode on. Behind him trod the first of several thousand troops. They were mostly Missouri men, who must have abandoned their state when it didn't leave the Union, and Texas men, who thought they should've been a nation all to themselves. Generally I preferred Texans to smallpox, Republicans, and tax collectors, but little else. They thought they were tougher than the rest of us because they were still fighting Indians at home. I thought they were just ignorant. Us folks in Arkansas were smart enough not to settle the Ozarks until after the Indian problem had been cleared up.

Sprinkled among all the Missourians and Texans were a few Arkansas units. As each one passed, Rankin asked if it was the 34th and if anyone knew of the Lomax brothers. After a spell a regiment passed with a few faces I recognized.

"Thirty-fourth Arkansas?" yelled Rankin.

"Yeah," answered several men in unison.

I felt my heart pounding. My brothers were near.

Then I saw them—gaunt and haggard, slouched under the weight of their shouldered rifles, eyes and heads drooping with exhaustion. "Jim, Andy, Van!"

All three looked around before Van spotted me. He elbowed Andy, then pointed me out. The three broke rank and ran to me.

"Henry," Jim scolded, "what the hell are you doing here?"

I straightened up on my mule. "Came here to tell you to duck."

They laughed.

"We figured that out long ago," Andy replied.

"He just wanted an excuse to run away from home," Jim said.

As I was introducing them to Corporal Rankin, the regimental colonel rode up. "Keep marching," he commanded.

Corporal Rankin saluted and volunteered to fight with the 34th until the battle was over and the Yankees were driven back to hell or wherever they bred. When the colonel accepted his offer, I hopped down, tossed my reins to the corporal, and ran with my brothers as they took their places in the formation.

They wanted to know about Momma, Pa, and the girls. Though they had passed close to home on the way to Prairie Grove, they hadn't had a chance to stop. I told them that between the Yankees and the homely Burke sisters, they probably couldn't have gotten within a half mile of the place without being shot or uglied to death.

"You shouldn't've left home, Henry," Jim scolded. "Momma'll be worried sick." He pointed to the mule. "You took one of Pa's mules, didn't you? And he didn't know you were going to do it, did he?"

"He does now, and I'll buy him another mule," I said softly in case Rankin was about.

Andy jumped me next. "Henry, this is war, and there's not a decent mule to be found around."

Van said, "You need to skedaddle home quick.

There's a Union Army behind us and a Union Army ahead of us. We're here for a fight, not a visit."

"Momma was right," Andy said. "You're the stubbornest, hardheadedest of her children."

Van grabbed my shoulder and jerked me to him, then patted me on the back. "It's the truth, but you're still our kid brother. We're pleased you came to see us. Tell us more about home."

I grinned, feeling I had been forgiven. "With Gordon Burke taking to the hills, the Burke women and Pooty are staying with us. Night riders burned the Burke place and our outhouse."

"Know who they were?" Andy asked.

"Beryl Fudge was one of them."

Andy said, "The bastard doesn't have the balls God gave a gnat. It figures he'd stay to pester women, children, and old men."

The column began to slow as officers assigned different brigades to different positions on a low wooded ridge that rose maybe sixty feet above the Illinois River valley toward Fayetteville. The Fayetteville road crossed the river about three quarters of a mile to the northeast of the ridge.

A hush fell over the troops at the sound of gunfire up the road.

"Sounds like our cavalry has found some Unionists," Van said, then turned to Jim and Andy. "What do we do with Henry?"

"No place is safe now, not if the Yankees are closing in," Jim replied.

Andy piped in, "The rear guard may not let him pass for fear he'll give information to the Yankees at our tail. We'll keep an eye on him here."

Jim sighed. "If something happens to him, Momma'll blame us, not him."

The gunfire picked up and came closer. Already batteries of Confederate cannon were taking up positions on either side of the road. The colonel raced up on his steed,

reining the gelding hard and pointing to a position behind
an apple orchard on the east side of the road. "Get in
battle line behind the trees, and stay hidden until the
Yankees advance. I'll call for your advance." He paused a
moment. "Look around, boys. This is Washington County.
This is your home, where your mothers, sisters, and
sweethearts live. Let's drive the abolitionists back to Bos-
ton and be done with this ugly war."

The men of the 34th Arkansas let out a cheer, then
began to fix bayonets and check the loads of their rifles.
The gentle click of metal against metal seemed even more
ominous than the approaching gunfire. Almost in unison
the soldiers trotted forward, fanning out into three lines,
grim and determined. I struggled to keep up with the
troops, who seemed to run as fast as the wind, even with
their heavy loads. Once I glanced around to see if Rankin
was following me. I didn't spot him, but when I turned
back I lost sight of my brothers. I panicked until I felt a
strong hand grab my arm and jerk me even faster toward
the orchard. It was Jim. I jumped in line with Van and
Andy.

The guns fell silent, and everything went quiet. We
listened to our own heaving breath and waited. Some soldiers ate squares of hardtack, read their Bibles, or wrote
last-minute letters to their folks in case they should die.
Others just fidgeted.

I talked to my brothers until a smattering of gunfire
gradually turned into a roar on the west end of the line,
to our left.

The colonel rode along our front, waving his sword.
"It's a diversion. The real attack will come from the road."

"How's he know?" I asked.

Andy pointed to a ridge across the river at activity I
didn't recognize.

"They're setting up artillery to support the infantry."

I thought my brothers were as smart as any general.
"If they start firing, hide behind a tree," Van said,

"but don't lean against it. If a cannonball hit it, the impact'd kill you."

My knees were shaking. I felt the earth rumble beneath me as Rebel batteries on both sides of the orchard fired at enemy artillery. Holding my ears against the deafening noise, I watched the artillerymen swab the cannon barrels, drive home the charge, load the cannonballs, tamp it all in, then jerk the lanyards to fire. With each shot the cannons jumped and rolled back. At a buzzing sound overhead the soldiers ducked, and Andy shoved me down. A cannonball thudded to the ground behind me.

"Stay low," Jim ordered.

It seemed our artillerymen were firing without effect against the Yankees; cannonballs from their side soon began to rain down on ours, knocking out our cannons one by one. Some artillerymen abandoned their damaged weapons while others tried to pull their cannons out of range.

Instantly Union soldiers charged off the ridge and down the road, crossed the river, and fanned out in battle lines.

"Here they come!" yelled the colonel, who must've thought his men were blind. "Get ready!"

The men rose to a crouch, awaiting their commander's orders.

I watched the Union soldiers charging, their yells carrying clearly in the crisp air. They came down that road like angry ants pouring out of a hole in the ground. A few began to fire. I never saw anything so grand as that charge, and I gazed in awe as those fools ran at us, more soldiers following behind them.

The colonel yelled to the 34th, "Hold your fire!"

Glancing at my brothers, I saw their jaws clenching, their eyes glazing over, and their grips tightening around their muskets.

The air buzzed with angry lead as the Yankees neared us.

"Fire!" screamed the colonel.

Now the 34th Arkansas entered the fray. The first line of men squeezed off a volley that blinded me with its acrid smoke. The second line did the same. Then my brothers stepped forward for the third volley while the others reloaded. The men of the 34th were firing as fast as they could load their guns.

Corporal Rankin appeared beside me, firing his carbine and then crouching down, bumping into me as he attempted to reload. In his excitement he dropped the carbine. As I reached to push it to him, I heard a sickening thud and felt my neck splattered with something wet. I glanced at Rankin and gasped. The side of his forehead was gone. I swiped at my neck, then looked at my hand. My fingers were smeared with his blood.

The corporal seemed frozen for an instant, as if he could not believe he was dying. As he tumbled over, I screamed. All three of my brothers glanced at me, then fired again at the now shattered Union line teetering between defeat and retreat. A cheer arose from the 34th as the Yankees fell back.

His face smudged with powder, Van grabbed me by the shoulder. His fingers bit into my flesh. "You've got to stay down, Henry, or you'll get killed."

All around me men were gasping for breath or moaning from injuries. The firing tapered off. As I looked around, I counted twelve men down but moving and three men perfectly still and perfectly dead.

"Let's go!" yelled the colonel. "Advance!"

Van shoved me to the ground. "Stay low and stay here, Henry." Then he fell in line with the others and trotted through the orchard as the 34th gave chase to the cowardly Yankees.

"Advance," the colonel yelled, "until you run up Old Abe's ass!"

Cheering, the entire regiment raced across the field. I raised my head and watched as our boys chased the backsides of Yankee cowards, a wall of butternut running through the gray haze of smoke. During a brief lull in the shooting I arose and raced through the orchard past dozens of downed men to get a better view of the impending Southern victory. I halted at the edge of the rise and watched the 34th drive the Yankees toward the river, knowing the Arkansas boys would give them a good whipping just like Pa had said.

Only problem with Pa's prediction was, he had never seen Yankee cannon loaded with grapeshot. Just when I thought the 34th was about to destroy every Yankee who had charged into the orchard, the cannons opened up.

The canister raised terrible screams and cut great swaths through our lines. The Washington County boys faltered, their charge ending in a trickle of Southern blood atop Yankee blood. They began to retreat, collecting their wounded colleagues as they limped back toward the ridge and the protection of the orchard. But many wounded and dead remained on the field, their bodies mingled with those of the Yankees. I understood now why Corporal Rankin had cried the day before. My eyes watered as I screamed at the Yankees, "Bastards, bastards!"

The 34th straggled back, its lines ragged, tattered, and broken. I ran among them looking for my brothers, but everything was disorganized. The men wore wild looks on their faces, having stared death in the eye.

"Jim, Andy, Van!" I shouted, darting among the wounded and dazed. Their faces, powder-smudged and streaked with sweat, all looked alike. No one answered my calls. They had to prepare for a second charge, if it came.

I ran by one man whose arm was bloodied. He reached out and grabbed me with his good hand. "Henry, stay down, whatever you do."

It was Jim.

"Where's Andy and Van?"

"Don't know about Andy," he gasped.

"Where's Van?"

He didn't answer.

"Where's Van?" I screamed.

Jim hung his head and refused to look me in the eye.
"Where's Van?"

Jim began to sob. He hung his head and pointed
toward the field the 34th had tried to cross. "He's out
there, Henry."

"I'll go get him."

His grip tightening on my arm, Jim shook his head.
"It won't do no good, Henry, not anymore."

"It can't be," I sobbed. "I talked to him a moment
ago."

"You'll never be able to talk to him again, Henry,
never."

Chapter Ten

"Kill them," I sobbed. "Kill the bastards."

Jim patted me on the shoulder. My whole body trembled as I cursed. Here I was, as good as rich with that Confederate payroll, but for all that money I couldn't bring Van back.

As I cried, Andy stumbled up and fell to his knees, gasping for breath. "Damn cannons," he heaved. "We'd whipped 'em if it wasn't for those guns." Then he realized Jim and I were crying. His eyes turned jittery, flicking from man to man around us. "Where's Van?"

"The canister killed him," Jim answered.

Andy took a halfhearted swipe at his eyes, then lifted his head in anger, his jaw jutting toward the Union cannons. "They're spent." Jumping to his feet, he waved his fist over his head, then grabbed his slouch hat and shook it. "Rally, boys! We'll get 'em!"

The colonel, now horseless, dashed to Andy. "Be patient, man. Shaver's and Parsons's infantry and Roane's cavalry are preparing to attack. We'll provide support."

The men of the 34th reloaded their rifles, their faces as hard as their resolve, their eyes fixed upon the enemy.

"We'll clear the field of Yankee invaders!" the colonel shouted.

Having caught Andy's fire, the soldiers yelled wildly.

Andy, though, sank when he saw blood on Jim's shirt. He knelt beside him and tossed his hat down. "Not you, too?"

"Just a crease," Jim replied, "nothing more."

I reached for a discarded rifle, planning to charge with the regiment.

"What are you doing?" Andy demanded.

"I'm going with you. I want to kill a Yankee."

"No, dammit!" cried Jim.

"Hell, no," Andy echoed. "When we get them on the run, we may chase them to Fayetteville or beyond. I want you to stay here, find Van's body, and see that he gets a decent burial. You must carry the sad news to Momma. One son is enough for her to lose on this day."

"But what about you two? She could still lose more."

They shrugged. "We've got to follow orders," Jim said. "You don't."

I angered quick. "But I'm old enough to."

Andy stood up, lifting his Enfield rifle like it was an oar. "See the butt of this rifle?"

I nodded.

"It can put a knot the size of a melon on your head. I'll see that it does if you don't promise to stay here and bury Van. It's the least you can do for your brother."

My shoulders slumped. I wanted to kill Yankees, but Andy was right. I had a greater obligation to my dead brother in the valley.

The colonel trotted by, waving his sword. "Be patient!" he yelled. "Then we'll throw Southern steel against Yankee flesh."

The men of the 34th were grim and determined. They checked their Enfields and formed a line through the orchard, ready to give support when the fresh brigades attacked.

When the firing to our west started, I cheered, but the men around me showed surprise and looked with fear in that direction. I could see in my brothers' eyes that something was wrong.

The firing became the roar of thunder.

"The enemy's down the Fayetteville road," Jim shouted, "not that direction."

The soldiers regrouped, swinging around to face the northwest rather than the northeast.

What I didn't realize at the moment, but what the men of the 34th feared, was that the Union Army units that had been trailing them had circled around in front and attacked our flank just as the men were getting ready to drive the first force from the field.

Damn bastards that would do something like that probably cheated at cards, kicked puppies, stole from the blind, and voted Republican.

The federal charge rolled up the flank of Hindman's army before braver men in the 34th helped knock the attack back, giving the Southerners a chance to regroup and mount a counteroffensive. The colonel ran by yelling something, and several men followed him to the west. When the enemy soldiers turned tail, the Southern brigades whooped and hollered and followed them into the fields along the river plain. But Yankee artillery drove them back.

"Where's our artillery? Why can't we shoot back?" I screamed.

No one answered. That was when I realized Jim and Andy had abandoned me. Frantically I looked all around, trying to find them among the handful of men still in the trees, but I didn't spot them. It would be the end of the war before I saw them again.

I couldn't believe they had left without letting me know or saying good-bye. Then I saw Andy's slouch hat on the ground where he had tossed it. I swapped my hat for it to remind me of my brothers.

The rest of the day I waited for a break in the fighting that would allow me to escape. All afternoon each side tried to overwhelm the other. Back and forth the battle went, the Confederate soldiers unable to take the Union artillery and the Yankees unable to wrest the high ground from the Confederates.

Come dark the South still held the high ground, and the Yankees were still scattered across the opposite side of the river plain. I wandered a bit among the troops looking for my brothers, but men were edgy and firing shots at anything that moved.

The night was bitter cold, and I no longer had even a blanket, just my coat. Few men lit fires for fear of giving away their positions to Yankee snipers. It was a miserable night, made eerie by the groans and wails of the wounded and dying. Only the dead slept peacefully, Van among them. Every time I thought of him I cried, the tears freezing on my cheeks. I slept in snatches, shivering and waiting for the sunrise and warmth.

Well before dawn, though, the Southerners had formed up and started retreating. They lit no fires and gave no shouts, just tramped down the road. The officers took soldiers' blankets and coats to wrap around the wheels of the surviving cannon carriages and muffle the noise. A group of cavalry and about fifty mounted irregulars were left behind to create enough commotion in the camp to disguise the retreat and delay the Yankees if they caught on to the ruse and tried to strike the Southern rear.

Come dawn I could see the Yankee infantrymen across the river plain rising and building fires that they clumped around for warmth and coffee. I wondered if it was smart to wear my brother's hat, it being of Confederate issue, but I couldn't throw it away because it had been Andy's.

Between me and the Union troops I could make out splotches of dead and wounded scattered across the plain and up the slopes of the ridge. There were more than I could count, but only one mattered to me. If I had to inspect every body on the plain, I would do it until I found Van and gave him a Christian burial.

I was cold and hungry and scared. I'd seen Yankees

at Cane Hill, but these were much more numerous. They seemed to multiply every time I looked, as more and more emerged from the woods.

The Confederate cavalry rode around the remnants of the Southern camp, helping the wounded to some of the farmhouses at our back. The dead they left on the field. A couple of cavalrymen challenged me, but when I explained I was waiting to bury my brother from the 34th Arkansas, they left me alone.

I didn't have as much luck with the irregulars, though. A group of them gathered just beyond the orchard, tied their horses, and fanned out along the edge of the ridge, then started searching the grounds. They were looking for something more than bodies, though. I tried to ignore them, but as they drew nearer, a couple began to whisper, and one of them pointed in my direction.

"That's got to be him," he said.

Looking behind me, I realized they must've been talking about me because there wasn't another man close. The two irregulars walked cautiously toward me. One looked fifteen at most, and the other was likely not yet twenty. I feared they thought I was a Union spy. "Morning," I said, trying to sound confident.

Beneath their unbuttoned gray longcoats I saw twin gun belts around their waists. The younger man was blinking incessantly. I caught my breath. It was Blinky. I wondered if he recognized me. His fluttering eyelids gave him a nervous look, and the cold, steely blue of his eyes made me feel just as nervous. In the freezing cold that morning I didn't think I could get any colder, but the venom of his gaze raised goose bumps on my goose bumps.

"Think that's him, Buck?" asked Blinky.

"Don't do anything that might flush him, Dingus."

I felt like a cottontail hiding under a bush, wondering whether to hop away or stay put.

There was a bit of a resemblance around the nose between the two men. Blinky wore a blue-and-white-checked work shirt and carried his pistols butt forward in the holsters. He sported a hat with the brim tied to the crown so his pale, rounded face was clearly visible beneath dark brown hair. His eyes were narrow, but his lips were on the thick side. He stood about five foot ten and weighed maybe a hundred and fifty pounds, us all being a little skinnier during the war years when decent food was hard to come by.

Unlike the first two times I had seen him, now I stood eyeball to blinking eyeball with Jesse James. I was glad I wasn't a Yankee, and I hoped he didn't remember me calling the bushwhackers who had burned our outhouse sons of bitches and insulting his poor ugly momma.

I learned later that the irregulars he rode with had taken to calling him Dingus because that was the most profane word he ever used.

"Buck," I learned later, was Jesse's older brother, Frank. He was taller than Jesse, and his blue eyes were not as cold and steely. His hair was lighter, his eyes wider, his lips thinner, and he, too, wore two pistols butt forward.

They studied me like a wolf eyes a lamb. I shivered. Buck seemed to realize I was edgy, but Dingus didn't seem to care.

"What you up to, boy?" Buck asked casually.

"Waiting for the Yankees to clear out so I can bury my brother." I pointed toward the river. "He's out there in the field."

"Yankees have spilt a lot of good Southern blood," he drawled as the two split apart to approach me from different sides.

Dingus grunted. "We're looking for a body, too. A corporal named Rankin. You know what happened to him?"

I doubted I could trust those two. "He died yesterday."

Buck took off his hat. "The South will be irrigated

with good Southern blood until we send those Yankees packing."

Dingus stared hard at me, and his hand slid to the butt of one of his revolvers. "Do I know you?"

I shrugged. "Nope," I answered, and that was the truth—I didn't know his real name at the time, and he didn't know mine.

"You wouldn't happen to know where Rankin's body is, would you?" Buck asked, still shaking his head at the news of Rankin's death.

"Not far," I answered, "unless he's been moved."

"Our boys didn't spend much time moving bodies after yesterday's fighting," Buck said.

Shrugging, I led them through the orchard. It took me longer to find Rankin's body than I expected, because your memory can be rattled when you're being shot at by every damn Yankee this side of Abe Lincoln. Dingus was growing impatient, so I was relieved when I finally stumbled upon the corporal's body.

I pointed at the corpse. "That's him."

Buck nodded his thanks, then searched the corporal's pockets. Not caring to watch, I turned away. I had planned to walk to the edge of the rise and see what the Yankees were up to, but Dingus had other ideas.

He poked a gun in my stomach. "You're not going anywhere."

"I'm no Yankee. I didn't kill him," I cried.

"Yeah," Dingus answered, "but you're the secesh we're after."

"What do you mean?"

Buck stepped up to Dingus, put his hand on the gun barrel, and pushed it toward the ground. My stomach muscles unclenched, and my heart, which had been bobbing like a fishing cork in my throat, settled back into place.

"Where's the payroll?" Dingus growled.

It was easy to look dumbfounded, because I didn't know how these two strangers could possibly know about the payroll. "What are you talking about?"

Dingus's eyes flared, and I knew he was itching to hurt me, but Buck spoke very softly. "Dingus, go tell the rest of the men we've found the kid."

Dingus sighed loudly and shook his head. "I intend to find that payroll." He sounded too pompous to be sincere.

"Go on, Dingus. Have the men mount up."

Dingus kicked at the dirt and marched away.

"Now," Buck said, turning to me, "the cavalry captain said a Corporal Rankin gave him news that the payroll had been hidden to keep it out of Yankee hands. Only the corporal and a kid thirteen or so knew where it was. The corporal's dead, and you're the kid."

Momma had taught me not to lie, but she must never have had a personal fortune depending upon a fib. Now that I did, I just couldn't bring myself to tell the truth. Fact was, I figured if I did, I'd be killed on the spot. "I came to see my brothers with the Thirty-fourth Arkansas. Now I've got to bury one of them." I hemmed and hawed until Dingus returned.

"He told you yet, Buck?"

"We're just getting there," Buck answered.

Dingus put his hand on his revolver. "I can scare it out of him quicker than you can sweet-talk it out."

"It's hard to think straight on an empty stomach," I announced.

"You want your last meal before you talk?" Dingus threatened.

Buck chewed him out, then turned to me. "You'll be treated square as long as you tell us where the gold is. It ain't yours."

It wasn't Buck's or Dingus's, either, though I didn't express that opinion out loud.

With those cold eyes Dingus glared at me. I could feel my blood thickening to an icy slush. Then I had a grand thought. If he killed me, he'd never find that payroll. I gave him a big grin.

Dingus seemed confused for a moment. "He's as dumb and ugly as the captain said."

"You haven't seen the Burke sisters, have you?"

Just then we heard shots in the distance, and Buck turned toward the Yankee line. I was tempted to make a run for it, but I had nowhere to run. Dingus spun around and dashed to his horse.

"The Yankees are coming!" cried a passing cavalryman.

A minute later Dingus and some other irregulars came galloping up on their horses, reining to a stop in front of Buck. Before I could react, Buck grabbed me under the shoulders and handed me to a burly fellow with a beard as dark as his heart. The fellow shoved me down in the saddle in front of him and wrapped a ham of an arm around my chest.

"I got to bury my brother," I cried out. I wrestled against him and tried to break free, but he held me firm. The more I squirmed the harder he shoved me into the saddle horn, which settled in at a most uncomfortable spot between my legs. It had never been my ambition to be a gelding, so I relaxed, and he growled something that I didn't understand. His breath was rank enough to gag an outhouse.

Dingus tossed Buck's reins to him, and the older brother mounted quickly. Behind us I heard the cavalry begin to fire at the approaching Yankees. The irregulars, being the cowards they were, didn't linger to help but turned their mounts to the south and started racing to safety.

I sat as high as I could in the saddle, but it wasn't high enough, and I took to bouncing between the bushwhacker's lap and the saddle horn. I admit I much preferred his lap. I screamed with each unfortunate bounce and thanked God for every fortunate miss. Between screams and gasps for breath, I prayed to God for deliverance from this foul-smelling idiot. I wasn't one to pray like some people, over every meal, every misfortune, every lucky break. I figured God didn't want to be bothered all the time. So I prayed mostly when Pa and Momma made me or when I really needed something. This was one thing I really needed or I wouldn't be able to walk for a year or father children for a lifetime.

I should've saved my prayer, though. No sooner had I got started than I'll be damned if some fifty Union cavalry didn't charge out of the woods, straight for us. They were screaming like men at a cockfight and shooting my way.

My captor couldn't hold the reins, me, and his gun at the same time, so he put the reins in the hand that held me and drew his revolver with the other, shooting a couple times at the enemy. I grabbed the reins and tried to turn the animal toward the Yankees, but all I did was annoy him.

He steered his horse away from the charging cavalry and turned his back to them. It must've made a good target. I felt him flinch, then slump forward against me, pressing me even harder into the saddle horn. I screamed and shoved back against him. This time his arm fell away, and he swayed over to one side.

I grabbed the reins from his dying fingers and drew back on the horse. The animal slowed suddenly, and the bushwhacker slid off, his foot still in the stirrup.

The Union cavalry charged toward me. I looked at the retreating bushwhackers and saw Dingus turn his stallion savagely, then start racing for me. I leaned over in the saddle and backed up the terrified horse until I could free the dead man's foot. I managed to release him, then tried to slip my foot in the stirrups but missed. Dingus charged, no more than twenty-five feet away, his revolver pointed at me. I had the choice of facing him or the whole Union Army.

I chose the army, praying the Yankees' aim was as bad as I'd been told. I hoped they didn't aim for Dingus and hit me, though it'd been okay if one aimed for me and hit him.

The Yankees were fast approaching. Behind me I heard Dingus yell in disgust. "Dingus, dingus, dingus," he cried, then turned around and raced away like the coward most bushwhackers were.

Then I rode headlong into the whole Union cavalry.

Chapter Eleven

I hunkered low in the saddle and charged toward the Yankees. "Don't shoot! Don't shoot!" I yelled as a line of cavalry bore down upon me, fifty men with pistols or carbines aimed in my direction.

I was too scared to stop my horse, and the cavalry never hesitated. When I was no more than fifty feet from the line of charging Union steeds, a gap opened up in their formation, and I raced right through it.

Three cavalrymen whirled their horses about and came after me. When I heard a shot overhead, I reined up, lifted my hands, and prayed.

The cavalrymen circled me, their pistols drawn, eyeing me suspiciously.

"This is the youngest bushwhacker I've seen yet," said a corporal. "You want to hang him or shoot him?"

"Shoot him," said a private.

"Hang him," offered the other private.

"I ain't a bushwhacker."

"Explain the hat," demanded the corporal.

"It was my brother's."

"So you're secesh kin. How old are you, boy?" asked the corporal.

"Almost thirteen."

"What's your birthday?"

"January 9, 1850."

The corporal nodded. "That works out right."

"Shoot him," said the second soldier.

"Hang him," suggested the third.

I talked fast, telling the corporal how I had treated Yankees around my home after the battle of Cane Hill.

The corporal smiled. "One of my men was treated by three of the prettiest girls he'd ever seen, the Burke sisters. You know them?"

I about gagged, wondering if there was a brain in the entire Union Army. "Know 'em? They're prettier'n speckled puppies, and they're staying with us."

The corporal holstered his pistol.

"Can I go now?"

He shook his head. "We've got to check with the lieutenant." He turned his horse and rode away.

Shortly the cavalry came back, disgusted that the bushwhackers had disappeared into the woods. They'd turned back to avoid riding into an ambush. Several troops stared at me with hate-filled eyes.

I was relieved when the corporal came back with the lieutenant, a slender man with a golden mustache and narrow eyes. He studied me hard as the two privates saluted him.

"Shoot him," said the first.

"Hang him," called the second.

"He was riding with the bushwhackers, sir," said the corporal. "He's not quite thirteen. He was one of two on the same horse. We plugged the other one."

The lieutenant pointed his finger at me. "Why're you riding with those bastards?"

My mind froze over like a rain barrel in winter, and my tongue stuck to it. I wished I'd saved my earlier prayer for now. But the heat in the two privates' threats gradually warmed my brain, and I lied as best I could. "I knew one of them. They feared I might tell you his name if I stayed."

"Why you wearing a gray hat?" the lieutenant wanted to know.

"It was my brother's."

"Bushwhacker, was he, son?"

"Infantry," I said. "Thirty-fourth Arkansas."

"Shoot him," the first private repeated.

"Hang him," grated the second.

The lieutenant turned his hard gaze from me and nodded to the two privates. "Dismissed," he said.

I grinned. I wanted to shoot the first and hang the second.

Turning back to me, the lieutenant stroked his chin, mulling over my fate. He did what all soldiers do when confronted with an obvious decision—he consulted someone higher up. "We'll take him to the captain after we take his horse."

The corporal ordered me to dismount. After I did, he searched me, finding nothing except my pocket knife, which he allowed me to keep. Then he opened the saddlebags and found a Navy Colt revolver and two cartons of ammunition. "This yours?"

I twisted around and pointed at the dead bushwhacker in the meadow behind me. "It's his."

"What's his name?" asked the corporal.

"Don't know."

"Who'd you know among the bushwhackers?"

"I didn't know any of them."

Sitting all high and mighty on his horse, the lieutenant crossed his arms over his chest. "A minute ago you said you knew one."

He had a point. I could almost feel a bullet hitting my chest or a noose tightening around my neck, if Shoot Him or Hang Him had their way. Then I had a good idea. "Most of them were Missouri boys, though there were a few from Arkansas. I'm scared to say the one that's our neighbor back in Cane Hill."

"Cane Hill?"

"That's where the boy's from," the corporal answered.

Behind me Union infantry congregated, looking at the scattered dead. I pointed to the soldiers. "Once you fellows leave, no one'll be around to protect me and my folks. The bushwhacker and his gang will kill us or worse."

"Worse?" asked the lieutenant.

"Torture and maim us," I answered.

"You're assuming we won't." The lieutenant smiled.

I didn't know if he was joking or wishing. "Maybe it's better to get tortured by secesh," I said, "but I'll tell you the bushwhacker's name." I could hardly keep a straight face. "The one from Cane Hill was Beryl Fudge."

"Make note of that name, Corporal," ordered the lieutenant. "Now let's go see the captain."

The corporal tied my horse behind his, then re-mounted and pointed toward a captain inspecting the damaged Rebel artillery near the orchard. I walked over and waited a half hour while the lieutenant explained to the captain that I wasn't quite thirteen and I wasn't quite a bushwhacker, but they didn't know what to do with me. The captain considered my fate but a few seconds, then pointed to a farmhouse a hundred yards away. "Check with the colonel."

The way I was moving through the ranks, I half expected to be shaking Old Abe's hand before sundown. The colonel had me wait on the front porch while he and his subordinates discussed their glorious victory and whether they should give chase.

The house was a modest log cabin. At the opposite end of the porch sat a skinny woman and her four kids, all gaunt-faced and hungry. I wondered if they were to be shot as bushwhackers, too.

Me, the corporal, and the lieutenant waited about an hour so the colonel could have his lunch. The aroma of fried bacon and boiled potatoes sent my stomach to tumbling. But hungry though I was, I felt sorrier for the momma and her little ones, the oldest being no more than six. They stared at me with their big, listless eyes, like I was a condemned man.

When the colonel ordered us inside, he didn't offer

me a bite of anything. He leaned back in his chair and inspected me while the corporal and the lieutenant explained my situation.

"Should we execute him or let him go?"

The colonel stroked his ragged gray beard, then lit up a cigar and studied it. "It'd be a shame to shoot a boy that wasn't a bushwhacker," he said.

My spirits rose.

"It'd be a bigger shame to let him grow up to be a bushwhacker."

I wondered if he'd assign Shoot Him or Hang Him to execute me.

The colonel sucked hard on his cigar, then spewed a cloud of smoke with all the other hot air he was passing. "If we kill him now we won't lose any men by him in a few years."

"I'm no bushwhacker."

The colonel nodded. "And you never will be after today."

My knees went as mushy as sour mash.

"Take him out and have him shot," the colonel ordered.

The lieutenant saluted. "Yes, sir."

"Yes, sir," echoed the corporal.

I have to admit I was mightily disappointed on missing out on my chance to shake Old Abe's hand.

I started to call the colonel a bastard and a son of a Yankee whore, but before I could compliment him on his bloodline, the woman from the porch barged through the open door.

"You animals," she spat, "don't you think there's been enough killing?"

The colonel was stunned. The lieutenant was shocked. The corporal grinned.

"Ma'am," said the colonel, "this is an army matter and no concern of yours."

She pointed her finger at him. "No concern of mine? You're sitting at my table in my house after me and my young ones have been in the cellar for two days hiding from your bullets. Now that our boys are gone, your soldiers run me out of my cellar and steal what little food we had to get us through the winter. And you're telling me this is no concern of mine."

"You'll be reimbursed by the government."

The lieutenant took her arm to escort her outside, but she shook herself free.

"Pay me today, then."

"We don't have money for that," the colonel told her.

"We can negotiate, then."

The colonel threw up his arms. "Okay, ma'am, what is it you want? How much do we have to pay?"

"I want the boy turned over to me. I'll not stand by and watch a mere child be executed by you and your men."

The colonel sighed, his frustration as big as the cloud of smoke he blew across the room. "Lieutenant," he commanded, "let the boy go." He turned to me. "If any of my men ever see you with secesh again, I'm ordering them to shoot on sight. You understand?"

I understood him as much as you can a crazy man. I nodded.

"Then get out of my sight now and forever," he said.

I darted out of that house like a cat with its tail on fire.

"Wait," the woman called after me.

I stopped behind the house. Inside I could hear the colonel laughing at how scared I'd looked. Now I understood why the Burke sisters got along with Union soldiers—they were *all* dumb.

The woman scurried around the cabin, her children following her. "In my cellar," she said. "You'll be out of sight there."

"Thank you, ma'am," I said, running and hugging her. She lifted the wooden cellar door, and I climbed down the steps into a dark pit that smelled of earth. After she sent her kids down, she shut the door. As I took a corner stool, two of the kids came over and crawled into my lap, asking me questions about how many Yankees I had killed and if I'd fired a cannon and why cannons made so much noise.

We spent about an hour in the dim cellar before the door opened and the kids' momma returned.

"Are they ever gonna leave?" I asked.

She shrugged. "Seems to me they're too 'fraid to chase the Southern army and too 'fraid to go to Fayetteville and pester folks there. My name's Annie Belle Higdon. My husband Tanner's in the Thirty-fourth Arkansas."

"Three of my brothers—I mean, two of them now— are in the Thirty-fourth."

"What about the third?"

I grimaced. "He's dead down by the river. I stayed behind to bury him. What about your husband?"

"He came by before the retreat and is okay, just hungry like all of us. You aren't with the bushwhackers, are you? Or the army?"

"No."

"What's your name?"

"Henry Harrison Lomax from Cane Hill."

She smiled. "The colonel's gone. Maybe we can find some eats."

"I need to look for my brother."

"We'll help."

Before leaving the cellar I poked my head up and looked all around for the colonel, then stepped outside into bright sunlight. The warmth felt good on my back. We wandered among soldiers making fires and cooking meals. At one fire the infantrymen offered us a boiled potato apiece, which we ate greedily before marching on.

Union burial parties had already begun digging holes for their dead, but the Confederate soldiers lay where they fell, stripped of their valuables. Their bodies were beginning to darken and bloat. We marched down into the river plain, where more than fifty broken Southern bodies were scattered across the ground. Mixed among them was a dead horse, fully bloated, its legs angling up at the sun.

We moved tentatively among the dead. I stepped from body to body in awe and horror. Some men had contented looks upon their faces, as if they had met death peacefully, while others wore contorted grimaces as if they had fought it all the way.

Annie Belle and I walked together, but the kids lagged behind, ignoring the dead men and looking for playthings. It sounded out of place when we heard a low thumping noise and then giggling. I didn't pay much attention to it until Annie Belle turned around. "What are you kids doing?"

I stopped and looked behind me.

"Bouncing horses," cried the oldest.

The four of them stood not ten feet from a bloated horse.

"Watch," laughed the youngest. He turned and charged at the horse, then flung himself on the animal's bloated belly. The horse hide gave a bit, then flung the boy back in the air. He giggled as he landed on his feet and then fell on his behind.

"Quit that," Annie Belle scolded. "If that hide breaks, one of you'll disappear inside that animal's innards. You want that?"

"No," answered the little girl, her face twisting at the idea.

I moved on, wondering if I would ever find Van Buren Lomax. Some of the soldiers' features were distorted by the bloating; others had their faces shot up so badly that God couldn't identify them. War up close was not as glorious as the parades.

As we gradually made our way toward the river, I inspected each body. I had about given up on finding Van when I saw one soldier who had charged farther than the rest. Even before I reached the body, I knew it had to be Van. He had fallen face toward the enemy, dying while advancing, not retreating. Because his body had begun to

swell a bit, I hesitated to turn him over, not really wanting
to know what grapeshot had done to flesh barely four
years older than me.

Annie Belle sensed my reverence. "Is it him?"

I nodded, then knelt beside him, patting his shoulder
as if I could rouse him from a deep sleep. His skin felt
mushy.

Holding my breath, I slipped my hand under his
shoulder and gently turned him over. His face, unblem-
ished by Yankee lead, had a peaceful look about it, as if
he had not struggled with death. I wished for a drizzle to
show that his soul had been accepted in heaven, but too
many Yankees had fallen nearby for God to send such a
sign.

Van's chest was caked with blood and matted with
grass and dirt. I took off my coat and placed it over his
head and chest. "I'm sorry, Van." I closed my eyes and
began to sob. I felt Annie Belle's hand on my shoulder.

When I opened my eyes, I could've sworn I saw a
dove take to wing almost within reach and fly toward the
heavens. I took it as a sign that God had accepted Van's
soul. I stood up and looked back to where the Yankee
burial parties had gathered their dead. There were no
doves rising around them.

"We can bury him behind my cabin," Annie Belle
said.

"As long as he's not near any Yankees."

She understood.

We couldn't carry him, so we each grabbed an arm
and started dragging him across the river plain. The kids
trailed us.

A couple Yankees approached. "Kin?" asked one.

I nodded.

"Want us to carry him for you?"

I shook my head. They had killed him, and I didn't
want them touching him now.

"We understand," the first Yankee said and moved
away.

It seemed to take forever to get him up the ridge and across the flat rise, where many Yankees were eating their meals and throwing tents like they planned to stay a few days. I hoped the colonel didn't spot me before I got Van buried. After that I didn't care. Maybe the colonel was right. Maybe when I got older I would join the bushwhackers or the army and kill dozens of his men for taking the life of my brother.

The Yankees we passed removed their hats reverently. *He died the nearest to your lines with his face forward,* I wanted to say to the bastards, but I couldn't. It would demean Van and his noble charge. I said nothing, just kept dragging him toward the cabin.

I bit my lip to keep from shedding tears the Yankees could see. When we reached the cabin, I dropped his arm and let him lie where I wanted to bury him. I felt exhausted from exertion and weak from too little food over the last three days. Leaning against the back of the house, I cried where no one could see me.

I was suddenly startled by gunshots and turned around to see seven riflemen firing a final salute over the graves of several Union dead. I shook my head in disgust. Then I heard the sound of someone digging nearby and was surprised to see two Yankees digging a place for Van.

I broke down sobbing one last time for my brother. Annie Belle tried to comfort me, and her kids moved beside me as well. When the soldiers had finished digging, a chaplain brought over a shroud to wrap Van in. I removed my coat from his head and slipped it back on as more Yankees came up to help lower him into the grave.

The chaplain read the Twenty-third Psalm, one of the few Bible verses I knew. I mouthed the words with him. Then, to my surprise, the seven riflemen approached the grave and upon command lifted their rifles to their shoulders and fired a seven-gun salute. The men who had killed him had given him a better tribute than I could ever have done alone.

Chapter Twelve

Though it was right decent of the Yankees to give my brother Van an honorable burial, that couldn't make up for murdering him in the first place. I wanted to avenge his death, but I was no longer sure who owned vengeance. I'd buried a stranger killed by a Southern bushwhacker and buried a brother killed by a Yankee cannon. None of it was right, but I mostly blamed the Yankees for leaving their affairs up north and coming south to tell us how to run ours.

Annie Belle and I retreated to the cellar, closing the door behind us. The flame of a single candle lit the earthen room. The kids were moaning about how hungry they were. I could hear Yankee cooks up in the house clanging pots on the stove, and I could smell bacon frying. The aroma was delicious but not very filling.

"There's no food," Annie Belle said.

"But they're cooking on our stove," said her oldest boy. "It's our house."

She nodded. "This is war, son."

"Then war's bad."

"It will be okay, son," she said, then reassured herself, "if only your pa comes home whole."

We slept that night hungry and cold, all huddled together between a couple quilts. I awoke to the sound of the army waking and decided to leave without disturbing Annie Belle, but she stirred as I edged to the cellar door, wearing my slouch hat and coat.

"I'll take care of your brother's grave."

"You just take care of those children. Van would understand."

"You be careful getting by the guards and pickets," she said.

"Thanks for saving me, ma'am."

"I did it for your momma in case another momma someday has a chance to save one of my boys."

"You think the colonel really would've shot me?"

"He's Yankee," she said.

Which meant he was smart enough to feed himself but not smart enough to dress himself. I climbed the steps in a crouch, then gently pushed the cellar door up. The morning air slapped me as I poked my head out like a squirrel and inspected the field for the colonel. He was probably in the cabin sleeping in Annie Belle's feather bed. I saw Yankees everywhere, but they were stretching, yawning, building fires, and opening up their spigots after the cold night's sleep. I slipped out and lowered the door.

With my hat tugged down and my coat pulled tight I started walking toward the southwest and the Cane Hill road, figuring I could follow it for a few miles, then swing back toward Fayetteville—if I wasn't followed by Yankees—and fetch my money.

The soldiers seemed more interested in standing by their fires or slipping into the woods to mark the trees, but one red-eyed guard who could barely keep his eyes open challenged me.

"Halt."

"Huh?" I was going to play lost and dumb.

"What's the password?"

I didn't know the password, but I figured his Yankee brain was no match for mine and answered with about as obvious a choice as I could. "Abe Lincoln."

The guard lowered his rifle. "Proceed." That confirmed that the average Yankee couldn't match wits with Pooty Burke, much less me. I skirted the Cane Hill road a quarter of a mile or more before slipping into the woods to make sure I wasn't being tailed. I was no more noticed than a fart in a whirlwind. After lingering a while to be certain no Yankee was trying to wait me out, I circled through the woods, not even bothering to look over my shoulder. I walked until noon, clinging to the brush for cover. At high sun I swung north to search for my fortune.

I'd never been rich before, and I didn't know how I was going to spend so much money. Fact was, I didn't know that I could spend that money at all, the countryside being stripped of all goods and food worth buying. I wasn't going to be able to buy anything—not a good horse, not a good gun, not a good knife, not good shoes, not a good hat.

Twice I heard riders in the woods, so I lay under some bushes. I didn't care if the riders were friend or foe. In my recent experience there hadn't been much difference.

Before dark I managed to knock a squirrel from a tree with a well-thrown rock and then clubbed him to death with a broken branch. I skinned and gutted him with my pocketknife. Though I was hungry enough to eat him raw, I risked a fire, which I built by rubbing sticks together over a bed of dry grass. That sizzling meat was music to my ears. When I could stand the aroma no more, I started eating that squirrel so close to the bone that a bed of ants couldn't have picked his carcass any cleaner. I'd like to have eaten his momma and his pa and all his brothers and sisters, I was so hungry, but he must've been an only child because I didn't see sign of another squirrel before dark. Maybe they didn't like the smell of their kin frying.

By dark I wasn't certain where I was or if I was anywhere near the hidden payroll. All I knew was I was tired and needed a good night's rest, which would be hard to get sleeping on the frigid ground without a blanket. I lay down on the cold earth and used the slouch hat for a pillow. It wasn't a comfortable sleep, but I did manage to doze off. A couple times I heard noises among the trees but figured them to be varmints and not men. I slept as good as could be expected and was really sawing logs about dawn when I should've been getting up.

Problem was, I kept having this dream about someone rubbing a wood file across my cheek. It was a wet wood file, and it smelled rancid. Slowly I emerged from my sleeping trance. Though the dream went away, that damn file kept stroking my cheek. I shook my head, then opened my eyes to find two round eyes and two wide nostrils staring back at me.

I screamed, and that monster backed off. In the dim light seeping through the trees I made out about the best-looking mule I'd ever seen. He had a contraption on his back, and he seemed a bit skittish.

Slowly I got up, not making any sudden movements for fear of spooking him. "Easy, boy," I said, slipping toward him. He dipped his head and watched me. I moved cautiously, figuring it would be nice to replace the mule I had borrowed from Pa and the Confederate Army had borrowed from me.

The mule blew, then stepped forward.

"Easy, boy," I repeated, then grabbed the halter line that dragged beneath his feet. The mule nuzzled my chest, pushing me with his strong neck. Holding the leather line, I backed away, and the mule followed, limping slightly on his right rear foot. I tied the line tightly around the low branch of an oak tree, then stepped over to the mule, patting his head with one hand and stroking his neck with the other. I made my way down his side, patting his gray hide as I advanced to his back leg. When I realized the contraption on his back was a pack saddle, I knew where the mule had come from: It was the pack animal that had carried the payroll when Corporal Rankin escaped the Yankee ambush.

Branded in the mule's rump were the letters *U.S.*

Rankin or some other good Southern boy must have stolen him from the Yankees. I thought it'd be safe to ride a Yankee mule as long as I didn't discuss politics with him. After all, the mule had carried payroll for the Confederacy and Jefferson Davis, so I thought I might be able to trust him.

I squatted and gently lifted his leg, bent it, and inspected the hoof. Even in the soft light I was able to make out a small stone wedged between the hoof and the iron shoe. Holding his leg in my left hand, I retrieved my pocket knife with my right and propped my knee under the donkey's leg so I could open the blade. With it I pried the stone from beneath the shoe. The mule had a small bruise on his hoof, but nothing that would keep him from carrying me home.

After I folded my knife and slipped it back in my pocket, I patted that mule on the rump, stroked his back, rubbed his neck and his head, and massaged his ears so he would like me. I was feeling damn proud of myself until I looked into his eyes. I swallowed hard, not so certain my find had been that good after all.

I could see the white all around the eyes' dark centers. That was a bad sign, a sign most Ozark folks took to mean that the horse or mule was a killer. I studied him mighty close after that, uncertain just what I should do. If I asked him point-blank if he was a killer, it might give him some ideas. I had to outsmart him, beat around the bush a bit for my own peace of mind.

"You wouldn't be the type of mule that would harm a man, woman, or child, would you?"

As the mule eyed me, those white borders seemed to widen. I was getting a bit nervous.

"You wouldn't be the type of mule that would harm a fellow who took a rock from under your shoe, would you?"

The mule didn't say anything, didn't blink, didn't twitch a muscle, didn't break wind, didn't do a thing that would give me a clue what to expect.

I grabbed his ear and whispered into it, "You're a good mule, one a fellow can trust, aren't you?"

I've seen rocks that were more responsive than that mule. I blew in his nostrils, trying to convince him by my scent that I meant him no harm and wanted none from him. He never nodded or shook his head, just stood there. So I blew in his nose again, then wondered if I should remove the pack saddle. I decided to leave it on so I would have something to grab in case the mule turned killer and tried to throw me. I eased toward the branch where I'd tied the leathers, stopping to whisper again in the mule's ear.

"You're the finest-looking mule I've ever seen in these parts. Your poppa was a fine donkey and your momma a great mare. And you're gonna have the finest-looking offspring Arkansas's ever seen."

Of course, I lied a little about his offspring, but I didn't care to disappoint him by letting on to the truth, not just yet.

I untied the single line from the oak branch, half expecting him to grow horns and gore me right there, but he was as mannerly as a politician's wife. Smiling, I started back toward him before I realized it could be a trick. My smile wilted like a fat gal in the sun.

"How's your hoof feel with that rock gone? I removed it," I reminded him. As I slipped past his nose, he turned his head and watched me draw up beside his middle.

"Easy, boy." My voice sounded girlish as I grabbed the pack saddle and pulled myself atop him. The mule must've been a Southern sympathizer in spite of the brand, because he didn't do a thing except straighten his head and wait for me to rattle the line.

I turned him deeper into the woods, trying to find the trail where the payroll escort had been ambushed. It was midafternoon before I came across it and another hour before I came upon four bodies bloated and stinking in the road. The mule tossed his head and informed me he didn't want to pass them too closely. The stench was bad, so we circled them and started up the trail to my fortune.

My stomach began to churn—and it wasn't from the emptiness. I was just minutes away from being the richest twelve-year-old in all of Arkansas. I figured I'd buy my brothers' freedom from the Confederate Army, then take the family to California and forget about the war that had cost me a brother and my sack of marbles—damn Amanda Fudge.

I rode at a walk, fighting the urge to hurry the mule. When we finally came around a bend in the trail and I saw the limestone cliff up ahead, I caught my breath. The mule must have sensed my excitement, for he pranced forward like he was the finest Tennessee walking horse around. He was probably gloating over my good words about his family.

When we reached the wall, I jerked on the line, but the mule shook his head. Instead of stopping he jumped into a trot, and I just knew he was going to fling me into the cliff and bash my brains out by the crevice where the payroll was hidden.

"Whoa!" I called, but he never slowed. Instead he turned into the woods and trotted away from the cliff. Then I heard noises on the trail from Prairie Grove way. This was a damn smart mule, getting me off the trail before I was spotted. I thanked him several times as we slipped deeper into the woods to a hiding place.

As I jumped to the ground I'll be damned if the mule didn't drop to his knees and roll over on his side like he was hiding, too. He was way smarter than the average Yankee soldier. Only question remaining was whether he was smarter than Pooty Burke. I took off my hat and plopped down beside him, laying my head on his chest and stroking his neck to make sure he didn't make any noise as the riders neared.

By the jingling of the equipment and the sound of the horses, I took it to be a small cavalry patrol, probably looking for deserters. I owed the mule a great debt. If he hadn't run into the brush, I might've been uncovering the payroll when the soldiers rode up. I don't figure the Yankees would've let me keep the money since they'd steal just about anything that wasn't too hot or too heavy.

As the riders went by, I stayed where I was, listening to the pounding of the mule's heart. I had plenty of time now to think about that money and how dangerous it would be if word got around I had it. Even a rumor would start folks coming from miles around—Yankees who would steal the curl out of a pig's tail, bushwhackers who would as soon shoot you as greet you, and just plain folks the war had driven to desperation. I decided to leave one bag in the crevice and hide the other three. I mentioned my plan to the mule, and he didn't object.

I hoped the money was all gold and not Confederate paper. Us southern folks weren't too impressed with Confederate dollars. I'd seen an orator pass through Cane Hill once trying to raise money to equip General Hindman's army. This orator was a pompous fool who was better at talking a good fight than fighting one. If hot air could've won the war, this fellow would've assured a victory for the South. After making his grand speech he took off his hat and extended it to the small crowd.

One of our oldest Cane Hill men jerked a five-dollar Confederate bill from his pocket and waved it in the air. "I'll give two-fifty." The crowd hooted. The orator didn't get much because people didn't have much. Sure, their sons, husbands, and fathers were in the army and we wanted to support them, but we didn't have enough to fend for ourselves, much less equip the whole Confederate Army. Of course, I'd take four bags full of paper money, but I preferred something hard in my hand, something that glowed, whose worth people didn't question.

Finally, when I could wait no longer, I got my mule up and led him back toward the limestone wall. My hands were trembling when I reached the crevice. I was so excited I didn't even tie the mule.

"I'm about to be rich," I told him as I leaped toward the ledge and pulled away the branches and leaves hiding the treasure. When my fingers touched the canvas pouches, I was as happy as a rooster in a full henhouse. These sacks weren't filled with paper money. No, they had metal in them. I pulled out all three and untied the rope around one sack, shoved my fingers inside, and pulled out a handful. I grinned at the cold feel of gold in my hand.

I wanted to shout, but I whispered to the mule instead, "I'm rich, I'm rich." Mule, though, didn't pay me no mind. He'd turned his behind to me and was nibbling at some grass by the roadside.

I fastened the heavy bag, picked it up by the neck, and started toward the mule to load him up. As I approached, I said, "Thank you, Jefferson Davis."

Instantly the mule brayed and with a rear leg slashed out at me, knocking the bag from my hand and spilling a couple dozen coins.

I jumped away, angered. The whites of his eyes hadn't lied.

"Jefferson Davis will—" I started, but before I could finish, the mule brayed and kicked again. I leaped back. "—hear about this," I finished.

I was stumped. Even though the mule was kicking at me, he made no attempt to escape. "What you got against me and Jefferson Davis?" I asked, and the animal kicked again.

"What you got against"—I paused—"Jefferson Davis?"

Once more the animal brayed, his steel hooves flashing through the air.

"Jefferson Davis, Jefferson Davis, Jefferson Davis," I said quickly. Once, twice, thrice did the mule bray and kick.

"Abe Lincoln." The mule did nothing.

"Abraham Lincoln." The mule never flinched.

"Jefferson Davis." The mule bawled, and its hoof

flew. All I could figure was, the U.S. teamsters had taught him that trick before Confederates stole him. I stopped mentioning the President of the Confederacy and fastened the bag of coins to the pack saddle, then retrieved two more and lashed them on as well. After that I started picking up the spilt coins.

For some reason the mule was fidgeting. Not wanting to risk losing him, I grabbed the halter line, squatted over the coins, and began gathering them again. That was when I heard the crack of a twig behind me.

I spun around and gulped. A bearded fellow stood there with a pistol pointed at my heart.

"What ya pickin' up, boy?" he asked.

I realized I had just lost my fortune.

Chapter Thirteen

As I studied this cowardly thief, I thought about trying to match him up with one of Pooty's sisters. He was uglier than a wart on a hog's butt. I've seen better-looking hairballs—which is what I figured he was set on becoming, what with all the shaggy hair hanging from beneath his sweat-stained hat and colliding with an even shaggier beard. He looked like he'd never been acquainted with anything sharp, which pretty much squared with his feeble mind.

This fellow's eyes were as muddy as his tobacco-tinted teeth, and I could see white all around the black centers. I couldn't remember if that was a sign for a killer in men or just in horses and mules. He was heavyset, his gut hanging out over his gun belt, and wore no coat. I guessed he had enough fur under his clothes to keep him warm all winter. Behind him in the woods I could make out a fair-looking horse, and I wondered how my mule and I had let him slip up on us. Of course, we'd been discussing Jefferson Davis at the time.

The fellow wriggled his gun at me and spat a chaw of tobacco about fifteen feet. "What ya pickin' up, boy?" he repeated.

"I spilt my hardtack, I did, and I was just sacking it back up. I'll just finish up and head for home."

He wrinkled his nose. "Looks like coins to me."

Bending down, I picked up another coin. "I do believe you're right. I thought the last one I ate *was* a little tough."

The fellow snorted, and his nose started running. With his free hand he clasped his nostrils between his finger and thumb and blew. Snot flew everywhere. If I was lucky, he'd step in a puddle, slip, and break his neck. He wiped his hand on his shirt and the beard.

"If you're hungry, I can leave a sack of hardtack here with you," I offered.

He pointed his pistol at the pack saddle. "I want all the hardtack I can get." He laughed like he was being clever.

My fortune was draining away like the snot out of his nose. I had to think fast. "We can split it fifty-fifty. Plenty for you and me!"

He considered the offer, then shook his head. "There's more than a hundred dollars there."

I'd dealt with smarter tree stumps. He was dumb enough to be from the North. "You a Yankee, or you just think like one?"

"I ain't no goddamn, egg-sucking, yellow-bellied, son-of-a-bitching jackass Yankee."

I got the message and prayed he wouldn't have to blow his nose again. "I figure you're due all the hardtack you want, then."

He grinned. "I ain't a bad thinker, I ain't. And now I'm gonna be rich and you ain't. Gimme those sacks."

Having no choice, I moved to the mule, untied one bag, and tossed it to the ground behind my mule. More coins cascaded free.

"I ain't never seen so much money." He dropped to his knees beside the sack. "Unload those other two sacks."

I eased beside my mule, patting him on the neck and acting like I was untying another bag. It was time to discuss politics. Carefully I backed the mule toward the robber.

"There's more money here than I can count." He was as happy as a drunk in a brewery.

"How high can you count?"

"Near a hundred," he said proudly.

"How old are you?"

"Thirty-two."

"You sure?"

"I am," he answered. "Why?"

"I didn't think a man could get that dumb in thirty-two years." I backed my mule a little closer.

"I ain't dumb."

"Then who's the President of the Confederacy?"

"Why, Jefferson Davis."

The mule brayed, cocked his hoof, and plowed into the robber's abundant belly. Dropping his pistol, the robber grabbed his gut and leaned forward.

"Jefferson Davis!" I yelled. My mule kicked him again. The thunk of hoof against head told me I was rich again.

Hairball fell over, his nose smashed, his teeth broken and jagged, his beard soaked with blood. I ran over and snatched his pistol, but he was so far gone he could've been in Texas, where we Arkansas folks had always sent the ugly and dumb ones, the Burkes excepted.

I unbuckled his gun belt, slid it from under him, rebuckled it, and hung it over my shoulder, then dropped the pistol inside. On hands and knees I grabbed as many of the coins as I could, not wanting to leave him a single one but scared to linger for fear another dumb son of a bitch might come along and think *he* was rich.

I tied the top of the canvas bag still in his hand, then scurried to my mule and secured it to the pack saddle. Turning around to check on the robber, I saw a dozen more coins scattered across the road. I ran and picked them up, shoving them in my pocket. I was about to mount my mule when the robber's horse nickered. If I didn't take the horse, the fellow might come after me.

I abandoned my mule for the barrel-chested bay,

which had a slight swayback, likely from toting that tub of lard around Arkansas. As I untied the horse, I saw a carbine in the saddle boot and bulging saddlebags I didn't have time to inspect right then. I mounted and trotted over to my mule. Leaning over, I grabbed his halter rope and tied it to a ring in my saddle, then started for Cane Hill.

I angled through the brush, taking my time and trying to stay as quiet as possible. With a gun belt over my shoulder and a carbine beneath my leg, I was as cocky as a rooster at dawn. I'd never had my own gun before, much less a revolver and a carbine. I guess the army mule really belonged to Pa, since I'd borrowed his, but I now had a horse, my own saddle and bridle, three sacks of gold, and a fourth well hidden. I was the richest kid in all of Arkansas, but that robber had gotten me to thinking: I could die young, too. Then I remembered the man I had buried on the way to Prairie Grove. Beryl Fudge had killed him for money that didn't exist. I'd been thinking how fine it would be to return home and show off my riches in front of Pooty, but I knew I shouldn't talk about having any money at all.

I rode a long way, thinking about dying and what it must be like. I have to admit I was scared. Van was the only one of my family who knew what dying was like, but as much as I missed him, I didn't care to join him. I decided the only way to stay alive was to hide the money and not tell anyone. I'd keep a few coins in my pocket but hide the rest—if only I could figure out where.

By suppertime I was hungrier than a woodpecker with a headache, but I kept on riding and worrying, looking over my shoulder every other step, not knowing whether I was blessed or cursed by the riches within my reach.

By dark I was as lost as a short dog in tall grass. I directed my horse and mule to a small hill and made camp inside a circle of trees. I tied the horse and mule to separate trees and opened up the saddlebags. One was filled with cartons of ammunition. The other had an Arkansas toothpick as well as a bag of jerked beef, a canteen with a broken strap, a tin of matches, a Confederate army blouse, a pair of socks, a worn deck of cards, and a plug of chewing tobacco.

For supper I ate a dozen strips of jerky and wound up with a powerful thirst. Much as it pained me to drink out of the same canteen Hairball had, I swallowed a few sips anyway. The water had a slight tobacco taste, but it was wet enough to quench my thirst.

As the night deepened, it turned colder. I untied the bedroll from the back of the saddle and made myself a place to sleep, keeping the pistol nearby. I slept poorly, but at least I had a bedroll to keep me warm—though it was probably home to a thousand of Hairball's fleas.

Come morning I studied the rising sun for a moment to get my bearings. I ate a couple strips of jerky but held off drinking anything from that canteen, figuring I'd run across a stream where I could drink some fresh water and refill the canteen. After untying the mule and hitching him to the bay, I mounted up.

I worked my way west and south through the woods, avoiding the occasional cabins I saw. Early afternoon I rode out of the brush to find a new grave between a burnt cabin and a barn that had a familiar look about it. It was the widow woman's place, and the grave was the one I had dug. Seeing no sign of the widow or her daughter, I started to ride on, but I had an idea.

"Hello," I called. "Anybody about?"

Only silence answered me.

"Ma'am, it's me, Henry Lomax, the one that buried your husband. You've nothing to be afraid of, me being armed and all."

Still no answer.

I rode the bay over to the barn and kicked open the door without getting off my horse. The barn was as empty as a Democrat's head. Then I looked around the woods and bushes but saw nothing except those same bushes and trees looking back at me. Back at the grave I spotted the shovel where I had left it. After dismounting, I tied my horse to a tree and looked around once more before digging a narrow hole in the grave, careful to keep the first shovelful intact. When the hole was about two feet deep, I impaled the shovel in the ground and moved to the mule, careful not to mention Jefferson Davis within earshot. I untied one of the bags and planted it in the grave, then scooped the dirt back in the hole, careful to replace the top shovelful as near to the way it had been as I could. When I was done, I untied and mounted my horse, then rode him back and forth over the grave, the mule following.

The more I rode across the grave, though, the more suspicious it looked to me; I figured anybody that happened by would know that someone had buried gold there. I decided to cover the plot with stones. So I walked down to the creekbed, gathered stones, and carried them to the grave. It was late afternoon before I was satisfied with the rock pile and mounted up again.

Though I was near Cane Hill, I didn't want to arrive home until dark so I could hide the two remaining bags. I clung to the side of the road for a mile, circled Cane Hill—or what was left of it—and finally hit Jordan Creek, which I followed.

On Lomax land there were plenty of places to hide the two bags. When I came to the white tree trunk that had tumbled years ago from the top of an embankment into the water, I knew my home was just beyond. The trunk made a natural footbridge from the creek to the top of the steep bank. I drew up my horse, jumped down, untied a bag of gold from the pack saddle, and clambered up the tree. Near the top I slid the bag between two slabs of limestone and screened it with other rocks.

After scurrying back down I mounted my horse and led the mule downstream until I was well past the house. There I climbed the embankment and headed into the woods on the back half of our property. I knew where another dead tree was, this one with a hollow trunk, and found it easily in the dark. I removed the last bag and shoved it inside a chest-high hole that a raccoon had used for a home. The sack clinked to the ground. It was a sound I hated to hear, because I would rather have speut that money than hidden it. Now all I had on me was the coins in my pocket.

I turned my bay for the creek and traveled upstream to the regular crossing, then aimed for the house. As I approached, I noticed a dim light through one of the windows, but the hounds started to howling and the light was snuffed.

I was about thirty yards from the house when Pa called out the door, "Name yourself or ride on. We don't want no trouble."

"It's me, Pa."

No sooner had the words passed my teeth than I heard a scream and an awful commotion. The door swung open, and a dark form ran out, crying my name. It was Momma. At first I thought she'd learned about Van, but she charged toward me, spooking my horse and mule until I reined them in. She grabbed my leg, pressing her cheek against it and crying. "You're home. I was so worried."

Pa came out behind Momma. He wasn't quite as happy to see me. "Where in tarnation have you been, Henry? I ought to get my razor strop and teach you a lesson for running away and stealing my mule."

"I brought you another one, Pa, and a horse."

That seemed to satisfy him for a moment. Then he frowned. "What'd you do, steal 'em? Lord knows you didn't buy 'em."

"Enough of that, George. Let me enjoy his return."

I agreed with Momma. "You heard anything from my brothers?" I asked, trying to get a sense of what they knew.

"Nothing," Momma replied.

My heart sank. I would have to tell her. I looked to the cabin and saw dim lights in two windows.

"Let me put my mule and horse up," I said.

"I thought they were *my* mule and horse," Pa corrected.

"As long as everything else is mine."

"Okay," Pa said, not being able to see all that I had.

"You two go on in the house," I said, "before some bushwhacker takes a potshot at us."

They did as I suggested, and I turned the animals toward the barn. Quickly I tended them, then took the saddlebags and tossed them over my shoulder like I had seen men do after a long trip. Picking up the carbine and bedroll, I started for the house. I thought I looked pretty important, a pistol under my left shoulder, a carbine in my right hand, and saddlebags draped over my right shoulder. On top of that I had gold in my pocket.

The walk from the barn to the house felt longer than usual because I had such terrible news for Momma. When I walked in the door, everyone was staring—Momma, Pa, Lissa, Harriet, and the whole Burke family, though I wasn't quite sure whether SincereAnne was staring at me or the fireplace, her eyes still being ajar.

Pooty's eyes grew bigger than washtubs when he saw the pistol and carbine. "Where'd you get those guns?"

"I whipped a bushwhacker and took them from him."

"Did not."

"Left him lying in the road, all bloodied and battered, I did." It was true, every word, except I didn't give the mule and Jefferson Davis their due.

"You stole them," Pooty said, "when he was taking a leak."

"Joe Don, watch your language," SincereAnne scolded.

Pa came over and took the carbine and pistol from me. I offered him the saddlebags. "Here's plenty of ammunition."

Pa grabbed them. "We can sure use this. The bushwhackers have ridden up a couple times, just to scare us."

"Where you been?" Lissa asked.

"Prairie Grove."

Momma's hand flew to her mouth. "There was a battle there."

I nodded. "I saw it."

She closed her eyes. "Thank God you're okay."

My lip quivered. "The Thirty-fourth was in the fight, Momma."

"Did you see your brothers?" Hope glinted in her eyes.

"Yes, ma'am." My head drooped like my spirits.

"Oh, no," she said, crying as she ran to me. "Which one? It *was* just one, wasn't it?" She grabbed my shoulders and shook me.

I nodded.

"Which one?"

I couldn't tell her.

"Andy?"

I shook my head.

"Jim?"

Again I shook my head.

"Oh, no, it was Van, wasn't it?"

I nodded. She fell to her knees, and Pa moved quickly to her side.

"He charged artillery, Momma. Got farther than anyone else. He's buried at Prairie Grove. I buried him myself."

Lissa and Harriet started crying. The Burkes shook their heads in sympathy.

"No, no, no," Momma groaned, reaching for me.

I felt so helpless, I didn't know what to do to console her. I dug into my pocket and pulled out a couple gold coins. "Here," I said, prying her hand from my shoulders. I tried to give her the coins.

She looked at them and knocked them across the room. "Money'll never bring him back."

SincereAnne jumped on those gold coins like a chicken on a june bug. She eyed them, then me, and I knew she was wondering where that money had come from and just how much more I had. If it wouldn't've wasted ammunition, I'd've shot myself for giving away my secret.

Chapter Fourteen

A bit of Momma died that night. She'd been lucky with her children, getting them all past childhood without losing a one. Until now. She talked more about Van than she ever had when he was alive. Periodically, when we were alone together, she'd ask me questions about his death.

"He wasn't disfigured, was he?"

I shook my head. "He took a chest wound, but his face was okay, Momma. He seemed at peace."

Momma started crying. "It should've been me, so Van could live a full life."

"A fine woman helped me bury him, Momma. Annie Belle Higdon said she'd care for the grave so if something ever happened to one of her sons, someone might do the same for him."

Momma cried harder.

I tried to soothe her feelings but felt about as effective as a bucket of spit at a barn fire. "He was buried with a prayer and a salute by the Yankees."

"The same Yankees that killed him?" she asked.

"He was brave, Momma. They respected him."

"Then why's he dead?"

I didn't know. I couldn't answer. What could I say?

Momma lifted her head, her eyes spilling tears down

her cheeks. "When this war's over and we make some money, I want to buy a good stone for his grave, maybe move him to a plot here."

I looked around the kitchen to make sure no one else was around. Although I didn't see anything, I smelled an odd aroma. "I've got money, Momma," I whispered. "I can get a stone for him now."

"You got money like you gave me when you came home?"

"Not so loud, Momma." As I tried to keep her quiet, I realized that odd aroma could only have been Pooty, trying to live up to his name. "Where are you, Pooty?" I called out.

He crawled out from behind the water barrel in the corner, hanging his head like an egg-sucking dog.

"You been listening?" I demanded.

He stood up, shaking his head. "I didn't hear nothing about you having money."

I took a step toward him, deciding I'd beat some sense into him even if it took me the rest of my life, but Momma grabbed my arm, and SincereAnne came into the room. Her appearance reminded me of the Prairie Grove battle when the Yankee bastards attacked the Confederate flank.

Coldly Momma said to her, "Your boy's been listening to talk he shouldn't've been."

SincereAnne crossed her arms over her bosom to match her eyes, then held her nose in the air like she owned the place. "What you been talking about? Where Henry got the gold?"

"None of your business," Momma shot back.

"Joe Don's got as much right to be in here as you do."

"This isn't Pooty's home, nor yours."

"His name's Joe Don, and we ain't your slaves."

"Your boy don't have no right to go sneaking about like a bushwhacker and listening in on our talks."

"Joe Don wasn't doing that, were you, Joe Don?"

Pooty shook his head. "No, ma'am."

"Liar!" I shouted, then charged for Pooty, but Momma caught my arm and jerked me back.

SincereAnne spat. "Henry's nothing but an ignorant ruffian."

Before I could grab her, Momma charged Sincere-Anne, slapping her across the cheek and knocking her eyes straight for an instant. The two of them started slapping each other and grabbing for hair. I'd never seen Momma so mad. I stood dumbfounded, then looked at Pooty, and we charged across the kitchen, grabbing our mommas and pulling them apart. Fighting was our job, not theirs.

Pa came barging into the kitchen, followed by the girls. "What's going on?" he demanded.

"SincereAnne insulted my sons and my house," Momma said, "and I'll not put up with her arrogance anymore, not in my house. She can go back to her own."

Stroking her reddened cheek, SincereAnne shook her head. "Secesh like your sons burned my home. I don't have a place to go."

Momma pointed her finger at SincereAnne's nose and was mad enough to have pulled the trigger had it been a gun. "You ever stop to think you're alive because we invited you into our place?"

I knew the answer to that: The Burkes weren't smart enough to think. Momma and SincereAnne argued back and forth, Pa just standing there and shaking his head. Watching the dispute was a lot like shearing a pig. There was a lot more wailing and screaming than wool when the chore was done. Pa didn't know how to stop a catfight, so he just listened and made sure the women didn't take to slapping each other again.

SincereAnne finally marched out of the kitchen into the dogtrot, taking her brood with her. "We're pulling out," she said, slamming the door behind her.

I shuddered at the cold that entered the open door, but SincereAnne was even colder than the weather.

Momma looked at Pa and shook her head. "War's

hard enough without living with a family that's against everything our boys are fighting—and dying—for." She sobbed.

Pa went over and put his arms around her. "It'll be okay."

"No, it won't. I'll never have Van back, no matter how much I cry. And that mean woman and her ugly kids are no help around here. Her biscuits are harder than cannonballs but softer than her head."

Shaking his head, Pa spoke. "Maybe it wasn't a good idea to let them stay here. I was just trying to protect ourselves and them from all the meanness. Just like it didn't work to yoke Henry and Pooty together, maybe this was a bad idea, too."

I thought it was a bad idea having to look at those ugly Burke girls all the time. I was confident the scenery around the Lomax place would improve when we booted them out. But no sooner did that thought make me smile than SincereAnne opened the door and walked in, her head lowered, her ugly kids behind her.

"We don't have a place to go in the cold."

"The barn," I offered, "with the mules."

Pa released Momma and thumped my ear.

"Ouch!"

Pooty grinned.

SincereAnne began to eat the biggest piece of humble pie I'd ever seen, saying maybe she'd been a bit rash in threatening to leave and she didn't know where her husband was or if he was even still alive. "No one else'll take us in if you kick us out."

Pa nodded, then turned to Momma. "What do you say?"

"As long as she and her kids stay clear of me and quit trying to overhear every conversation, they can stay. SincereAnne can do more chores—except cooking, because her biscuits are ruining our teeth."

SincereAnne flinched at the mention of her petrified biscuits, though I was right pleased that Momma had got that out in the open. She nodded meekly. "That will be fine."

The Burkes climbed the ladder into the loft, leaving me and my sisters with our parents.

"Momma," I said, digging into my pocket for the gold coins I still had, "I've money enough to go to Fayetteville, buy a stone for Van, and see that it's put over his grave."

Pa shook his head. "Where'd you get the coins, horse, and mule?"

I shrugged. "Just happened upon them."

"You steal them?"

I didn't think I had. "I just found them."

"The carbine and pistol, saddle and tack?"

I shrugged. "A fellow tried to take away what I'd found. We got to discussing politics, and I talked him into giving me all his belongings."

Pa's eyes filled with frustration. "Henry, sometimes I wonder about you. I'm never certain when you're telling the truth or not."

Momma smiled. "I'd like a stone for Van."

"I can get it," I offered.

"You sure you won't just bring more trouble upon us with your gold?" Pa asked.

"I ain't told a soul, and no one knows about it unless Pooty overheard something," I whispered.

The way it turned out, lots of people figured out I might be wealthier than I let on. Word of the lost payroll spread through Washington County. Word had it the payroll was all in gold. Word got around from SincereAnne that I had come back after the battle of Prairie Grove with a handful of gold coins. It seemed like we had more visitors coming around to see how well we were eating. Mostly the visitors were women, though a troop of Union cavalry came by, stopping to offer their thanks for helping the wounded soldiers after the battle of Cane Hill. We heard later the troop had checked the Fudge place for Beryl Fudge, who'd been sighted with bushwhackers at Prairie Grove. I smiled.

I was anxious to go to Fayetteville and get a head-stone, but Momma and Pa would have none of it until the federal troops left Prairie Grove. The troops lingered more than three weeks at the battlefield before deciding they had stolen all they could from the locals and packing up.

Winter, normally the worst season in the Ozarks, became the safest for the decent residents of Washington County. Bushwhackers, being the cowards they were, didn't have near the number of bushes and trees to hide behind once the leaves fell. So they cleared out of the state, many of them heading for Texas, where the mentally infirm were wont to congregate like maggots on a carcass.

Food was in short supply, though Pa and I were able to bring in enough game to feed ourselves. We were also running out of salt. So Pa, Pooty, and I dug up the smoke-house floor. We boiled the dirt in water, then strained it through a cheesecloth. The salt water that was left we put in tubs in the sun to evaporate and ended up with some salt, though not nearly as much as we had hoped.

It was sure hard with money in my pocket not to go buy what we needed, but if I made a purchase with coin, the rumors would pick up. We made it past Christmas and into 1863 before I left for Fayetteville to buy a stone for Van.

I rode my mule, which by then I'd taken to calling Old Abe since Lincoln hated Jefferson Davis almost as much as the mule did. We didn't say when I'd leave so the Burkes wouldn't know. I just got up one morning like I was preparing to do my chores, saddled Old Abe, and rode out. Even though it was colder than a Yankee's heart, I was glad to get away. Pooty had started clinging to me like moss to a rock. He wanted to find out where I'd hidden the gold.

With it so cold and most of the vermin bushwhackers gone, I didn't worry much about keeping to the brush. I followed the Prairie Grove road, riding off only once when I reached the farm where I'd buried the bag of coins. The barn had been burned since I last stopped by, but the grave and my hidden gold seemed undisturbed. Happy as a squirrel in a tree full of nuts, I rode on.

At Prairie Grove I went to Annie Belle Higdon's home, stopping behind the house to check on Van's grave. True to her word, Annie Belle had tended it, even outlining it with a rectangle of stones. I tied my mule, went to the front door, and knocked. I knew someone was inside because I could smell the woodsmoke in the air. When Annie Belle opened the door, I was shocked at the sight of her. Her face was gaunt and her eyes hollow.

She smiled, hugged me, and invited me in. Her four kids stared with hungry eyes. "What brings you here, Henry?"

"Going to Fayetteville to buy a headstone for Van's grave."

"I had the kids collect stones for it. Keeping them busy helps keep their minds off being hungry. The soldiers cleaned us out, didn't leave us much of anything in the way of food. We've made do, but we're none of us good hunters, though the boys get us an occasional rabbit. Some women have husbands who've deserted for the winter to help out, but my man's not that type. He'll stick with the army until this war's over."

Never in my life had I felt sorrier for a woman and her family. The gold coins were burning a hole in my pocket.

"Would you join us for our noon meal? It's not much."

"I'll stay a bit, but I want a little time to visit with Van."

I slipped outside, took off my hat, and talked to my brother. "Momma misses you, Van, and I promised her I'd buy you a stone. I came to do just that, but the woman and her kids in there need money for food. Could you wait? The woman's a fine one, she is, and her young ones've been carrying stones to mark your grave. I promise you a stone later."

Van didn't raise any objections. I know it was foolish to be talking to a dead man, but I felt better when I marched back inside.

"I've got something for you, Annie Belle," I said, "but you've got to promise you won't tell anyone where you got it, just that you found them on the battlefield."

"What is it, Henry?"

"Just promise me what I asked."

She nodded.

I motioned her toward the back corner where the kids couldn't see us as well, pulled the nine remaining coins from my pocket, and pressed them into her hand.

Her eyes went as wide as saucers. "It's so much money."

"Don't tell anyone," I said, "and don't show more than a single coin when you buy anything. Sometimes folks get killed when word gets out they've got money."

Annie Belle hugged me and started crying. I never understood women—they cried when they were happy and cried when they were sad and expected men to understand them. But I felt as good about what I had done as anything since Van's death.

"You're a good boy, Henry."

"You just take care of your kids and Van is all I ask."

She nodded, her eyes overflowing with tears.

Feeling uncomfortable with her crying, I stepped outside and mounted Old Abe so I could hunt a few rabbits for the family. I was gone about an hour, killing three rabbits, all of them skinny but with enough meat on them to satisfy a few hungry stomachs for a while. Annie Belle fried up the rabbit and fixed a few sourdough biscuits. That was our meal. Afterward we visited for a bit in front of the fireplace. She said she would like to meet my momma someday and show her how well she was keeping Van's grave.

After giving each of the kids a hug, I left on Old Abe. I went down the Cane Hill road, then cut back into the woods, circling away from Prairie Grove and toward the

spot where I had left the last bag of gold in the limestone
wall. I found the site easily, though I rode past it in the
opposite direction for a quarter of a mile to make sure no
one was nearby. When I returned, I jumped down from
my saddle and slipped over to the crevice.

The leaves and branches I had used to disguise the
hiding place were gone. My heart sank when I saw a
couple gold coins on the limestone floor of the crevice,
and when I stuck my hand in, my fingers closed around
an empty sack. Cursing, I jerked it out, shoved it inside
my coat, and pocketed the two coins. At least the thief
hadn't gotten them all.

As I walked back to Old Abe, I studied the ground
for other dropped coins but didn't see a one. I mounted
up and started back for home. I was down to three bags
of gold, but to my way of thinking that still made me the
richest kid in Arkansas. I wondered whether Hairball had
found the money or if someone else had happened upon
it. As dumb as Hairball was, he probably wouldn't have
known how to spend it if he *had* found it. I considered
tossing the empty sack away but was struck with a better
idea: I wanted Pooty to know what it felt like to be rich.

I circled wide of Prairie Grove and hit the Cane Hill
road for home, wondering how to trick Pooty and let him
find his own riches. At dusk I stopped at the wagon
crossing near home and filled the empty money bag with
five or six pounds of stones. Then I rode into the woods
behind the barn and hid the sack under a rotting tree
trunk. The sack would be the bait.

From there I rode straight to the barn and left Old
Abe, then walked up to the house. I whispered to Momma
that I had failed to order a stone. She seemed hurt until
I told her why, and then she seemed proud. When Pa
came in, I saw Pooty's head poking down from the loft,
so I knew he was trying to eavesdrop.

"Pa," I said, "I brought the bag of gold." My voice
was louder than it should have been.

"Hush, boy," Pa scolded. "You lost your mind saying such?"

He didn't understand that I knew what I was doing. I whispered to him that I needed to hide it in the regular hiding place. Then I ran out the door, and I hadn't made the barn before Pooty stepped out after me. I circled the barn and headed to the outhouse, where I attended my business. While I was sitting on the throne, I came up with a great idea.

As soon as I was done, I ran into the woods. Pooty followed me, of course. Every now and then I would spin around like I was looking for someone behind me, and he would dive to the ground. After a roundabout trip through the trees and down the stream I wound up at the rotting tree trunk and paused until Pooty was close enough to see me in the dark. Then I bent down and removed the canvas bag.

"I'll take a couple coins and hide the rest," I said aloud for Pooty's benefit. I picked up the bag, looked all around, and slipped back toward the house. Pooty followed me like a hound follows a coon. I broke out laughing a couple times. Pooty must've heard me and thought I was laughing because I was rich.

I'm sure he thought he'd have his own money before long; I would've thought the same thing if I was as dumb. I angled for the outhouse and went inside, then waited. Through the cracks between the planks I saw him sneaking up. When he was near, I started talking to myself.

"There must be ten thousand dollars in here," I said. "I wish I could spend it."

Pooty came closer. That was just what I wanted.

"I'll hide this gold where no one will ever think to look," I announced. Then I held the bag of rocks over the hole and let it fall into the pit. There was a splash and then a groan that could only have been Pooty realizing his fortune had vanished.

Chapter Fifteen

Poor Pooty was beside himself the next couple days. I could see it in his eyes every time someone went to the outhouse and he thought about that gold getting buried deeper and deeper. Even when it was colder than a spinster's drawers I'd linger in the outhouse, making noises with my mouth so Pooty'd think I was unloading on his fortune.

When I came out, Pooty'd be standing there, his face longer than a thief's alibi. I'd just smile and tell him the seat was still warm. He'd frown like he'd lost his peter and couldn't remember where he'd left it.

"You sick, Pooty? You've been to the outhouse a lot," I said.

He shrugged. "Been better."

It took Pooty about a week to figure out the best way to get at that money bag. One night at supper he turned to Pa. "Can I borrow your cane pole and fishing hook?"

"If you'll share your catch with us," Pa replied. "Henry, show him the fishing pole in the barn."

I nodded, trying to keep from laughing. Pooty was going to fish that bag out of the pit. I finally couldn't stand it. "I don't know that I'd be interested in splitting everything Pooty catches." I laughed, and everyone thought I was crazy. LouAnne stared at me, and I stuck my tongue out at her, knowing full well she was gonna slap me the next chance she got.

Come morning I took Pooty to the barn after breakfast and got him a cane pole with a fishing line attached. "You want me to show you the best fishing spots?" I offered.

He shook his head. "I don't need your help."

I pointed him toward the creek. "If you need me to hitch up the wagon to haul in your catch, whistle."

He hesitated.

"I've gotta go take a dump," I said.

"Me, too," he replied.

We both started in that direction.

"You go first," I said.

"No, you go first," he countered.

I knew he wanted me to empty my system first, then depart and leave him alone to do his trolling. "I'd hate to slow down your fishing. You go first."

"No. The fish won't be biting until it warms up."

"That a fact?"

"Honest Injun."

Then I stopped and put my hands on my hips. "You just want me to warm up the seat first, don't you?"

"No, no," he answered with a wave of his cane pole. "It just may take me a while."

I nodded. "I don't want to freeze my butt off."

Pooty sighed like he'd just cut the biggest fart in Arkansas history. I knew he was pretty pleased with himself.

Not having to go, I slipped in the door, latched it, and killed a few minutes, making noises with my mouth. I figured I should taunt him just a bit when I got out, so I shoved my hand in my pocket and pulled out one of the two gold coins I still had. I made a few final noises, then let out a long breath like I was buttoning my pants and admiring my handiwork below. I lifted the latch and stepped out.

"Look what I found, Pooty."

His eyes and mouth widened. "Where?"

"Damnedest thing. Right between the seat slat and the wall, like somebody dumped a bag of them in the pit and this one fell out."

Pooty licked his lips. "Okay, I guess I'd better go." He stepped toward the door, carrying the cane pole and all, but I snagged it from his hand. "You won't need this in there."

Reluctantly he handed me the pole and stepped inside. It didn't take him near as long to do his business as it had me. He was out in a minute flat, grabbed the pole from me, and strode toward the creek. Just to keep him mad, I walked with him and stood on the embankment as he tossed his hook in the water.

"No bait?" I asked.

Pooty shook his head, then rolled his eyes. "If you keep making noise, you'll scare them away."

I walked away from the embankment until I was out of sight, then bolted for the outhouse, hoping to wait there until he returned with his fishing pole. I grabbed the door handle and flung it open just in time to see LouAnne pulling up her drawers. Well, I remembered what I'd seen under Amanda Fudge's skirt, and I was curious if LouAnne's matched. To my surprise she motioned for me to come closer.

With my eyes focused on her waist, I moved within reach.

She hauled off and slapped the fire out of my cheek. "That's for sticking your tongue out at me."

Then, before I could react, she slapped me on the opposite cheek. I was beginning to think a Yankee couldn't fight without attacking you from two different directions.

"That's for looking at my drawers."

"I bet I'll be the only fellow that ever looks at your drawers."

She straightened her skirt, lifted her head in the air and marched back to the cabin.

"You look better from behind," I reminded her.

She ignored me, like she was too good to respond to an insult.

I glanced toward the creek to make sure Pooty wasn't watching, then jumped in the outhouse and pulled the door to. I sat down on the seat to wait, hoping Pooty'd be the next one to come, even though it might be funny for SincereAnne to open the door and for me to jump out and scare her eyes straight up.

It must've been thirty minutes before Pooty came back. He'd almost waited me out, but I finally spotted him coming, pole in hand. Struggling to keep from laughing, I pulled down my pants and waited. Pooty had a wide grin on his face when he opened the door. When he saw me, that grin clabbered faster than warm milk.

I covered my crotch. "You can't have my worm for bait."

"I need to fish . . ." he stammered, ". . . I mean pesh . . . pee."

"Pooty, haven't you ever written your name on the ground?"

"I forgot."

"You're dumber than I thought." I made out like I was finishing my business, then hauled up my britches. When I stepped out of the throne room, I took his cane pole. "Go ahead, Pooty."

He shook his head, stepped into the outhouse, and shut the door. I didn't hear the sound of water draining into the pit.

"Pooty, you forgotten how to pee?"

He barreled out of the outhouse, jerked the pole from my hand, and started toward Jordan Creek again. After he disappeared down the embankment, I slipped back to the house and scrambled under a bench on the dogtrot. I could hear the women inside around the fireplace, talking as they sewed. Pa happened by on his way to the barn. He stopped suddenly and looked down at me.

"What in tarnation are you doing, Henry?"

"Just waiting for Pooty to bring his fish back."

"Is this more of your mischief?"

I pled innocence.

Pa shook his head and continued on. I lay in the cold while he finished feeding the stock and returned to the house. Pooty waited an hour before he came sneaking back to the outhouse, looking all around as he advanced. I ducked behind the end of the bench so he couldn't see me. I heard the door creak open, then shut.

When I peeked out, I could barely keep from laughing. Pooty had taken his fishing pole into the outhouse with him. Anybody with half a brain would have untied the line from the end and left the pole outside. The pole had to be too long for Pooty to drop the line in the hole and still move it around.

The thought was no more out my mind than Pooty poked his head out the door and stared at the cabin first, then in both directions. Certain no one was watching, he backed out of the door with the pole in his hands. Apparently he had snagged the bag of rocks, because he was fighting and trying to lift something out of the pit.

Gritting my teeth to keep from laughing, I slipped from behind the bench to the kitchen door. As I opened it, everyone looked at me. I held my finger to my lips, then gestured for them to follow me. "I've something for you to see."

One by one they came out onto the dogtrot. I pointed at Pooty struggling with that fishing pole in the outhouse. Me and Pa started laughing. It was the funniest thing I'd ever seen.

SincereAnne, though, didn't think it was funny at all, and she didn't appreciate us laughing at her son. "Hush up," she scolded, then called to her son. "Joe Don, what are you doing?"

Pooty froze, then let the pole slip from his fingers. He turned around all sheepish and shrugged.

"You latch onto a big one?" I called. Pa and me

slapped our knees and almost fell on the porch with laughter.

Momma, Harriet, and Lissa had smiles on their faces, but the Burke girls looked like they had been sucking a trainload of lemons. I stuck my tongue out at LouAnne, daring her to slap me in front of everybody else—and I'll be damned if she didn't do it, marching past Pa and popping me on the cheek.

"Whatever Joe Don's doing, you're the cause of it," she said.

My cheek had been violated and my honor besmirched. But I didn't mind, not with Pooty fishing in the outhouse.

After the shock of being discovered melted away, Pooty ran to the house. "I can explain, Ma. I followed Henry the other day."

"What?" I cried, putting on a good show.

"I saw him find a sack of gold, I did."

LouAnne pointed at me. "See, I knew he was the troublemaker."

I shrugged. SincereAnne gave me the evil eye, but I wasn't sure which one it was, the way they went in different directions.

Pooty continued. "I followed him and saw him drop the sack of gold in the hole. I know the gold's down there."

Pa looked at me. "That true, Henry?"

Looking Pa straight in the eye, I told him the truth. "Pa, there's no gold down there."

"Is too," Pooty argued.

"Not either."

SincereAnne screeched like a wounded cat. "Why won't Henry leave my Joe Don alone?"

"Why can't Pooty keep from following my son about?" Momma shot back.

Pa got worried, thinking the women might go at each other again. "They're just boys." He turned to me.

"Henry, for the last time, I want to know and I want to know straight. Did you put anything down that hole?"

Taking a deep breath, I nodded. "I put things down that hole a lot, Pa. So's everybody else around here." I looked straight at SincereAnne, though I'm not sure she saw me. "At least I'm not so prissy to think mine doesn't stink."

"No more of that, Henry. No gold, right?"

"Cross my heart and hope to die if I put gold down that hole."

Pa looked at SincereAnne. "You satisfied?"

"Absolutely not. My boy don't lie like—"

Momma lifted her finger and pointed it at her. "Don't say it, or you'll be sleeping in the cold tonight."

SincereAnne just puckered up her lips, then marched over to Pooty, put her arm around him, and escorted him to the outhouse. Together they picked up the cane pole. She agreed something was snagged on the end of it and showed him how to grab the line and pull it from the slop without using the pole. Pooty seemed impressed by his mother's smarts. But in trying to lift the bag of rocks they snapped the line, and the bag disappeared beneath the muck.

"Did you see that, Ma? It was a bag, wasn't it?"

"I couldn't see straight, Joe Don. I couldn't see straight."

Truer words were never spoke by that woman.

Well, I was mighty pleased with myself for making Pooty look like the idiot he was. My prank didn't help the Burkes and Lomaxes get along any better, but it didn't make it any worse. Pooty pretty much stayed clear of me and me of him, though we still shared the same bed at night. We didn't speak to each other for a couple weeks or more, but then Momma didn't speak to SincereAnne, and our sisters hardly spoke to each other.

It was about February when Pooty and I started talking again, less because we wanted to than because we found ourselves competing for the same girl—Amanda

Fudge. It was damn stupid for either of us to see much in her. Pooty came from a family of abolitionists, and Amanda believed in everything Confederate. She thought she was better than me, and I didn't trust any child of Beryl Fudge, no matter how pretty she was or how few underthings she wore.

I figured her father was the meanest man in Washington County. I'd had second thoughts about insulting his daughter's virtue the last time we met. Of course, since I'd lied about seeing him with the bushwhackers at Prairie Grove, the federal cavalry had made a few trips to his place to arrest him, but he was never around to accept their invitation for free room and board in prison. Most said he'd gone south to Texas until the forests greened up in the spring and he could resume his back-shooting ways.

Amanda Fudge walked over on a warm February day. She was all smiles and lies when she stepped into the kitchen with all of us. When she saw me, she smiled like I was her beau.

"Played any marbles lately?"

"Found your drawers?"

"That's not a nice thing to say," Momma chastised me.

Amanda ignored her. "I'd like to go for a walk, if one of you boys would like to go with me."

"Why ain't you on your father's black stallion?" I asked.

"He left the county so the Union bastards wouldn't steal it."

"Amanda," Momma interrupted, "that's not proper language for a fine young woman like yourself."

"It's true about them, Mrs. Lomax. Didn't they kill your son?"

Momma nodded.

"How could you feel otherwise about them?"

Momma shrugged. "It's not that I don't feel that way, just that I don't believe it's proper to talk like that in front of others." She turned away. "I don't think we've enough for you to eat with us today, Amanda."

Amanda smiled. "I thought the boys might want to play marbles."

"We don't have any marbles," I reminded her.

"I hear you can buy some more."

By those words I knew she'd heard the rumor about me and the Confederate gold and that she'd try to find where I'd hidden it. I was getting of the age where I was interested in trying a few things out, and I knew she was gonna tempt me mightily.

Purring like a kitten, she stepped over to Pooty and took his arm. My jaw dropped. Pooty looked as bewildered as a fish out of water as Amanda marched him out the door.

"Don't wander far," SincereAnne reminded them.

"Take her fishing, why don't you, Pooty?"

As he closed the door, he gave me a look that would've scorched iron.

During her brief stay inside, Amanda hadn't said a thing to the other girls. In fact, she seemed to scorn them. I'll say this about the Burke girls: They may not have been the prettiest around, but they were decent, unlike the deceitful Amanda. To my way of thinking she was as cold-blooded as a reptile and had a memory only half as long.

That wasn't what Pooty thought after he returned. He had this cockeyed look on his face that sure made me curious, but us not being on speaking terms, I didn't inquire, though he apparently wanted to tell me about it.

After we retired to the loft that night, he whispered, "You ever done it?"

"Done what, Pooty, fish for turds in the outhouse?"

"No, I mean, felt a girl's, you know, her tits?"

I was jealous but not about to admit it. Of course, Pooty could've been lying, too, but I figured he was too dumb to lie, much less to see that Amanda was a conniving female.

"She said I could do it again," Pooty said wistfully.

"She's dangerous, Pooty. She doesn't care for you."

"You're just jealous because she doesn't like you, told me so herself."

"I ain't jealous. She's trying to see if we've gold hidden around here. She's gonna lead us on until she finds it."

"Is there gold around here?"

I shrugged. "You won't trust me, whatever I say."

"It's in the outhouse, isn't it?"

"No, Pooty, it's not. Just believe me. Amanda Fudge is dangerous."

"She likes me."

"No, she don't. She's using you, that's all. You remember the night the bushwhackers came and burnt the outhouse?"

"Yeah."

"Her pa was leading them. I think she's been spying on your folks for him. The Union Army—the army you side with—thinks he's a bad man. They keep sending troops to catch him. Why would you want to get tied up with her?"

"You wouldn't know, Henry, because you ain't experienced it. She kisses good, Henry."

"What's her tits feel like, Pooty?"

"It's hard to say. Kinda soft, kinda firm. Just right."

As soon as he said that, I could feel my sap rising. We talked a bit more before Pooty dozed off, but it took me a long, hard time to fall asleep.

Chapter Sixteen

Winter seemed like it would never turn into spring in 1863. Pooty had his hands all over Amanda, and I was getting nothing but his word about what her tits felt like. Finally he asked for my best sock and said he'd show me. He took me out to the barn and filled the sock with some seed corn, but he said that felt too lumpy. So we went down to the creek and filled the sock with sand. That was closer, he said, but Amanda's skin was softer than a sock. We might've kept trying, but Momma got upset when she saw my sock with sand in it.

Amanda'd meet Pooty at least once a week. She'd come to the cabin, or he'd meet her between our places. At first it bothered me, but then I realized that whenever he was off feeling her, I could go about my business without being watched. When he wasn't with her, he stuck to me like a shadow.

"Why you hanging around me so close, Pooty?"

"She said she'd let me do more than just feel her if I found where you'd hid the gold." By that admission I knew he was desperate, since she wasn't doing anything more for him than helping his sap rise.

One spring day when everything was budding out and the branches were covered with new leaves, Amanda came over and caught me alone behind the barn.

"Hello, Henry," she said, batting her long lashes at me. "Played any marbles lately?"

I shook my head without looking at her. "No marbles left."

"Seeing my bottom rattled your aim." She laughed.

I didn't see anything funny about it. "Pooty's probably waiting to rub you down."

She smiled and curtsied. "He'll wait, Henry. All boys will." Holding the pleats of her skirt, she slowly lifted it.

I licked my lips when the hem passed her knees, then inched up her thighs until I could see her patch of corn silk. When she dropped the skirt like a stage curtain, I sighed.

She scowled. "I don't like Pooty, never have. Don't like his sisters, either."

"You got a fine way of showing your dislike to Pooty."

"He's a Yankee-lover, the whole family is. I don't care for that. Now you, you're secesh."

"Then why are you letting him feel you all the time?"

"To make you jealous, Henry."

She'd succeeded. My sap was rising again, and there wasn't a thing I could do about it but grit my teeth.

"I know you've got gold, Henry, and I got this." She lifted her skirt again, then twirled around so I could see her front and bottom. "I'll share what I've got if you share what you've got." She was as brassy as a prostitute in church. "When you start sharing with me, I'll drop Pooty faster than you'll drop your pants. Until then, Pooty gets my goodies."

I was as wobbly as an hour-old colt when she turned around. Below the waist I was ready to sell my soul to dip my wick in her basket, even though I knew she was evil. Though I was smart enough to know not to trust her, it was still a tempting offer. I was glad I didn't watch where she went, or I might have run after her and given her the two gold pieces I still carried in my pocket. Instead I went into the barn and saddled Old Abe and rode him out into the woods, a couple of Pooty's hounds following me.

When I got among the trees, the hounds picked up the scent of something and began to sniff at a trail. I stopped Old Abe, and as one of the hounds sauntered up behind us I called out, "Jefferson Davis." The mule brayed and lashed out with its hind leg, catching the hound full in the stomach. Knocked ten feet on its haunches, the dog yelped and turned around, running back to the cabin, the other hound following.

I meandered through the woods, wishing I'd brought my carbine when I jumped a deer that would've made several good meals. Whether I intended to or not, I wound up by the hollowed-out tree trunk where I had hidden the last bag of gold. I dismounted, picked up a broken branch, and inserted it into the knothole. Even stretching my arm I could just barely touch the top of the money bag with the branch. It was a comfort to know it was still there.

Then I thought I heard a noise. I spun around, wishing I hadn't scared off the hounds so they could've warned me of somebody's approach. I didn't see a thing, but I walked all around the trunk, looking for spies in the woods. Now that it was spring, the bushwhackers would be making the woods dangerous again.

Remounting Old Abe, I made a wide swing, hitting Jordan Creek on the southern boundary of our place and riding back up the stream, figuring to check my second cache of gold in the ledge. My plans changed when I saw Pooty approaching from the wagon crossing. He had a long face, not the joyous look of a fellow who had been feeling the goods in Amanda's basket.

"You seen Amanda? She was supposed to meet me at the wagon crossing, but she never showed up."

I shrugged. "I saw her out by the barn. I guess she was looking for you."

"She must've forgotten where we were to meet."

"She don't like you. You're a Yankee-lover. She's using you."

"And I suppose she likes you?"

"She don't like nobody but herself, Pooty. She'd eat her young if it would make her a dollar."

"They might be our young," he said proudly.

"Pooty, I want to tell you something. I've called your sisters uglier than homemade sin from the day I first laid eyes on them. And they are. And LouAnne, always slapping me around. I can't say I like any of them. But they'd make damn better wives than Amanda Fudge. She's got a heart of stone."

Pooty doubled up his fists. "You don't say that about Amanda. Step down from your mule and I'll whip you like you deserve."

I kicked Old Abe in the flank and started home. A fellow that would take up for a girl like Amanda instead of defending the good name of his sisters was in too far over his head.

Back home I put Old Abe in the barn, careful not to discuss politics with him. At supper nobody said much except Pa.

"Henry, we start plowing tomorrow and getting ready to plant. At least we've still got two mules to do the work. That's more than most folks have around these parts. We'll plant crops we can eat."

"More likely the Yankees will eat," I answered.

"We got to do something."

I went to bed early but wasn't asleep by the time Pooty came up. We lay there, not saying a thing. In the still night, sound carried well, and a thumping noise came to my ears. I heard Pa stirring downstairs and stepping out in the dogtrot. He said something to Momma, who shortly poked her head up in the loft.

"Henry, your pa wants you."

I jumped out of bed and scurried down the ladder, wondering what the problem was. When I stepped outside, I saw Pa holding the Spencer carbine I had swiped from Hairball. The thumping noise sounded like someone chopping dead wood.

"What is it?"

"Don't know," he answered, then pointed toward the woods.

My heart sank. Though the foliage was returning, I could make out the small flicker of a torch.

"Is someone cutting wood on our place?" Pa asked.

Now I knew why Amanda Fudge hadn't met Pooty. She'd followed me into the woods that afternoon. She was what the hounds had taken scent to. Every time her dress went above her waist, it spelled trouble for me. I thanked God I wasn't Pooty—he'd have to be in a heap of trouble before he let loose of her goody basket.

"Maybe we better check on it, Henry."

"I know what it is, Pa."

"What?"

"I hid some gold I found. I checked today to see that it was still there. Somebody must've followed me and come back for it."

"Was it Pooty?"

"Amanda Fudge."

Pa spat. "That little bitch. And she's got Pooty's doodle tied in so many knots he'll never get it untied."

"Beryl Fudge was with the night riders that threatened us."

Pa cleared his throat. "I know. That's why he kept his horses when the Confederate quartermaster took everybody else's."

"I know for a fact, Pa, he murdered a man between here and Prairie Grove, because I helped bury him."

"And he's bound to be the one that burned down the Burke place. He's no better than a rabid cur. Maybe I should go out there to kill him, but a man like that always travels in packs."

I grabbed Pa's arm. "Don't even talk about going out there."

"The money wasn't ours to begin with. It's not worth dying over."

"But, Pa, it ain't theirs, either."

Pa thought a long time. "I guess, son, none of it's really ours. I've always heard that money talks, but what I've come to figure is, all it ever says is good-bye. It'll say good-bye to Beryl and the others, just like it does to everyone else. Only difference between them and us is, we'll still have our decency when our money's gone."

We didn't say much else, just listened to the thunk of the ax against the wood and watched for the occasional glimmer of the distant torch. When the sound of the chopping stopped, we heard a shout of joy, and then the torch flickered out. We stood in the darkness, not saying a thing.

Pa put his arm around my shoulder and led me back inside. I was glad he was still with us and hadn't taken to the hills or been forced into the army.

"We best check the shutters, son, and make sure they're tight. I don't trust Beryl. I figure he'll take to bushwhacking again."

After inspecting the shutters I returned to bed.

Pooty was still awake. "What was that all about?"

"Night riders in the woods," I said, falling into bed. I pulled my pillow over my head because I didn't want to talk. I just wanted the damned war to end so things would get back to normal and I could go to Fayetteville and buy Van a headstone.

Pa woke me early the next morning, then fetched the carbine and asked me to hike into the woods to see if we could find any game. I knew he intended to check on the mischief that had taken place the night before. We moved cautiously and quietly until we came to the tree trunk. As I had expected, it had been chopped down and the bag of gold taken.

"That's where I hid the gold, Pa."

"Is there more?"

I didn't know how to answer him. My hesitation, though, was all the answer he needed.

"Where is it?" he asked.

"Two bags, one on our place and the other one north of Cane Hill."

Pa shook his head as if he was greatly disappointed in me. "If you don't have something in this war, you starve to death. If you have something, you get killed over it. I guess it's best I don't know about it. Just tell me one thing, Henry. Is the money under the outhouse?"

A grin wormed its way across my mouth. "It's a bag of rocks down there."

Pa snickered, then laughed loudly. "Pooty was trying to fish up a bag of rocks?"

I nodded, and we both laughed as we walked back to the barn. He gave me the carbine to take up to the house while he hitched up the two mules to plows and led them out to the field. Our mule went about his chore with me trailing him. But Old Abe figured plowing was beneath the dignity of an animal that had once carried gold for the Confederate Army. Pa struggled all morning with him and finally gave up before lunch.

He shook his head at me. "You took a plow-broke mule, though a mite worn down, I admit, and traded him in for the most obstinate animal I've ever seen."

"Just don't discuss politics with him," I warned him.

"What do you mean?"

"Unhook the plow so nothing gets broken or hurt."

Pa unhitched the plow and nodded.

"Don't stand behind him." Pa moved out of range. "Now, name the president of the Confederacy."

"Jefferson Davis," he said.

Old Abe lifted his head, brayed, hoisted his hind leg, and slashed at the air with his hoof.

"A fellow tried to rob me, Pa, but Old Abe saved me when he kicked the robber. That's how I got the carbine and the bay."

Pa chuckled as we walked to the house for the noon meal.

It was a modest lunch of fried squirrel and corn

bread. We'd taken to consuming so much meat and so little of anything else that our systems were plugged up pretty good. Momma made us take some of her sassafras medicine to loosen our innards. I didn't think it wise for us to take it on the same day we started plowing, as it could interfere with the progress of a man's work and the straightness of his rows.

After lunch Pa rested about fifteen minutes on the dogtrot, then returned to the plow. Since we only had one good mule, he told me to stay home and draw water for the women. I made a dozen trips down the creek and was starting another when I heard a gunshot from the woods near the field.

I saw Pa fall in the plowed ground, and I screamed, tossed my bucket aside, and ran to the field. From the woods I heard the sound of a galloping horse. Pa didn't move as I ran up. I expected to find him dead, but he was wide awake and alert.

"I'm okay," he explained as I knelt beside him. "I wanted him to think he'd hit me."

Momma and the girls came running out of the house, screaming as well, and fell to their knees beside him.

"Everything's fine," he said, but it took them a minute to believe it.

"George," Momma said, "I couldn't bear to lose another family member. The crops can wait."

"Winter won't, though."

Momma said, "I'd rather go hungry than lose you."

Lissa and little Harriet echoed her sentiment.

"Who would've done it?" Momma asked.

"No telling, these days," Pa answered.

We helped him to his feet and escorted him back to the cabin like he was wounded. I returned to the field, unhitched the plow, and led our old mule to the barn, cursing the son of a bitch that would take a shot at my pa. I don't know whether the assassin had wanted to kill Pa or just scare him.

The rest of the day we all stuck by the house, afraid

even to go to the outhouse. We had a cold supper of leftover biscuits and nothing else. When dusk came, we felt more vulnerable, especially when we heard gunshots in the distance. It was hard to tell which direction they came from, making it all the more frightening as we sat in the dark waiting. Pa took the carbine and gave me the pistol and Pooty a shotgun, instructing us if riders attacked to run up in the loft and shoot back through the portholes. We still had barrels of water positioned around the cabin in case attackers tried to fire the place.

What we feared would happen finally did a couple hours after dark: The night riders came.

We could make out about two dozen of them riding up the embankment. Pa, standing watch at one of the windows, saw them first. They lit a torch and approached as slowly as a funeral procession.

"Don't shoot unless I say so or they start shooting at the house," Pa ordered. "You women, stay low and don't lift your heads for anything."

Momma herded Lissa and Harriet to the back wall, pushed them down on the floor, and screened them with her body. SincereAnne dropped to the floor with her daughters as well. One of the women was whimpering.

"They're coming," Pa said, pointing me and Pooty to different windows.

My stomach was flipping over like griddle cakes as I looked out. I gritted my teeth when I saw a rider atop a black stallion. It was Beryl Fudge. If ever a man needed killing, it was him.

The riders drew up not thirty feet from the front of our house.

"Boys," Pa whispered, "if the one with the torch looks like he's going to throw it at the house, shoot him."

"Lomax," called the man on the black stallion. I recognized Fudge's voice.

"Yeah," Pa answered.

"Folks say you was working the field today. That true?"

"Until some bushwhacker took a potshot at me."

"He was trying to tell you something, Lomax."

"Then why didn't he just come right over and say it to my face?"

"He's shy," Fudge answered. "He wanted you to know there'll be no crops this year."

"How'd you expect us to eat? There's women and children under this roof."

"Some of them's Yankee bastards," Fudge yelled back. "Fact is, soon as you get a crop, the Yankee soldiers will come and steal it. You'll still be starving, but their bellies'll be full. This way, they starve, too."

"You bringing us food, then?"

"Not as long as you got Yankee vermin living under your roof. Send them out now, and we'll leave you good secesh folk alone."

"No, please don't," SincereAnne whimpered.

Pooty spoke up, but his voice cracked. "It's okay, Momma, I'll take care of you."

Pa called out, "Leave us be. The women and children haven't harmed anyone."

Fudge laughed. "That Burke boy's a Yankee in waiting. Better to get rid of him now than fight him later."

SincereAnne sobbed. "Don't give him up, please."

"Hush, woman. I'll die before I let them take him," Pa said.

"Lomax," Fudge called, "we found a sack of gold last night."

"Don't know what you're talking about," Pa answered.

"Your son Henry does. I've talked to the Confederate paymaster. There were four bags of gold before the Yankees ambushed the guards. We've got one. We'll be back for the other three when we need them." He ordered the torchbearer to toss the torch on the ground.

"Don't shoot," Pa whispered desperately to us as the flaming torch fell on the hard-packed dirt in front of our porch.

"Next time we come back," Fudge said, "we'll want more gold. And don't you think we won't be back." He and his men turned about and rode away as calmly as a family on a Sunday ride.

It would be weeks before we saw them again, but there wasn't a day we didn't dread nightfall and the possibility of their return.

Chapter Seventeen

The summer of '63 was bad. We had no crops and little food beyond the game we killed and the wild berries and nuts we collected. We didn't have flour for bread or biscuits, our salt had long been depleted, and coffee was a luxury. Our summer shortages tormented me because I had the gold we needed to survive, but the moment I spent any of it, we'd all be in jeopardy.

We were thankful that Beryl Fudge hadn't returned since the spring. He had been right about the Yankee troops; their foraging parties roamed the country and took all the crops and vegetables they could find. Even if we *had* grown food, we'd've gotten very little of it before Abe Lincoln's men took it. The Yankees stole the horse I had taken from Hairball, but we managed to keep Pa's mule and Old Abe. When soldiers came to look at him, I assisted by whispering "Jefferson Davis" in his ear, and they figured he was too dangerous for them.

That summer a troop of federal infantry set up camp on our land to dig up the Yankees buried there after the battle of Cane Hill. Pooty and I watched the burial crews uncover bone and cloth and little more. I thought of the excitement and parades when Thomas and John had marched off with the 3rd Arkansas Infantry and wondered if the dead Yankees had had such a send-off up north. If so, the glory was gone. All was now decay. I thought about Van in his grave back in Prairie Grove and wished I wasn't watching these graves being uncovered. I remembered him as a flesh-and-blood brother, with a sense of humor and a good look about him. Now he was little more than these men were. I hid my tears from Pooty.

Occasionally we got word about the 34th Arkansas from Washington County boys who'd deserted for a few weeks to check on their loved ones. Generally Andy and Jim were as well as could be expected, living on poor rations and dodging bullets every time they ran into the bluebellies.

Things didn't go well for the South that summer. Vicksburg fell on the Mississippi River, cutting Arkansas, Louisiana, and Texas off from the rest of the Confederacy. Then we heard about a place in Pennsylvania called Gettysburg, where Union troops had killed thousands of our boys. We worried because we hadn't received a single letter from Thomas or John since they left Arkansas. We didn't know whether they were alive or dead.

In August, fortunately, we finally got a letter from Thomas. He said he and John were alive and well, but the Yankees were harder to spank than Pa had thought. He said he'd seen Richmond and even caught a glimpse of Washington from afar, but he'd be glad to get back to Arkansas where cities were manageable and quiet. He sent his love to us all and asked that Momma give his best to DeeAnne Burke.

That seemed a bit odd to me, him wanting Momma to greet DeeAnne, but Thomas didn't know, I reckon, that the Burkes and Lomaxes were living together. After reading the letter aloud to us and the Burkes, Momma sighed. "At least they're both alive." She smiled.

"What's the date on the letter?" Pa asked.

"May third." Her smile drooped.

We all realized the letter had been written before Gettysburg. I noticed DeeAnne's eyes watering, and then she began to sob. "I sent him letters, but he never answered them."

"DeeAnne," SincereAnne said, the surprise apparent in her voice, "you've been writing Thomas Lomax?"

She nodded. "He promised me he'd write. We'd taken to seeing each other before he left." The way she said it, it sounded serious and genuine, unlike the words that came from Amanda's mouth.

Momma looked at Pa as if this was all news to them, too.

"He's secesh," SincereAnne reminded her daughter.

"I don't care. He's a decent sort," DeeAnne said.

I was getting nervous. If DeeAnne and Thomas were fond enough of each other to get hitched, that would mean Pooty and I'd be related. I was as despondent as a toothless squirrel in a barrel full of nuts.

"Your pa wouldn't approve," SincereAnne scolded.

"My pa's not here and neither's Thomas, so it doesn't matter." She seemed embarrassed that everyone was staring and started crying again. I hate to admit it, but in that moment I saw in her the deeper beauty that must've appealed to Thomas.

Pa nodded. "I had suspicions of a sort, DeeAnne. Thomas asked me to look after you. That's one reason I invited your family to live with us until this thing was settled."

DeeAnne smiled through her tears.

"Don't put stock in not getting any letters," Pa went on. "Mail's not dependable. We don't even know where to write Thomas or John."

Lissa stood up and marched to DeeAnne, throwing her arms around her. Then Harriet joined her along with LouAnne and RuthAnne, and Momma and SincereAnne hugged. By then me and Pooty were ready to gag. We jumped up from our seats and stepped out on the dogtrot, Pa following on our tails.

"We better put on boots, boys, before the flood hits," he said.

Pooty nodded. "I've never seen so much crying."

"I bet Amanda never cries," I said.

Pooty clinched his fists. He knew I was right.

Somehow Thomas's letter and DeeAnne's confession drew the Burkes and Lomaxes together. We seemed almost to have forgotten the threats of Beryl Fudge and the night riders.

In early September some bushwhackers and Yankees ran into each other during the night on the far edge of our fallow field. They spent about five minutes shooting at each other and making us nervous, then rode away. Come morning Pa, me, and Pooty took guns and went out to check.

We found two dead horses, removed their saddles and rigging, and collected two dropped pistols and three cartons of ammunition. We carried the tack to the barn and the guns to the house.

I waited a couple days until those horses were ripe, then sidled up to Pooty.

"You ever bounced a horse?"

"Huh?"

"You ever bounced a horse?"

"Horses don't bounce."

"I bet I can bounce one farther than you can."

Pooty looked at me like I was stupid. "This a trick?"

"I wouldn't trick you, Pooty."

"I remember the times you knocked the 'coon on me or had me flush out that polecat or shoved me off Amanda's horse."

I shrugged. "It wasn't me that sent you fishing in the outhouse. Are you betting or not?"

Pooty scratched his head. I knew I was taking a risk, but I just couldn't pass up the bet, not with Pooty to pay.

Though we had been ordered by Pa not to stray, we slipped out to the field and to the horses, now bloated to twice their size.

Pooty looked at me and shook his head. "You're

gonna pick up one of those horses and bounce it like a
ball, is that right?"

"Nope. We're gonna see who can bounce a horse the
farthest."

I had Pooty confused, but he never was a fast thinker.

"Watch." Hoping this prank didn't burst in my face,
I took a deep breath, jogged toward the horse, and
dropped gently against its bloated side. The rotting flesh
gave, then bounced me back three or four feet. I grinned
at Pooty. "That's bouncing horses."

He laughed. "I get it." He started running awfully
hard for the horse, but I held up my hands and stopped
him.

"Go slow the first time. Get the feel of it."

Pooty started again. He slowly approached the carcass, then fell against it, bouncing back a few feet. He
giggled.

"You ready to see who can bounce the farthest?" I
asked him.

"I can, and I'm ready."

"Good," I said. "Get ready to mark where I land."

Pooty moved aside, and I stepped back about twenty
feet. I couldn't hit too hard for fear the hide would burst,
but I couldn't hit too softly or Pooty might smell a trick.
I started running as hard as I could, then braked a bit at
the end. Flinging my arms out and gritting my teeth, I
hit the bloated flesh. When it gave I was afraid I had
failed, but suddenly the bloat bounced me back a good
ten feet, though Pooty only marked me at eight.

He laughed. "I can do better than that." With his
foot he plowed a line in the dirt where I'd landed, then
turned around and ran about twice as far from the carcass
as I had.

"You sure you want to do this?" I asked, feeling
guilty about stealing the oars from Pooty's boat once
again. But he wasn't about to be stopped now.

He stamped at the ground, tossed his head, and
charged. If the bloat had held, he might've bounced all

the way to Texas, where he'd've been among his own kind—people with mush for brains. He ran with his legs and arms churning, his eyes wide, his mouth open. I thought he was smart enough to brake when he neared the carcass, but I was wrong. He plowed ahead full speed, then tucked his arms against his chest and ran into the horse, screaming like a Yankee on leave.

I held my breath when Pooty hit the inflated hide and vanished. Then I heard the hide rupture—and damn if it wasn't about the worst thing I had ever smelled. With a loud pop the carcass spewed gasses and entrails and then deflated, snaring Pooty within its rot. For a moment everything was quiet. Then the hide started bouncing.

Pooty had fallen in and couldn't back out.

I ran over, plopped on my knees, stuck my arm in, grabbed an ankle, and pulled him out like I was birthing a calf. He emerged spitting and flailing, smelling almost as bad as the time the polecat sprayed him, though he wasn't green. No, sir, he was a rainbow of putrid red and yellow and brown and purple. He jumped to his feet and gagged and puked and started running for home.

I took out after him. "Wait," I called, fearing he would run inside, stink up the house, and ruin my reputation.

Pooty ran faster than I'd ever seen. SincereAnne saw him coming and screamed because he looked like he'd been hit with a cannon blast of grapeshot. She ran out to catch him, but he dodged her.

No matter how fast I ran, I couldn't gain on him. He disappeared over the embankment by Jordan Creek, and a second later I heard a loud scream and a splash. When I topped the embankment, he was flailing in the stream, dousing his face, gargling and spitting, ducking his head under water—in short, doing everything he could to remove the innards and the stink that covered him like a coat of rotting whitewash. He didn't stop cursing me, not even when SincereAnne ran up and demanded to know what was going on.

"What happened?"

"He ran into a horse," I said.

"I'm talking to Joe Don," she snapped.

Instead of listening to his momma, Pooty was cursing me from sunup to sundown. Figuring I wouldn't get a fair hearing from SincereAnne, I returned to the cabin.

Pa was standing on the porch steps. "What's going on?" he demanded.

"Pooty dove into one of those dead horses. Good thing I was there to pull him out, or he might've drowned."

Pa shook his head. "Go wash off your arm."

I went to a washbasin and used some lye soap to get rid of the odor. I was drying my arm when SincereAnne came striding back toward the cabin, her eyes ablaze and Pooty dripping wet at her side. I figured I was in for it, in spite of my heroism.

"Mr. Lomax," SincereAnne shouted, "your boy's done something horrible to my Joe Don and needs to be punished."

Pa moved to the shade of the porch, crossed his arms, and cocked his head. "I hear my boy saved yours, is that right?"

"What? There's no more truth in that than there is in the Southern cause," she answered. "Henry made Joe Don run into one of those vile dead horses."

Pa asked me straight. "That true?"

"No, sir. We was bouncing horses."

"Bouncing horses?"

"We'd run into their bellies and bounce back."

"Did you put Pooty up to it?"

"Not until after I did it," I answered. "I bounced off of it once real easy, him too. Then we both made runs at it, me first."

Pa looked at SincereAnne. "Ask your boy if that's true."

She turned to her son. He took a deep breath and

sighed. "He bounced twice. He bet me he could bounce farther."

I felt vindicated.

Pa said, "It could've happened to either of them, SincereAnne."

"No, no," she argued. "Henry planned it this way."

"Are you saying Henry's smarter than your son, SincereAnne?"

"No! No!" She was so flustered she didn't know what to say for an instant. "He stinks, and we've got to get him a decent bath."

"Henry'll be glad to help," Pa answered.

"But, Pa!"

He answered in a low voice so SincereAnne couldn't hear. "I know what happened. Pooty doesn't have the sense God gave stump water. You put him up to that, and now you can help wash the stink out."

That afternoon I carried wood, hauled water, and built a fire beneath a black washpot. When the water was hot, we doused the embers and gave the pot a chance to cool before Pooty stripped and jumped in.

As it turned out, we should've waited until that night to clean him, because the night riders returned. They slipped up at midnight when we were near asleep. The hounds set up a cry, but by then it was too late for us to do anything.

"Lomax!" yelled a rider.

I recognized the voice of Beryl Fudge as I scurried from the loft. Pa gave me a shotgun and grabbed his rifle.

"What do you want?" Pa asked.

"We want more gold."

"You got the only bag we had."

"Paymaster said there was four, Lomax." Fudge whistled for a moment as a couple men lit torches. "Pay up or I'll burn your place down."

Pa looked at me. "Henry, you got more gold?"

"Yes, sir."

"Give it up. All money ever says is good-bye. Where is it?"

"Show us, Lomax!" Fudge called.

"I don't know where it is. Only my boy knows."

Momma hurried to Pa's side. "Don't let Henry go out there."

"It's our only chance," Pa replied.

"We're getting impatient, Lomax," Fudge called. "Hurry or we'll fire the house and shoot you all when you run out."

SincereAnne screamed. "Tell them, Joe Don, tell them."

I heard a shuffling in the loft, and then Pooty came barreling down the ladder. "I know where the money is," he called out a window.

"No, Pooty," I said. "It's not in the outhouse."

"It's in the outhouse!" he shouted.

"No, Pooty, no," I cried.

"Who's talking?" Fudge wanted to know.

"Joe Don Burke," Pooty answered.

"Why don't you come out, then."

"No harm to him," Pa yelled, "or we'll come for your kids."

"You don't know our kids," Fudge replied.

"Amanda'll be close enough," Pa shot back.

Pooty shot out the door and led the riders to the outhouse. We couldn't see and couldn't hear much of what they were saying.

SincereAnne bolted into Pa's bedroom, shaking and crying, "My boy, my boy." Her daughters trailed her.

It was a brave thing Pooty did, no more than he knew about the gold cache, but a dangerous thing, too. We heard a brief commotion at the outhouse, then hooves thundering across the field, followed by gunshots. It seemed like total chaos had erupted. Pa stuck his head out the door, me right behind him.

By the torchlight I saw a man carrying a bag from the outhouse and other bushwhackers scurrying for their horses and firing across the fallow field. Then I spotted Beryl Fudge, in his distinctive plumed hat, firing three times into the pit.

Running out onto the dogtrot, SincereAnne screamed, "No, no, no!"

Quickly dropping their torches, the bushwhackers mounted up and charged toward Jordan Creek as a troop of cavalry came thundering past, shooting at the fleeing figures.

Pa and I ran to the outhouse, picked up a still-burning torch, and held it over the inside. The bushwhackers had pried the seat board off. I knew Fudge had killed Pooty, and I felt terrible—until I saw him in muck up to his neck.

Pa bent over the hole, lowered his hand, and grabbed Pooty's arm. When he lifted him out, Pooty smelled worse than ever.

Chapter Eighteen

SincereAnne charged for the outhouse in her night-gown, screaming, "Joe Don, Joe Don!"

"He . . . he tried to kill me," Pooty sputtered, flinging muck around.

SincereAnne threw her arms around her son, then took a whiff and stepped back, looking at her hands in the flickering light of the discarded torch. She held them to her nose, then slung them around, trying to shake everything off.

"We'll have to heat more water," Pa said.

"He tried to shoot me," Pooty kept repeating.

"You know who that was?" I asked.

He shook his head.

"Amanda's father."

"The bastard," Pooty said.

"The bastard," SincereAnne echoed.

"But you got even with him," I announced.

Pooty looked bewildered, like any sane person drenched in thunder water up to his neck would. "How?"

"There was nothing but rocks in that bag."

Shaking his head, Pooty walked to the creek, his mother trailing behind.

In the distance we heard shooting, like the soldiers had caught up with the bushwhackers. Pa picked up the torch and started down to the river. "You women get in the cabin," he said to my sisters and the Burke girls. "I want to be sure Pooty and SincereAnne don't have any more problems." He looked at me. "Henry, run back to the house and get some lye soap."

I dashed to the house, took soap from the washstand, and ran to the creek, where I handed it to SincereAnne. She nodded her thanks.

"I don't want to rush you two," Pa said, "'cause I know you've got a lot to wash off, but it ain't safe out here, not at night, not with the bushwhackers about and me holding a torch."

Pooty replied, "I'm scrubbing as hard and fast as I can." He pulled his nightshirt over his head and washed himself some more. SincereAnne didn't have as much muck on her, but she couldn't take her gown off, not with me and Pa and her own son within sight. When Pooty stood up, he wrapped his nightshirt around his waist and started up the bank. His momma followed.

At the top of the embankment we heard the sound of horses approaching. By the rattle of their gear I took the riders to be cavalry. With Pa holding the torch, the soldiers could see us before we could see them. I heard an officer issue orders for the soldiers to set up camp in front of our house and to post guards immediately.

Twenty yards down the creek we could hear them crossing over. A single officer approached on horseback. In the flickering light he was hard to make out, his face hidden by the broad brim of his hat. He was Yankee, no doubt, but something about him seemed familiar. He stopped and studied us as we squinted back, then clucked his tongue and started the horse across the creek.

SincereAnne gasped. "Can it be?" She stared at the officer, then straightened her wet nightgown, which clung to her skin like flesh to ribs, and patted her hair hurriedly. Then she took to bawling like a lost calf.

"I'm home, Sincey," the officer said as he rode to us.

"Pa!" yelled Pooty, charging the officer and flinging his arm around his leg.

SincereAnne trembled so hard I thought she might break, but otherwise she seemed frozen to the spot on the ground. Gordon Burke dismounted, handed Pooty the reins, and stepped to his wife. He took her in his arms and pressed his lips against hers. They held each other tightly, the only sound being her sobs.

"Welcome home, Gordon," Pa said.

He nodded but spoke only to SincereAnne, running his fingers through her hair. He kissed her a final time, then released her, but she clung to him like a vine to a tree.

By the markings on his uniform I took him to be a captain.

"We're grateful, Gordon, you saving us like you did."

Pooty's pa turned to mine. "I'm indebted to you for taking my family in. I know it hasn't been easy, Sincey being hardheaded on occasion, but she's a good woman, a godly woman."

Pa nodded. "We've had our good times and our bad. Henry and Joe Don've had their ups and downs, but we've managed. Even if we ain't eaten that well, we haven't starved, either."

We started walking toward the house, SincereAnne still crying and hugging her husband like she hadn't seen him in two years.

"I know our sentiments are on opposite sides of this war, George," Burke said, "but tell me who was causing the trouble."

Pa sighed. "Our politics aren't as far off as you might think, Gordon. I've never been for slavery. It's an abomination, but I'm crippled and can't fight. Five of my boys joined the Confederacy to get the Yankees out of Arkansas, and I can't go against my boys."

"How are your boys?"

"Van died at Prairie Grove. Andy and James are fine, last we heard. Just had one letter from Thomas. He and John were in Virginia."

"Who was raiding your house?"

"Beryl Fudge's the only one I know for certain."

As we neared the cabin, Pooty bolted ahead, struggling to lead his pa's horse and hold the nightshirt around his waist. "RuthAnne, DeeAnne, LouAnne," he yelled, "Pa's here! He's rescued us." He jumped on the plank dogtrot, tied the horse's reins around a post, and disappeared inside the house. His three sisters bolted out like they'd been shot out of a cannon. Screaming and shouting and carrying on, they jumped around their pa, hugging and kissing him in turn. LouAnne even darted over, grabbed my arm, and did a dance around me before planting a kiss on my cheek. I had to admit I liked that better than being slapped, but I didn't feel right kissing back.

Pooty ran back out wearing his pants and shirt. Now their whole family was together, and I was jealous. Ours would never be together again, not with Van dead and four brothers still in danger.

My sisters and Momma stepped out onto the porch to greet Gordon Burke. As Pa tossed the dying torch aside, I saw Yankees around a dozen campfires, staking their mounts, setting up camp, unfurling their bedrolls, and following orders.

Captain Burke stood on the porch and turned to face his soldiers. "Men," he called, "this is my wife, SincereAnne."

The men cheered. Then he introduced his daughters. The men whistled, the girls still being in their nightclothes and most of the men wishing they were in them as well.

"This young soldier," he said, running his fingers through Pooty's hair, "is Joe Don, my boy. His friends call him Pooty."

I figured that would be the end of his introductions, but he didn't stop there. "All you Lomaxes get up here."

I feared he might tell them to shoot us since we were Southern by our sympathies, but he treated us like family.

"This is George Washington Lomax and his wife, Abigail."

The men cheered.

"Now," he said, "their boys have been fighting for secesh"—the men hissed, then laughed—"but they've been fighting like men in uniform, not like the cowards we were chasing tonight."

The men cheered my brothers, and I felt proud.

He pointed to my sisters. "Little Harriet has a voice like a songbird, and Melissa there, you can see she's as cute as they come. The boy there's Henry. He's been known to get into some trouble, but what boy hasn't?"

I felt embarrassed and proud at the same time.

Then Burke asked us all to go inside while he issued orders to his men. We waited in the kitchen ten minutes until he returned, carrying a burlap sack that he plopped on the kitchen table. "There's sugar, coffee, and flour in there. Some salt as well. The boys thought you deserved it." He dropped his hat on the table and removed his sword and gun belt, looking at his wife. "There's a lot to talk about."

"The house is gone," SincereAnne said.

He nodded. "I know. Did Beryl Fudge do it?"

Pa cleared his throat. "We think so. He came here threatening us for keeping your family and flying the American flag."

"What?"

"It was one I had. Pooty found it and flew it over the house. Beryl didn't like it. Threatened us and burnt your house."

Burke smiled. "Tomorrow we'll return the favor."

We spent about an hour talking and trading news, Burke wanting to know why Pooty had been in the outhouse, what was hidden there, and what had led him to believe such nonsense. Pooty pointed at me.

I couldn't deny it, not with his pa commanding a troop of cavalry outside. "I was greening him," I admitted.

Pooty started to describe all the times I'd tricked him, but Burke waved the complaints away. "No harm done, as long as you're alive and not maimed." I breathed a little easier.

It was well after two o'clock in the morning when Pa told me, Lissa, and Harriet it was time for us to find our beds in the loft. Then he turned to Burke. "Why don't you and SincereAnne take our bed for the night and as long as you're here?"

Burke hugged his wife. "It'll beat sleeping on the ground."

Us Lomaxes retired while Pooty and his sisters visited with their pa a while longer. It seemed odd, Pa and Momma in the loft, but I knew it was the right thing to do.

Morning came early the next day, and we were roused by the sound of the cavalrymen rising and fixing their breakfast. Captain Burke had a grin on his face when he came into the kitchen. Momma was fixing biscuits. Pooty and I were waiting at the table for him, both of us interested in his stories about the war. He didn't care to talk about it, saying he'd seen too much to describe and hoped the terrible war ended before Pooty and I had to fight because we'd likely be fighting each other.

One thing bothered me. "Were you at Prairie Grove?"

"No, son, I wasn't. I'm sorry about your brother."

I nodded. "The Yankees treated him fine, once they killed him."

"There's no glory in war or killing, not when you're fighting your neighbors," he said.

"The damn bushwhackers don't see it that way," Pa said. "They're snakes in the grass who'd as soon steal from their friends as their foes."

Burke rubbed his chin. "Beryl Fudge is the leader of the bushwhackers in these parts. He's run with Bloody Bill Anderson some and then terrorizes these parts when he's homesick for his wife. With the leaves turning, I figure he's heading for Texas."

Pa agreed. "He's a back-shooting coward, brave

around women, children, and crippled men, but that's all."

When the girls joined us, we talked about more civil things until Momma finished the biscuits. Then we gobbled them down, enjoying the wonders of a little flour, water, baking soda, and salt.

After breakfast Burke grabbed his gun belt, sword, and hat and stepped outside to talk to a lieutenant. Shortly we heard the cavalry saddling their mounts. When Burke returned, he announced he and his men were about to ride over to the Fudge place.

"Mind if I go along?" Pa asked.

"Me, too," Pooty and me piped in.

"You probably shouldn't"—Burke winked—"but I can't stop you."

"We've a couple mules in the barn."

"I know. The lieutenant told me." Burke turned to his son. "You and Henry can ride double on one of the mules, George on the other. If there's trouble, you three return here quick as you can."

Me, Pa, and Pooty jumped up from the table and ran out the door.

"You be careful, Henry," Momma chided.

"That goes for you, too, Joe Don," called Sincere-Anne.

With the saddle I'd stolen from Hairball and the two we'd taken from dead horses in the field, we had more saddles than mounts. We threw the best two on the mules. Pa decided to ride Old Abe and give me and Pooty our plow mule.

When the cavalry got in formation, we were up front with Captain Burke. "Forward," he ordered.

It was exciting riding with the cavalry, even if they *were* Yankees. We crossed the river and angled toward the Burke place. Captain Burke halted the cavalry and studied the charred remains of what had once been his home, his barn, his toolshed, his smokehouse, and even his outhouse. Not a one was left standing.

"A lot of hard, honest work went into that place," he said.

"At least you haven't lost any kin," Pa said. "If you get your family through this war, you'll be better off than most."

The captain looked at Pooty and me. "I hope the war's over before it gets to them."

Pa wiped his hand across his forehead, then pinched the bridge of his nose. " 'Seed corn' is what the Confederacy calls them. I don't care to see any more of my flesh planted in the soil."

Burke pointed at the ruins of his home. "My neighbor did this, a man I'd help patch his roof and catch his loose stock. It'll be years before the folks of Washington County get over this war." He cleared his throat. "Time for me to be neighborly."

He motioned with his right hand for the troops to advance. They followed him past the blackened ruins of his home, across a weed-infested field, and up a forested hill, where they stopped among the trees overlooking the Fudge place. Burke lifted his field glasses and studied the area. "Don't see any horses in the corral."

"Fudge rides a black stallion," Pa said.

"No horses, unless they're in the barn." Burke lowered the glasses, then twisted around in the saddle. "Lieutenant, take a dozen men around back and make sure no one escapes. Be in place in five minutes, then we'll approach."

"Yes, sir," the lieutenant responded, then ordered a line of cavalrymen to cling to the hilltop as they circled the house.

Shortly Captain Burke motioned for the soldiers to advance. We rode down the slope and emerged from the trees at the foot of the hill. Though the soldiers had ridden two abreast until then, now they spread out in a battle line with Burke in the center.

By the smoke from the chimney we knew someone was there. We rode within fifty feet of the place before we saw any other sign the house was occupied—a quiver of a lace curtain, as if someone had touched it.

Burke drew the soldiers up in front of the house and ordered them to dismount. Every third man held the reins of his own and the adjacent soldiers' horses while the free soldiers pulled their carbines from their scabbards and advanced toward the house. As four men positioned themselves on either side of the two front windows, the others stepped to the door and at Burke's nod kicked it open and burst inside.

The air was pierced by the screams of two females screeching like wounded mountain lions. They caught their breath, then started shouting profanities like a medicine-show barker shouts remedies until two grimacing soldiers dragged them out. Amanda came first, biting and clawing until the trooper grabbed her golden hair and tried to lift her off the ground with it. She went instantly quiet and struggled to fight back her welling tears.

Her mother, a chunky woman, was anything but ladylike. She spat at the soldier holding her arm, then cursed everybody from Abraham Lincoln to the soldier's mother. "Don't you damn Yankees know to knock? You don't have the manners God gave a pig."

Burke took off his hat. "Morning, Corrine. Is Beryl around?"

She hushed and stared like she'd seen the devil in blue. "Gordon Burke."

He replaced his hat. "Just being neighborly," he said, his voice tainted with bitterness. "Would your husband be about?"

She grew defiant. "We thought you'd turned yellow and run."

"The only yellow is the stripe down my cavalry britches. You ought to've learned more about cowardice from your husband."

"You Yankee bastards got no business down here. Get on home."

"Your husband burned my home."

She lifted her chin defiantly. "Yankee bastards don't deserve a home down here. Go up north and leave us folks alone. Take your cross-eyed wife and your ugly daughters when you go."

Captain Burke pointed his finger at her nose. "Your husband dumped my boy in an outhouse last night and tried to kill him. He'll answer for that, whether I'm in uniform or not."

"That's a lie. My husband ain't been home in days."

"I hadn't seen my wife for two years until last night," Burke replied, "but I don't go hiding behind her. I wear a uniform and fight like a man, not a coward." He turned to his soldiers. "Men," he said, "search that house for Beryl Fudge." He directed other men to the barn.

"Pa," Pooty said, "Amanda stole some marbles from me and Henry. Could the soldiers get them back?"

"Bastard!" Amanda screamed.

"Sure," Burke replied. "You heard him, men."

The soldiers moved like locusts in a wheat field into the house. We could hear dishes breaking, pans falling, furniture being smashed. One soldier came out with a couple sacks of marbles. "These them?"

Pooty nodded and took them. Soon the other soldiers reappeared, all shaking their heads.

"Nobody inside," the lieutenant said, "that we found."

"He could be hiding in places you didn't find," Burke said. "See if we can burn him out."

Mrs. Fudge and Amanda took to screaming and pleading for the house to be left alone, but their pleas were futile. The soldiers torched the house and barn. Soon both were blazing.

"Mount up, men. He must not be home." Burke turned to the women. "Good day, ladies."

As Burke led his men away, Amanda and her mother threw dirt at them.

Chapter Nineteen

Autumn became winter, 1863 changed to 1864, and I turned fourteen in January. With Captain Burke's cavalry roaming Washington County, I had hopes of making it to my next birthday. As predicted, the bushwhackers had left for Texas when the leaves fell. Others likely to make trouble were less bold with the cavalry about, especially after word got around of what Captain Burke had done to the Fudge place.

The soldiers visited our place regularly. Pooty came near to becoming their mascot and would have had he another two legs, a hide of fur, a wagging tail, and a drooping tongue. He and I were always arguing about who made better soldiers—men in blue or gray.

"Yankees can't even pee straight, much less shoot straight."

"How come no secesh is brave enough to show his hide in uniform in Washington County?"

Pooty had a point, but then so did a saber and that didn't make it smart. Whenever he brought up such a point, I'd throw up my arms and shake my head like I understood the military, then change the subject. "Want to shoot some marbles?"

"Nope," he replied. "I want to shoot secesh." Of

course, he'd say those things when his pa's soldiers were about, but he wasn't near so bold after they left.

Among the soldiers, Pooty seemed closest to one from Kansas everyone called Cap Andrews. Like most of the others Cap was small and wiry, but he had mean eyes. All the cavalrymen had eyes hardened by three years of war, but none had the same simmering evil within them. He wasn't to be trusted, but Pooty confided in him more than in the others.

One spring day I was heading out to the barn to feed the mules when Cap Andrews fell into step beside me, eyeing me like he knew a secret. I was no more comfortable around him than a lawyer is around the truth, so I broke into a jog, figuring I'd leave the bluebelly behind. But he ran beside me all the way to the barn. I opened the door and slipped inside, looking for the pitchfork to protect myself, but some Yankee must've stolen it.

Andrews closed the door behind us. As I scrounged around in the dim light for some fodder for the two mules, he searched the barn stall by stall and then checked the hayloft. I eased over to Old Abe, figuring to discuss politics if Andrews threatened me.

Certain we were alone, Andrews sauntered to the stall, licking his lips like he was approaching a platter of pork chops. His grin made me as nervous as a pig passing a slaughterhouse.

"It true you know where gold is hidden?" He stared at me with those evil eyes.

Shrugging, I began to stroke Old Abe's neck. "If I knew where a treasure was, I'd dig it up and spend it."

Andrews rubbed his hands together. "So it's buried? Where?"

"Pooty's been known to make up things, like saying his momma can see straight or his sisters are pretty."

"They are," Andrews answered.

Only thing I could figure was, all Yankees were stupid—or blind. I maneuvered Old Abe around to defend myself if the Yankee tried to enter the stall.

Andrews's right hand disappeared behind his back, then reappeared with an Arkansas toothpick. He waved the knife at my nose. "I could slit your throat, you damn secesh."

My knees started shaking like leaves in a breeze. I was beginning to wish I'd never found that Confederate gold. When the Kansan sliced the air in my direction, I bent and slipped under Old Abe's neck and went to the opposite side of the stall, putting the mule between me and the crazy Yankee.

"This war won't last forever," Andrews said. "When it's over, maybe even before, I'll be back for the gold."

"You'll be coming back for nothing."

Andrews shook his head. "I'd hate to be you when I do come back. You'll die a slow death." He backed away from the stall, holding the knife in front of his neck and making sawing motions until he disappeared out the barn door. I waited several minutes, then slipped outside, looking all around for him. I spotted Pooty and ran over to him.

"What are you telling these bluebellies about gold?"

"Nothing that ain't true," he said, holding his chin in the air like he thought he had the whole U.S. Cavalry behind him. "You've hid gold somewhere. That's what Beryl Fudge wanted, and the way I figure it, I'd sooner a Union soldier had it."

I would've knocked a couple inches of arrogance off Pooty's chin, but there were a lot of cavalrymen about, and if they were as crazy as Cap Andrews they might just haul me out and tie me to a tree and shoot me like a dog.

Although the family felt safer that winter than they had since the war started, I was worried with Cap Andrews about. He always seemed to be watching me, and Pooty always seemed to be trailing me. I couldn't so much as fart without one of them being close enough to share the aroma.

As spring approached, though, we all grew nervous. The bushwhackers would be coming back, and Beryl

Fudge'd likely seek to avenge the burning of his house. We'd heard that Amanda and her momma had been blaming us Lomaxes as well as the Burkes for it and vowing that Beryl would kill us all when he came back and then claim our place.

But with the Union cavalry about, me and Pa felt safe enough to plow the fields and prepare a new crop since we'd missed last fall's harvest. Captain Burke helped get us enough seed to plant corn, beans, squash, and potatoes. As long as Captain Burke was in the vicinity, we had reason to hope that we'd be able to grow, harvest, and eat this crop ourselves.

One of the things I learned early in life was, once things get to going good, something comes along and changes everything for the worse. That was what happened in May, when the federal army ordered Captain Burke's outfit to abandon Washington County and give chase to the Confederate Army. I would be glad to see Cap Andrews leave, at least; I hoped he'd run into Beryl Fudge so maybe at least one of them would die and I'd have less to worry about.

Captain Burke had more to worry about now that he was leaving his family. Even though he admitted he shouldn't do it, he left us a couple extra carbines and more ammunition to defend our place against bushwhackers, and he suggested we tie the hounds around the house at night to give us some warning if men approached.

We were all nervous, not knowing what would happen after the troops left. I figured Beryl Fudge would be back. He might still stink if he had carried that turd-soaked bag of rocks all the way from our outhouse to Texas. Being the cowards they were, the bushwhackers probably hadn't stopped until they were halfway across the state. And the Texans, being used to the smell of each other, probably hadn't given the odor a second thought.

The next morning the cavalry arose early and broke camp. We all got up to see them off. RuthAnne seemed taken by anything in a blue uniform. DeeAnne was courteous to the men but hung around her father. I couldn't shake LouAnne, though, who seemed nervous and kept edging over to me. I'd step away; she'd step closer. I rolled my eyes at her, shook my head, tapped my feet, crossed my arms over my chest, and sighed loud enough that the captain thought a locomotive had pulled up to the house. LouAnne had slapped me so many times in the past I was surprised my eyes weren't as crossed as her momma's. I'd had about all I could take of her pestering— even though she hadn't said a thing—and I was sorely tempted to take my chances and haul off and slap her.

Then I saw her lower lip tremble and a single tear slide down her cheek. Feeling about as useless as a two-legged milk stool, I stepped to her and patted her on the shoulder. She actually leaned against me and held my arm.

"I'm scared, Henry, with Pa leaving us behind."

"Things'll be okay. He left us extra guns and bullets. There's nothing we can't fend off." There probably wasn't a true word in what I'd said, but I never felt better about telling a story. LouAnne nuzzled my shoulder and gave me a nice, warm feeling. She wasn't so ugly after all, I told myself. And I began to wonder the thing that all boys wonder about any girl: Would she let me feel her tits?

LouAnne patted my hand. "You're so brave."

If she liked me so, I hoped she'd show it a little better than she had in the past, always slapping me, but I have to admit I didn't understand my own sisters, much less other girls. My feelings were as mixed as loyalties in Washington County.

Captain Burke stepped to his daughters, kissing each one on the cheek. LouAnne left my arm to kiss him good-bye.

Then the captain shook my hand. "Take care of LouAnne and her sisters, will you, Henry?"

"Yes, sir."

"And you and Pooty don't stay at each other's throats."

"Yes, sir."

Then Gordon Burke turned to Pooty. "Son, you behave yourself and do what Mr. Lomax tells you to do."

Pooty shook his head and bit his lip. "He's secesh."

"You do what I say, and I'm telling you to mind him. He's helped keep my family together and alive."

"Yes, sir," Pooty replied.

"I hope to help end this war before you and Henry have to go fight." He shook Pooty's hand vigorously, then saluted him. We didn't know it then, but it would be the last time Gordon Burke ever shook hands with his son.

The captain stepped over to SincereAnne and kissed her softly upon the cheek. She was springing more leaks than a sieve, and he finally had to pry himself away from her. "Take care, Sincey."

She sobbed something, and LouAnne began crying, too. I put my arm around her and pulled her against me.

Captain Burke strode to his gelding and mounted. When he gave the command, the whole column started forward. LouAnne pulled me by the hand, running after her pa, waving and crying.

Pooty had fallen in beside the column, running to keep up with Cap Andrews. As Andrews rode past me and LouAnne, he called to Pooty. "I'll be back, Joe Don. Keep one eye on you know who and the other on the lookout for you know what."

"What was he talking about, Joe Don?" LouAnne asked.

Pooty shrugged. "You know how soldiers are."

LouAnne shook her head. "That one's a bad man."

"You're imagining things, LouAnne." Pooty backed away from us and toward the house, his gaze never leaving the column until it disappeared in the trees.

For the first time in months we all feared the bushwhackers. They would return with Beryl Fudge in the lead and vengeance on their minds. But there wasn't much we could do except say our silent prayers and hope the war would end. It seemed it never would—or if it did, it would be in Confederate defeat. The news was all bad from all over, with no sign of change.

That afternoon Pa instructed us on how to defend the house and gave assignments to everyone. If the hounds started barking, all three of us men would take a carbine and fire out of the house to try to scare the bushwhackers off. Pooty and I were to take positions at the portholes in the loft, and Pa would stay downstairs and shoot through the gunports in the shuttered windows. The two shotguns would be handled by Momma and SincereAnne. All the girls were to keep low, help us reload as fast as possible, and stay near the water barrels with buckets close by to douse any flames if they tried to burn us out.

That night we were all on edge—me more so than the others, because when LouAnne and I were alone in the kitchen after supper, she leaned over and kissed me on the cheek. She did nothing more, but I sure thought about the possibilities.

The next day Pa gave instructions for no one to leave the house without letting others know about it. That afternoon I took one of the carbines and told Pa I was going hunting to see if I could get a few rabbits or a wild hog for supper.

"Can I go with him?" LouAnne asked.

Pa shrugged. "Ask your momma."

LouAnne turned to SincereAnne. "Let me go with him, please."

SincereAnne nodded halfheartedly. "Remember your upbringing."

I didn't know what SincereAnne meant by that, but I figured it wasn't too good. I grabbed a carbine and a handful of bullets and was out the door, wondering with every step just what LouAnne had in mind.

When we entered the woods behind the barn, I told her to keep pace behind me in case I had to do some quick shooting. I never saw any game and never had to shoot. LouAnne was looking hard, too. Once I turned to find her plucking something from a low branch. Whatever it was, she hid it from me real quick.

We went about an hour with no luck—at hunting. I took a swing by the hollow tree trunk where I had hidden the bag of money the bushwhackers had stolen.

"What happened here?" LouAnne asked.

"Somebody chopped a tree."

"But why? Wasn't it dead already?"

I nodded, catching a glimpse of what she was trying to hide in her hand. It was an old wasp nest. I didn't see the point in picking something you couldn't eat, but then again I wasn't a woman.

I sat down on the log and rested the carbine across my knees. LouAnne sat down beside me.

"Do you like Joe Don?"

"You mean Pooty?"

"Ma doesn't like it when we call him Pooty."

I laughed. "That's why I call him Pooty."

She swatted my leg.

"Why are you carrying a wasp nest?"

"My affair and none of yours. Do you like my brother?"

"He's okay. He's easy to green about things."

"He believes you have gold hidden around the place. Is that another of your tricks?"

"Pooty falls for lots of things."

"That's why the tree was chopped down. You'd hidden gold there."

"Who told you that?"

"I figured it out on my own," she said.

"What's it matter if there is gold? You want some of it if there is, is that it? Pooty's put you up to sweet-talking me into telling where it is, hasn't he?"

She shook her head. "So there is gold?"

"No, that's not what I said."

"Yes, it is."

"So you want the gold, too?"

LouAnne's eyes clouded over again. I couldn't understand it. "No, I don't want any gold. I just don't want you to get hurt because of it." She leaned over and kissed me on the mouth.

I figured that was an invitation to reach for her blouse, but she broke away from me and jumped up fast.

"We best be getting home before our folks get worried."

She charged through the woods. I followed her, though I must admit walking was a bit awkward, as tight as my britches had become.

Everyone was disappointed when we returned without any game, but I promised to go again the next day, early. LouAnne agreed to go with me.

After a breakfast of fried saltpork and biscuits the next morning, I was gathering my carbine when Lissa approached. She looked over her shoulder to make sure no one was listening. "You know what LouAnne's pinned under her skirt?" she whispered, as if anyone else would care.

If it wasn't my hand, I didn't care what was under her skirt.

"A wasp nest," Lissa said. "It's a sign she's trying to make you her fellow, Henry."

I shrugged, trying to hide my excitement.

Lissa pointed to my hat on a peg by the door. "See your hat?"

It was a dirty felt work hat with a stained band. "I ain't blind," I answered back, starting for the door.

"If one day you find the band missing, then that's another sign she's trying to make you fall for her."

"Sounds like thievery to me."

"If she makes a garter for herself out of the band, it's a sure sign she's in love with you."

When LouAnne approached, Lissa went quieter than a corpse.

"I'm ready, Henry. How about you?" LouAnne asked.

I grabbed my hat and started out the door.

"Mind if I have your hatband?" LouAnne asked.

I looked back over my shoulder to see a broad grin on both LouAnne's and Lissa's faces. I almost tripped off the porch.

"Be careful with that carbine," Pa chided me as I rounded the corner of the house and headed for the woods again.

LouAnne was scurrying to catch up. I strode into the woods far enough that I couldn't see the house and no one there could see me, then propped the carbine against a tree and waited for LouAnne.

I felt a bit awkward because I'd never just started in on kissing a girl, but this seemed like the right time to begin. LouAnne stopped two paces away from me and smiled. I walked toward her, wrapped my arms around her, and kissed her. She kissed me back. I ran one hand up and down her back, and she liked that. I moved my other hand up her side and lifted it up along her ribs. She liked that, too, and I decided to see how much she liked *me*, so I moved toward my real target, her tit. She didn't like that. She hauled off and slapped me so hard I saw double. Then she spun around and charged home, angrier than I'd ever seen her.

Sighing, I shook my head, certain I'd never understand women. I stayed out in the woods for about an hour, like I was hunting, before I returned home. When I entered, everybody was waiting and all the women were crying. I never got to feel LouAnne's tit, but the women were so worked up I figured she'd told them all.

Then Pa rattled a piece of paper. "A letter from Thomas came while you were gone. John was killed at Gettysburg."

Chapter Twenty

The letter was only the second from Thomas since he had marched off to war, and we received it seven months after it was written. He said he might not write again as he had been wounded as well, but he gave no details.

Momma took John's death poorly. She had lost two of her six sons to the war, and a third one talked of a vague injury. DeeAnne fretted, too, over what had happened to Thomas and what it might mean to their future.

SincereAnne grabbed Pooty and hugged him. "Let it end, Lord," she prayed, "before even the seed corn is taken from us."

Lissa and little Harriet gathered around Momma, patting her shoulder, trying to help her forget what she could never forget. I noticed LouAnne looking at me with her soft eyes. She stepped toward me, shyly at first. When I nodded, she came the rest of the way.

"I'm sorry," she said.

"No, I'm sorry," I said, "for, you know, in the woods."

She shook her head. "That was nothing like this."

LouAnne was right. It was bad enough losing Van, but at least he was buried in southern soil we could visit on occasion. But John was likely buried in Yankee soil with no stone to mark his passing.

As the summer went on, Momma sank lower, her spirits as poor as I'd ever seen. She would sit on the porch in her rocking chair and just stare into the distance. We didn't have much to eat, but she quit eating her share of what we had. She was going to waste away. Lissa and Harriet took care of her mostly, with some help from the Burke sisters and SincereAnne. Momma seemed to have lost the will to live.

Pa and I were helpless around her. It was almost like she didn't want to get too close to us in case she lost us to the war. After Van's death we had laughed on occasion, but John's death seemed to take away what little merriment the war had left us.

The summer was a poor one for me, except for LouAnne. She was budding into a fine-looking young woman, and I found myself enjoying both her company and her looks. I don't know whether I changed or she changed in the three years she'd been living with us, but one of us had. Maybe it was just that my juices were flowing and she was the closest girl about, but I never tried to paw her again, and she never tried to stop me from kissing her when I got the chance. Time with LouAnne kept my mind off Momma and her low spirits.

We had a scare in the middle of the summer. All of us were on the porch late one evening, enjoying the cool after a hot, humid day. As usual Momma sat in her rocking chair, staring off into nowhere. Pa was leaning up against the wooden wall behind her chair. It was still light enough to see when a gunshot exploded from the woods and thudded into the wall over Pa's head. Everyone except Momma dove to the wooden planks and scrambled inside the house. Pooty and I shot up the ladder into the loft and carried our carbines to the gunports. Down below I heard Pa screaming for Momma.

"Abigail, get in here! Hurry!"

Another shot exploded from the woods, and I heard

it strike the house. Cursing because my gunport did not face the bushwhacker, I raced to join Pa. I scrambled from the loft in time to see him dash outside, grab the back of Momma's rocking chair, and pull it toward the door. Momma barely moved as two more shots hit the side of the house.

I jumped out into the dogtrot and blindly squeezed off a shot toward the woods. After Pa pulled Momma inside, I felt him grab my arm and jerk me inside, too. SincereAnne slammed and barred the door.

"Are you crazy, Abigail?" Pa yelled.

She didn't answer. Pa growled in exasperation and ran from the kitchen into the dining room. He flung open the shutter over the window and emptied his carbine toward the woods. Then he grabbed mine and emptied it as well.

I reloaded Pa's carbine with bullets DeeAnne handed me, but Pa grabbed it before I had finished. No more shots answered his. Tensely we waited as the night crept over us. Who was shooting? Why? Had he meant to kill us or just scare us?

We didn't know the answer. All we knew was, we were all scared, save possibly Momma.

"Why didn't the hounds bark?" Pa turned angrily to me. "Get to your gunport, Henry."

"I'll go with him," LouAnne said.

I scurried up the ladder, LouAnne right behind me.

"See anything, Pooty?" I asked.

"Nothing but the dark," he replied.

I took my position by my gunport and waited. It was a long night. LouAnne fell asleep after midnight, and I lasted a couple more hours, then leaned against the plank wall for a little rest.

Come morning Pa waited until good sun to step outside and whistle for the hounds. Not a one came, so he went out to check the woods. With carbines at the ready me and Pooty covered him from the downstairs windows. He crept to the edge of the trees, looked around, then returned, holding the hulls of bullets meant for us. He said he had found the tracks of a single gunman.

"It could've been anybody," he said. "Whoever it was poisoned the hounds. All are dead."

Us men were tired from insufficient sleep and nervous that the assassin would return. Though he didn't come back that night, we stayed on edge and the next morning toted buckets of water from Jordan Creek to fill the water barrels throughout the house. Then we fed the mules and attended to other chores.

Just after noon Pa and I took our carbines and walked carefully around the house and the barn, through the north woods over to the creek, and then along the creek to the south woods before returning. As we ambled back to the house, we had no idea what to make of things or whether to expect more trouble when darkness fell. We were near the back of the house when RuthAnne came barreling off the porch, pointing toward Jordan Creek.

"There's a man coming."

I tensed, sliding my finger against the trigger, ready to kill the son of a bitch if he gave me the slightest excuse.

"What's he riding?" Pa asked. "Nothing," answered RuthAnne as we ran past her to the front of the house.

I don't believe I'd ever seen a leaner, raggedier man in my entire life. His clothes were tattered, and his feet were bare, perhaps explaining the slight limp. He wore a dirty slouch hat that, along with his long hair and unkempt beard, helped hide his features.

When he looked up and saw us, I thought I saw a smile crack his beard. Then he lifted the hat to greet us, and a dirty bandage was visible across the left side of his face.

"You think it's a trick, Pa?"

"I don't know, Henry. Nothing would surprise me anymore."

"You want me to send him on his way?" I took a step toward the fellow, but Pa grabbed my arm.

"Stay close to the house, in case there's something to this."

As I studied the man, I realized he was wearing what looked like the threads of a Confederate soldier's uniform. "Deserter," I suggested as he came within thirty feet of us.

Pa nodded, then spoke. "Sorry, friend, we don't have food nor room to spare."

The man shook his head. "Not even for your own son, Pa?"

Pa began to tremble. I didn't understand. Then it hit me: This scarecrow of a man was Thomas Jefferson Lomax.

"Henry, you've grown since I last laid eyes on you."

I shouted with glee, placed the carbine on the plank porch, and bolted for Thomas, who flung his hat away and threw open his arms. We grabbed each other and hugged for a minute.

"My, you've grown," he said.

Thomas and I were laughing and staring at each other. I turned about and looked at Pa. Tears were streaming down his cheeks.

RuthAnne shouted who our visitor was, and soon everyone spilled out of the house, Lissa and Harriet running to him and throwing their arms around him and laughing. Seeing Pa frozen in his tracks, Lissa ran to him, grabbed his hand, and tugged him to Thomas.

"Come on, Pa. It's Thomas."

Pa began to sob. "Get your momma, get your momma."

I looked at the porch and saw Momma behind Pooty and the Burke women, staring blankly at her firstborn child. Lissa darted up and grabbed her hands. "It's Thomas, Momma. He's come home."

Momma seemed confused by his bandaged face, his long hair, and his beard. "It's not Thomas. He was a handsome boy."

At Lissa's insistence Momma stepped awkwardly

from the porch. Thomas released Harriet and walked slowly to her.

"Thomas," Pa whispered, "don't bring up John's death. Momma's not taking it well, not with that and Van's back in '62."

Thomas sighed. "I didn't know. I was hoping John was the only one." He wrapped his arms around Momma, then seemed to realize more people were on the porch. He looked up. "Oh, my God. DeeAnne, you're here? I didn't want you to see me like this." He released Momma and stepped aside.

DeeAnne charged from the porch and threw herself into his arms, hugging and kissing him wildly. "I'm glad you're home. I wrote you but never heard back." She started crying.

"I never got your letters. I didn't know if you still cared."

"It's no matter now. You're home, alive."

We all clumped around Thomas until Pa broke us up. "Get inside 'fore somebody takes a potshot at us again."

"Again?" Thomas asked.

"There's been trouble, Thomas, with bushwhackers."

I picked up my carbine as we all moved inside to the dinner table, SincereAnne helping Momma, who still seemed dazed by it all.

"We don't have much to offer, son, but you're welcome to whatever it is after you tell us a few things."

"I'd like a warm bath, a shave, a haircut, some clean clothes."

We told Thomas how the Burkes had come to live with us. I told him how Van died. All of us explained how tough life had been with the bushwhackers about. Thomas spoke of life in the Confederate Army and the hardships he faced from Malvern Hill to Sharpsburg and from Fredericksburg to Gettysburg, where he lost John. He cried at the memory.

Then he told of hand-to-hand fighting at Chickamauga, where a rifle butt to the face had gouged out his left eye and scarred his face. As he talked about the wound, he stared at DeeAnne, then bit his lip.

She patted his hand. "It doesn't matter as long as you are back. I've missed you so."

Thomas took her hand in his, lowered his bearded face, and kissed her fingers. Then he lifted his head and looked around at everyone. "I guess Dee and I should've told you we'd taken a fancy to each other, but politics being so bitter, we thought it best to keep quiet. We saw each other before I went off to fight and decided to get married."

Lissa and LouAnne clapped and squealed while the rest of us congratulated them. It was nice to have something to celebrate.

Momma smiled. "Where's John and Van?" she asked.

"Van's at Prairie Grove," I replied.

"John's in Pennsylvania," Thomas said.

"They need markers for their graves," she said.

"Momma," Thomas said, "I'll do what I can."

She smiled vacantly again, then settled into her rocking chair, staring far beyond us.

It was late afternoon by the time Pa boiled water in the black pot outside and hauled the water inside to the washtub Momma used. We shooed the women to the next room so Thomas could undress. When he stood naked before me, I'd never seen a man so skinny. He'd walked all the way from Virginia except for occasional stretches when he hitched a wagon ride. I gasped when he unwrapped the bandage around his head. His left cheekbone seemed flattened, and his empty eye socket was purple and pink where it had yet to heal.

"Ugly, isn't it? I've worried DeeAnne might not want me now."

All those years I'd been making fun of SincereAnne's eyes, and now my brother'd be maimed for the remainder of his life with just one. I turned my head away, wondering what DeeAnne would think.

Thomas washed his hair and beard, then began the descent down the body. Pa got Momma's sewing scissors and trimmed his hair, explaining as he worked our predicament with the bushwhackers.

"We don't know whether they'll be back tonight or not."

Thomas shook his head. "Give me a carbine and some ammunition, and I'll sleep outside. If there's trouble, I'll surprise them."

"No," Pa said. "You need rest on a feather mattress tonight."

"I've been sleeping on the ground for going on three years," Thomas answered. "Another night won't make much difference."

"You sure you'll be safe out there?" Pa asked.

Thomas started laughing and couldn't stop. "Sleeping on a railroad track'd be safer than where I've been. I'll slip outside after dark. I saw no one I recognized, and I told no one who I was. I just want some time alone with DeeAnne before I go out."

When Thomas finished, he looked better, but the left side of his face would take a while to grow accustomed to. He dressed in some of his old clothes, which were now three or four inches too big around the waist. He stood with his face to the wall and asked Pa to send DeeAnne in. "I'll wear a patch over my eye," he said, "but she needs to see me like this to make sure she still wants to marry me."

Pa and I left the door open and called for DeeAnne. She was there instantly. "Thomas wants to have a word with you," Pa said.

DeeAnne smiled, her eyes filling with tears. "He wants to show me, doesn't he, because he thinks I'll change my mind? I'll not." She stepped inside the door and pushed it shut. Pa and I joined the others in the next room.

No one knew what to say. We just waited, everyone wanting to overhear what was being said in the other room. About ten minutes later the door opened, and they came in arm in arm, Thomas's eye still unbandaged. He looked better with his beard gone and his hair clipped, but the wide smile was what made him look like the brother I remembered.

"We're getting married," he said.

Everyone but Momma shouted congratulations. She gasped and stared at his scarred face, then took to bawling.

"I want everyone to see what I look like so you're not curious. It doesn't look pretty, and people'll stare at me because of it."

SincereAnne smiled. "Folks've stared at me since my eyes crossed years ago. I've made do, and you will, too."

Pooty was the only one with reservations. "But he's secesh."

SincereAnne turned on him. "This isn't politics, it's love. Thomas is good folk like all the Lomaxes, even Henry there."

I was obliged to be included, though I couldn't figure out if it was praise or an insult.

"There not being any preacher about," Thomas announced, "DeeAnne and I figured we'd get married tomorrow in front of all of you. We'll make our vows over the Bible."

We visited some more and celebrated the occasion, having a slim supper of hardtack boiled in water until it became mush, then sweetened with a little brown sugar SincereAnne had been hoarding for a special occasion. Before it got dark, Thomas and Pa looked over the place from each house window, trying to decide how to position Thomas. He figured to hide in the woods behind the outhouse. If shooting started, no one in the house was to fire in that direction.

"We're probably worried about nothing," Pa said.

When darkness came, Thomas slipped out, carrying a carbine, a shotgun, ammunition for both, and a blanket for a bedroll. We sat watch once again, but it was so quiet I dozed off.

I don't know how long I was asleep before I was awakened by the sound of gunfire, horses galloping around the house, and bullets thudding into the wooden walls. Grabbing my shotgun, I jumped for my gunport. Pooty had already fired a couple shots by the time I took a bead on a fellow and fired. The room exploded with the noise of the shotgun.

Outside I heard a man scream, though I had no idea if it was my shot that caused it. Suddenly there was the sound of a commotion among the riders, and the shooting stopped except for one gun. I knew Thomas had pitched into the bushwhackers.

"Let's get out of here!" yelled Beryl Fudge's familiar voice.

I fired blindly at the sound of a horse passing.

"I'm down!" cried Fudge. "Somebody come get me!"

I saw a horseman flash by and squeezed the trigger, but my shotgun was empty. I scrambled to reload.

Thomas's shotgun joined the fray. Then I heard the noise of a single horse galloping away to join the other cowards.

Pa yelled, "Thomas, you okay?"

"Sure thing, Pa."

We stayed alert the rest of the night and were glad for the dawn. Come sunup I slid down the ladder and marched outside to inspect the damage. Thomas was already up and about. "Don't go around the side of the house. There's a man there without his head. Took a full shotgun load."

As I turned in the opposite direction, I saw a black stallion lying on its side. I pointed to it. "The stallion tells me what we need to know."

"How's that?" Thomas asked.

"That stallion belonged to Beryl Fudge. He's the

worst man in all of Washington County." Hoping Fudge
had been killed like his horse, I walked around the end
of the house to inspect the headless body. Even without
a head the corpse was taller than Beryl Fudge.

I cursed that he was still alive.

Chapter Twenty-one

Thomas spent the morning of his wedding day helping me, Pooty, and Pa drag the dead horse away and burying the headless bushwhacker on the far edge of our land. He dug a shallow grave, dumped the body inside, and quickly mounded it over.

"No deeper than it is, hogs'll dig it up," Pa said.

Thomas looked up, his gaze hard. "If he'd been man enough to fight men, I'd've dug him a man's grave. I hope to God the hogs dig him up and scatter his bones from here to Texas."

Pooty stared at him. "He was secesh and you still hate him?"

Thomas nodded.

"Then you really must hate me and the Yankees."

Thomas shook his head. "They killed many of my friends, and they killed my brother, but they fought face-to-face instead of trying to shoot me in the back."

The four of us started toward the house. Thomas had a faraway look in his eye that reminded me of Momma, but it softened as we neared the house. Except for Momma and DeeAnne, the women were all out on the porch, wearing shy smiles and the nicest dresses they had.

I wasn't sure how to feel about the wedding, since it meant I'd somehow be related to Pooty, but the smile on

LouAnne's face perked me up a bit. I sidled over to Thomas. "Did DeeAnne ever take the band from your hat?"

He nodded. "Before I left, she did. Made a garter of it. She also pinned a wasp nest inside her skirt."

I swallowed hard. That's what LouAnne had done. I didn't believe all those superstitions—unless they were true, and Thomas had pretty much confirmed that these two were. The more I thought about it, the more I figured it had to be right. Why else would I have thought LouAnne and her sisters uglier than a mule's behind, then found myself liking one of them and actually thinking she was pretty?

At the house we men got cleaned up and ready for a ceremony. I joined Pooty at the washstand. "Me and you'll be related after this," I said.

He buried his head in the towel. "Only thing worse would be losing the war," he mumbled through the cloth.

Thomas dressed in his best suit, which was too big for his skinny frame. He looked like he was wearing an army tent. Then RuthAnne brought him a piece of cloth and told him it was from DeeAnne. He unfolded it and found a patch with a band for his eye. He worked the patch down his forehead and wriggled it in place over the empty eye socket.

None of us men had seen DeeAnne, and I'd begun to wonder if maybe she'd been frightened away by the prospect of marrying into my family. But when Thomas was dressed and the rest of us had cleaned up as best we could, Lissa and LouAnne escorted us out on the dogtrot, where the women had set up a couple benches in front of a chair that held both family Bibles. RuthAnne motioned for Thomas to approach the chair, which served as an altar. After Harriet sang, RuthAnne asked us to stand. Only Momma remained seated as DeeAnne came out the door, wearing a yellowed wedding dress and carrying a lace handkerchief. She was smiling, and her eyes fairly glistened with tears.

All the hardness I had seen in Thomas at the bushwhacker's grave had melted. As Harriet hummed a song, DeeAnne marched to him. I'd always figured weddings were something women had created as the final fence men had to climb to get what they wanted from a woman, but I was touched by this, especially when LouAnne took my hand and leaned against my shoulder. There had been so much death and suffering over the last few years, it was good to witness a happy moment.

When Harriet finished humming, RuthAnne acted like the preacher and asked us to pray silently. I was too busy thinking to pray, but I looked at LouAnne and saw her eyes closed and her lips mouthing the words to her own prayer. I wondered if she mentioned me.

Then RuthAnne prayed aloud. She seemed to want to impress God with her oration. With the war still going on I figured God had enough on his mind—particularly as much as the Yankees were stealing and sinning—without worrying about every little marriage that took place without benefit of a real preacher or a real justice of the peace. RuthAnne must not've agreed with my philosophy, because she kept praying for a happy and long-lasting marriage. I figured if the marriage lasted as long as her prayer, God would judge it a success. When she finally said amen and told us to sit down, I wanted to break out and cheer.

She asked Thomas and her sister to state their names, even though everybody there knew them. Then she asked them to promise to be true to one another and to stand by one another in sickness and in health. Thomas and DeeAnne said their I do's. When they were done, SincereAnne took the wedding ring from her own finger and handed it to Ruthanne, who gave it to Thomas, who slipped it on DeeAnne's finger. Then RuthAnne picked up our only pencil from between the two Bibles on the chair.

"To seal this bond, we shall now enter the name of the husband and the wife in their own hand in each family Bible," RuthAnne said.

Thomas took the pencil and wrote his name in both books, then said to DeeAnne, "When this war is over and we can afford pen and ink, I'll write my name in ink to be as permanent as our marriage."

All the women started crying as DeeAnne took the pencil and wrote her name beside his in each Bible. After that Thomas kissed her. We all cheered, except Momma, then congratulated the newlyweds. Pooty and me volunteered to take our guns into the woods and bring back some rabbits so we could have a nice wedding feast. Pa agreed as long as we took only one shotgun, so we grabbed a scattergun and scampered into the trees, glad to escape all that silliness.

"LouAnne likes you," Pooty announced. "Did you know that?"

"I had an inkling."

"I figured you and I'd be fighting each other until this war ended, but if it keeps going, we'll all be family. I don't know if I like that or not."

Neither did I, but I knew I'd taken a shine to LouAnne, and she seemed worth the risk. We didn't find any rabbits, but as we moved deeper into the woods we heard the grunting and snorting of a hog.

Pooty and I looked at each other, nodding that we knew where the sound was coming from. We moved downwind from the bushwhacker's grave, then crept toward it and slipped within range. I lifted the shotgun to my shoulder and fired at the hog's head. He stood for a moment, then toppled over.

We rushed out of the brush like soldiers and approached the stilled hog. In the soft dirt he had managed to unearth one of the bushwhacker's hands. We stomped on the hand to push it back beneath the soil, then each grabbed a hind leg of the hog and dragged him back to the house. He was only about a hundred and fifty pounds, but that was plenty to make a fine wedding feast. Pa cleaned him and turned him over to the women.

Thomas and DeeAnne spent the afternoon strolling

around the house hand in hand. Pa offered the new husband and wife his and Momma's bed for the next week,
and the two of them gladly accepted, though not without
a blush of red across DeeAnne's cheek.

For the wedding supper we had fried pork chops and
some small potatoes Pa had unearthed. Then LouAnne
made some skillet-fried pies with brown sugar filling.
Though the women tried to get the supper finished before
dark, they couldn't do it. We shuttered the windows and
ate by the light of a single candle, our guns at the ready
in case the bushwhackers returned.

Fearful they would, Pa announced we'd follow the
same plan as the night before, except tonight one of us
would sleep out by the barn rather than the outhouse.
Though Thomas volunteered again, Pa waved him off. "A
man should spend his wedding night with his wife. I'll
hear nothing more about it."

Thomas sure didn't argue. We all wanted to chivaree
the couple, but we knew we shouldn't make noise or be
seen outside.

We all hoped the wedding would help Momma get
over her sinking spell, but she seemed as lost as ever.
She kept repeating, "We need to put stones up for John
and Van, we do."

"We will one day," Pa answered, patting her shoulder.

After supper Pa slipped outside to stand watch. Pooty
and me took our carbines into the loft and took positions
at the gunports. Thomas took his wife to bed. The girls,
though, weren't about to let them have a peaceful night.
They climbed into the loft and held their ears to the
planks just above Pa and Momma's bed. Every time they
heard the bed creak or even a whisper from the newlyweds, they knocked on the ceiling and giggled.

The night passed without incident, at least as far as
the bushwhackers were concerned. I'm sure Thomas had
an eventful night, but he didn't talk about it the next
morning, just grinned and ate a cold pork chop.

That wedding was a turning point. For the rest of
the summer we didn't see any sign of the bushwhackers
and were able to gather enough of a crop to get us through
the winter. We kept Thomas hidden from view as much
as possible in case some Yankee sympathizers decided to
settle some score.

Even so, rumors began to circulate about the attack
by the bushwhackers the night he arrived. Word was that
George Washington Lomax's son had killed one of the
bushwhackers and knocked Beryl Fudge's prized horse
from under him. Since most folks thought I was still the
only one of Pa's sons at home, I began to develop a reputation that was greatly exaggerated.

It's surprising how word *did* get around, since we
had little contact with folks other than an occasional rider
who dropped off a letter as he passed by or folks crossing
our land to escape from something or somebody or Union
soldiers, primarily cavalry, who were on the move to
someplace else. There were still a few skirmishes in
Washington County between Union troops and Confederate patrols, but they weren't major battles and few soldiers were killed. The major problem remained the
bushwhackers on both sides.

Though conditions improved, Momma seemed to
worsen. "We need stones for my sons," she said. "We
need stones for my sons." Staring vacantly into the distance, she seldom acknowledged anyone's presence. Even
word that DeeAnne was with child didn't perk her up;
she was still lost behind her grief. Day in and day out,
she kept reminding us about the need for stones.

"Momma'll drive us all crazy this winter if we're
cooped up in the house with her," Pa told me one night.
"If we could just get those stones, maybe she'd shut up."

I thought long and hard before I opened my mouth
but decided there was no better time than then. I whispered, "Pa, I've got some gold hidden. I could take some
to Fayetteville, buy a stone."

Pa shook his head, then told me he'd talk it over with

Thomas and see what he thought. They pondered it for a week, as much as anything stalling so the leaves would fall and reduce the cover any bushwhacker might make use of.

Finally they agreed it was worth the risk or Momma would drive herself crazier. In mid-November we decided the leaf cover had thinned enough. Early one morning, when Pooty went to the outhouse, I slipped from the front of the house while Pa stood watch down by the road and Thomas kept an eye on Pooty. I ran down to the creek and had just reached the embankment when I heard LouAnne behind me.

"Henry, where're you going in such a hurry?"

I waved her back, but she started after me.

"LouAnne," cried Thomas, "wait here. Henry can't wait for Pooty to finish in the outhouse."

LouAnne turned back. I reached the fallen tree and walked down it until I was out of sight of the house. Then I sat down and straddled it, inching back up toward the top and the ledge where I had hidden the gold. I moved the rocks and breathed easier when I saw that the money bag had not been disturbed.

Hurriedly I untied it, shoved my hand in, brought out a fistful of coins, and stuck them in my pocket. I reached for a second handful just as Thomas yelled, "Next!" That was my signal that Pooty had emerged from the outhouse. Without taking time to retie the bag, I shoved it back in place and rearranged the rocks in front of it. I got up on my knees, then to my feet, and ran along the log to the top of the embankment.

As I raced back to the house, I saw LouAnne watching. She didn't say a thing, just looked at me and shook her head. I darted past her toward the outhouse, where Pa and Thomas were waiting.

"You'll leave before dawn tomorrow," Pa said.

"I want to ride Old Abe."

"I'll saddle him," Thomas said. "Take the gold and

split it up—some in your shoe, some in your britches, some in your coat, some in your saddle."

The day seemed to take forever to pass. Before dark I visited the outhouse. When I came out, LouAnne was standing a few feet away.

"What are you up to?" she asked.

I played dumb. "What are you talking about?"

She shrugged. "Maybe I'm just imagining things." She held out her hand. "You dropped this."

When I reached out, she plopped a gold coin in my hand.

"Where'd you find this?" I asked nervously.

"Where you dropped it."

I shook my head. "Don't tell anybody."

"I will unless you tell me."

I sighed. "I'm going to Fayetteville come morning, but don't tell anybody, and especially not Pooty."

"I won't," she answered. "It's for stones for your brothers?"

I nodded.

LouAnne leaned over and kissed me on the cheek. "Be careful."

After supper Pa and Thomas kept Pooty occupied doing chores while I divvied up the gold, putting a piece in each shoe, some in my pocket, some in my coat. Early the next morning I was roused by Pa, who retreated down the ladder while I got dressed. Grabbing my coat and hat, I went downstairs.

Outside I heard Thomas bringing Old Abe around. I was too nervous to eat. Pa and Thomas had debated whether to give me a gun or not and had decided against it. Since I was riding an army-branded mule, someone might mistake me for a soldier and shoot or capture me.

Before I mounted, I put some of the gold in the saddlebags. I nodded to Pa and Thomas, then rode away, getting past what was left of Cane Hill before sunrise, then clinging to the side of the road into Prairie Grove.

I reached Prairie Grove in the late morning and stopped to check Van's grave. It was well tended, but

Annie Belle Higdon was gone, though the house seemed to still be occupied. I rode on, reaching the outskirts of Fayetteville before dark, and spent the night in the woods, deciding to ride into town early in the morning, order the two headstones, and leave quickly. It was a cool night, and my blanket provided little warmth, so I was glad when morning came and I could get up and move around.

I rode into town and found a mason who would carve the stones, drive them to Prairie Grove, and set them over Van's grave. I decided to put John's stone beside Van's even though John was buried somewhere in Pennsylvania. After paying the stonecutter well I still had the money I'd hidden in my shoes and in the saddle.

Fayetteville was sprinkled with Union soldiers. At times I thought a few were following me, but I guess I was just too nervous not to be scared. As soon as I finished with the stonecutter, I mounted Old Abe and started back for Cane Hill.

It was near dark when I arrived at Prairie Grove and stopped by Annie Belle Higdon's cabin. Through the window I saw her, her kids, and a man seated at a candlelit table. I was hungry and nervous, still fearing I'd been followed from Fayetteville.

When I knocked on the door, the room went silent for an instant. "Who is it?" came Annie Belle's voice.

"Henry Lomax," I replied.

I could hear her unbarring the door. When it flew open, she put her hands on her hips and just stared. "Henry, my, how you've grown."

Embarrassed, I took off my hat. "I just dropped by to let you know I ordered two headstones from the stonecutter in Fayetteville. He'll be by in a few weeks to place them."

"Them?" she asked, motioning for me to come inside.

"I lost another brother at Gettysburg. Momma wanted him to have a stone, and there's no way we can get one there for him."

She grimaced, then pointed to the table. "This is my husband, Tanner. He came back."

I nodded, thinking him rude for not getting up, but I saw he had lost a leg. He put a revolver back in his lap. "Can't be too cautious."

I stepped to him and shook his hand. Annie Belle whispered in his ear that I was the one who had given her the gold to buy food.

He nodded. "Thanks."

"There's some biscuits and gravy left, Henry, if you like." Annie Belle pointed to her chair. "Why don't you finish up my plate. I was done."

I knew she wasn't through eating, but I was too hungry to be mannerly. I polished off what was left, then visited with them.

"I'm obliged for what you've done for my family," Tanner said.

"They helped me find Van's body and bury him on your place. That means a lot to me."

After supper Annie Belle cleaned the dishes, then offered me one of the kid's beds while Tanner took care of Old Abe. We were in bed early. I slept soundly, not arising until midmorning, and after saying good-bye to the Higdons I saddled the mule and was back on the trail to Cane Hill.

Much of the way I had a strange feeling I was being followed, but I never could glimpse any true sign. Then as I got near Cane Hill, I saw a man not a hundred yards away and five more behind him, all wearing Union cavalry uniforms. The one in the lead sent a chill up my spine.

It was Cap Andrews of Captain Burke's cavalry.

Chapter Twenty-two

I slapped Old Abe on the flank and sent him to charging down the road. My heart was beating harder than the pounding of the mule's hooves. I glanced over my shoulder and breathed easier when I saw the soldiers weren't giving chase, but even so, I raced home. Pa, Thomas, and Pooty stood on the porch, weapons in hand, when I galloped up.

"What's got into you, Henry?" Pa asked.

"Bluebellies, Pa. Six or seven of them."

Pa shook his head. "They've treated us square."

"It was that Kansan Cap Andrews that rode with Pooty's father."

Pooty grinned widely. "Must mean Pa's nearby, too."

"I don't trust him, Pa."

"I wouldn't worry about it, Henry, not with Captain Burke around to keep him in line."

Pooty ran into the house, shouting that his pa was coming. SincereAnne and her daughters ran out into the dogtrot and stood looking and giggling. DeeAnne seemed especially anxious to see her father and tell him he would be a grandfather come summer.

Fact was, I hadn't seen Captain Burke, just Cap Andrews and some other men I didn't recognize. I took Old Abe out to the barn and unsaddled him, removing the coins from my saddlebags and shoes and dropping them in my pocket.

When I got back to the house, the women had abandoned the porch to the November chill. I joined them inside, where they were fanned out in a half circle in front of the fireplace, soaking up the warmth and discussing why Captain Burke hadn't shown up.

"Did you see Gordon?" SincereAnne asked.

"No, ma'am, just one of his troops, Cap Andrews."

SincereAnne grimaced. "I didn't care for him, nor did Gordon."

I cocked my head at Pooty and grinned.

"Cap's okay," Pooty protested.

"Your pa said he had a mean streak in him."

"He's wrong."

"No back talk, Joe Don." SincereAnne ended the conversation.

The women went back to their sewing and handwork while Pa and Thomas stood at the window, carbines in hand, watching for the approach of the soldiers. They never came, though around dusk we heard shooting from Cane Hill. Pa and Thomas slipped outside to see if they could tell anything about the ruckus, but they came back knowing no more than when they'd left.

We went to bed and tried to stay warm. I had a fitful sleep, made worse by Pooty hogging all the covers. When we arose the next morning, Pa had made a roaring fire, and we all gathered in the kitchen for some potato cakes. When breakfast was done, Pooty left for the outhouse.

He was gone a while. Just as SincereAnne got worried about him, he pushed open the door and entered. "Look who I found," he said, and we all turned around, half expecting his pa to be with him. It was Cap Andrews.

I bit my lip.

"Morning, folks," he said, taking off his hat and holding it at his waist. "Sure have missed your hospitality." He sauntered around the room like he owned the place.

"See, Momma, I told you he was okay."

"Where's Captain Burke?" SincereAnne asked.

Andrews laughed. "Well, ma'am, I can't say. Your husband and I parted ways a while back. No profit in army pay."

"You deserted?" she asked.

I saw Thomas edging toward a shotgun in the corner, but Andrews must've seen him, too. He jerked his revolver out and pointed it at him. "I wouldn't try nothing if I was you, One-eye."

Thomas stiffened, and DeeAnne jumped from her chair and ran to stand between him and the gun.

"You'd be a lot smarter woman," Andrews said, "if you gave me some of your sugar. You might live longer."

DeeAnne didn't budge.

"Boys," shouted Andrews, "come on in the house. We caught them doing their sewing, the men, too."

I could see terror in the girls' eyes and was getting nervous myself, fearing the men would ravish them.

Four more soldiers entered the room, guns drawn. They were rough, scraggly men, the meanest I'd seen since Dingus and Buck at Prairie Grove. There was more mercy in a gallon of rattlesnake venom than there was in their souls.

"A few of the fine ladies of Cane Hill shared their beds with us last night, so you ladies are lucky this morning. But we'll be back later to collect some sugar. Like I say, we left the army because we didn't like army pay, not when there was so much more money and sugar to be taken out here." Andrews turned to me. "We want to know where the gold is, Henry."

I caught my breath, then licked my lips. "What gold?"

"The gold Pooty told me about."

"There is none."

Andrews shook his head. "I's afraid you'd be this hardheaded, but I figure you'll want to talk to us before long."

I didn't say a thing.

Andrews nodded. "Boys, tie up the old fart and the

one-eyed bastard, and let's see if we can get Henry to cooperate."

The soldiers pulled lengths of cord from their pockets and roughly tied Thomas and Pa, leaving me and Pooty unbound. The women backed into the corner by the water barrel as Andrews stepped to the fire, picked up the iron handle of an ash scoop, and waved it around like a sword. Then he squatted and shoved the scoop into the fire, slowly twisting it around in the flames.

"Henry, it's been a bit cold outside. Maybe it's time we warmed you up. I bet your feet are cold."

Shaking my head, I answered, "They're fine."

"Boys," said Andrews, "why don't you take off his brogans and socks, and we'll see just how cold they are."

Two soldiers grabbed my shoulders, and another fell to his knees and ripped my shoes and socks off. I kicked wildly, but the three men pinned me. Andrews picked up the ash scoop, its head red-hot and sizzling, and stepped toward me, holding it over my face until I could feel the searing heat. "Where's the gold?"

"I don't know what you're talking about."

"Then you'll limp for the rest of your life." He squatted down and inched the iron closer and closer to the arch of my right foot. I could feel the unbearable heat even before he touched me.

"Last chance," he said.

"I don't know," I cried.

I gritted my teeth against the expected pain, then screamed when my foot felt a strange sensation, a cold sensation. I heard the sizzle of the hot iron and realized I was wet instead of burned.

Andrews cursed, then turned to the side. LouAnne was standing there with the bucket of water she had emptied on the hot iron. Defiantly she glared at him. Snake quick, he drew back the ash scoop and swung it at her. It caught her full on the side of the face, and she toppled to the ground, out cold.

Bucking against the iron grip that held me, I screamed and fought to get away. "Bastards!"

SincereAnne fell to the floor and grabbed her daughter, cradling her bruised head against her chest.

"Damn you," Andrews said to me, shaking the scoop in my face. "This is your last chance. Speak up, or we'll kill you all."

I quit fighting. The gold wasn't worth the risk, not with LouAnne hurt and the others threatened. "I'll show you where the gold is if you let everybody alone."

Andrews laughed. "Glad you came to your senses. A lot of folks were about to get hurt and still may, if you don't show us the gold."

"It's not far," I cried. "In a ledge, down by the creek."

The soldiers released their grip on my arms and legs. One of them kicked my shoes and socks toward my feet.

"Put them on," Andrews said. "If the gold's not there, I'll gouge out your eyes so you'll be twice as blind as One-eye."

My hands were trembling as I pulled my socks on. I saw SincereAnne sobbing over LouAnne.

"How is she?"

"She's breathing. That's all I know."

Then something transpired that shocked us all. Momma seemed to finally comprehend what had happened. She bolted from beside the fireplace and flew into Andrews, screaming, "Bastards, bastards!" and clawing at him like a mountain lion.

Andrews drew back the iron scoop and hit her on the head, but it barely slowed her. Another soldier pulled her off, and a third slammed the butt of his carbine into the back of her head. She collapsed in a heap on the floor.

Andrews tossed the iron scoop down on her, then cocked his pistol and pointed it at her head. The women screamed, Pa yelled out, and Thomas cursed as he struggled against his bindings.

I shoved my feet in my brogans and jumped up.

"Come on, come on," I cried. "I'll show you where the money is." I grabbed Andrews's arm and pulled him toward the door.

The cavalryman pointed the gun at me. "Get moving."

As he marched toward the door, he grabbed Pooty by the arm. "Come on, Joe Don. If you've been lying to me about there being gold, I'll kill you, too."

Pooty cursed. "Pa was right about you."

I stumbled off the porch toward Jordan Creek. Andrews kept shoving me, and I kept stumbling. My hands were trembling, my heart was pounding, and my mind was racing, for I feared what they would do once they found the gold.

Reaching the embankment, I straddled the downed tree and inched my way up to the limestone ledge. When I came to it, I held my breath. Something didn't look right—the rocks appeared to have been moved. I reached for the first rock and jerked it aside. My heart was pounding so I could barely make out what Andrews was yelling.

"Where is it?" he shouted.

I didn't see the the money bag.

"Hurry up!"

I grabbed the other rock and shoved it aside. It fell from the ledge like my hopes.

The bag was gone!

I shoved my arm between the ledge and the overhang, slapping at the rock, hoping my hand would find what my eyes could not see.

There was nothing but stone.

"Where is it?"

"It's gone," I croaked, fearing my family was about to die. "It's gone."

"You bastard," Andrews cried, crawling out on the log and looking for himself. "Start killing the others," he said. Two soldiers turned to go back to the house.

"Wait!" I screamed. "I know where there's another bag. If you kill anyone, I'll never tell where it is."

"Hold it," Andrews called out to the soldier. He grabbed my arm and jerked me back up the log, then flung me to the ground. Bending over me, he pressed his knee against my chest until I could barely breathe and stuck the barrel of his pistol in my ear. "You better not be lying this time, or I'll kill you first."

"I'm not, I'm not. There were four sacks. Three were stolen, but I know where the other one is. It's buried in a grave the other side of Cane Hill."

Andrews lifted his knee from my chest.

"Leave the others alone and I'll show you. Promise me that?"

"Sure, boy, whatever you say."

"I'll saddle up my mule and show you."

"You better be telling the truth this time."

I never prayed so hard in all my life that the gold was still there. I knew God had a lot on his mind with the war and all, but I hoped he was listening.

One of the soldiers shoved me toward the barn. I knocked open the door, charged to Old Abe's stall, and quickly saddled him, hoping to discuss politics with Andrews. I backed the mule out of the stall, then led him out of the barn. Once in the open, I mounted up. A couple soldiers disappeared into the trees and returned with their mounts, while others searched the house, bringing out our rifle, three carbines, two shotguns, and four pistols. Without weapons my family was helpless against any threat.

Mounting up, the soldiers gathered around me as Andrews approached, dragging Pooty. "Get in the saddle with Henry," he said, shoving Pooty to the ground at the feet of Old Abe. Then he turned to our families, gathered on the porch. "We'll take a boy from each family. If Henry's lying and there ain't no gold, we'll kill them both, then be back to kill you and burn your place to the ground."

Pooty scrambled to his feet, pulled my foot from a stirrup, inserted his, then boosted himself behind me on the mule's back.

Andrews jumped on his gelding and motioned for me to join him. "Lead the way, Henry."

Behind me I could hear the girls sobbing. I rattled the reins and started Old Abe toward the wagon crossing on Jordan Creek, then turned north and passed through Cane Hill. On the edge of what was left of the town, I saw three old men hanging from a tree.

Andrews laughed. "They once owned slaves, but they don't own nothing now. We've killed slavers ever since the early days in Kansas. Ain't that right, boys?"

The men shouted and cheered.

"You're all from Kansas?" I asked.

"That's right. We're the ones that made bleeding Kansas bleed, and we're damn proud of it. We've done more than John Brown ever did, because we survived to kill more slave owners. Abolition will triumph because it is right."

Maybe so, I thought, but even if abolition was right, these abolitionists weren't.

The ride seemed to take forever. I thought we'd never reach the trail to the grave. When we finally did, I led the Kansans to the clearing where the house and barn had once stood. All that remained were the blackened shards of walls overtaken by weeds. As we neared the grave, I hopped down from Old Abe and was relieved to see the shovel just as I had left it when I buried the remaining bag of gold.

It gave me hope for myself and my family.

I picked up the shovel and pried some of the rocks from atop the grave. As I dug, the soldiers dismounted and gathered around me. I breathed easier when the shovel finally snagged against something.

Andrews grabbed it and pushed me aside, then quickly uncovered the bag. "Well, I'll be damned boys, Henry didn't lie to us this time. How're we gonna thank him?"

The soldiers laughed.

"How about a party?" one shouted.

"A necktie party," answered another.

I saw a soldier hold a coil of rope in the air, then start toward an oak tree and toss it over a limb. The bastards had been planning to hang me all along.

Enraged, I jerked the shovel from Andrews and swatted him in the face, then swung it toward the groin of the nearest soldier. It didn't take them but a moment to subdue me. After they pinned me, I looked up and saw Andrews's bloody face glaring at me. I had a feeling he didn't much care for me anymore, even if I had made him a rich man.

"It's a shame I can't hang you twice, you secesh bastard," he growled, then jerked me up and shoved me toward the noose, now dangling over the oak limb.

Chapter Twenty-three

Even though the war had been around us for three years, I hadn't thought much about dying. Kids never do. But as they dragged me kicking and screaming toward that oak tree, I had a chance to think about it, and I decided I didn't care for it. Especially not by hanging. I took some deep breaths, knowing my number was dwindling. I figured every word might be my last so I made good use of every one, calling the Yankee bastards every bad word I'd learned in my fourteen-plus years in Arkansas.

"You're cowards!" I screamed.

They laughed.

"We're Kansans," one shouted back.

To my way of thinking they were one and the same, particularly when they would hang a fourteen-year-old and that fourteen-year-old was me. "You egg-sucking bastards ain't got shit for brains."

Cap Andrews laughed. "At least we ain't getting hanged."

As they dragged me to the hanging tree, I caught a glimpse of Pooty. He was pale as a ghost, his eyes wide as a coffin. He was too scared to help, but there was nothing he could do against these snakes. They'd just as quickly turn on him as they had on me.

They jerked me toward the tree and the noose swinging from the branch. I fought harder, digging my heels into the earth, and when that failed, I tried to pull the men past the noose. But they were too many and I was too few. Cap Andrews grabbed the rope and widened the loop, then shoved it over my head.

"No, no, no!" I cried.

Andrews laughed in my face as he tightened the noose. I felt the stiff rope cutting into my skin, scraping against my flesh as he jerked it tight under my jaw and lifted the knot behind my ear.

"Pull!" Andrews cried.

The slack rope went taut, jerking my heels off the ground, then relaxed enough for me to stand flat-footed.

"Any last words, you secesh bastard?"

I suddenly relaxed. There was nothing I could do—and nothing Pooty *would* do—that would change the outcome. I turned calm, as if I weren't afraid to die, though my knees were quivering. I cocked my head as best I could with my neck in the noose. "Eat shit, you Yankee sons of bit—"

Before I could finish, the bastards began to hoist the rope. I took the biggest breath I had ever taken, hoping it would last me the rest of the day. The rope stiffened against my neck. My toes curled in my brogans as they tried to cling to Arkansas soil.

The tight rope went even tighter.

Around me men cheered.

My feet were lifted from the ground.

The rope began to strangle me.

I couldn't breathe. My eyes were watering. I clawed at the rope, trying to wriggle my fingers between my neck and the raw hemp. I tried to scream, but I had no breath. I felt myself swaying. My chest burned like fire from the breath that was trapped there, my sight began to blur, and every noise seemed to float into the distance—every noise save one, a loud, horrible scream.

Through the haze I thought I saw an avenging angel,

breathing fire as he charged toward me, a sword held high over his head. I heard explosions as he raced by, swinging the sword for my neck. I knew I was going to hell, because that angel was surely no messenger of God.

Without understanding why, I fell hard to the ground. All around me the earth trembled as demons raced by, shooting and firing.

My fingers gouged into my neck as I fought the noose. Then it gave, and sour air exploded from my lungs. I sucked in air tinged with gunpowder. Even though it was acrid, it was the sweetest breath I'd ever taken.

The more air I took in, the more my head cleared. I realized that the Yankees had been ambushed. All around me must've been twenty men firing at them, and right in the middle were Dingus and Buck—Jesse and Frank James.

Nearby I saw Cap Andrews fall with a gunshot to the shoulder. He scrambled to his hands and knees and lifted his gun to shoot at Dingus. I screamed and charged him, kicking the gun from his hand and pounding my fists on him until he fell on his face. I jerked the noose from my neck, then quickly looped it over Andrews's head and tightened it around his neck. He groaned and resisted a minute, but I kicked him in the jaw, then shoved my foot in his back and pulled on the rope as hard as I could.

As calm as a preacher on the way to church, Dingus rode past and shot a wounded Yankee not ten feet away. He was smiling like a groom on his wedding night, but his eyes were hard and cold and looked even more dangerous and disturbing because of their constant blinking.

I tugged on the noose around Andrews's neck until my hands burned. Then I collapsed with exhaustion onto the ground beside him. As I lay there, still trying to catch my breath, I saw another rider go by. The blood in my veins turned to ice.

It was Beryl Fudge.

I rolled over and tried to crawl away, but a horse blocked my path. I looked up and saw Dingus smiling down at me. He lifted his revolver in my direction and cocked the hammer.

The bastards had saved me just to shoot me like a dog. At least they'd think I was a tough bastard in hell, what with the noose burn around my neck and the bullet hole wherever Dingus put it.

The gun exploded in my face, the puff of powder stinging my eyes. For a moment I thought I must be all gristle and bone, so tough I didn't even feel the bullet. Then I realized Dingus had been shooting behind me.

I rolled over in time to see the resurrected Cap Andrews standing over me, staring at the hole leaking blood from his chest. He tried to say something, but only bright red blood came out of his mouth. He collapsed in a heap at my feet.

The firing stopped. Everything went quiet except for the heaving of the horses, the agitated breath of the men, and the clink of fresh cartridges being loaded. Pooty was all balled up and cowering on the ground, his hands over his ears.

Dingus looked down at me. "Ain't I seen you somewhere before?"

I didn't remind him I'd escaped from his band at the battle of Prairie Grove. I looked around at the bushwhackers dismounting and stripping the dead Yankees of their guns and cartridges. Beryl Fudge rode among the dead, firing extra shots into the corpses. Nearby I saw Buck kneeling over the grave and picking up the bag of coins. He slapped away the dirt, then opened the bag.

"Dingus," he called, "we've found gold."

Everyone stopped looting the dead and stared at Buck, who pulled a handful of coins from the canvas bag. A wicked grin cracked Dingus's face as he wiggled his gun at me. "We saw you at Prairie Grove after you'd hidden the payroll. Looks like we got it now after all."

"I'd've showed you where it was then if my horse hadn't gotten away from me and the Yankees caught me."

Dingus shook his head. "That's not how I remember

it. I thought you were a damn bluebelly the way you rode from us, but after seeing how you tore into that Yankee after we cut you down tells me your heart's in the right place."

Maybe my heart was in the right place, but I wasn't so sure about the rest of me. I looked around and saw Pooty peeking from between his fingers at the bushwhackers just as Beryl Fudge rode up beside Dingus and scowled at me.

"Well, you little son of a bitch," he said, jerking his revolver from his holster, "I knew I'd run into you one day and get even for burning my place down and sending my wife and daughter on the run." He waved the gun at me.

"Yankees burned it. Wasn't nothing I could do."

Fudge cocked the hammer on his pistol and took aim. But Dingus shoved his arm skyward, and the revolver discharged harmlessly.

"Leave him be," Dingus said. "He's a friend of mine."

Fudge glared at him.

Dingus glared back and answered the unspoken challenge. "You do as I say—and I say he's a friend of mine."

I remembered the first time I saw those two together, when they had threatened to burn our house. Fudge had been giving orders then, but no more. Though he was older than Dingus by fifteen or twenty years, he didn't have the guts to challenge those cold eyes. He let out a deep breath and slowly holstered his pistol.

I heard another sigh behind me and saw Pooty stand up, thinking he was safe now. I motioned for him to get away before Fudge recognized him, but Pooty was so relieved that he didn't realize the new danger he was facing. I glanced up at Fudge and saw his eyes flare with anger.

"Get our mule, Pooty," I ordered.

"Wait," said Fudge.

Pooty went pale with fright.

Fudge pointed at him. "He a friend of yours, too, Dingus?"

Dingus studied Pooty briefly. "Nope."

"His pappy is the Yankee bastard that burned my place."

Pooty's eyes widened in terror. Fudge jerked his revolver from his holster faster than I could stop him.

"No!" I screamed.

Fudge squeezed the trigger. Though I was blinded by the powder, I could hear the sickening thud of the bullet.

"No, no!" I cried. I spun around, my stomach churning at the sight of Pooty falling on his back, a bloody hole in his chest. I moved toward him, but Fudge cut me off with his horse, leaned over in his saddle, and put a bullet in Pooty's head.

Then he turned to me. "You tell the Burkes I'll kill them all, women, too." He shoved his pistol in its holster, pulled his carbine from the saddle, and held the stock so I could see several brass brads embedded in it. "Another dead Yankee, another brad. He'll make twenty-four." He spat at Pooty, then rode off to join the looting.

Though I'm ashamed to say it, I turned away from Pooty for fear Dingus might change his mind about me. Dingus nudged his horse toward the grave.

"There's several thousand dollars here," Buck announced.

"Good," Dingus answered. "It'll give us a little spending money while we winter in Texas."

The bastards were going to spend the money on themselves rather than the cause. Dingus turned to me. "You're welcome to a cut if you want to winter in Texas with us, then start killing Yankees again in the spring. You look like you'd be good at it."

"I got to see my momma through the winter," I lied.

Dingus sighed. "I wish my ma didn't have to fend for herself. She lives up in Missouri—Clay County, near

Kansas City. Zerelda Samuel, that's her name. When the war's over, come for a visit."

I nodded, though I didn't care to visit any of these bastards, even if they were for the Confederacy. I tried to make an excuse. "I don't know *your* name."

"Jesse James." He pointed to Buck. "That's my brother, Frank James. Don't believe we caught your name."

"I'm Henry Lomax."

Frank wore a sincere grin as he stuck his hand out and shook mine. Jesse, though, never offered his hand to me. There was something cold about the man, even when he was being hospitable. Giving orders, he turned and rode among his men.

One by one the bushwhackers mounted up. One caught Old Abe and led him over to me. "He yours?" he asked.

When I nodded, he tossed me the reins. I led Old Abe over to Pooty's body and straightened him out. Trying to hide my tears, I started to pick him up so I could put him on Old Abe.

Jesse rode over. "What are you doing?"

"Gonna take him to his momma so he can be buried."

"Is his pa a Yankee and him a sympathizer?"

I nodded.

Jesse shook his head. "Let him rot."

It went against my constitution to leave Pooty, but I didn't have a choice. I promised myself I'd see a decent burial for him unless something happened to me. As Frank secured the gold to his saddle, I mounted Old Abe and waited for instructions from Jesse.

"Where you live?"

"South of Cane Hill."

"We're riding that direction. You can ride with us a ways."

I guess I could've argued, but I didn't. I rode away with them, glancing over my shoulder and hoping no hogs would come out of the woods and eat Pooty before I could get back. Jesse sent Beryl ahead to scout.

"You sure you don't want to go to Texas? We'll trade that mule for a good horse and give you a split of the gold."

I shook my head. "I've got to see Momma through the winter."

He sidled closer to me. "You ought to reconsider. Beryl Fudge won't be going to Texas with us, which is fine with me. He's crazy as a loon, accused me of sleeping with his daughter." He shook his head. "That girl's too hard for me. She's got a heart of stone."

I nodded, knowing well how her looks could deceive.

"Beryl Fudge's staying in these parts to avenge the loss of his place. About half these men are his, and they'll be around, too."

"Thanks for the warning."

Jesse laughed. "Thanks for the gold. I guess God just planned for us to have it."

I don't know that God had a hand in the gold at all, because several people had died over it. I felt lucky to have survived.

Before we reached Cane Hill, Jesse and his men skirted off to the east side of the road and took to the bushes.

"Come see me if you're ever in Missouri," he offered.

I nodded, but I'd as soon visit that hellhole Texas as go to Missouri, where the men were too scared to secede from the Union.

After the men disappeared into the woods, I continued riding toward Cane Hill, then circled back around to the site of the ambush. Pooty was there just as I had left him. The tears I had been holding cascaded down my cheeks as I jumped off Old Abe.

"I'm sorry, Pooty," I sobbed. "I greened you a mite too much, I know, but I didn't mean nothing bad by it."

With one arm under his neck and the other under his knees, I lifted him from the ground and draped him over the saddle, then tied his feet to his hands under the mule. Old Abe was skittish with the body on his back, but I managed to grab the reins and lead him back toward the road. It would be a long walk, but it was the least I could do for Pooty.

I didn't know how I was going to tell his momma and LouAnne; I figured both would hold it against me. I felt nearer fifty than fourteen with the load I was carrying home.

I looked back to check on Pooty and saw Old Abe's ears flick forward. Beryl Fudge emerged from the trees.

"I circled back, too," he said. "I knew all along you loved the bluebellies."

I figured I had a better chance convincing a bear to shave his fur than I had of surviving this encounter with Beryl Fudge. I didn't answer, hoping he'd talk himself to death so I could escape.

"You're the one that insulted my Amanda, talking about Jesse getting into her britches."

"Jesse'd liked to've gotten into her britches, all right," I said, "but she preferred Old Abe." I pointed to my mule.

"She did no such thing," Fudge growled.

I shrugged. "She'd deny it, and he can't talk. Fact is, she had itchy britches."

Fudge grumbled. "Just like her mother."

Seeing how well I was rattling him, I lifted my hands and shook my head. "I never saw Old Abe take a poke at your wife. Seemed she liked the black stallion."

Fudge's eyes flared. "You son of a bitch. That's not true."

I shrugged. "I ain't saying it's true, just what I heard some folks say."

He pulled his pistol and waved it at my face. "It's not true, not a bit of it."

"Okay," I said. "It's not true what other folks've said."

He pointed the gun toward the woods. "Get on in

those trees. I want to kill you so far in the woods that God couldn't find you in a month of Sundays."

I nodded, then turned Old Abe about so his behind was aimed at Fudge's gelding.

That's when I decided it was time to discuss politics.

Chapter Twenty-four

"Jefferson Davis!" I yelled.

Old Abe brayed.

Beryl Fudge's horse shied away.

Old Abe's back leg exploded into the horse's side.

"Jefferson Davis!" I screamed.

Old Abe brayed.

"What?" yelled Beryl Fudge.

My mule loosed another slashing hoof. I was glad I had tied Pooty down tight.

Beryl Fudge aimed his revolver at me.

Old Abe's hoof hit his horse again.

The gelding reared in the air just as Beryl Fudge fired. The bullet went wide.

"Jefferson Davis, Jefferson Davis, Jefferson Davis!"

Old Abe kicked the horse again and again.

The horse reared up, then bolted, throwing Fudge hard to the ground, his plumed hat and revolver falling beside him. I pulled Old Abe about as Fudge, stunned and groggy, crawled to his hands and knees and reached for his gun in the dirt.

"Jefferson Davis, Jefferson Davis, Jefferson Davis!"

Beryl Fudge screamed, but his shout died full on his lips as Old Abe's hoof caught him straight in the mouth.

"Jefferson Davis, Jefferson Davis, Jefferson Davis,

Jefferson Davis!" I yelled and yelled and yelled. I was in a blind rage, dragging Old Abe back and forth over Beryl Fudge's body. I yelled until I was hoarse.

And for all my yelling and noise-making, Beryl Fudge never once raised an objection nor even blinked an eyelid. He was as limp and lifeless as an old man's peter.

After calming Old Abe down, I grabbed Fudge's revolver. Deciding to take no chances, I held it to the dead man's chest and pulled the trigger, but the gun snapped on empty. I cursed him and spat on him, hating him more than any man I'd ever known. "You're the bastard," I tried to shout, but my voice was little more than a rasp.

I stripped him of his holster, then did a foolish thing. I took his plumed hat and plopped it on my head. I'd killed him, and I was damn proud of it. Me and the mule had avenged Pooty's death.

After shoving the pistol back in the holster, I buckled the gun belt and draped it over my shoulder. I tied Old Abe and started for Beryl Fudge's horse, which was standing among the bushes. Though the horse was wary of me, I managed to grab the reins, calm him, and check both the carbine in its scabbard and the ammunition in the saddlebags. After examining his leg and the gashes from Old Abe's kicks I decided the horse was still strong enough to ride and led him to Old Abe. The horse was skittish around the mule, but I kept him calm enough to tie the mule's reins to the saddle. Then I mounted up and started once more for Cane Hill.

Along the way I cried for Pooty, feeling bad for all the jokes I'd played on him, regretting he'd ever taken up with Cap Andrews, wishing there was something I could do to bring him back. I circled Cane Hill. South of town I reached the wagon crossing, turned the gelding through the cold water of Jordan Creek, and headed up the sloping embankment toward home. I screamed for help, but no one answered. I put the gelding into a trot and rode up to the porch, where I jumped off, quickly tied the reins, and ran inside. The doors were all open, and the house was empty. I crawled up the ladder into the loft, but no one was there, either.

They had abandoned the place. But what other choices had they had once the Kansans took all their weapons? They'd had to leave to protect the girls.

I was alone except for Pooty, and he wasn't saying anything. I cried a while, then untied him and carried him inside and laid him out on the table. His flesh was cold, and his eyes stared blankly at the ceiling until I closed the lids over them. I spit on my finger and washed the trail of blood off his forehead, trying to make him look better for SincereAnne, then folded his arms across his chest to hide the bloody splotch on his shirt and coat.

I went back outside, grabbed the carbine, and walked around the house, trying to pick up tracks to lead me to everyone.

"Pa!" I yelled with what was left of my voice. "Thomas! Somebody, come home, please." I was tempted to fire the carbine to get their attention, but I figured it would only scare them farther away.

"Come home! It's safe!" I yelled again. I sat down on the porch, examining the carbine as I waited. It had twenty-three brads embedded in the stock. At least Beryl Fudge hadn't lived to add another one for Joe Don Burke.

For a long time I sat there, feeling lonely and helpless. Then I heard my name being called.

"Henry, you home? Pooty? Anybody?"

It was Pa. I jumped up and ran to the back to see him limping out of the woods.

"You all right?" he asked.

"Yes, sir, but Pooty's not." I bit my lip.

Pa grimaced. "Dead?"

I couldn't answer, and that told Pa it was true. He buried his head in his hands. "How am I gonna tell his momma?" He stared at me, then realized I was wearing a plumed hat. "Is that Beryl Fudge's?"

I nodded. "He killed Pooty, but he won't kill anybody

again." I told Pa about the ambush by the Rebel partisans and Fudge's cold-blooded shooting of Pooty.

Pa was shaken. "You shouldn't've have taken his hat. Folks'll know you killed him."

"I don't care, Pa. He needed killing."

Pa shook his head again. "When will this damned war end? We've been sinned against by all sides, and it won't stop even when the war's over. Feelings are too deep. Get rid of the hat where no one'll find it. I'll fetch the women and Thomas in the woods. Then we'll bury Pooty."

"Take this," I said, offering him the carbine.

He looked at the brads, then at me. "Beryl Fudge's?"

I nodded. As he turned and limped away, I angled for the outhouse. I flung open the door, jerked off the plumed hat, and shoved it in the hole. I hoped Beryl Fudge could see it from hell.

Leaving the outhouse, I went back around to the mounts and led them to the barn. I removed the saddles, fed and watered the animals, then went back to the house. I waited in the kitchen, crying and scared to face Pooty on the table in the next room, not knowing what I would tell SincereAnne when she returned.

Finally I heard the sound of voices and stepped out onto the dogtrot to see Pa and Thomas herding the women to the house. Momma and my sisters were trailing SincereAnne and her brood. SincereAnne saw me and began to wail, then charged toward me. I stood my ground, ready to take whatever she did to me, figuring I deserved it for all the misery I had caused her and Pooty.

She flung her arms around me. Instead of beating me she hugged me and sobbed. "Thank you for bringing him back instead of leaving him for the hogs and buzzards."

"I'm sorry," I said. "Beryl Fudge did it."

She grabbed my arms and pushed herself back from me. "Your pa says you killed Beryl Fudge for murdering Joe Don."

"He threatened to kill you and your daughters."

"Thank you," she said, then released me and stepped to the kitchen door. RuthAnne and DeeAnne caught up with their momma and accompanied her inside.

LouAnne lingered a moment, looking at me with tear-filled eyes and shaking her head. I thought she was angry at me.

"I'm sorry. I couldn't stop it."

She lifted her finger to her lips, then stepped toward me with an expression on her face I'd never seen before. I feared she would slap me across the cheek like she had so many times before. Instead, tears streaming down her cheeks, she said, "At least you're safe."

I felt helpless at first and uncertain what to do. Then I closed the gap between us, wrapped my arms around her, and kissed her hair, whispering my regrets.

Lifting her head from my chest, LouAnne kissed me on the cheek. "I know you did all you could." I would've felt better except for the wailing from SincereAnne and her two eldest daughters. "I best join Momma," LouAnne said, sliding from my grasp and going inside.

No sooner had she stepped away than Momma came up and hugged me, her eyes moist and red. She ran her fingers through my hair. "I'm glad you're okay and so sorry Joe Don's dead."

"I funned him a lot, Momma," I said, "but I did everything I could to keep him alive."

"Your pa said how brave you were, that you killed his murderer."

Momma seemed herself again. I didn't know how to explain it except that maybe her attack on Cap Andrews had released her grief over Van and John.

Thomas walked by, patting me and Momma on the shoulder, then went inside to comfort his wife. Lissa and little Harriet hugged me and Momma. Then Pa hobbled over, holding his hat in his hand.

"When will this war end?" Momma asked no one in particular.

"Even after it ends," Pa replied, "it won't be over."

Momma began to sob. "That's what I fear most. Even when it's done, some folks may still be after Henry."

I wasn't too worried. I was fourteen and invincible.

Pa motioned us inside. "Maybe we best comfort SincereAnne."

In the dining room SincereAnne was kissing Pooty's pasty face and wiping his forehead with the end of her sleeve. His sisters were sobbing and hugging each other. Thomas tried without success to console his wife.

Momma went over to SincereAnne and patted her shoulder. "I'm sorry. We're all sorry."

"It's my fault," I cried.

SincereAnne turned from Momma to me. "It's the war's fault. If those Kansans hadn't taken the two of you and our guns, he'd still be alive. I'd feared my husband might die in this godawful war, never thinking Joe Don could be hurt. If this war doesn't end, we may all die. Now I just want to bury him."

Pa spoke up. "Where'd you like us to dig his grave? You're welcome to any spot on our place."

She shook her head. "I want him resting on our place where I can tend his grave and grow flowers when the war is over."

"Where? Thomas and I will go dig the grave."

SincereAnne nodded. "DeeAnne knows. She can show you."

"I'll help," I offered.

"No," SincereAnne said. "I want you to tell me what happened."

I nodded. It was the least I could do.

Pa escorted DeeAnne and Thomas from the room. SincereAnne told RuthAnne and LouAnne to go through one of their trunks and find the best clothes they could to bury Pooty in. Momma and Harriet went to fetch water and soap to clean Pooty with while Lissa climbed up in the loft to find a blanket to wrap him in. When everyone left, it was just me and SincereAnne.

"How did it happen?"

I told her about the Kansans taking us to the place where I had hidden the gold.

"There was gold, then?" she asked.

I nodded. She looked at my neck, then pulled my collar away from my throat and touched the tender rope burn.

"Did Joe Don try to stop them from hanging you?"

"He did what he could," I said, knowing that wasn't entirely true.

She sighed. "I should've kept him from that evil Cap Andrews."

My momma told me not to lie about things, but this was one time I felt it was necessary. Instead of telling that Pooty had cowered in fear while the damn Kansans tried to string me up, I made up a story. "Pooty tried to save me. He flew into a couple Yankees, but they pushed him aside and threatened to hang him, too. Even that didn't stop him from trying."

SincereAnne smiled. "He was a good boy. We raised him right."

I nodded. "As they were starting to hang me, the bushwhackers swarmed out of the woods and killed them all. Pooty rushed to free me and would've lived if Beryl Fudge hadn't recognized him and shot him before anyone could do anything about it."

SincereAnne sobbed.

"The bushwhackers forced me to leave with them, but I circled back to get Pooty. That's when Beryl Fudge jumped me and threatened to kill me, but I got a jump on him. He won't be bothering any Burkes again."

SincereAnne nodded. "Thank you." She hugged me once again, then released me as Momma came into the room with a pail of water and a chunk of lye soap. Harriet carried a clean cloth to wash him with. SincereAnne and Momma washed his face, then removed his shirt and cleaned his bloodied chest. They excused Harriet and told her to shut the door as she left.

Lissa returned with a tattered blanket and offered it to Momma.

"We can do better than that," Momma said. "Find a nice one."

SincereAnne held up her hand. "That one will do. We've got to think of the living and their needs, too."

"I've something that'll do," I said. I ran into the kitchen and scrambled up the ladder to the loft. In the corner where I had hidden it, I dug out the United States flag Pa had given me from his days in the California Gold Rush. I held it to my chest for a moment, then kissed it. I loved that flag and wished I could keep it, but it was the least I could do for Pooty. I slid back down the ladder and returned to SincereAnne.

Pooty was all decked out in his father's suit. It was too big, but his own suit was too small. They had worked a smile on his lips and put a couple stones on his eyelids to weight them down.

"You can wrap him in the blanket, then cover him with this." I extended my hands with the folded flag.

SincereAnne and Momma both began to sob.

"Thank you," SincereAnne said. "I know how much that means to you."

I still felt bad for all the tricks I'd played on Pooty.

SincereAnne took the flag and gave it to Momma. As Momma unfolded it and draped it lengthwise across Pooty's chest so we could still see his face, SincereAnne hugged me again. I felt sorry for all the times I had mocked her and made comments about her crossed eyes. When she released me, I left the room and went outside to the dogtrot, where I sat on the bench alone for several minutes.

LouAnne came out and joined me. "Momma's grateful for all you've done." Hand in hand, we sat in silence until Pa and Thomas returned a couple hours before dusk.

"The grave is ready," Pa told us as he went inside. A few minutes later he came back and announced that it was time to carry Pooty to the Burke place for burial. Thomas and I hooked up the mules to the wagon, drove it up to the house, and went inside to help Pa carry Pooty out.

SincereAnne and each of his sisters gave Pooty a final kiss, then wrapped him in the ragged blanket and covered him with the flag.

"I'm giving away the flag," I told Pa.

"It's the right thing to do."

Pa, Thomas, and me gathered Pooty up and carried him out to the wagon, then loaded the womenfolk around him and got in ourselves.

As we rode toward the Burke place, little Harriet began to sing, her voice prettier than I had ever heard it. She sang a couple religious hymns, and the others joined in. I never was much of a singer so I just listened.

When we reached the grave, beneath a copse of trees just a stone's throw from the blackened ruins of their home, we all helped carry Pooty to his grave. We lowered him into the earth as far as we could, then dropped him the rest of the way. We'd forgotten our Bibles, but Momma led us in the Twenty-third Psalm. Then she spoke a few words that I figured mommas all over Arkansas could agree with.

"Oh, Lord, please let this horrible war end so the healing can begin. Let no other mother anywhere lose a son. Too many sons have died already. If it keeps up we will have no sons and no husbands."

"Amen," we all said.

Thomas and Pa picked up shovels and began to cover the flag-draped body. I took the shovel from Pa and did my part for Pooty, working hard to cover that grave.

I was glad I had killed Pooty's killer, but I never thought that the death of Beryl Fudge would make me a Cane Hill legend—and a marked man.

Chapter Twenty-five

That winter was the hardest of the war for us. Pooty was dead. What food we'd managed to harvest that autumn was short. The weather was cold. Our nerves were on edge. And I was a marked man. Rumors began to circulate about how viciously Beryl Fudge had been murdered. I had been seen riding through Cane Hill on his horse, wearing his hat, carrying his easily identifiable carbine, and bragging about the killing—or so they said. I was beginning to wish I had given Old Abe his due in Beryl Fudge's demise.

All we had to defend ourselves after the Kansans took our guns was Fudge's pistol and carbine. We had more meat than anything else and maybe an occasional potato or piece of bread or hardtack, followed by a dose of sassafras tea that Momma would brew up to purge our systems. Sometimes when we'd had too much tea, we'd line up at the outhouse, ready to explode. Then our bottoms'd be on fire.

Between trips to the outhouse I'd likely have gone crazy locked up in the house all the time had it not been for LouAnne. Many a night we never lit a candle for fear some bushwhacker might try to assassinate me, so we sat away from the fireplace and talked about dreams and ambitions. I enjoyed those visits. Unlike Amanda, LouAnne was as innocent as a kitten, and I took a liking to her. Sometimes she'd even let me kiss her, and I felt about as good as a boy could feel without getting a feel. I could remember how much I had despised her and how ugly she was when she moved in with us, but either she'd gotten prettier or I'd gotten less picky.

In January of 1865 I celebrated my fifteenth birthday. LouAnne made a small stack cake from what flour Momma had managed to save up. As LouAnne cut the cake, Momma made a big deal out of making sure I understood who had baked it for me. I took the first bite and nodded my approval. "Sure is good," I said, my mouth full.

"She'd make some fellow a good wife," Momma said.

LouAnne blushed, and I felt my cheeks heat up. I figured I was still too young to get married. If LouAnne had pushed herself on me I don't know what I would've done, but she was as patient as time itself and getting better looking each day.

When I finished my slice of birthday cake, she gave me hers. I did what any boy approaching manhood would do: I ate it. She seemed all the more pleased. Afterward, when the others retired to bed, she and I sat on the bench in the kitchen.

"I never had better cake," I said.

She moved closer to me and squeezed my arm, then leaned her head on my shoulder. "I'm glad."

We held hands, and I kissed the top of her head.

"What are you gonna do when this war's over?"

I shrugged. "Seems like it'll never end."

"It has to end. What'll you do when it does?"

I couldn't see the future any better than I could change the past. "Seek my fortune somewhere."

"Do you think you might settle down?"

"There's no money in farming. Besides, I've always figured to see the West," I answered.

"Would you take someone with you? Like a wife?"

At that moment I understood where she was going.

I'd never given much thought to settling down, figuring there wasn't a sane woman around that would be interested in hitching up with me. I was growing to like LouAnne more and more by the day, but I didn't know if I was ready to settle down. It was like that noose was tightening around my neck again. "I'd consider it, if my wife could be you."

LouAnne cuddled against me, letting me know I had given her the right answer. "When the war's over, maybe we can get married."

"Not before I'm sixteen," I answered.

"I can wait." Her voice was sweet. "With the money I've saved, you'd have enough to start out with."

I laughed. "How could you've saved any money? We haven't had the cash to buy anything to eat, much less save."

She just smiled. "Whatever I had I'd share with you."

I figured that was true as far as it went, although she'd shown no signs of wanting to share what was between her legs or on her chest. I was naturally curious, especially since Pooty and I had experimented with that sand-filled sock, but that was the randy side of me. The good side respected her innocence . . . though I couldn't help being curious about claiming it.

The way I read our conversation, I had me a wife anytime I wanted once the War Between the States ended. That gave me a lot to think about, even more so when she lifted her head and pressed her lips against mine. Her lips were sweeter than a hive of honey. Deciding we'd best get to our beds, I kissed her back and suggested she retire.

"I hope you had a fine birthday," she said.

"It would've been no different from the others except for you and your cake." She seemed pleased by that.

After I crawled up the ladder and into my cold bed, I thought a long time about LouAnne and how nice it would be to have her warm my bed with me. I'd never thought much about marriage, figuring it was pretty much a self-imposed prison sentence, but I had to admit there was something to be said for having a place to stable your mule every night, particularly with someone as decent as LouAnne. I had to admit she wasn't as comely as Amanda—on the outside, at least. But LouAnne Burke had an inner beauty that made Amanda Fudge look like a mule's behind.

The winter passed slowly, LouAnne being my only diversion from boredom. We saw far more federal troops ranging around Washington County than we did Confederate soldiers. Once, though, a band of Confederate cavalry did approach. Fortunately Pa and Thomas had taken the mules and the horse into the woods to hunt for wild hogs and bring back firewood, or the soldiers would've stolen them. The cavalry lieutenant announced himself and ordered us to turn over any horses or mules we might have.

Momma shrugged. "They were taken years ago."

"That's not what we hear, ma'am," the lieutenant answered.

"Check the barn, then," Momma challenged.

The Confederate officer pointed to two men and ordered them to see for themselves. Five minutes later they returned, carrying manure in their hands.

"There's fresh droppings in the barn," one announced.

"How'd you know they're fresh? Did you take a bite?" I asked.

"Hush," Momma said.

The lieutenant leaned over his mount's neck and stared at me from under the wide brim of his hat. "How old are you, seed corn?" he demanded.

"Fifteen," I answered.

The lieutenant nodded. "Old enough to join up and fight, unless you're a bluebelly or a yellowbelly."

Momma stepped off the porch, waving her fist at the lieutenant's nose. "I've lost two sons to this war, and I'll not lose another."

"Whose side did they die for?"

"Your side," she answered, her voice rising. "The losing side."

As he stared at Momma, he ordered his two soldiers to mount. They threw their handful of manure at me, then climbed into their saddles. "We'll be back," the lieutenant threatened, "and we'll get seed corn there."

I was madder than the devil at a prayer meeting. Here I'd been supporting the Confederate cause against the Yankee hordes, and now I was being threatened by Confederate cavalry in addition to Beryl Fudge's friends. My own side in this damn war was causing me more harm than the Yankees were.

As we watched them ride away, Momma took to crying. LouAnne ran outside and flung her arms around me. She was crying, too. So were the other women. But their tears were for nothing. Those were the last Rebel troops ever to set foot on our place during the war.

Through March and on into April Yankee troops came by regularly on patrol. Pa and Thomas took to plowing the fields, hoping to put in a crop.

In late April word came down that the war was over. General Lee had surrendered the Army of Northern Virginia in Appomattox and with it all the other armies of the Confederacy.

The Confederacy had lost, taking with it two of my brothers. The Burke women had more reason to celebrate than we did, but they were subdued out of respect for us. We had had our differences over the years, but now we were tied together by Thomas and DeeAnne's marriage and by the common experience of having survived the war.

We sat out on the porch that night in the cool April breeze. All around us the trees and plants were leafing out and blooming.

"The earth's springing back to life," Momma said.

"It's so pretty," SincereAnne added. "I'll plant flowers on Joe Don's grave, and maybe we can forget the war and all its hurt."

Pa grimaced. "The surrender couldn't have come at a worse time."

"What do you mean?" Momma wanted to know.

"The war may be over, but the bickering's not. There'll be bushwhacking and killing for years to come."

Thomas nodded. "We've been lucky. No one's shot at Henry because the Yankees have controlled these parts. That'll change."

LouAnne came over and put her arm around me. For a long time nobody said much; we all just watched the light fade.

Momma finally spoke. "When it's safe to travel, I'd like to go to Prairie Grove and see the stones for Van and John."

It seemed like a century since I had traveled to Fayetteville and paid the stonecutter to make markers for the two. I hoped he had produced the tombstones rather than taking my money for nothing.

Though we retired that night glad the war was over, we were uncertain what the peace would bring. It turned out it brought carpetbaggers, opportunists, thieves, and lawyers. During Reconstruction, as the Yankees called it, I came to hate lawyers and respect thieves. At least thieves had the decency to steal behind your back. Lawyers'd steal to your face and smile while they were doing it. They had no more conscience than a reptile.

The Yankees we had fought to be shed of grew in number, though few of them wore uniforms. They came down to Arkansas after the fighting and took over the legislature and all the political offices. Nobody who had fought for the South could vote, and the elections were as crooked as a corkscrew. Jim and Andy returned home but stayed only briefly. They saw that the carpetbag law was stacked against them and decided to leave Arkansas. If they'd gone anywhere but Texas I'd have joined them, but I was still drawn to LouAnne.

We would've lost our land except that Gordon Burke returned home in midsummer and started rebuilding his own place. He was devastated by the death of his son, and though he cared very little for Confederate sympathizers, he was forever grateful to my folks for taking his family in and to me for killing Beryl Fudge. Burke took over Fudge's place, made the biggest farm in the Cane Hill vicinity, and turned it over to Thomas and DeeAnne to work. It was there that DeeAnne gave birth to a daughter, whom they called JoAnne in memory of Pooty.

When the carpetbag lawyers came to steal our place by phony laws, Burke told them to leave my folks alone because they had protected his family during the war. When word got around what he had said, a lot more folks took us to be Union sympathizers, and we became a target of animosities for reasons beyond my killing of Beryl Fudge.

After the Burkes returned home, the place was quiet. I couldn't believe how much I missed LouAnne. Sometimes after I did my chores I'd walk to her place, or we'd meet by Jordan Creek to spoon and visit. I decided I should marry the girl and hope her father would let us work his place. Then we'd be close to Thomas and DeeAnne as well as our own families.

The problem was, embittered secesh wouldn't allow it. They still had grudges to settle with me.

It was late on a June evening when they struck first. Me and LouAnne were sitting beside Jordan Creek, pitching pebbles in the water. I caught a noise but didn't think much of it until I heard a metallic click. I'd heard guns being cocked before and knew just what it was. I shoved LouAnne to the ground and dove atop her as the woods exploded with a gunshot. I don't know how close it came, but if I hadn't heard the click I'd've been dead or wounded for sure.

LouAnne screamed, and I scanned the woods, hoping to recognize a face or a horse. I heard the sound of someone dashing away, but nothing else. For an instant all was quiet until I heard Pa shouting from one direction and Gordon Burke from the other.

Burke arrived first, his carbine in his arms, ready for action. When he saw LouAnne and heard her sobs, he hurried down the embankment toward us. "Are you hurt, Lou?"

"No," she sobbed. "Henry saved me."

Pa limped up next, carrying the gun that had belonged to Beryl Fudge. "Did you get a look at him?"

I pointed down the creek. "He fired from over there."

Burke and Pa charged down the creek. They fired a couple shots in frustration, but never saw anyone and returned out of breath.

"Beryl Fudge'll be with us forever," Burke growled.

Pa nodded. "Henry, you don't be taking LouAnne outside her home anymore. I'd hate for her to get hurt or you, either."

"I don't want you hurt," LouAnne said to me.

I kissed her before we went home with our pas.

"Don't go out unarmed again, Henry," Pa commanded.

We didn't have enough guns to go around, just Beryl Fudge's pistol and carbine, which was easily identifiable by the brads nailed in the stock. When we got home, Pa took his knife and pried the brads free, leaving the holes as the only reminder of the carbine's previous owner.

Nothing happened for weeks after that, and we began to hope the partisans had forgotten their grudges. By late fall I'd taken to meeting LouAnne by the creek again, though we didn't tell our folks.

One day Pa was pulling ears of corn from dried stalks when he took a bullet to the shoulder. Me and Momma ran to rescue him. As we did, three more shots came out of the woods, one knocking my hat off. I dove among the cornstalks and hid, lifting my head briefly to scan the woods. I didn't see a thing, but I heard Pa moaning.

I crawled on hands and knees toward the noise. Momma, though, never ducked. She ran straight to Pa, daring the assassin to shoot.

When I reached him, he looked up at me. "You okay?"

I nodded. "What about you?"

"I ain't dead yet."

Lissa and Harriet came barreling out of the house and ran toward us, oblivious to the possible dangers. In the distance I heard the sound of a horse galloping away.

We managed to get Pa to the house. I took the carbine and looked around for a while, hoping for a clean shot at a bushwhacker. After Momma and the girls got Pa to bed and dressed his wound, Momma called me inside.

"We've been talking, son, your pa and I, and we think it's time for you to leave home for your own good."

All my life I had been waiting for this day. Now that it was here, I didn't know what to do. I thought first of LouAnne.

"Pa thinks they just grazed him to draw you out for a clean shot. I think he's right." She came and hugged me tightly. "Feelings are still running high against you, son. It may take years to change. You need to leave soon."

"How soon?"

"Tomorrow isn't too soon."

I grimaced. "I need to see LouAnne."

"Go after dark and let her know, but be careful."

The trip was the longest I had ever made. LouAnne greeted me at the door, but the smile withered on her face. "What's the matter?"

"I've got to leave," I said.

She invited me inside. "But why?"

"They shot Pa this afternoon. He thinks they were after me."

LouAnne began to cry. She threw her arms around me. "I'll go with you."

"I'd like that, but I can't risk you being hurt," I said.

"You can write for me, and I'll join you."

"Somebody can intercept the mail."

"Take me with you, then. I've worn a garter made

from your hatband and a wasp nest pinned to my skirt to make you love me."

I took a deep breath. "I do love you," I said, "but I can't risk you getting hurt by someone trying to kill me."

She hugged me and buried her head in my chest, sobbing. "Don't leave. You'll never come back to me, Henry. I know you."

"I'll come back one day, LouAnne, when we can live together safely."

"I've got gold," she said. "We can move away where no one has ever heard of us."

I feared she was telling me a story just to keep me there. I didn't know how she could have gold, because there still wasn't even much paper money circulating around northwest Arkansas.

"Please let me go with you. When are you leaving?"

"Seven in the morning," I replied.

"I'll be there," she answered.

I knew I couldn't stop her from showing up, just as I knew I could never take her with me. I smiled and kissed her a final time.

"I'll see you then."

I turned and ran home to gather my belongings, which didn't take long. I spent my final night with my parents, Lissa, and Harriet. It was the saddest night of my life, for I knew I might never see them again. Then I went to bed. And slept poorly.

I awoke at five o'clock and climbed down the loft for the last time, carrying my belongings over my shoulders. Momma had a bundle of food for me, and Pa told me to take the carbine, the pistol, and the ammunition. I kissed them both good-bye, ran to the barn, saddled Old Abe, and left by five-thirty so LouAnne would be too late to join me.

Now that I was finally out on my own, I didn't know where to turn for certain. The only invitation I had was to see Jesse James on the Samuel farm in Clay County, Missouri.

Chapter Twenty-six

I never felt lower than I did then, running out on LouAnne. I didn't want her to get hurt, but I hurt her in ways I didn't understand at the time.

I passed through Cane Hill, didn't see a soul about, and rode on, passing the place where Pooty had been killed. I couldn't bear to look. At Prairie Grove I stopped at Annie Belle Higdon's place. She was milking a cow as I rode up.

"Henry Lomax, is that you?" she called.

I howdied her.

"The stones look fine." She pointed behind the house.

I aimed Old Abe to the back and looked for myself. She was right. The stonemason had done a good job. "Momma'll like that."

Annie Belle ambled over with her milk pail. "You're up early."

I nodded. "Leaving Arkansas."

"It true you killed Beryl Fudge? Beat him to a pulp, I heard."

"I had a hand in it," I admitted.

"Good," she said. "He was nothing but a rabid animal. I hear his wife and daughter've taken to running a bawdy house in Fayetteville. May be nothing but vicious gossip, I don't know."

I didn't know either because at that age I wasn't sure exactly what a bawdy house was. I shrugged.

"Can you stay for breakfast?"

"I best be riding on. I wish I could pay you for tending the grave, but my fortune's changed since the war ended."

She smiled. "The money you gave me carried us through the war. We owe you, and we'll take care of the grave. Did the rest of your brothers make it back alive?"

I nodded. "Thomas lost an eye. Jim and Andy came back, but left for Texas."

"You heading after them?"

"Nope. Texas is a big state, and I wouldn't know where to look for them. I'll head to Kansas City or St. Louis, see a big city, find a job long enough to make me some money, and head west."

"Good luck, Henry Lomax. I hope the West is better to you than Arkansas has been."

I tipped my hat and turned Old Abe toward Fayetteville. Arriving before noon, I found the town flooded with men who spoke with Yankee accents and wore fancy clothes that no Confederate supporter could've afforded.

At one street corner I was shocked to see a young lady with a strong resemblance to Amanda Fudge, though she was dressed all fancy in a bonnet and bows. She carried a parasol and had two Yankee-looking men beside her, all of them giggling and drawing the disapproving stares of more plainly dressed women. I was tempted to ask the lady to skin a cat for me so I'd know for sure if it was Amanda, but I figured I best ride on.

Fayetteville showed a few signs of war, but the countryside north of town was devastated. Homes were burned, fields were overgrown, white bones of dead animals were strewn along the road. It was much the same all the way into Missouri.

I never knew for certain when I crossed into Missouri, though I did detect a foul odor I could explain no other way. I still didn't think much of Missourians, them being too yellow to secede with the rest of us, but at least they were better than Kansans, who were not nearly as bad as Texans, who were arrogant, crude, and mean without the manners and refinement of us Arkansans. At least we knew not to spit tobacco on the floor or fart in front of company or blow our noses without kerchiefs—excepting Hairball, of course.

Once I got used to the odor of Missouri, I found the people were either dumb or suspicious. I figured they'd been in the outhouse when brains were passed out, so they had to substitute what was at hand for what they'd missed. Maybe that was why Missouri smelled so bad—from the fumes seeping out of their ears. I'd've thought a lot more highly of Missourians if they'd just answered a simple question.

"Which way to Kansas City?"

I must've asked that a thousand times, and all I got was stares that were emptier than a politician's promises. I knew Kansas City had to be somewhere in Missouri, but I don't think Missourians were so sure. After all, it was named Kansas City. Bad as things had been in Arkansas with bushwhackers, I gathered things had been even worse in Missouri and weren't likely to get any better for a while. That's why folks feared talking to strangers or giving directions.

Thanks to Old Abe, I found Kansas City and avoided any serious encounters with the ruffians who kept terrorizing the countryside, neighbors still settling old scores. Old Abe was a dependable, likable mule and the only true friend I had in Kansas City. He was smarter than the average Missouri man, prettier than the average Missouri woman, and more honorable than the average Missouri politician.

Kansas City was the biggest town I'd ever been in, and I stayed around for a spell, working at odd chores for food for myself and hay for Old Abe, figuring I'd make a few friends and a few dollars. I came up short on both counts. As the nights turned cold, I decided it was time to find the Samuel farm and see if I couldn't at least get a warm place to spend the winter.

I lasted in Kansas City through December and was never more depressed than that first Christmas away from my family. For a Christmas gift I stole a worn deck of cards and a full bottle of whiskey when a bartender wasn't looking, went to the barn where I'd stabled Old Abe, and finished off that bottle. I got drunk and sick and soiled the straw. I can't say that I liked the taste of hard liquor, but I can't say that I *didn't* like it, either. It always seemed to taste better before I drank it than after, but for a bit I felt about as happy as could be expected of a man dead broke and sleeping in a stable with the stock.

The next day I filled my empty whiskey bottle with water from the horse trough and rode toward Liberty on the way to Kearney to look for the Samuel farm. Everything went fine until I reached the north side of town and tried to board the ferry to take me across the Missouri River.

"Fare's a nickel," said the squinty-eyed ferryman, who hadn't shaved in so long his face looked like a porcupine's behind.

"I'm broke."

"I'd be broke, too, if I let every no-account drifter ride my ferry for free. Looks like you'll be staying in Kansas City, unless'n your mule and you can swim."

I started bargaining, promising to return and pay him once I got a job. He must've taken me for a lying sort because he didn't want to have anything to do with my offers. Finally I twisted around in my saddle, unbuckled the flap to a saddlebag, and pulled out my water-filled bottle of liquor. "This is a near full liquor bottle that's yours if you just get me across the river."

"Give me a sip," he said, poking his hand toward the bottle.

I jerked it away and shook my head. "No, sir. You

can have a single sip now or the entire bottle once we're across."

The ferryman was no smarter than the average Missourian, which meant I could smell his brains. "Ride your mule aboard, then."

Old Abe marched up the ramp, and the ferryman pushed off from the bank. We were soon crossing the muddy waters, the ferryman watching the river and me studying the ferryman to make sure he wasn't armed. He didn't appear to be, which was good because I figured he'd turn mad once I gave him the liquor bottle.

When we reached the other side of the river, I started Old Abe down the ramp.

"You're forgetting my whiskey."

"You mean your whiskey bottle," I replied, tossing it to him.

He grabbed the bottle like a spider snagging flies, uncorked it, and took to suckling like a newborn on his first tit. The moment he came up for air, though, he cussed like a circuit rider after an empty offering plate. "This ain't whiskey!"

"It's watered down some," I admitted, "but the deal was for the whiskey bottle, not a bottle of whiskey."

"I don't see no difference."

"And you don't see me swimming." I laughed.

The ferryman cursed. "It won't be funny the next time you need to cross the river."

Laughing again, I nudged Old Abe toward the trail and into the trees. I rode through Liberty, then to Kearney, arriving in that modest community about dusk. I began to inquire about the location of the Samuel place and Jesse James. There were few people about at that hour, and I couldn't have pried information out of those folks with a crowbar.

I spent a couple days about town trying to talk to someone, anyone, who would point me in the right direction. Then I visited the farms around the town, hoping by accident to run into Jesse or Frank. I figured once I did find them my troubles would be over, because at least then someone would talk to me.

But I was wrong. Once I found them my troubles were just beginning.

Not once did I approach a farmhouse in all of Clay County without children scurrying to hide or women grabbing their throat in fear. Men who'd gotten back from the war would greet me with guns in their hands. When I asked for directions to the Samuel farm, folks would shrug their ignorance.

"Don't anybody know where the Samuel place is?" I asked one farmer, who had sacrificed his leg to the war.

With a crutch under one arm and a carbine under the other, the fellow eyed me. "The problem is, don't anybody know you. It's better to keep our mouths shut than open them to the wrong folks."

"I'm friends with the Samuels."

"If that's a fact, why don't you know where their place is?"

"I met them in Arkansas."

"You didn't meet any Samuels, then."

I tried to explain, but he waved the explanation away with the barrel of his carbine. "You're riding a federal mule. That won't make many friends in these parts, especially not with the Samuels."

"Hell, Old Abe didn't have a choice on what side he joined."

The one-legged farmer cocked his head at me. "Who?"

I gulped. "Old Abe. That's my mule's name."

The farmer spat. "I don't suppose he picked his own name?"

Once again I tried to explain. "I gave him the name 'cause he's got this odd habit every time you say the name of Jefferson Davis."

Old Abe brayed and kicked.

The farmer grinned. "Jefferson Davis."

Again Old Abe brayed and kicked.

"Looks to me like your mule's a Yankee clear through."

"How about if I change his name to Robert E. Lee or Stonewall Jackson?"

"Why don't you name him Skedaddle and do just that?"

Old Abe might've been a mule, but at least he wasn't a jackass like that tight-lipped farmer. "Just a bit of advice," I offered.

"I'm all ears," he answered, which told me why the stench was so thick about his place.

"I wouldn't be entering no butt-kicking contests, if I was you."

"Won't be a need for such contests, once all you strangers leave Clay County to those of us that call it home. But don't you worry, the leg that counts still works."

I shook my head. If that were true, there'd be a lot more dumb Missourians born on his place. I turned Old Abe back down the road and went to the next place.

That was the way it was for days. The only thing I was getting less of than straight answers was food, and I was beginning to weaken. In the January cold I felt about as miserable as a fellow can, short of being forced to listen to a long-winded preacher. In fact my stomach was growling so much it sounded like a bad song on a pump organ. Being so hungry I lost track of the days and had about decided to give up my search. I was so desperate I thought about heading southwest to Texas. As much hot air as Texans spouted, it was bound to be warmer there than in Missouri.

It was a Confederate sky overhead, all gray and dreary, raindrops falling like tears, when Old Abe turned off the main road and down a trail that followed a shivering creek for a bit. A long, dingy house sat back among the barren trees. I approached from the back side, which was made of rough-hewn logs and chinking; the other end of the house, where the road curved around, looked more respectable with its milled and whitewashed lumber. Hounds took to barking as I steered Old Abe through an opening in the split-rail fence.

"Hello, the house," I called. I saw the curtain move behind one window, then watched one of the doors open onto the porch.

Out walked a stocky old woman with deep eyes, sunken cheeks, lips that seemed to fold back into one another, and gray hair slicked back and tied in a bun. I'd always thought SincereAnne was the homeliest woman I'd ever seen, but this woman made ugly a sin.

I doffed my hat, trying to show what respect I could in the face of overwhelming ugly. I'd always heard that beauty was only skin deep, but in this case ugly went clear to the bone. She seemed to be eyeing me as much as I was her, but I couldn't be certain since I couldn't make out her eyes beneath her heavy brow.

"What's your business?" she asked, her voice deep and rasping.

"I'm looking for the Samuel place. Would it be around here?"

She crossed her arms over her broad bosom. "It would."

"Would you just point the way?"

Slowly, deliberately, she shook her head. "That wouldn't be neighborly, as much back-shooting as been going on."

"I'm an old family friend."

"That a fact?"

I nodded.

"Any friend of the Samuels is a friend of mine." She eyed me and Old Abe some more. "Why don't you set your feet on the ground and stretch for a minute? You look like you could use a little food."

Licking my lips, I agreed. "I sure could."

She pointed to Old Abe. "That a Yankee mule, is it?"

"He was until I freed him," I announced. "Lincoln may've freed the slaves, but I freed this here mule."

She didn't crack a grin, but I figured the weight of

all that ugly made it difficult for her to manage a smile, however slight.

"I'll be back with something for you to digest." She waddled back in the house.

I was pleased with her being more neighborly than any other Clay County resident I'd yet encountered. I was so hungry I figured I could hold down her food, whatever it was, provided I didn't have to stare at her while I ate it. She must've gotten in the line for cooks when they were handing out looks.

Leisurely I dismounted, led Old Abe back to the fence, and tied the reins to a post. Not wanting to frighten the first Clay County resident to offer me food, I undid my gun belt and hung it over the saddle horn. Then I turned around and started back to the porch, noting the coffee bean tree and smokehouse to the west of the house and the large barn north of them. On the perimeter of the clearing were several sassafras and oak trees.

I was halfway to the house when the old woman barged back onto the porch. She had her hands full—of shotgun. And she was smiling like nothing I'd ever seen. "You ain't no friend of the Samuel family," she cried out in that husky voice.

Thinking this wasn't the proper time to debate the question, I swatted at my waist, then remembered I'd removed my pistol.

She cocked the twin hammers on the double-barreled weapon.

I considered trying to tackle her, but feared some of the ugly might rub off and then no decent-looking woman would ever care to be seen with me. Too, she might cut me in half with that shotgun before I reached her.

"Stay still!" she cried.

Not being one to take orders very well, I turned and ran toward Old Abe, hoping to escape or turn my own guns on her and improve the looks of the entire state of Missouri.

The old woman had another idea, though. She fired

off a barrel of that shotgun, and it kicked up dirt and pebbles between me and Old Abe. The mule took to kicking and stomping as if he had been discussing Jefferson Davis. I changed directions, figuring she'd sighted in on me. My only hope was to jump over the rail fence, hit the ground at a roll, then get up and run. Texas looked better and better with each step.

"Run, you skunk, run!" I heard the woman yell.

I could almost feel her glare knifing into my back and expected any moment to be peppered with shotgun lead. I knew I couldn't vault the fence, so when I reached it I dove headlong for it.

"Don't shoot, Ma!" I heard a man's voice yell, but he was too late.

Instantly on the tail of his command I heard the explosion of the shotgun and felt the sting of shot in my behind as I cleared the fence. Overhead the air whizzed with the sound of other shots. I landed hard on the ground, writhing in agony at the pain in my behind and the back of my calves. I swatted at my backside, trying to put out the sting.

"Don't shoot, Ma. He's a friend of mine!" the man yelled again. I recognized the voice. It was Jesse James.

"He ain't a friend of the family," she answered back.

After my welcome I doubted the family had many friends.

"Henry Lomax, that's you, isn't it?"

"As long as I don't bleed to death," I answered.

"I thought it was you. I recognized your backside." He laughed and turned to his momma. "Lomax fought and shared his gold with us during the late war."

Jesse stole the gold was more nearly the truth, but I didn't figure that was the best time to mention that to Jesse, not with his momma toting a shotgun and a disposition that would scare a grizzly.

"But he's riding a Yankee mule," she replied, as if she wanted to shed more of my blood. "You certain you ain't one of them?"

Jesse laughed. "He's more mule than Yankee."

I shook behind the nearest fencepost like a scared dog until I was certain Jesse wasn't going to let her reload that shotgun. He was standing with his arm braced against the doorway, a bandage wrapped around the right side of his shirtless chest and a revolver tucked in his beltless pants.

"Just see if you can tend him, Ma. I got to save my strength." He turned to go back inside.

Ma James kept her eyes on me, still debating my future. "I don't like his looks." She was sure someone to be talking about looks. If ugly could kill, I'd've been dead the moment I laid eyes on her. "He's not one you can trust."

"Ma," Jesse answered in exasperation, "if we can't trust him, we can kill him later. Anyway, what kind of fool planning harm would ride to our place on a mule when our horses could run him down in an instant if he tried anything?"

Jesse had a point, though it wasn't any too comforting to my mind or my butt. I managed to get to my feet, then held the fencepost to steady myself. I didn't know whether it would be more painful to climb the fence or go around it to get to the house. Of course, I was assuming Jesse's momma'd let me in.

I decided to climb over the fence, and it felt like my backside was lit by a hundred tiny fires. I patted my bottom and realized the seat of my pants was shredded. My hand came away sticky with blood. I jumped down from the fence, wincing at the pain jolting through my legs and bottom, and staggered up to the door. I was about to enter when Jesse's momma stopped me.

"Wipe your feet."

Fighting the urge to slap the woman, I obeyed, then stepped inside to the warmth of the kitchen.

She pointed me to the table. "Bend over it, and I'll dig the shot out. It's Jesse's idea, not mine."

After I saw the shotgun in the corner, I did as she

suggested. She jerked my shredded pants down and looked at my naked backside, trying to comfort me. "I was shooting for your head."

Her words soothed me. I twisted my head to the side and saw Jesse sitting in a rocking chair near the fireplace and grinning.

"Jumping the fence saved you," he said. "Odd that a man can survive by putting his butt where his head was."

Jesse's momma took a wet rag and wiped the blood off my bottom. "You're lucky. Looks like most of the shot just creased your behind, and only a few dug in."

I didn't care as long as the pain subsided. Jesse's momma walked to the corner and came back with a can of coal oil. She doused the rag with it, then shoved it against my flesh. Screaming at the burn, I bucked against her.

"It'll kill the poison," she said.

I just hoped it didn't kill me. "What's the date?"

"What's it matter to you?" Jesse answered.

"I want to know the day I die."

"It's January ninth," Jesse replied.

Between gritted teeth I said, "It's my sixteenth birthday."

"Well, happy birthday," growled Jesse's momma as she poured more coal oil on my backside. Her sincere wish was the last thing I remember before passing out.

Chapter Twenty-seven

I was laid up for a week, either lying on my belly or standing up. Jesse thought it was funny. I don't think Ma James thought anything was funny. She did give me a pair of old pants that were a couple inches too big in the waist, but she left my pistol and my carbine with Jesse, so I didn't have any weapons to defend myself against either of them. She tended Old Abe as well, and though I asked her to discuss politics with the mule, she ignored me.

Jesse introduced his momma as Zerelda Samuel, but I just called her Ma James. It seemed she was more James than Samuel. Jesse's stepfather, Reuben Samuel, had abandoned Missouri, taking his and Zerelda's children with him until the animosities died down. Ma James felt the Yankees had singled her Jesse out for persecution—after all, they had shot him in the chest and shot off the tip of the middle finger on his left hand. She didn't concern herself with any of the wrongs Jesse had done.

Probably the worst thing he'd ever done was take my gold. When I was feeling better and could sit without thinking about sitting, I confronted him at the supper table.

"Where'd you hide my share of the gold, Dingus?"

Jesse looked at me. Ma James filled his bowl with

stew, then put but a few bites in my bowl before emptying the pot into her own.

"I want more," I protested.

Ma James held up the pot. "It's all gone."

"So's the gold," Jesse added. "We spent it for the cause, just like you'd have done."

I had hoped that Jesse had enough honor to save me a bit to grubstake the rest of my life, but I was pissing into the wind. All I had to show for the four sacks was stones on my brothers' graves. At twelve I had been the richest boy in Arkansas, and not days past my sixteenth birthday I was broke and in Missouri. I couldn't have gotten much lower than that without going to Texas.

Jesse pointed his spoon at me. "Now I've got a question." He blinked incessantly, like he was always nervous, and his voice was deathly cold. "It true you killed Beryl Fudge? He was a good fighter."

"That's what rumor has." I spooned at my paltry stew.

"Is the rumor true? Your carbine looks like his, though someone's removed the brass tacks from the stock."

I studied Jesse, trying to figure his angle. I couldn't recall if he and Beryl had been friends. I licked my lips and nodded. "I had a hand in it."

Jesse leaned back in his chair. "Who else was involved?"

Figuring he wouldn't believe Old Abe's part, I deflected the question. "It doesn't matter. I'll stand for the blame or for the credit, rather than bring another man down."

Jesse squinted at me. "He was one of us, you know?"

"He was until he threatened my family," I replied.

Lifting his spoon, Jesse blew on his stew, then took a bite as his momma handed him a hunk of corn bread. She gave me a piece about a fourth the size of Jesse's, then hoarded the rest for herself.

As he swallowed his bite of stew, he nodded. "A man's got to be true to his blood."

I figured I'd come up in Jesse's estimation by defending my kin. I should've kept my mouth shut, but I'd been curious about Frank.

"Where's Buck?" I asked.

Jesse's blinking eyes narrowed.

Ma James scowled. "I told you he couldn't be trusted."

Jesse rubbed his chin. "Just why you asking? You ain't spying on us for no carpetbaggers, are you?"

"No, no, no! I ain't heard if he made it through the war."

That didn't satisfy Ma James, though nothing short of my hanging would.

Jesse seemed to understand. "Buck's on business. You best not ask too many questions, Henry. They make Ma nervous. She thinks you're spying for the Yankees."

I was surprised the woman was smart enough to think, but I didn't consider it wise to mention that. "Maybe it's best I ride on. Your momma don't trust me, and she's trying to starve me."

Jesse shook his head. "Don't think of leaving right yet, Henry. Once your bottom's healed, we've got work you can do while I recuperate. Too, maybe we can go for a ride. I need to see how my endurance is in the saddle. You never can tell when I might have to leave in a hurry."

"If I don't get more grub, I'll starve to death here."

Jesse told Ma James to fix more food and give me a bigger share, but she must not've heard him over the smacking of her lips, because I didn't see any increase on my plate over the next several days.

About a week later Jesse told me at breakfast he felt strong enough to go for a ride and test his stamina. It sounded like a chance to get away from Ma James. I saddled Old Abe, then the chestnut that Jesse favored. When I returned to the house, I found Jesse with two gun belts strapped around his waist and a carbine under his arm.

"Where's my guns?" I asked.

Ma James looked up from the table where she was kneading dough.

Jesse grinned. "You won't have cause to use a gun."

"And you're saying you will?"

He nodded.

I grimaced.

"The mounts saddled?"

"They are."

"Then why don't we go for a ride." Jesse slipped his coat on and stepped out the door with me.

"Be careful, Jesse," Ma James called. "Don't let yourself get hurt." She didn't say a thing to me.

I knew how a calf felt being led to slaughter. I came pretty near attacking Jesse right there, figuring I could do him more harm by punching him in the chest than he could by slapping me on the butt. But knowing Ma James was behind me with that damn shotgun made me reconsider. If Jesse planned to kill me, I'd have to defend myself away from his mean momma.

Side by side we walked to the barn, Jesse giving me a slight, almost sinister smile. I didn't know what to make of him. Maybe he was better friends with Beryl Fudge than he'd let on.

Jesse's hounds caught up with us as I opened the barn door. He bent down and roughed the dogs' ears, then motioned for me to go ahead. In case he pulled his gun I looked for a weapon and saw a shovel. When he finished with his dogs, he shooed them away and came inside.

"Mount up," he said.

I lingered. "I figured you might need some help."

Jesse laughed. "The day Jesse James needs help getting in the saddle is the day he's dead."

I hesitated, drawing Jesse's stare.

"You seem to be a mite fearful. You think I'm gonna kill you?"

"The thought's entered my mind," I admitted.

"I give you my word I won't kill you," he said.

I felt a mite better until he finished his thought. "Not today, at least."

Untying my mule's reins, I said, "Come along, Old Abe."

Jesse cocked his head at me. "What's his name?"

"Old Abe's what I call him."

Jesse grimaced. "That's what I feared you said." He grabbed the reins to the chestnut and pulled himself into the saddle. I could tell by his clenched jaw that he hurt considerably.

I stuck my foot in the stirrup, hauled myself atop Old Abe, and followed Jesse out of the barn. "How'd you get shot?"

Jesse's eyes glazed over, and his fingers tightened into fists around the reins. "I went to Lexington to surrender. A lot of us irregulars did. Seems the terms left something to be desired. A federal soldier, irregular or not, is pardoned for any crimes he committed during the difficulty. But not us Southern boys. No, sir! We could still be brought up on state crimes by those damnable carpetbaggers."

It didn't sound fair to me, but nothing the government ever got involved in seemed fair. It wasn't enough to have the federal government standing on our necks with the same foot that had kicked our Southern butts, but we had the state government kicking us around, and the county government. We'd lost a war over slavery, but the damned government was making slaves of us all. It didn't make sense to me.

Then Jesse made an admission that shocked me.

"I wanted to be a preacher."

"If you fought sin like you fought Yankees, the devil'd be running for cover come sundown," I said, trying to make a joke of it. But Jesse didn't think it was funny.

"You ever heard of the Drake Constitution?"

I shrugged.

"April a year ago, the state adopted this new constitution. Now it gives amnesty to Union soldiers but not to

Confederate soldiers or sympathizers. Not just that, but us Southern boys can be indicted, tried, and punished in any county in the state, regardless of where we committed a crime. No way a Southern boy can get a fair shake, not when we can't even get our own kind on juries.

"This Drake Constitution won't let a Southern boy practice law or medicine or any profession," Jesse continued. "On top of that, it won't even let a Southern boy preach without risk of a five-hundred-dollar fine and six months in jail. How do you answer that?"

Not much I could say, politics being a game of lawyers, a species of reptile that even the snakes looked down on.

"That's a lot for a man to think about when he goes in to surrender," Jesse said. "I had to give it some time. I knew it was best to put the war behind me because hatred can ruin a man's soul, but I couldn't sell my soul to a law that was unjust, either. I was at Lexington with other irregulars under a flag of truce, talking about surrender with one bunch of Yankee vermin when another bunch rode up and started shooting. Didn't take me long to make up my mind after that. I was shot in the chest and just barely escaped.

"You know what it's like to cough up blood into your fist? Or empty your boot of blood? You know what it's like to lie two days in a stream, trying to cool your fevered body and fearing you'll pass out and drown?"

I shook my head that I hadn't and considered asking him if he'd ever been shot in the butt by his momma, but he kept on yammering.

"That's what amnesty was to me. Friends got me to Nebraska where my family was and my stepfather still is. When I got better, I swore I was gonna return to Missouri and repay those Yankees for all they did to me."

"An eye for an eye," I suggested.

"No, a lie for a lie," he snarled. "All we wanted before the war was to be left alone. They wouldn't let us.

All we wanted after the war was to get on with our lives. They wouldn't leave us be."

"Maybe you should move out west."

"There's Yankees there, too. Missouri's my home, and I don't plan on leaving. And if they won't let me live the way I want to live, then I'll make their lives as miserable as they've made mine."

We rode into the woods and along the creek, not saying much. I kept watch on Jesse out of the corner of my eye. He frowned and grimaced a lot, but I couldn't tell if it was from the pain of the memory or the pain of the wound.

"This is the boundary of the Samuel place," he said as we passed a pile of rocks near the creek.

I almost came to feel sorry for Jesse until I heard the hammer on his revolver click. When I turned in his direction, he had the gun cocked and wore the evil look I remembered from when he ambushed the Kansans and took my last sack of gold. "I don't like things Yankee."

I lifted my hands, mad I had trusted him. "I ain't Yankee." I was resigned to meeting my death then and there.

Jesse shook his head, then aimed his pistol and fired into Old Abe's ear. The mule collapsed on his front legs, then tumbled forward, tossing me clear before he fell on his side.

I hit the ground and jumped up, prepared to run for my life, but Jesse had already holstered his pistol.

"What'd you do that for?"

"He was a damn Yankee mule," he answered. "You called him Old Abe. He had *U.S.* branded on his flank."

"But he was just a dumb mule," I pleaded. "You take my guns, you shoot my mule. What's the matter with you?"

"I'll give you your guns when the time's right. I'll get you a good horse, one that's better than a damned old mule."

I could only shake my head.

"You'll need your saddle and tack," Jesse informed me.

I looked up at the heavens and bit my lip. Jesse'd've made a hell of a preacher. I walked over to Old Abe, bent down, and patted him on the neck. He'd saved me several times, and it didn't seem fair for him to die like that. I leaned over and whispered thanks in his ear, then started to remove the tack.

"It was just a damn mule," Jesse said. "The way we stayed alive with the irregulars was good, strong horses. A mule could run all day in the shade of an oak tree."

"He saved me a couple times."

"Hurry up. I'm tired and ready to go back."

Getting the bridle off was easy, but I had to struggle to remove the saddle from beneath the mule. Jesse didn't offer to assist, and I didn't ask him to. I didn't figure he was a good enough man to place his hand on Old Abe's hide. After tugging unsuccessfully at the stirrup under the mule's body, I scrounged around the brush and found a dead limb I could use to pry up the carcass while I extracted the saddle and saddlebags.

"You can toss the saddle behind mine," Jesse offered.

"I'd as soon carry it," I answered.

I threw my saddlebags over my left shoulder, then hoisted the saddle over my right and started back for the James place.

Jesse reined his horse around. "I didn't want a Yankee mule rotting on my place."

When we reached the farmhouse, Jesse dismounted and gave me his horse to unsaddle. I cared for the chestnut, then did a few chores in the barn, preferring the cold of the outdoors to the cold of Ma James's glare. Around noon I went into the house hoping to find a more adequate portion of food at my place, but I was disappointed as she dished out some bland mush. Jesse got the most. She gave herself a generous portion, then doled out what was left to me.

I shook my head, ate the mush, then spent the afternoon doing chores. I chopped and carried in wood for her fireplace, made a dozen trips to the creek hauling buckets of water, and milked her cow. Come supper I received the same treatment. Jesse was expecting me to help his momma until he got better, but here I was being treated like a redheaded stepchild.

I decided I'd have to do a few things for myself. I watched as Ma James cleared the table. I knew she had a few jars of preserves hidden in the pie cabinet, and by the aroma in the kitchen I knew she'd baked bread that day.

I visited some with Jesse until he got tired, then hung around the kitchen while Ma James read her Bible and eyed me warily. I outlasted her bladder, though, and she scurried outside into the cold wind to visit the outhouse.

As soon as the door shut behind her, I jumped up from my seat and ran over the the pie cabinet, jerking open the doors and finding what I had expected—a whole loaf of bread and plenty of wild plum preserves she hadn't a thought of sharing with me. Though I was tempted to tear off a hunk of bread, I heard her footfalls on the porch. I closed the pie cabinet and managed no more than a step back to my place before she charged in shivering and huffing. She eyed me suspiciously, then took her place back in the rocking chair and picked up her Bible again.

I stretched, yawned, and acted sleepy. "I'm turning in."

"Good," she answered without looking up from her Good Book.

To get upstairs to my bed in the small attic, I had to go out onto the porch and into the front bedroom, where stairs gave access to my quarters. The front bedroom was where Ma James slept while Jesse was recuperating in the back bedroom, which shared a wall and a door into the kitchen. You couldn't get from one bedroom to the other without going out onto the porch. To get back down to the kitchen I'd have to pass through Ma James's bed-

room—a challenge that would strike terror in any man—
but I was so hungry, I was desperate.

I waited a good hour after I heard her retire, then
slipped back down the stairs and angled for the door to
the porch. I heard her heavy breathing and figured she
was asleep, but the moment I touched the doorknob, she
sniffed and snorted.

"Where you going?"

"To the outhouse. I got the runs."

"Then run along." She snuggled under the cover.

I stepped outside in the cold, dashed to the outhouse,
slammed the door to sound authentic, then retreated back
to the house. Cautiously I eased onto the porch, cringing
at the sound of the creaking wood, then slipped to the
kitchen door, slowly twisting the knob and pulling it open.
I slid inside the dark room and made my way carefully
toward the pie cabinet, trying to be quiet so I wouldn't
disturb Jesse snoring in the next room.

My eyes adjusted to the darkness enough for me to
see the odd shapes of the furniture and the pie cabinet. I
made it to the cabinet without stumbling. Proud of my
stealth, I reached for the handle.

Then I saw a big shadow beside the cabinet. The
shadow moved.

"Oh, no, you don't." It was Ma James's husky voice.

The next thing I knew, my head exploded with
thousands of shooting lights. I didn't remember a thing
for a good while.

When I finally came to, the room was yellow with
low lamplight and Ma James was standing over me, her
arms crossed over her bosom and a cast-iron skillet in her
right hand.

"Looking for something?" she asked.

"Not anymore," I replied.

Chapter Twenty-eight

Jobs weren't easy to find in Missouri after the war, and good money was hard to make. That was why I was willing to risk death at Ma James's hand, either from starving at her table or being beaten with her skillet, until the weather turned warmer. Then there was Jesse—any man who would shoot an innocent mule could turn on me like a hen on a june bug.

While I was worried about living out the winter and then finding an honest job, Jesse was planning how to make an easy living. There he was resting in bed, pus still draining from his chest wound, and he was thinking about a new occupation. He wasn't interested in farming, not with me hanging around the place and doing all the winter chores. I could tell by the look in those cold blue eyes that even when he recuperated, he wasn't going to be happy working the fields.

Farming is damn boring work, unless you enjoy watching a mule's butt as you wrestle a plow through the stubborn earth. It takes patience and provides little profit for a man and his family, especially a man that wants some of the finer things in life, like a sewing machine for the little lady and a subscription to *Police Gazette* for himself. Too, farming had changed. Before the war, most folks farmed to survive. They grew their own food, made their own clothes, and bartered with their neighbors and the local storekeepers for whatever else they needed. After the war, though, crops got bigger, since most of the fields had been fallow for two or three years. If folks managed to get a crop in the ground, they generally grew more than they could eat, use, or barter.

By then the railroads had extended their iron fingers into more and more areas. The railroads meant that you no longer had to barter with your neighbors or the local storekeeper. You could sell to markets all over the place. Of course, to get your crops to those markets you had to pay steep freight rates to the railroad lines, which were mostly Yankee owned. And on top of that you probably had to take out a loan from a Yankee-run bank to get your crop in the field or your harvest to market.

If there was anything Jesse hated more than Yankees, it was the railroads and the banks they ran. I learned a lot about his politics in the evenings. When all my chores were done and Ma James was reading her Bible by the fireplace in the kitchen, I'd slip into Jesse's room to talk. His politics were simple: Do unto Yankees, then run like hell.

Every time I entered the room, I'd see his revolver pointed at me. I didn't know what he was so worried about. He had my pistol and carbine, and Ma James had knocked me so woozy I still saw double.

"A man can't be too careful, not with Yankees thick as maggots in these parts."

"You don't trust me, do you, Dingus?" I asked one night.

Jesse licked his lips, then grimaced as he shifted in bed. "I've had my doubts about you. Lord knows Ma can't stand the sight of you. She says you're a Judas."

"I ain't betrayed you."

Jesse nodded. "Not yet, but Ma says you will, and she's probably right. She don't trust Arkansawyers."

I clenched my teeth, then let out my breath, figuring I ought to go in the front room and whip the stuffing out of Ma James. I knew Jesse'd be a tad angry if I did that, but I thought certain he'd forgive me after he realized how much the beating had helped his momma's looks and disposition. I took a step toward the door, then figured my chances were better fighting Jesse than his momma.

I spun around so fast Jesse grabbed for his gun again until he realized I was no more armed than I had been when I entered the room.

"At least us Arkies had the good sense to secede from the Union," I told him. "You Missourians weren't brave enough or smart enough to figure how."

"You couldn't keep the Yankees out after you did secede, so what difference did it make? To my way of thinking that proves we're smarter than you Arkansaw-yers."

I could tell I was riling Jesse because his voice was rising and I could hear a slight wheezing from his lung wound, but I didn't care. If he shot me, his momma would have to clean up the mess. I didn't like him looking down his nose at me just because I was born in Arkansas. The way I saw it, a man born in Arkansas had as good a chance as a man born in any other state to succeed, plain and simple.

"Hell, who knows, one day we could have a president from Arkansas," I offered.

"He'd be a dumb son of a bitch," Jesse answered.

"He'd still be president."

"Only a weak-minded son of a secesh would want to be president of the Union."

Jesse had a point. Jesse also had a gun. As his hand inched toward it, I decided I didn't want to mess up Ma James's house after all.

"Maybe you're right," I admitted.

He stared hard at me, and I know I must've wilted under his gaze. "You ain't like us," he finally proclaimed. "The day those Yankee bushwhackers strung you up, you had a sour look on your face when Beryl Fudge shot that Yankee boy."

"I was about to whip him myself," I lied, still pained by Pooty's murder, "and teach him a lesson."

Jesse laughed. "Killing them's the best lesson you can teach a Yankee, because you don't have to teach him but once. And you're talking to a pretty fair Yankee teacher."

"Among the best." As I stared at Jesse, I realized just how much he enjoyed killing Yankees. It also dawned on me that you don't have to hang from a tree to be a nut. I wasn' t fond of Yankees, I admit, but I had suffered no more from them—probably less—than I had from Confederates during the war. Fact was, I just didn't have the stomach for killing Yankees the rest of my life. That's what Indians were for, anyway.

Pointing to the bandage on his chest, Jesse reminded me of something. "It was a Yankee that put a bullet in my lung when I was surrendering." He held up his left hand, wriggling his middle finger at me. I was offended until he pointed with his right hand at the missing fingertip. "It was a Yankee that clipped my finger."

My brothers Van and John had lost their lives to Yankees, and my brother Thomas had sacrificed an eye to them. That was enough, but that was war. This was peace. "The war's over, Jesse."

"No, it's not," Jesse answered angrily, "not as long as there's Yankee soldiers prowling Missouri, not as long as there's Yankee railroads overcharging us, not as long as there's Yankee banks mortgaging our places, not as long as a man can't preach if he wants. It's not safe for me to be out in the field. I can't go back to farming. Besides that, there's no excitement or money in it."

That was the nub of the matter. Farming wasn't as fun or profitable as bushwhacking had been. I could only shake my head at him. "Maybe it's time for me to move on."

Jesse raised up in his bed. "Why?"

"I'm a Judas, remember?"

"We need you."

"To chop wood, tote water, and do the other chores until Frank gets back from wherever he is? Your momma hasn't done nothing but torment me."

Jesse grinned. "The frying pan was an accident. She thought you were an assassin."

"Not just that," I answered, getting madder the more I thought about it. "I'm doing all these chores and she won't even wash my clothes when she washes your bandages. Then she calls me a Judas."

Easing back down on the thick mattress, Jesse could only shake his head. "Ma's a strong woman."

And ugly, mean, and hardheaded to boot, I thought. On top of that her cooking was so bad that if she'd prepared the Last Supper, Judas would've shared his shame with the other eleven disciples.

"She's treated me worse than a mule. At least you had the decency to plug Old Abe and put him out of his misery, rather than starving him to death." I rubbed the side of my head. It was still tender where she had walloped me with the skillet. "At meals she doesn't serve me enough to plug up a gnat's ass."

"I'll have a talk with her," Jesse offered, "tell her to loan you some of my clothes."

"I can't eat your clothes."

"No, no," Jesse said. "To wear while you're doing chores."

"I don't want any with bullet holes in them, either."

Jesse grinned. "I don't know that any of my clothes haven't been nicked by Yankee lead."

"And I want more food, even if it is bad. You've been getting a hog's share of it."

"I'm recuperating, Henry. Ma's just trying to get me well."

"While she's doing that, she's starving me. Hell, I'm doing all the work around here and you're resting in bed. Who's to say I shouldn't just move on?"

"The weather's cold, Henry. Anyway, I've been thinking about a new line of work. One that could make us wealthy."

That got my attention. I still remembered how great it felt when I hid all that Confederate gold and knew I was a rich. "This line of work wouldn't involve killing Yankees, would it? I'm not going to do that."

Jesse clucked his tongue. "Here I am trying to do you a favor and you think I'm up to no good."

I snorted. Like with most bushwhackers, his cause was his own. "Exactly what kind of work will you be doing?"

Jesse shook his head. "I'm not talking about it until Frank returns. If it doesn't stick in his craw, I'll let you know." He rolled over in bed, his sign that he was tired of talking. "Send Ma in when you leave so I can talk with her."

I returned to the front room, where Ma James glanced up from her Bible and scowled at me. "Jesse wants to see you," I announced, though I couldn't believe any man—even her own son—would ever want to see her. She looked like she'd had a severe beating with an ugly stick. I pitied the stick.

She pushed herself up from her rocking chair, then bent around and placed her open Bible in the middle of the seat. "Don't you touch my book." She wagged her finger at my nose.

"I can't read," I lied.

She lifted her nose in the air. I was tempted to plant my shoe right in her behind and see if I couldn't put it on a level with her nostrils, but she escaped before I could pay my respects.

I backed up to the fireplace, enjoying the warmth of the strong flames devouring wood I had chopped for Jesse and his momma. It wasn't long before I heard Ma James's voice rising.

"He can wash his own clothes."

Shoot her, I thought.

"And I'll not let him borrow any of yours."

I glanced at the open Bible in her chair and wondered what verses she was reading. Had to be from the Old Testament. If ever there was an eye-for-an-eye and a tooth-for-a-tooth family, it was Ma James and her brood.

"Ma, you gotta let him wear my clothes," Jesse said, his voice rising in agitation.

"And why?"

"He's doing chores outside, mostly. If some Yankee bushwhacker comes by and mistakes him for me, they might shoot him, rid us of the problem."

I heard Ma James snort, then laugh like she had swallowed some snuff. "That's a fine idea you have, Jesse, a fine idea."

Well, whether Jesse was serious or merely trying to trick his momma into loaning me some of his clothes, I felt I needed to retaliate. I looked around the kitchen and spotted her skillet. I was sorely tempted to show her how it would work as a hat, but that was the same eye-for-an-eye outlook I didn't like in the Jameses. My gaze fell upon the open Bible again. Carefully I inched toward the rocker, checking the door to Jesse's room to make sure she wasn't coming out.

Then I took a deep breath and flipped a handful of pages in the book, losing her place but good. I returned quickly to the fireplace and stood as innocently as a choirboy when she came out.

It was one of the rare times I ever saw Ma James smile, and it was a sight I hoped never to see again. Her teeth—what there were of them—looked like weathered wood.

I smirked, then edged a little closer to the fire and a little farther from her, checking to make sure she didn't have another frying pan within reach. I felt as edgy as a barrel of knives with her and a frying pan in the same room, but I clenched my jaw in defiance.

As she neared the rocker her smile melted like grease over a flame. She looked at her Bible, narrowed her eyes, and glanced up at me. I had faced cannon at the battle of Prairie Grove, but it wasn't as fearful as her cold gaze. She pointed her crooked finger at me. "Did you lose my place?"

Shaking my head, I hoped my voice didn't crack when I answered. "Nope, didn't touch it."

Wagging her finger at me, she shook her head. "You sure?"

I nodded confidently.

Her scowl evaporated. She dropped to her knees so suddenly I thought she'd been shot, even though I hadn't heard a gunshot. I figured it must be a trick to lure me to her side where she could pull a skillet from beneath her skirt and slap me up 'side the head.

"It's a sign," she cried, tears streaming down her cheeks as if a dam had broken behind her eyeballs. "It's a sign from above."

I looked at the ceiling and didn't see a damned thing. To my mind it was a sign she was another of those treeless nuts that ran in the James family.

She snatched the Bible up from the rocker and skimmed the print. "This is a miracle. There's a message here from God about my son."

I still suspected it was a trap. She'd draw me within her reach, then pound my brains into the floor with a skillet.

"It's a miracle. It's a miracle," she kept repeating.

I looked around the room. It was me and her and nobody else. No ghost and no God. It was just the two of us, and I was beginning to wonder if one of us was all there.

"I've found it!" she shouted. "I've found it!"

Finding a pot of gold couldn't have excited her more. She looked at me all wide-eyed and believing. I felt sorry for her, and for myself. My prank had turned into a religious experience. That's the way it is with zealots. No wonder Jesse had wanted to turn preacher.

Ma James held up the Bible and pointed to a verse. "First Samuel, sixteen-eighteen," she whispered, her voice breaking with emotion as she read it aloud. " 'Then answered one of the servants, and said, Behold, I have seen a son of Jesse.' "

I knew the Jameses were religious folks, but this was no more religious than drawing an inside straight in a crooked poker game.

"You don't believe me, do you?"

I shrugged.

She struggled to her feet and waddled over to me, wiping tears from her cheeks with the sleeve of her dress. She handed me the Bible and pointed her fleshy finger at the offending verse. "It means Jesse's gonna have a boy."

I jerked the Bible from her and read the passage. She was right, though she left out the part about Jesse being a Bethlehemite and his son being a cunning player of the harp, a valiant man and a man of war.

"Hey, Jesse," I called into the bedroom, "do you play the harp?" I'd about decided Jesse wasn't smart enough to play with himself, taking after his Bible-toting momma in that respect.

"What?" Jesse called. "A harp? What are you talking about?"

As I skimmed down the page, I couldn't figure out why she selected verse eighteen rather than verse twenty, unless it was because she was Baptist.

"You sure verse twenty isn't God's sign?" I challenged. " 'And Jesse took an ass laden with bread, and a bottle of wine, and a kid—' "

She interrupted me. "I thought you couldn't read."

She'd caught me. I checked to make sure no skillet was within reach before I replied. "It's another miracle," I cried, trying to display the emotion that she was feeling.

It must've worked, because she stepped closer to me and threw her arms around me, hugging me out of religious joy and crushing the Bible between our two bodies. I hadn't been this scared since I wrestled a bear cub in Fayetteville before the war.

By the time I pried her arms off me, my knees were shaking and I figured I best retire before I went crazy and took to her brand of religion.

"It's a miracle," she kept repeating. I escaped from the kitchen into the front room and up the narrow stairs to my attic bed.

The real miracle came the next morning when I got up for breakfast. I had eggs, bacon, and biscuits aplenty. She piled my plate with more food than she had in all the weeks since I had first appeared on her doorstep. After breakfast she gave me a set of Jesse's clothes to do chores in. I went outside—minus a hat so any would-be assassins would know I wasn't Jesse—and except for a quick lunch I worked all day, then past the regular supper hour. I chopped plenty of wood, as the signs showed a cold spell was approaching. Jesse'd already eaten by the time I got to the table so I didn't figure there'd be much left for me, but I had to put sideboards on my plate to hold all the ham, taters, and creamed corn she kept piling on.

When I finished up with that, she placed a bowl of cherry cobbler in front of me. Afterward she suggested I go upstairs and change, then visit some with Jesse. I went up in the attic and found she had washed and ironed my clothes.

I put on the clean clothes quickly and scurried downstairs to see Jesse and tell him his talk with his momma had worked. When I entered, Jesse's room was dark except for a single candle on the washstand. Propped on a pillow, he didn't lift a hand for his gun. I didn't understand why until I reached the foot of his bed.

Something was wrong.

The floor creaked behind me.

Before I could turn around, I felt a hand cover my mouth and the barrel of a gun poke me in the back.

There was only one explanation. Ma James had been fattening me up for the kill.

Chapter Twenty-nine

I figured I was as good as dead. What made it more galling was that Jesse just leaned back on his pillow and grinned at me.

"Looks like you need another miracle, Lomax."

I would've spat in his eye if my mouth hadn't been covered, but it was a good thing that it was because Jesse wouldn't have cared for that. I didn't know who was behind me, except that it wasn't Ma James. As many bushwhackers as there were roaming these parts, it could've been any of a hundred men or more. Whoever it was had slipped inside without rousing the hounds, though, because I had been outside all day and hadn't heard a thing. Then it hit me. Only one person could've slipped inside without the hounds barking: Frank James.

Jesse confirmed it by chuckling, not the sinister cackle he loosed when he was shooting Yankees, but a genuine laugh.

Emboldened, I opened my mouth enough to chomp down on a crescent of flesh from the palm that was smothering me. Frank howled and released his grip. He hopped back on his heels and took to mumbling something that no one could understand, Ma James not allowing curse words of any type under her roof.

Jesse laughed and slapped his thigh as Frank jumped around.

"How are you, Buck?" I said without turning around.

"Fine until you bit me."

Jesse shook his head. "Tell me what happened last night, Henry. Ma came in here this morning talking about a miracle and me gonna have a boy of my own. She said God turned the pages of her Bible."

I shook my head and pinched the bridge of my nose. "I was the only one in that room, not God." I took a deep breath. "I played a prank on your momma. It was me that turned the page, not God."

Jesse crossed his arms over his bandaged chest. "You sure it wasn't God?"

"Sure as I'm standing here."

"You don't think God might've used you to turn the pages?"

"We didn't have a talk about it, me and God. I just up and turned them myself."

Jesse smiled like he knew more about religion than I did. I didn't know how to answer him. I didn't pretend to know how God worked, but I figure he had more important things to worry about than whether I played a trick on Ma James.

"God works in mysterious ways," Jesse reminded me.

"Hell, Dingus, I just turned a couple pages."

"But it sure made Ma happy what she found, so maybe God's hand guided yours. Never seen her happier."

She'll get over it, I thought but didn't have the guts to say, not with Frank still holding his revolver.

I turned to Frank. "Where you been?"

"Kentucky."

"How was it?"

"Fine for winter. War didn't affect them up there as it did us down here. I brought us back some fine horses, barrel-chested, long-winded animals that'll do to escape any type of trouble."

Jesse nodded. "He even bought a couple extras for
you to choose one. Replace that damn mule of yours."

"Thanks," I said, thinking fellows that are planning
to escape trouble must know they're headed down that
road to begin with. I figured it was probably time for me
to cut and run.

"With Frank back, I don't reckon you'll be needing
me anymore."

Jesse pursed his lips and shook his head. "There's
good money if you stay and a chance to prove you're no
Judas."

"Money sounds good."

"Frank and I are figuring on going into banking, Lomax. You interested?"

"You gonna start a railroad, too?"

Jesse had a sinister gleam in his eye as he cocked his
head at Frank. "I hadn't thought of that, but there's a lot
of money in trains, too."

I figured they were just greening me, trying to twist
my tail and make a complete fool out of me. I had no idea
I'd given them an idea for more mischief, but apparently
I had.

"Railroads can come later," Frank said, "but right
now let's just worry about getting into the banking business."

Jesse nodded at Frank, then at me. "Lomax, you can
handle deposits. Frank and I'll handle withdrawals." Both
men laughed.

I didn't get it.

"You interested or not, Lomax?" Jesse asked.

"Is the money good?"

"It's better than farming and easier, too."

I looked at my hands, callused from chopping wood
and doing chores. "A desk job sounds fine to me."

Jesse and Frank just hurrahed.

"Good, but we'll have to bring in a few more part-
ners," Jesse said. "There's a lot to watch out for in banking."

Now, it didn't seem to me that a man who was bored

by farming wouldn't be bored by banking, though granted it would be more fun to count money than chickens.

"There's the bank over in Liberty," Jesse said. "Maybe we could ride over tomorrow and take a look around, Frank."

"You sure you feel up to a ride that long, Jesse? You're still a mite pale," I observed, thinking how odd this whole idea sounded.

I knew the boys had seen the Liberty bank before, but if they were serious about opening a bank, I guessed they needed to inspect it a little more closely, maybe even talk to the banker himself. It was just over fifteen miles from the James place to Liberty. And Kansas City wasn't but another six or seven miles beyond Liberty. "You could wait until you're feeling better and go on into Kansas City, where they've got more than one bank."

"Too far." Jesse grinned. "I want to start with a small bank."

"It may be cold tomorrow," I told him. "There was frost on the ground this morning, and clouds later."

Jesse nodded. "That's a good sign of colder weather and maybe some snow. That's not bad. It'll mean fewer people about."

Whenever he could, Jesse always saw to it that he was out when the fewest other people were. It was a habit he picked up from his bushwhacking days, and it didn't seem unusual at the time.

I was curious how much money a man stood to make in banking, but I figured Jesse didn't know. After all, he wasn't but eighteen. We talked a bit more, Frank telling about his trip to Kentucky. When it was pitch dark, Frank went into the woods and brought in the horses he had hidden there in daylight so no spy would know that he had returned. Then the three of us retired, Jesse saying we needed to get up early.

Ma James had another big breakfast for us that morning. She fretted over Jesse, saying he shouldn't be going anywhere until his wound quit draining, but he answered that it didn't bother him that much and he only wanted the doctor who visited periodically to think it did. He returned my carbine and revolver. "With Frank around, I've got someone to cover my back," he said.

Frank had saddled the horses before breakfast, so we gathered our guns and coats, leaving well before sunrise, when the air was crisp and thin. We didn't say much because our voices carried well in the morning air.

We stuck to the less-traveled roads and tugged our hats down over our eyes whenever we met someone. Even after the war, with emotions high, men like Jesse and Frank still had enemies roaming about, ready to kill them. Any chance meeting could turn deadly. Good horseflesh gave a man an edge when he was roaming the hills, and we were astride three magnificent geldings that were strong of lung and fleet of foot. Mine was a bay. I don't remember ever riding such a good-looking horse.

We arrived in town late morning and circled the courthouse, Jesse studying it intently. I thought he had come to Liberty to inspect the bank as the first step to becoming a banker. Instead it seemed like he wanted to become a politician or, worse yet, a lawyer. I always had a hard time deciding which did more damage to the regular man. I finally figured it was lawyers, because you never got a chance to kick them out of office at election time. Too, a fellow could just up and decide to become a lawyer, and nobody'd have any say in it. At least politicians stood for election and were known to buy a few votes from those of us who couldn't tell a dime's worth of difference between them. I never knew lawyers to put money in anybody's pocket but their own.

After Jesse had all but toured the courthouse, he headed down the street to the Clay County Savings Bank, a stone building with barred windows and a thick front door. Frank motioned for me to ride on with him, and we went to the other end of town, examining the place as we rode, then on down to the ferry. Frank seemed to be studying the town awfully closely for someone who'd been there many times before.

At the Missouri River ferry we waited for the flatboat to cross. The ferryman eyed me suspiciously, and I realized this was the same man I'd traded a whiskey bottle of trough water for passage.

"I seen you before, ain't I?" he asked.

"Don't remember."

"You remind me of a fellow that was riding an army mule. He owes me money for not paying me the last time he rode the ferry."

Frank rode up and gave the ferryman a nickel for each of our fares and an extra nickel for my previous trip.

"Obliged," the ferryman said, glancing at me. "The son of a bitch was riding an ugly mule, didn't have the sense to pick out a good horse like you."

Reaching the opposite bank, we stayed on the ferry to cross back over to Liberty. Frank inquired about the usual times the ferry crossed, then paid a nickel apiece for the return trip.

Riding back toward town, it dawned on me that Frank and Jesse were gathering a lot of information that didn't pertain to banking, but I couldn't quite figure it out. Frank was studying the cross streets and the buildings. As we neared the bank, we saw Jesse come out, walk to his horse, and mount. If he'd even talked to the banker, he hadn't spent much time with him.

"How'd it go?" I asked as I started to rein up my bay.

"Shut up and keep riding," Frank said under his breath.

Then I knew something smelled worse than Ma James's cooking, but for the life of me I couldn't figure out what. We rode on, never looking back over our shoulders.

Once we were out of sight of Liberty, Jesse caught up with us. "What do you think, Frank?"

"It'll work."

"It's a stone-and-brick vault with a big iron door. The bank opens at eight. Vault was unlocked when I made change. We'll need to make sure it's open when we go in. It'd save time instead of having to have a cashier open it."

"What the hell's all this have to do with starting up a bank?" I finally asked.

Jesse and Frank laughed.

"Who said anything about opening a bank?" Jesse asked me.

"You told me you've been thinking about new jobs."

"You Arkansawyers are dumber than horse manure. Have you ever robbed a bank, Henry?"

"I have to admit I haven't."

"No civilian has ever robbed a bank the way we're gonna rob it, Henry. Sure, bankers and carpetbaggers have been robbing the rest of us, but they do it all legal with the courts and the law behind them. We're just planning on getting back what's ours, what the Yankees have taken away from us."

"Somebody could get killed." A chill ran down my spine.

"And somebody could get rich, if he's got the guts for it." Jesse studied me with his cold blue eyes. "You a Judas or not?"

"I got to think about it," I answered.

Frank and Jesse shook their heads.

"No, you don't," Jesse said. "You're either in or dead. Which is it?"

It didn't take me long to decide. Jesse had a convincing way of making a point. "I'm with you."

"You Arkansawyers aren't so dumb after all."

All the way back to the Samuel place Frank and Jesse planned their new career. I thought back to the previous night and how Jesse had sounded all religious and pious when he was wondering whether God had used me to get a message to his momma. Now here he was planning to rob a bank and break one of the Ten Commandments. Dumb as us Arkansawyers might have been, we at least knew that thou shalt not steal.

It began to snow as we neared the farmhouse. Jesse

turned to me. "You're made of weak stuff, Henry, maybe because you haven't been wronged as many times as we have."

And, I thought, I hadn't been wrong as many times as he had.

"Now that you know our plan, Henry, you better not make a trip to the outhouse without letting us know, or we might think you're running away to tell the law. If you turn Judas on us, we'll string you up like the disciples hung him."

Though I knew Judas had hung himself, I didn't think Jesse would care to be corrected on a religious matter.

"You ride with us, Henry, and we'll make you a rich man. You ride against us, we'll make you a dead man."

Like I said, Jesse had a knack for convincing people to go along with him. When we got back to the place it was just after dark, and Ma James had a big meal ready, though I wasn't very hungry. I retired early that night. Sleep was long in coming, especially since I could hear Frank and Jesse through the ceiling talking about how they needed to keep an eye on me.

Over the next couple weeks nine different men visited the James brothers in ones and twos. They were bushwhackers and about as ignorant a collection of humans as I'd ever seen. There was Oliver Shepherd, Bud and Donny Pence, Frank Gregg, James and Bill Wilkerson, Joab Perry, Red Monkus, and Ben Cooper. They spoke in whispers, especially when I was nearby. They didn't trust anyone who hadn't murdered, maimed, and pillaged with them.

Jesse would send each man to Liberty to look over the town and get acquainted with it before the robbery. Knowledge of the terrain, good timing, and the best horses a man could buy—or steal—were essential.

Jesse planned the robbery like a military operation. He named three men to watch one end of the street, three to watch the other end, and three to hold the ferry. Frank and Jesse were going to rob the bank, and they ordered me to enter the building with them. I began to sweat, even if it was February. Though greatly honored to have such a distinguished place in what was to be the first civilian bank robbery in the United States, I couldn't help but fear they planned to shoot me on their way out.

Jesse finally announced the date of the robbery as the day before St. Valentine's Day. We left the James place the day before that, meeting the others near Liberty. We then split up into our groups and made separate camps so as not to create extra suspicion.

Morning came early. We arose without breakfast, saddled our mounts, and headed toward Liberty, arriving just after eight o'clock when Clay County Savings Bank opened up. Jesse, Frank, and I rode the length of town, Jesse checking that all the men were in place. Satisfied that everything was in order, he turned to Frank. "How does it feel?"

"Like old times," he answered.

They both looked at me.

I grinned as best I could.

"Lomax, you remember you're to cover the door and not let anybody come in behind us. If you skip out on us, the other men have instructions to shoot you down."

Shrugging, I nodded. "Thanks for your confidence in me."

As our mounts neared the bank, my stomach began to churn with the anticipation of being shot. The three of us dismounted and stepped up to the bank door.

I was about to learn that bank robberies are like marriages. No matter how well they're planned, something's bound to go wrong from the beginning.

Chapter Thirty

Before I entered the bank, I looked up at the cold, leaden February sky. How had I let myself get into this predicament? Placing my hand on the door, I realized my whole arm was shaking.

I followed Jesse and Frank inside. They were wearing long overcoats with their collars up and their hats low. After closing the door behind me, I stood there shivering. The bank was empty except for two clerks working at their desks behind stacks of bills and coins. One, an older fellow, frowned at us, but the other offered us the kind of smile that comes from handling someone else's money. The young fellow pushed himself away from his desk and stepped toward the counter, smiling all the way.

Frank eased over to the potbellied stove to warm himself while Jesse sidled up to the counter so it screened the movement of his hand as he lifted his pistol.

I was so scared I feared I'd wet my pants or get shot. Either way I'd be leaking something on the floor before we escaped.

The young teller looked at me. "That cold, is it, out there?"

My head was already shaking, so I don't know if the teller realized I'd nodded.

With a wave of his arm he motioned to the stove. "Help yourself. The warmth's free."

I was so nervous I stuttered. "I-I c-c-can't. I g-gotta to watch the d-d-door." Before the teller had a chance to consider my stupid remark, he found himself staring down the barrel of Jesse's revolver. I was supposed to watch the street but found my gaze fixed on Jesse and Frank instead.

"Morning," Jesse said, "We've come to make a withdrawal."

The teller backed toward his desk as Jesse bounded over the counter. Before I could blink, Frank ran around the counter as well and stood with his gun in the gut of the older banker.

"We want all your valuables," Jesse commanded.

The young teller stood in a daze while the older banker looked toward the open door of the walk-in vault. With his pistol Jesse hit the young clerk on the shoulder, then pushed him toward the vault. "We want the valuables *now*." He jerked a cotton wheat sack from his coat pocket and shoved it in the clerk's hand. "Move."

As the clerk turned about, Jesse pushed him again.

Frank waved his pistol at the older man. "Get in and help."

"Just a minute, good sir," he protested.

"Get moving or get shot." Frank cocked his pistol.

His eyes widening, the banker scurried to join the other teller. Together the two filled the sack as fast as their windmilling arms could move. They dropped a lot of bills, and I figured it was because they were as nervous as I was, but Jesse didn't see it that way.

"Quit dropping money. You're just trying to keep a little for yourselves," he said.

Not another bit of money hit the floor.

When they were done, the young teller looked up and offered the bag to Jesse. "That's all the money."

Jesse shoved the bag back and waved his pistol at the shelves lining the vault's back wall. "We want all the papers, too."

The tellers looked at each other and sighed.

"My trigger finger's getting impatient," Jesse observed.

The two men turned and started stuffing papers in the sack. By the time Jesse let them quit, they had cleaned that vault like a buzzard strips meat from bone.

Jesse jumped inside the vault, jerked the bulging bag from the cashier's hand, and backed out. Frank released the hammer on his revolver and holstered it as he stepped to the vault door. He pushed the heavy iron panel, its stiff hinges groaning.

"Don't lock us in," cried the older man. "No one else knows the combination."

Jesse laughed. "You should've told someone."

The door clanged shut on their protests, but Frank had trouble turning the spring mechanism that locked it. Jesse ran to the desks and scooped up the remaining cash. Frank fumbled with the door, growling at its stubbornness. "I can't lock it."

"Don't worry," Jesse yelled loud enough for the two caged bankers to hear. "If they come out too early, we'll shoot them."

During this whole time I was shaking like a leaf, trying to keep my bladder from releasing.

Jesse, though, was calm as a preacher at a Sunday picnic. He dropped his pistol back in its holster, then tugged down his hat and pulled up his collar. He tied a knot around the neck of the bulging wheat sack and looked at me with a wide grin.

"I enjoy banking, Henry, but I see you're not cut out for it."

"It-it's the c-c-cold," I managed, my words as broken as my confidence.

Jesse grinned. "Then why don't you just stay here by the fire while me and the boys leave town."

I didn't think that a good idea. I'd been roped into helping these fellows, but I didn't figure the law or the townfolk would look too kindly on that argument, espe-

cially not when they found out the gang had cleaned out
their savings. It was fine and good to talk about what
bastards the Yankee carpetbaggers were and how Jesse
planned to take their money, but in the vault the money
all looked the same. There was no way of knowing what
was carpetbagger money and what was not.

Calmly Jesse let Frank precede him toward the door.
Frank pulled it open, poked his head outside, and looked
both ways down the street. "All's quiet," he told Jesse,
then exited, Jesse following. Both moved calmly to their
horses.

For a moment I was petrified. It was as if I had
actually drained my bladder and then been frozen to the
floor in the puddle. Outside everything was quiet. Then
I saw the vault door begin to inch open and the old banker's head peek out and look straight at me.

Suddenly I was no longer paralyzed. I spun around
and ran for the door, slamming it behind me. Jesse and
Frank, both sitting easily in their saddles, looked at me
like I'd shot off a cannon.

"The bankers got out."

Jesse turned his horse toward the river. Frank fell in
behind him, both riding at a leisurely gait. I tried to walk
to my horse, but my feet wanted to run. What composure
I maintained was shattered when I heard a door slam,
then two men yelling.

"The bank's been robbed! The bank's been robbed!"

I heard footsteps around the side of the bank and
glimpsed the young teller running for the street. Someone
fired a gun and sent the teller retreating behind the building. All around us, men on the street reached for their
guns or dove for cover while others came out of buildings
to see what the ruckus was about.

At the hitching post I untied my mount, but the moment I did he spooked and reared. It was all I could do
to cling to the reins as I grabbed the saddle horn and
pulled myself aboard.

Gunfire broke out from all directions. Men on the

plank sidewalks shot at us, and Jesse's men galloped down the street firing back. They had grins on their faces and seemed to be enjoying all the excitement. I was still fighting my horse for a ride. The moment I got both feet in the stirrups, the gelding bolted. I ducked low as a half-dozen men fired at me.

Somehow I made it to the edge of town without getting hit. Only then did I recall Jesse's instructions to leave by the opposite end of town and the ferry instead of the road to Kearney. I'd made good time, but in the wrong direction. If I got separated from the others, I was as good as dead.

I jerked my horse around and galloped back toward the river, taking more shots. Everything was a blur as I raced through town again—everything except two bodies sprawled on the sidewalk. One was perfectly still, and the other was thrashing in pain. I pitied them both and instantly regretted my part in this crime.

But the city folks didn't seem to understand my regret, because they kept firing at me. Somehow I made it past the good citizens of Liberty again and figured I was safe.

But the feeling was only momentary. At the end of the road I saw the ferry inching away from the landing.

"You sons of bitches!" I yelled, then slapped my horse, whistled, and screamed. "Wait for me!"

Grinning, Jesse waved with one hand and held the wheat sack up with the other. I slapped the reins against my mount's neck, trying to get every ounce of speed out of the animal. He was strong, and his lengthy stride took me quickly to the landing. There he flinched and threatened to bolt, but I slapped him onward, and he leaped toward the ferry and Jesse.

Jesse's smile disappeared faster than a jigger of whiskey at a meeting of drunks. All the riders tried to get their horses out of the way as we soared toward them.

My horse's front feet landed on the space just evacuated by Jesse. I pulled back savagely on the reins. All around me men cursed and horses screamed in terror.

Next my mount's back feet landed on the edge of the ferry, then thrashed to get a hold on the slick deck. The collisions between my horse and others slowed us enough so I could stop him before he charged off the opposite end.

My heart was pounding so loud I didn't hear all the curses being thrown at me. It beat even faster when I looked behind me at Liberty. The townsmen were mounting horses and galloping to the landing.

My saddle was suddenly warm and wet. I prayed the others wouldn't notice.

I knew the Missouri River separated us and would until the ferry returned to pick them up. Even though our horses were bigger, faster, and stronger than theirs, it wasn't a good feeling knowing that men with guns'd be chasing and shooting at us.

It seemed forever before the ferry touched the landing on the other side. As we raced off, one of the robbers, a lean muscular fellow, rode by the ferryman and scooped him up. "Let's go for a ride," the ruffian said.

The ferryman struggled, but the bandit swung him around on the horse's rump. "Be still if you want to live!" he yelled. The ferryman grabbed his captor around the waist and held.

As we raced away from the river, the sky began to spit snow at us. About a mile from the ferry the ferryman's captor shoved him off the horse. The ferryman screamed and hit the ground hard, rolling in the dirt. I glanced around and saw him get up on his wobbly feet.

A half mile farther on, Jesse eased his mount to a trot, and everyone else slowed with him. He looked at me and shook his head. "We appreciate you covering our retreat, Henry." Everyone laughed but me. He twisted around in the saddle, taking a quick count of his gang. "We started with twelve and still got twelve."

"Henry only counts as a half," Frank said.

Once again everyone laughed but me.

"Anybody get hit?" Jesse wanted to know.

None of us had a scratch, unless you counted my damaged pride.

As Jesse talked, the snow came down harder. "It'll be a while before the ferry crosses the river again and brings men after us. If this snow keeps up, it'll cover our tracks, so let's split up and meet at the regular place tonight and divide out the loot."

I didn't know where the regular place was, but I didn't say a thing. I figured it would be best if I rode my own way once everyone split up. That way I could wash my hands of this sorry act and do something honest for a living. I'd about decided Jesse'd've made a poor preacher—but a hell of a lawyer.

As the robbers broke up, I started down the road, hoping my departure wouldn't be noticed. I was quickly disappointed.

"Henry," called Jesse, "where you heading?" He steered his mount toward me, shaking his head all the way. "Dammit, I knew you just didn't have the heart for this kind of work."

"It ain't decent, Jesse."

"Neither's the Drake Constitution. That's what drove me to this. If the damn Yankees won't give us what's ours by right, we'll take what's theirs by wrong."

I tugged my coat collar around my neck, trying to shut out the cold. Maybe Jesse was right. There'd been wrong on both sides, no doubt, but the damn Yankees were rubbing our noses in defeat with their damned unfair laws that took advantage of us. Even so, what Jesse had done was wrong.

"How come you didn't ask where we were to split the money?" he demanded.

"I figured on just riding on."

He grimaced and shook his head. "Can't let you do that, not so soon after we started into banking."

I bit my lip, realizing I should've just let my horse

keep on running out the opposite end of town so I'd never have to see Jesse or his kind again.

"You might run to the Yankee law and tell them who was involved. No, sir, you're staying with us until I say it's time for you to go or decide to kill you. What I can't figure, Henry, is how you had the grit to kill Beryl Fudge."

"We got to discussing politics," I answered.

About that time Frank sidled over on his mount. "We best ride, Jesse, in case someone crosses the river after us."

Jesse nodded, then looked at me. "Don't pull your weapon unless we run into trouble."

We started south, then circled to the east and hit the Missouri several miles downstream. We crossed the river on another ferry and paid the ferryman a quarter apiece for getting out in the bad weather. Then we circled back north and finally approached the Samuel farm well after dark.

While Jesse carried the money into the house, Frank and I fed and watered the horses, then took our carbines and Jesse's into the kitchen.

Ma James had cold bacon, taters, and bread waiting for us. Like all her cooking it left something to be desired, but it was food, and we hadn't had any since the night before. After she retired, Jesse grabbed the wheat sack and planted it in the center of the table.

"I'm a bit tired," he announced to me and Frank. "I'll rest until the others show up to divide out the money." He stood up and stretched, then slipped into his bedroom and reclined on his bed without taking off his muddy boots.

Frank was decent as far as bandits went and tried to convince me I shouldn't be worried. "None of us'll hurt you as long as you play straight and don't turn against us."

Shrugging was the only answer I could give.

"He would've taken your guns if he didn't trust you," Frank said. "Besides, if you tried to get one of us, the

other'd plug you. Just don't leave here without us agree-
ing it's time."

"Yankees won't let you Missouri boys practice the
profession you want, and you won't let me come and go
as I want."

"War's an odd thing," Frank replied, "but peace is
even odder."

"The war goes on as long as you ride with the irregulars."

"Maybe." Frank nodded. "But those men you can
trust your life with. Those men are the only friends Jesse
and me've got and the only men we can trust."

As we waited, Frank made a pot of coffee. We drank
and visited until almost midnight, when the other robbers
began arriving in ones and twos. After they all crowded
into the kitchen, Frank roused Jesse, who joined us.

"Fellows, we hurt the carpetbaggers," he said. He
thumped the sack like it was a watermelon, then untied
the knot and dumped the contents on the table.

The bills and papers were all mixed together, and
everybody gathered to sort the loot. When it was done
and the money was in neat stacks, Jesse and Frank
counted the bills, ignoring the papers to the side. When
they added up the total, we caught our breath.

"There's more than fifteen thousand dollars there,"
Jesse said. "That comes to some twelve hundred and fifty
dollars apiece."

Everybody gasped.

"That's a lot of money," Jesse said, "especially for us
not to have taken any casualties."

I remembered the two civilians sprawled on the walk
in Liberty. The money had their blood on it. I didn't want
my share.

Then Jesse pointed at the papers piled at the other
end of the table. "Them's bonds. They may be worth
something, but you can't spend them like you can cash.
Anybody want any of them?"

"Get rid of them," said one of the bandits. "We want
things we can spend."

I saw Jesse grin at Frank. The son of a bitch had pulled one over on his band. I didn't know how much the bonds were worth, but the stack looked to be at least twice the value of the cash. Seemed to me Jesse was doing the same thing to his friends that he despised the Yankees for doing to them.

Jesse started doling out the money to each member of the gang. He shoved a pile of bills at me.

"It ain't right," I said.

Every man around the table stared at me.

Jesse nodded. "We'll sort yours out after everybody leaves. They need to get home so the Yankee law won't be suspicious."

After the money was divided out, it took another thirty minutes for all the men to slip out in ones and twos, leaving me and the James brothers around the table. When they were gone, Jesse shoved my stack of bills closer to me.

"It ain't right," I said.

Jesse's blinking eyes narrowed. "We can fix it."

I shook my head. "I'm tired and want some rest." I stood up and walked out of the kitchen onto the porch, careful not to let my hand near my pistol. As I closed the kitchen door, I saw Frank and Jesse gathering up the papers along with my stack of money. I lingered, my ear pressed against the wall, trying to hear what they were talking about.

"He's a smart one," Jesse said, "the only one that knew what the bonds might be worth."

For a minute they didn't say anything, and I wondered what they were doing until I heard a low whistle I took to be Jesse's.

"There's more than forty-five thousand dollars' worth of bonds here," he announced.

Both men laughed.

"He can cause trouble if he lets the others know," Frank said.

"He just wants his share. We'll tell him there's ten thousand dollars in bonds, give him three thousand dollars," Jesse suggested.

"Think he'll go for that?"

"I figure he doesn't have any choice."

They laughed again.

I swallowed hard, knowing I was running out of choices on the James place.

Chapter Thirty-one

Come morning Frank and Jesse were waiting for me at the breakfast table. Their mother stood behind them, frying bacon. At my place was a stack of money as well as a handful of bonds.

Jesse nodded. "There's your share of money and bonds, Henry. You knew these papers were worth something. Thanks for not creating a stir in front of the others."

I pulled up a chair and sat down.

"We counted them out," Frank said, "and they came to almost ten thousand dollars' worth."

Jesse announced, "We've figured out your cut. In addition to the money, there's four thousand dollars in bonds."

"I ain't interested in blood money," I said, "not this way. My momma taught me not to steal." I saw Ma James flinch.

Jesse and Frank looked at each other.

"We'll keep it a spell for you," Jesse said. "Just let us know when you're ready to leave, and we'll give it to you."

"I'm ready to leave."

Jesse shook his head. "Too soon after the robbery."

Biting my lip, I studied Frank, then Jesse. "You better end it now, boys. Maybe you can get away with this robbery, but every time you steal from a bank, you're shortening your life. Your momma was proud of that prophecy that you'd have a boy, Jesse. If you keep on robbing, you'll be nothing but a crook and wind up in jail or worse. You wouldn't want any son of yours to know you were a thief. If you keep robbing folks, some innocent people are going to get killed."

"Aren't no innocent Yankees," Jesse argued.

"The war's over, Jesse."

He nodded. "But the Yankees are still here."

"Give it up, Jesse. Don't rob any more banks. Lead a decent life like your momma taught you."

I thought I saw Ma James wipe a tear from the corner of her eye, but it was probably venom.

Jesse picked up my share of the money and thumbed through it. "You sound like a man that'd turn us in to the federals." He stared at me with those cold, blinking eyes.

Determined not to let him cow me, I glared back. "I sound like someone that's talking sense."

Jesse grabbed the bonds and pointed his finger at me. "Don't you be leaving this place until I tell you to. If you do, we'll figure you for a traitor—and you know what we do to Yankees."

"I know."

Nothing else was said during breakfast. The rest of that day we all moped around with our tails between our legs. Bad as I felt, I felt even worse two days later when Frank came in from Kearney carrying a newspaper with an account of the bank robbery. It was mostly lies, as newspaper stories tend to be. Jesse read it first and seemed pleased, but as I read it, I gritted my teeth. Two civilians had been shot, and one, a college student little more than my age, had died.

The story seemed to affect Ma James, too. A day later she took a bad case of the vapors and wouldn't leave her bed. She was as despondent as a mule with hopes for children. At the time I didn't realize she was giving me the chance I was waiting for to escape. All I could think

of was having to pass her every time I went up the stairs
to my room; there wasn't a time I went by that I didn't
pray her frying pan was still in the kitchen. My ears still
rang from the bashing she'd given me the night I was
foraging for food.

Jesse announced her condition and what it meant to
me. "Ma's not well. Sometimes she gets like this, and it's
a week or two before she's herself again."

I figured the new her might be an improvement over
the old but kept that sentiment to myself.

"So's we don't starve, Frank and I decided we'd have
you do all the cooking."

"That's woman's work," I said.

"Somebody's got to do it."

"Why don't you?"

"Because it's woman's work." He laughed.

I couldn't hide my scowl.

"You can always leave." By the way he said it I knew
it was a threat.

I swallowed my pride, figuring a little time would
help me plan my escape. For three days I chopped wood,
hauled water, cooked meals, and cleaned up afterward. I
quickly learned why a man needs a wife. One day I even
boiled and washed clothes. Of course, Jesse and Frank
were happy not to be doing woman's work, but they wer-
en't satisfied with my laundry or my cooking. They complained the bacon was burnt, the biscuits soggy in the
middle, the beans not done, the coffee too weak, and
something wrong with everything else I did. I took Ma
James her meals, but she had too big a dose of the vapors
to really care what I was feeding her.

I thought about poisoning the whole family but didn't
have any poison or know how to make any. It'd probably
take more than I could tote to kill Ma James, anyway, so
I gave up on that idea.

On the fourth day I announced to Jesse I was taking
the shotgun out in hopes of killing some game I could
make stew with. After gathering my coat, I took a butcher

knife from the table and tucked it behind my belt. Then I reminded Jesse I was going hunting, not running out on him. If he trusted me, I figured I wouldn't get shot in the back. If he didn't trust me, he'd be putting me out of my misery.

The air was chilly as I stepped out on the porch and angled for the woods. I hoped I might jump a couple rabbits for stew, although I didn't know how to make stew other than throw stuff in a pot, boil it, and hope for the best.

I was slipping through the trees and brush, trying to find a little game and not having much luck. I passed a thicket of sassafras bushes and then stopped under a sassafras tree to look around. All that sassafras brought back memories of Cane Hill and Momma slipping some in our coffee to purge our systems. I could remember my tail burning and everybody lined up at the outhouse, imploring whoever then occupied it to hurry up and give someone else a shot at it. Sometimes I'd be too sore to sit for a couple days. That sassafras brought back bad thoughts. I moved on.

Then it hit me like a preacher hits sin. Maybe it was time I purged the James family. I'd slip so much sassafras in their food and drink that the fire from their tails would scorch a hole in their drawers. And while they were purging and fanning their backsides, I'd get on my horse and ride away. I'd dose them up so good they couldn't sit in a saddle for a week.

I forgot about rabbits and returned to the sassafras tree. I sliced off slivers of bark and put them in my coat pocket until it bulged. I'd start with a small dose in their coffee in the morning, then hit them with so much they'd be fighting among themselves for the outhouse.

When I returned to the house, I put the shotgun in the corner by my carbine and carefully hid the sassafras bark behind the pie cabinet. Jesse startled me when he came out of his bedroom and found me bent over the floor by the cabinet.

"What's a matter?"

"Thought I saw a mouse," I replied.

"That the best game you could come up with?"

"So far."

Jesse shook his head. "You're no better a hunter than a robber."

He went out on the porch, heading for the front room to check on his momma. When he came back inside he was shaking his head.

"She's still down with the vapors."

"She don't like it you've taken to robbing banks, Jesse."

Jesse hotly disputed my claim. "She hates Yankees same as the rest of us. She knows what the Yankees did to us."

I was damned tired of hearing about the bastard Yankees. There're people who always blame their problems on somebody else. I know from time to time I've felt that way when life dealt me a poor hand and some lesser soul a better one, but I learned how to deal with it, usually turning to a bottle and drinking myself silly to forget. Ma James, though, didn't allow liquor in her house. She didn't even allow swearing. I figured there were other things she didn't allow, but I didn't know of any men who'd want to find out, judging by the looks of her.

Jesse went back to his room, and I went back to my chores. The next morning I built a fire, made double-strength coffee, had me a cup, then boiled the coffee again, doctoring it with some sassafras bark. Then I set about frying salt pork and making biscuits. I'd finally learned how to get the center of my biscuits done, the only problem being that when the center was done the outside looked like a lump of coal. When Frank and James came to the breakfast table, they looked at the biscuits, then held their noses.

"You'd make a poor wife for some old boy," Jesse said.

"How do you expect me to cook when I don't have

any tinned foods, no flavorings, nothing to make sweets with?"

Jesse nodded. "He's got a point. We do have money to spend."

"I'll go to town," I volunteered.

Grinning, Jesse shook his head. "Nice try, Henry. You're staying around here."

"I'll go to Kearney," Frank volunteered. "It'd be good to hear if they've pinned down anything on the bank robbery."

While they discussed that, I loaded up a plate of bacon and burnt biscuits for Ma James and poured her a dose of coffee. I excused myself and delivered the stuff. She sat up in bed, her jowls sagging like her spirits, looked at my plate, and grimaced. I could tell my food was contributing to her low spirits. I told myself I'd give her a double dose of everything.

When Frank left for town, I grabbed the shotgun and butcher knife and went out in the woods looking for rabbit or squirrel or possum or raccoon or anything that wouldn't attack me if I shot it. I didn't find any critters, though I sliced off some more sassafras bark, then dug up some roots. Back at the house I hid it once again, still biding my time. Frank returned before noon with supplies.

"You ain't got any excuses now for your sorry cooking," he warned me.

"And you won't have any excuses for not eating it and cleaning every bite off your plate."

"I don't know about that," Frank shot back as Jesse entered from his bedroom.

"Any news from town?"

Frank grinned. "The folks of Liberty have put up a reward for the bank robbers. Ten thousand dollars."

Jesse whistled. "That's almost as much as they lost. You don't think the tellers were holding out on us, do you?"

Frank shrugged. "I thought we cleaned them out."

"Let me ask you a question," Jesse said. "If you had

money, you wouldn't put all of it in a Yankee bank, would you? You'd save some back for yourself."

That ten-thousand-dollar reward worried me. I figured with that much money one or two of the gang might let their conscience and their greed get the best of them and turn the rest of us in. Fact was, I wasn't the only one with second thoughts.

Frank and Jesse looked at one another, then at me. Jesse lifted his finger and pointed at my nose. "You wouldn't be one that might turn us in for a reward, now, would you?"

"After all you've done for me? What'd make you think that?"

Jesse gave me a hard look, and I pretty much figured my days were numbered. As long as Ma James was bedridden with the vapors I figured I was safe, but once she was up and doing chores again, I didn't know that Jesse and Frank would need me for anything but target practice.

I offered the boys some of my sassafras-laced coffee and poured them each a steaming cup.

Jesse took a sip and nodded. "Your coffee's getting better, Henry, now that you're making it stronger."

"It's got a bit of a kick to it," Frank added.

I grinned, knowing it had more kick than a mule. They flattered me by taking another cup. After they retired to Jesse's room, I grabbed my coat, shotgun, and butcher knife and went out into the woods again, hunting for game and more sassafras. As I was pulling up roots, I flushed a pair of cottontail rabbits and killed them both with well-thrown rocks to the head. After stuffing my coat and pants pockets with sassafras root and bark, I grabbed the two rabbits by their hind legs and started back for the house.

Frank stood on the porch watching me approach.

I held up the rabbits. "Supper," I announced.

"Didn't hear any shots," Frank said.

"Killed them with rocks. I've always been a pretty good throw. Care to clean them?"

Frank shook his head. "Not my job. I'll take the shotgun inside while you clean them."

I handed Frank the shotgun and went to skin and gut the rabbits. They were skinny, not much flesh on their bones, but they would do for stew meat. I carried them inside, cut the meat off, and dropped the pieces in a pot. Then I looked at the supplies Frank had bought. There was flour, cornmeal, sugar, a sack of potatoes, a sack of carrots, a box of soda crackers, and all sorts of tinned food.

"Looks like we'll be eating well tonight," I said.

Frank nodded. "Plenty of food'll bring up Ma's spirits."

I didn't want that just yet, but I didn't care to announce that to Frank. I feared he was going to watch me cook supper, but he slipped into Jesse's room, where I could hear them talking quietly.

When I finally screwed up my courage, I emptied my pockets of sassafras and dumped it into the pot with the meat. Then I poured in just enough water to cover the roots. I wanted my medicine to be strong as an ox. To cover the aroma of the boiling sassafras I grabbed a blob of grease and dumped it in a skillet that I set on the fire. As the grease melted and sizzled, I peeled and chopped some potatoes and carrots and threw them into the pot, along with more water, canned tomatoes, corn, and beans. I let the stew simmer all afternoon, then removed the bits and pieces of sassafras as it got close to suppertime. Before I announced supper, I boiled another strong batch of coffee, set a cup aside for me, then added sassafras to give it a little punch.

Frank and Jesse came into the kitchen, and Frank went to check on his momma.

"Care for some mud?" I asked Jesse.

He nodded but seemed a mite uncomfortable when I glanced at the corner where they usually kept the shotgun. It was gone, as was my carbine. They obviously didn't want me handling any more weapons, and that was a bad sign.

I was surprised when Ma James came with Frank to the table. It was the first time she'd joined us in days. Nervously I filled three bowls with stew, hoping I'd removed all the sassafras pieces, and carried them to the table. "Ya'll go ahead while it's hot. I've got to get soda crackers."

I was relieved when everybody started eating. I got a platter of crackers and passed them around. After a few bites Ma James announced she'd feel up to cooking the next day.

Frank said, "This stew ain't bad. Ain't you gonna eat any?"

I shook my head. "It smelled so good, I ate some before you came to the table."

Jesse savored a bite. "Got a touch of a whang to it I can't identify."

"Coffee," I lied. "I spilt a bit in it when I was pouring a cup."

"Not bad," Jesse said. "Real shame we finally got you cooking better and Ma feels up to coming back."

After the meal I cleared the dishes and filled two bowls I left on the porch for the hounds. Then I retired to my room and gathered my few belongings, ready to escape at the first opportunity. For a long time I kept watch on the outhouse. I was starting to worry that my plan had failed, but sometime after midnight I heard Ma James scurry out of her room and onto the porch. I glanced out my narrow window and shortly saw her running through the moonlight toward the outhouse.

She was no more done than Frank was waiting, then Jesse. While they were all out of the house, I ran downstairs and into Jesse's room, found my carbine and revolver under the bed, carried them into the kitchen, and hid them behind the cabinet.

As they came in, I ran out like I was headed for the outhouse, but I went to the barn and saddled the bay. When I returned, I heard Jesse and Frank moaning in his room.

"I got a bad case of the runs," I announced. "Some of them tinned vegetables must've been spoilt. Maybe that was what gave it the whang, not the coffee."

No sooner were the words out of my mouth than Frank and Jesse raced each other outside. Quickly I got my carbine, strapped on my revolver, and ran outside, bumping into Ma James. I feared she would see I was carrying my carbine and belongings, but she just groaned and went on into her bedroom.

I stepped past the two hounds, but they didn't bark, just whimpered and rolled over. I ran on to the barn, shoved my carbine under my scabbard, and tied my bed-roll and belongings down on my horse. I cracked the barn door in time to see Frank jump out of the outhouse and Jesse run in. When he closed the door, that was the last I saw of Jesse James for sixteen years.

But I heard him for a bit longer, moaning between explosions, as I led my horse out of the barn toward the road. It was all I could do to keep from laughing and giving my escape away.

Once I got clear of the Samuel place, I did what I should've done when I left Cane Hill. I turned west to find my fortune, even if it did mean I'd have to start out in Kansas.

Chapter Thirty-two

When I ran out on Jesse James, he wasn't the bad man he would later become. If he hadn't robbed that first bank and gotten the taste for easy money, he might never have robbed the second and then the trains. Few people had heard of Jesse James when the war ended, but five years later his name was well known throughout the West.

I never planned on running into Jesse James again, figuring he'd shoot me on sight, particularly if his bottom had a memory of our final night together. After I left him in the outhouse, I spent the next sixteen years out west. I made some money on occasion, enough to be called a fortune, but I couldn't hang on to it any better than I had the Confederate gold.

Too, every time my luck started going good, something came along that changed everything. Things had been looking fine in Tombstone, Arizona Territory, for a while, until I got caught between two bands of skunks that couldn't stand each other but smelled about the same to all the rest of us. When I stood my ground and didn't throw in with either group, they both took it hard, deciding they'd just up and shoot me. Well, I got out of Tombstone and headed about as far north as I could go without speaking Canadian and wound up in the Dakotas, but it was cold there, and I got down in my boots, figuring I ought to go back home and see Momma before she died. I'd gotten word through Lissa, who'd taken up acting and occasionally ran into me out west, that Pa had died and Momma wasn't well off.

I always wanted to return home, but I wanted to return a success, not the miserable failure I was. I wanted Momma to be proud of me, and she couldn't be proud of a drifter who took to the bottle now and then and didn't have a wife and family or anything else to show for it. Some men I'd met over the years had made names for themselves, like Buffalo Bill Cody and Wild Bill Hickok. Me, all I made out of myself was a fool.

In March of 1882 I decided to head home. I caught a river steamer up in the Dakotas and floated down the Missouri River on the early spring thaw. My plan was to ride the river all the way down to the Mississippi, get off at Cape Girardeau or Memphis, and buy or steal a horse to get back to Cane Hill. I had a little money on me, so I was feeling pretty good until I wound up in a card game.

My luck was running hot, and I had tripled my money before one sorehead blamed my good luck on an ace that happened to have fallen out of my sleeve. Well, the bastard accused me of being a card cheat! I explained that I was merely trying to keep him alert so he couldn't accuse me of cheating when I cleaned him out. He didn't much buy that explanation but was a good sport about it and offered to give me a bath for free.

He and his buddies threw me in the Missouri. I was wet and cold when I crawled out onto the muddy banks that night and angled for the nearest town, every dog and rooster announcing my arrival. I was also broke and unarmed. My clothes looked like a wagon had run over them, and I didn't look much better. I didn't know what I was going to do, but I decided I had to do something so I wouldn't embarrass my momma when I finally made it back to Cane Hill.

I learned the town was St. Joseph, Missouri, and I

wandered aimlessly about until stores opened up. I inquired at several about jobs, but my shoes were still squishy with Missouri River water, my clothes hadn't fully dried, and I probably smelled like dead fish. That wouldn't have kept me from hiring a man for a job, but it sure kept those Missourians from offering me anything other than a scowl.

It was midmorning when I walked out on the street and bumped into a well-dressed, bearded gentleman carrying as a cane the biggest umbrella I'd ever seen. I looked at him, figuring to tell him to watch where he was going, and he stared back at me, his eyelids blinking like crazy. I thought the morning sun must've been angling into his eyes because I'd never seen a man blink so much since Jesse James.

My eyes widened to the size of wagon wheels, my mouth fell open, and my knees suddenly felt as mushy as my shoes.

I was standing face to face with Jesse James!

I thought—I prayed—he didn't recognize me.

"Good man," he said, "you look down on your luck. Care to come home to eat with me? My wife is fixing a pot of sassafras stew."

I gulped and was speechless for a moment. Jesse was wearing a coat, a fine derby, and leather gloves, probably to hide the missing fingertip on his left hand. By the bulges beneath his coat I took him to be well armed. He carried the umbrella in his right hand, and hidden among its cloth folds I saw the stock of a carbine. I knew I couldn't turn down his hospitality.

"Been a long time since I had sassafras stew."

"Sixteen years, I'd say."

I nodded.

Jesse pointed down the street. "Home's that way."

I started walking, and Jesse fell in beside me.

"Folks around here call me Mr. Howard, Thomas Howard."

"I'm Henry Lomax."

"I know. I wondered what ever happened to you, Henry. After you stole our horse, we got to figuring you must've dosed our stew with sassafras. Frank found where you'd cut the bark off a sassafras tree and dug up some roots. Mighty clever for an Arkansawyer."

"I thought you were going to kill me."

Jesse nodded. "We probably were. We couldn't trust you."

"You still mad?"

"I was mad for a few days and worried you'd turn us in. When you didn't, I got over my mad. Ma, though, she thinks about you every day."

"I thought she didn't like me."

"She hates you, Henry, but she thinks about you every time she visits the outhouse. That dosing of sassafras gave her the piles."

"It's nice to be remembered."

"Oh, about the only folks she hates worse than you are the Pinkerton detectives. They bombed our place and blew her arm off, killed my stepbrother. It didn't endear the Yankees to me any."

Jesse steered me through the streets, finally leading me to a hilltop that overlooked the town and pointing to a modest white cottage with green shutters. "That's home."

I was jealous. His little cottage was more than I had.

Then he said something that startled me. "A nice house and a little family, Henry, and I can't enjoy them without thinking everybody I run into'd kill me if they knew who I was. The governor's put ten thousand dollars on my head."

I grunted.

"Henry, I should've listened to you after the war. Let it all end right after the Liberty holdup. With all the bonds plus the money we stole, I could've done nothing the rest of my life but tend my wife and children."

"That's why I got out, Jesse," I reminded him. "I

could see I was getting dragged into something I couldn't control."

Jesse laughed. "Like the Jesse James legend. I enjoyed it during the early years when I was full of piss and vinegar, but time has a way of draining you. I'm weary, Henry. I have to wear gloves in public to hide my left hand. I can't go anywhere, not even to bed with my wife, without a gun at hand. I can't hold regular work. I keep two horses stabled out back, one saddled all the time so I can run away if I have to. I worry what will happen to my family if folks find out who I am. I can't have an unguarded moment with my children, whom I can't call by name and who don't know my real name." He looked at me with an odd expression on his face. "You remember that prophecy when you stayed with us?"

I shook my head and shrugged. I didn't know what he was talking about. I didn't figure God had used me for much, and certainly not for prophecy.

"Remember when Ma found her pages turned and she read a scripture about Jesse having a son?"

The crazy incident came back to me, slowly at first.

"I've got a boy. Best-looking fellow you ever saw. And a girl, too. She takes after her ma."

We stepped up to a knee-high picket gate, which Jesse pushed open with his umbrella. We walked up to the house, and Jesse opened the door for me.

"Zee," he called, "I've brought company."

A boy about ten and a girl a couple years younger raced out of the kitchen, then stopped when they saw me.

"Kids, this is Mr. Lomax," Jesse announced.

They nodded but shyly stood back. Jesse's wife emerged from the kitchen, wiping her hand on an apron. For a moment I saw the surprise on her face at my poor attire, but she quickly hid it with a warm smile.

"Zee, this is Henry Lomax. He lived with us for a bit right after the war."

She smiled and offered me her hand. I shook it.

"You're welcome to share our noon meal," she said, "though I didn't prepare enough for visitors."

"A little's better than none," I replied.

Jesse motioned for me to sit down on the upholstered furniture in the parlor.

I declined. "Don't want to soil your chair."

Jesse shooed his son and daughter into the kitchen to help their mother, then looked at me. "You never took any of the money from our dealings with the Liberty bank. I figure I can spare you a few dollars to get a new set of clothes."

"I'd be obliged," I answered. "I'd like to look decent when I get back home. I ain't been home since I stayed with you."

"Damn shame, when a man can't get home."

"How's your brother?"

Jesse looked to see that the kids hadn't slipped back in the room. "There's not a minute's peace for him, but he's a survivor, too."

We visited a spell, and a little before noon Zee called us to the table, where she'd laid out a platter of fried ham, boiled greens, and baked potatoes. I took a seat in one of the wooden chairs and waited. Jesse and his family bowed their heads as he offered a prayer, speaking softly but sincerely. I didn't understand how a man with such a bloody streak in his body could speak so humbly in prayer.

"Amen," he said, and his wife and children repeated the word.

"You'd've made a good preacher," I said.

He grinned. "Not many people know that's what I wanted to do. It'd be nice to have a little house in the country and a little church to tend." He spoke so wistfully I felt sorry for him.

After we cleaned our plates, Zee removed them, then brought out a dish of hot cherry cobbler.

"It's an excellent meal," I said, attacking the cobbler. She nodded and smiled. Jesse seemed pleased as well.

"You never got married?" Jesse asked.

I shook my head. "Closest I came was LouAnne Burke, but bushwhackers were trying to kill me after the war, and I figured she'd get hurt if I took her with me. It always bothered me, running out on her."

Jesse looked at his wife. "A good woman can make up for a lot of other things in life."

Zee blushed.

I thought of LouAnne and wondered where she was and how she was doing. I wondered how different—and how much better—my life might've been if I had stayed in Arkansas or taken her along.

When we finished the cobbler, Jesse motioned for me to rise. I got up from the table, thanking Zee for her hospitality. She smiled. "My husband doesn't invite many people into his house, so it's a pleasure when he has someone over."

"I apologize for my attire," I said, "but I had a bit of bad luck getting into town."

"Clothes and looks aren't as important as what's in a man's heart," she said.

Jesse ducked back into the parlor, where he grabbed his hat and his umbrella with the carbine inside. "Let's take a walk back to town, get you some new clothes."

We walked to the town square, where Jesse led me to a haberdashery. I was fitted for a suit, which the tailor said would be ready the next day, then picked out another pair of pants, three shirts, socks, drawers, a belt, and shoes. After I changed into new clothes, Jesse took me to a mercantile—and the man who despised carpetbaggers actually bought me a carpetbag. Then he took me to a barbershop for a haircut and a shave and a hat store to buy me a derby. I looked better than I had in years.

"Why you doing this?"

"Not many folks I can trust. Those that I can I'll do a favor for. My house isn't big enough for you to spend the night, Henry, but I'll put you up in the hotel until your suit's ready."

"I'm obliged." It was hard for me to believe that the most wanted man in all of Missouri was walking down the street with me, offering to pay for a night's lodging.

He took me to the hotel and, just as he'd done at each stop, paid for my needs. In my room he counted out a hundred and fifty dollars and put it in my hand.

"That'll be enough for you to get home on and have a little money left to impress people with how well you've done. I know that means a lot to any man."

I thanked him again and again as he started for the door. He stopped, then turned around and shook my hand.

"You wouldn't be interested in getting in the banking business, now would you? Did you ever know Charlie and Bob Ford?"

"They must've been after my time."

Jesse nodded. "They're coming over tomorrow to talk a little business. You wouldn't be interested, would you?"

I couldn't help but grin and shake my head. "You said you wished you'd never gotten into the business, yet here you are planning another robbery."

"I'm in too deep now to get out. The governor's put a reward on my head, so I might just as well torment him until he's out of office."

"I'll pass on the opportunity."

Jesse grinned. "You made the right decision back in '66. And again today. It's a life you can't escape." With a sigh he turned and left me in my hotel room. I counted the bills in my hand and saw that he hadn't shorted me. After stuffing the money in my pocket, I collapsed on the bed and stared at the tin ceiling, thinking hard.

There was a ten-thousand-dollar reward on Jesse's head.

Jesse trusted me.

I had enough money in my pocket to buy a gun.

I could get close enough to Jesse to shoot him.

I could collect the money and return to Cane Hill a rich man.

Forever I would be known as the man who killed
Jesse James.

Then I would be a somebody.

Out in New Mexico Territory I had known Pat Garrett. He was a nobody before he killed Billy the Kid. After
the shooting he became the man who killed Billy the Kid.
Men offered to buy him drinks; men wanted to shake the
hand that killed Billy the Kid.

I broke out in a cold sweat, thinking for once I could
make a name for myself. And some money. Then I realized what a cowardly act it would be to kill a man who
had trusted me.

I pondered that a long time. Maybe if I'd been a
lawyer or a politician I could've gone through with it, but
my heart wasn't that black.

All night I spent restlessly shifting in my bed, trying
to put the idea out of my mind. Ten thousand dollars was
a lot of money. Yet only a fool would try to kill Jesse
James. I decided I wasn't a fool, and a hundred and fifty
dollars tucked in my pocket was more than I'd had in a
while. Too, if I killed Jesse, I'd likely have to meet the
governor to collect the money, and I didn't want to stain
my palm by shaking hands with him.

Come morning I was so nervous I needed a drink,
but I didn't allow myself a touch of liquor. I feared if I
did, this wild idea might get the best of me, and I might
try to kill Jesse. A lot of Yankees, lawmen, and Pinkerton
agents had tried to kill him over the years, and he had
managed to survive their every attempt.

I was shaking so when I got up, like I was about to
rob the Liberty bank again. I gathered my belongings in
my new bag, marched down the street to the clothes store,
and picked up my new suit without even trying it on.
After rolling it up and stuffing it into my carpetbag, I
headed toward the river to catch a steamboat to the Mississippi.

I was in luck; there was one leaving at eleven o'clock.
I bought passage and went up the ramp and boarded. If

I'd had a chain I'd've tied myself down so I wouldn't change my mind at the last minute and try to kill Jesse James. I kept thinking about his decent family and how it was more than I had and how it would be a shame to rob his wife of a husband and his kids of a father. Even so, ten thousand dollars was a lot of money.

When the steamboat finally pulled away from shore, I rested easier, although I felt as two-faced as a politician and as greedy as a lawyer.

It seemed like the boat couldn't get me away from St. Joseph fast enough. I felt like asking the captain for an oar so I could speed the thing up. I felt better when we lost sight of the town.

Late the next afternoon we reached St. Louis. I got off the boat and headed for the Frisco Railroad depot to catch the train to Fayetteville, but I'd missed the afternoon train and would have to wait until the next morning.

I took a room in a nearby hotel and had a decent dinner that night, spending my money on food rather than liquor because I still wanted to impress folks when I got back home. That night I slept better than I had in St. Joseph or on the steamboat. In fact, I overslept and missed the morning train to Arkansas, so I got a ticket for the afternoon train.

After dressing in my new suit and packing my other clothes, I emerged from the hotel onto the street, where paperboys were trying to outsell and outscream each other. I didn't pay them much mind as I angled for the train station, but one of them ran up and shoved a paper in my face.

"Notorious outlaw dead!" he screamed. "Jesse James killed in Saint Jo!"

I grabbed the paper and started reading.

"Hey!" yelled the paperboy.

I dug a coin from my pocket and paid him, then read the story as quickly as I could.

The morning after I'd left, Bob Ford and his brother Charlie, a former member of the James gang, had gone to visit Jesse. Bob had apparently shot him in the back of the head when he turned to dust off a picture on the wall. The Fords said they had killed Jesse for the ten-thousand-dollar reward the governor had put on his head.

I was stunned. I carried in my pocket the money Jesse had given me and wore the clothes he had bought me. His wife was a widow. His kids would have no father for the rest of their lives.

But after I boarded the train, I sat there staring out the window, a single thought running through my mind: Bob Ford was ten thousand dollars richer.

Chapter Thirty-three

Just as the train was about to pull away from the station, there was a commotion at the back of the passenger car. Some woman lit into the conductor, complaining about the aisle being too narrow, about tickets costing too much, about the wooden seats not being padded. When I glanced at her, I decided she didn't need cushioned seats—she carried enough padding on her own. She waddled down the aisle, telling her two girls to stay with her.

Her girls weren't little ones but full-grown women with a hard look about them. I studied the woman a while because there was too much of her to catch in a single glimpse. She must've weighed close to three hundred pounds, and that wasn't counting the jewelry: rings on every finger, several bracelets on each wrist, three or four necklaces, and earrings that could've doubled as barrel hoops. She rattled so much she sounded like a regiment of cavalry passing by. She must've bought rouge by the keg, because her cheeks were coated with it. Her eyelids were painted gray, her eyebrows black, her lips scarlet, and one of her front teeth was capped with gold.

The respectable women on the train lifted their noses in the air and turned away, one young mother even covering her daughter's eyes until the old sow waddled by. I'd been around enough by then to know a madam. Her charges—one black-haired, the other brown-topped—behind her were younger, prettier, and slimmer.

"Come along, girls," the madam kept repeating.

"Yes, ma'am," they kept answering.

The madam took note of me as she walked by. "He's wearing a new suit, girls. Men like that have money."

"Yes, Miss Amanda," replied the black-haired one.

I coughed and sputtered.

The madam turned and grinned. "I have this effect on men."

I felt like I was going to puke. I squinted and stared at her, trying to figure if the only Amanda I'd ever known was buried in this woman's folds of fat.

"Girls," she said, "men that squint like that usually need to wear spectacles. When you get one like that, take your money from his wallet yourself. He won't know how big a bill you're really taking."

Was this woman Amanda Fudge? If she was, the girl I'd once thought was the prettiest thing in Cane Hill had aged beyond her years. Try as I might, I couldn't find the Amanda I remembered under all that lard.

"He likes me, girls, that's why he's staring," she said, resuming her awkward journey to a pair of seats that faced each other. She plopped down in a seat facing me while her two girls sat opposite her, placing their carpetbags on their laps.

I figured the only way to know for sure if that was her was to ask her to skin a cat, but I doubted there was a tree within sight that would hold her. I shivered and picked up my paper, unfolding it and holding it up in front of my face.

The train lurched forward and began the trip southwest. Every time I lowered the paper I saw her squinting at me. Later I noticed she had put on a pair of spectacles and was still looking intently at me. I tugged my derby down, wishing it had a wider brim so I could hide more of my face.

When the conductor passed by, punching tickets, I leaned over and whispered, "Where's the fat lady going?"

To my chagrin he looked over his shoulder at Miss Amanda, then at me. "To Fayetteville. She runs a bawdy house there."

The conductor had no more than finished his sentence than the madam called across the car.

"Don't be bashful, fella. If you'd like to get to know Miss Amanda any better, all you have to do is ask her, you hear?"

I preferred to ignore her, but it was impossible. "There room in any other car?" I asked the conductor.

"Oh, yes," he answered, "but I wouldn't move if I was you. She always picks out one man to pester. Looks like you're the lucky one today. Last time her victim moved to another car, she followed him and humiliated him, screaming at him like she was his wife. I never seen a fellow turn as white as he did, with everybody snickering about what a poor choice he'd made in wives."

"She ride this train often?"

"Once or twice a month, whenever she needs new girls from St. Louis. You're better off just ignoring her."

"What's her name, by the way?"

"Amanda Fudge."

I slumped in my seat and shook my head, figuring it was best not to press my luck. If she figured out I was the man rumored to have killed her father, no telling what she might do. I was beginning to wish I'd stayed in St. Jo and taken my chances with the late Jesse James. I kept reading the paper until I was blurry-eyed. Then I tossed it aside, leaned against the window, and tried to take a nap, but nothing worked. I couldn't escape her hard glare.

The weather being warm and sticky, I unbuttoned my collar and loosened my tie.

"I can help you finish taking things off," Amanda
sneered.

My cheeks burned with embarrassment. The young
mother who'd shielded her daughter's eyes gathered the
child and her things and marched out of the car.

"May your girl one day work for me," Amanda called.

I pulled my derby lower over my eyes, hoping she
would ignore me, but that only made matters worse. I felt
the train begin to shake. I thought we'd hit a section of
old track, but when I peeked from beneath my hat I realized it was Amanda approaching. I'd hunted buffalo in
Texas a few years back, but I'd never been near so fierce-
looking an animal.

To my horror Amanda grabbed my derby by the
crown and lifted it from my head. "You look familiar."

"That's what I say every time I look in a mirror," I
replied.

Amanda failed to see anything funny about that and
just scrunched up her face. Her breaths came in short
huffs and smelled like snuff. "I'm Amanda Fudge. You
sure we haven't met somewhere before, maybe when I
was younger? I've filled out a bit since then."

More like she'd filled out a whole eight bits. "Never
seen you before in my life."

"Where you going?"

"The end of the line."

"Aren't we all. What's your name?"

"What's the difference?"

"The difference is, I can embarrass the hell out of
you if you don't tell me. Why, just the last time I rode
this train, I humiliated a fellow, making people think I
was his wife. I can do worse to you."

I took her at her word.

"Now, what's your name?"

"Thomas Howard," I replied, "from St. Joseph, Missouri."

She eyed me and I studied her, wondering how many
days it would take to scrape the rouge off her face to get

down to bare wood. Her gaze slipped from my face down to my belt and pants buttons.

"I figure if I saw your equipment, I'd know if we'd met before. There's not two that're just alike, did you know that?"

"Can't say that I did."

"Take my word for it. I've been through hundreds of them."

I had no doubt that she had.

"My memory ain't what it once was," she told me.

Neither was her face, bosom, or hips.

"But somehow, Mr. Howard, I can't shake the fact that I know you from somewhere. What do you say to that?"

Then I made a very unwise comment. "I'd have to say you lost your marbles."

She shook her head. "If I find out you've been lying to me, I'll cut your marbles off."

I had no doubt about that, either.

Amanda kept staring at me, finally shaking her head and shoving my derby back at me. "It'll come to me. I never forget a face."

It sounded like that wasn't all she never forgot. I took my derby. "Now, if you don't mind, I'd like to get a little sleep."

She smiled, giving me a look at her snuff-stained teeth. "If you ever need a cozy place to sleep in Fayetteville, then ask any fellow. He can tell you where Amanda's is."

"I don't sleep that much."

Amanda laughed. "That's what all men say in public, but get them between sheets and it's a different matter."

I shrugged and plopped my derby back over my forehead, hoping she'd go away. I was also trying to forget the times we'd spent together as kids: the time we knocked Pooty off the horse into Jordan Creek, the other pranks I'd played on him, how she'd played me off against him. I missed Pooty more on that train ride than

I had in years. I hated Amanda for what her pa had done to him, and I felt proud I'd had a hand in the man's death.

That was the longest train ride I ever remember taking. Seems like we stopped at every two-bit town in Missouri, day or night, before we reached Fayetteville. It was the first time I'd been in the state since I ran away from the bushwhackers. I wondered if any of them still carried a grudge. Even Jesse James himself no longer did.

It was about four o'clock in the afternoon when the train reached the outskirts of Fayetteville. I was less than twenty miles from home and nervous about seeing Momma and what she'd think after all these years.

As the train pulled into the station, I grabbed my carpetbag and scurried off, trying to hide before Amanda Fudge waded out. The conductor grinned as I stepped onto the platform. "You survived." He pointed to a waiting buggy. "That's Miss Amanda's."

I walked over to the depot and stepped inside, staying out of sight until I saw Amanda and her two new girls pass. I stood at the door peeking out as the girls climbed aboard. Amanda hoisted up her skirt, shook her ample buttocks, and slowly hauled herself into the seat. It was like watching a newborn calf trying to crawl back inside its momma.

The conductor was watching and shaking his head.

"You got a bucket of grease there," I called as I stepped back out onto the platform.

The conductor strolled over and joined me. "I've seen tubs of lard that looked better from behind. I hear she was right cute as a girl, but took up with the wrong type."

I thought about her father. "She was born into the wrong type. Her pa was Beryl Fudge."

"The bushwhacker?"

I nodded. "As mean a man as ever rode in Washington County."

"That's what I heard."

Amanda finally seated herself, and the coach settled heavily on its springs. As the driver picked up the reins, I heard a loud scream and saw her twist around in the seat and point at me.

I gulped.

"Lost my marbles?" she shrieked. "You son of a bitch, you're Henry Lomax!"

The driver shook the reins, and the buggy lurched forward. "Stop!" she yelled at the driver. When he hesitated, she slapped him. He fell out of the buggy and spooked the horse, and the buggy charged down the street, Amanda yelling at me all the while. "If I ever see you again, I'll cut your marbles off and stuff them down your throat, Henry Lomax!"

I prepared to run, but the conductor grabbed my arm. "You're Henry Lomax?"

I nodded I was.

"Let me shake your hand." Before I could decline, he took my hand and pumped it vigorously. "You're the one that killed Beryl Fudge, beat him to a bloody pulp. Well, I'll be damned. You're more famous around these parts than if you'd killed Jesse James."

I grimaced at the thought of word getting around I was in Washington County. "Don't mention it to anyone, will you?"

"Thing like that's hard to keep a secret."

I doubled my fist and lifted it to my chest. "This fist beat Beryl Fudge to death."

The conductor paled. "I can keep a secret."

As I reached to pat him on the shoulder, he flinched. "Anything I can do for you?" he asked.

"A horse and saddle to get around Fayetteville."

"My brother lives here. I bet he'd loan you one, just to get to meet you."

I shook my head. "I'll meet him when I return the horse, not before."

The conductor was trembling slightly. "It'll just be a loan, right?"

"Two weeks at the most."

"Give me a few minutes," the conductor said, then scurried away.

I feared he might return with the law, but about fifteen minutes later he rode up on a horse. He pointed to a house down the street.

"That's where my brother lives. Just return the horse when you're done."

"Obliged," I said, tipping my derby as he dismounted. He held the reins while I tied the carpetbag to the saddle and climbed atop the gray.

I skirted the edge of Fayetteville, then hit the road to Prairie Grove on the southwest side of town. The ride brought back memories of childhood, many good and just as many bad. I reached the old battlefield, looked for the Higdon house, and found it deserted. Checking around back, I was disappointed to find the stones for my two brothers gone.

That saddened me. I rode on, feeling a lump in my throat. It had been twenty years since I had seen John and Van. Sometimes it seemed an eternity ago, other times just a moment. I remembered them both fondly and wished I had had more time with them. I turned down the road to Cane Hill, passing the place where the Kansans had tried to hang me and Beryl Fudge had killed Pooty.

Damn, it was hard riding back. I knew why I hadn't returned until now. There were too many memories to live down. I wished I'd returned before Pa died, and then I wished I'd never returned at all. There was something here I couldn't reclaim, but I didn't know what it was. The last time I'd ridden this road I was running for my life and leaving LouAnne behind. I bit my lip to keep from crying.

I found Cane Hill had been rebuilt, though it didn't look as prosperous as it had before the war. The college up on the hill remained the biggest building in town. The railroad—and progress, it seemed—had passed Cane Hill by.

At the wagon crossing I reined up the gray and sat for a moment, wondering if I really wanted to ride up the embankment and see the place. Momma could've died since I'd last heard from home; the place might not even belong to the Lomaxes anymore. But I'd come too far not to go on.

I shook the reins and started the gray through the water, then up the embankment. When I topped it, I was surprised at what I saw. The old barn was gone, but a newer, bigger one stood in its place. The fields of freshly turned soil were bigger and the woods smaller than when I left, and between the house and the river was a new stone pen, maybe twenty feet square. I couldn't figure out what it was for. Somebody had put in a lot of work in the years I was gone. I was just glad it wasn't me.

The house was still there, but it had grown and was now sheathed with whitewashed clapboards. The dogtrot had been enclosed, and a new, wider porch had been added to the front. Smoke was coming out of a stovepipe where the kitchen used to be, and I made out someone in a rocking chair on the porch.

As I neared the house, the figure rose. It was a man that I hoped would be one of my brothers, but as I got closer I realized I'd never seen him before. He seemed to be a few years younger than me and had a pleasant smile around the pipe clenched in his teeth.

"Evening," he offered, taking the pipe from his mouth.

"Is this the Lomax place?" I asked, doffing my hat.

"It is."

"Then who the hell are you?" I asked.

His smile disappearing, the man pointed the stem of his pipe at me. But before he could speak, the front door opened, and a woman poked her head out.

"Supper's ready," she said, then stopped to look at me.

It was Momma. She was an old woman now, frail and stooped, her hair gray.

"I'm sorry," she started, "I didn't know we had a visitor." Her words trailed off, and her feeble hand flew to her mouth. "Henry," she cried, "you've come home!"

As I climbed down off my gray, she shuffled out the door and across the porch, her arms outspread. I dropped the reins and caught her in my arms. She seemed so fragile I was afraid she might break if I hugged her too hard.

Momma cried and sobbed as I tried to calm her. Behind her I saw the door open and another woman come out. She began to cry, too, and I realized little Harriet was no longer little.

"Thank, God, Henry, you've finally come home. You don't know how Momma's prayed for this day."

She came and gave me a little hug while I held Momma, then went over and slipped her arm through the arm of the pipe-smoking stranger. I realized he must be her husband.

After Momma calmed down, Harriet introduced me to her husband, Jason Scott, but I could tell he wouldn't be giving me many more smiles. Momma ran her fingers through her hair and complained she hadn't known to pretty up and to fix extra for supper. Harriet opened the door and herded us all in, and Momma scurried to the table, setting another plate and fussing over me in spite of my protests. Harriet's husband whispered something to her, and she gave me a glare that told me she was not pleased with my greeting to her husband.

That didn't matter, though. I'd come to see Momma, not anyone else. After we sat down at the table, Momma said a long grace, thanking God several times for seeing me home safely. We ate and talked about relatives. Thomas and DeeAnne were still farming the old Fudge place and did most of the work on the Burke place. They had six children, all girls, so Thomas did most of the hard work alone, excepting those occasions when Gordon Burke was up to helping. SincereAnne had had a bout of apoplexy and was bedbound. Gordon was hobbled by a fall from a horse and the burden of caring for his paralyzed wife. RuthAnne, who had married one of the Yankee soldiers she had tended after the battle of Cane Hill, sent money each month to help. Her husband was a banker in St. Louis.

Momma doted on Harriet and especially her husband like she once had on me. He kept the farm working and food on her plate. Momma said it'd been two years since she'd seen Lissa, who was touring the West with an acting troupe, but Lissa was faithful in writing every month. Jim and Andy were both in Texas. Jim had taken up ranching and owned a small spread of his own, while Andy had joined the Texas Rangers. Momma mentioned just about everyone except the one person I really cared about.

"What happened to LouAnne?"

Harriet turned to me and scowled. "Why do you care? You never even wrote her."

I didn't have an answer.

"She finally got married," Momma said sadly.

"After five years, Henry, five years of waiting to hear from you, she married."

I felt lower than a snake's belly. I wondered again whether I should've returned or not, but Momma's tears washed away my doubts.

We talked late and arose early. Momma took me out to the stone enclosure where Pa was buried and Van had been reburied. The stones for both Van and John had been moved from Prairie Grove. Then Momma and I rode in the wagon over to the Burke place so I could pay my respects to SincereAnne, who didn't understand who I was. Odd though it was, the apoplexy had straightened her crossed eyes.

I went to visit Pooty's grave. As I lingered, Gordon Burke came over and patted me on the shoulder.

"Thank you for killing Beryl Fudge. Folks around here still talk about what a brave deed that was."

I nodded. I had envied Pat Garrett's reputation, never knowing I had one of my own closer to home. "Thanks," I said, not certain whether I meant it or not.

From there we went to Thomas's place. DeeAnne came out to greet me and seemed happy to see me. Thomas helped Momma out of the wagon, then ran around and hugged me. His grip was strong from hard work. "Glad you're home, Henry. There's work enough for you if you care to stay."

I shook my head. "I'm here only a week. Then I've got to go."

"Where?" DeeAnne wanted to know.

I shrugged. "Wherever the notion strikes me."

DeeAnne brought out my six nieces, all cute as a litter of puppies, though JoAnne, who'd been an infant when I left home, was sixteen. I looked at DeeAnne and found myself wondering why I'd ever found her ugly. She had a strong, steadfast dignity about her that was a beauty all its own.

Before we returned home that evening, DeeAnne made me promise I wouldn't leave before Saturday so we could get together Friday night for a dinner at Momma's. I promised.

I spent the next six days mostly with Momma. Though neither of us admitted it, we both understood this would be our last time together. She told me she'd always known I'd be a vagabond, but she didn't hold it against me like Harriet did.

The night before the dinner she had me help her up into the loft and led me to the spot where I'd kept my mattress. In a corner by the chimney, she picked up an old bull scrotum with a leather thong around it. She smiled and handed it to me. "It's your marbles."

I didn't understand why she'd kept them. "You should've given them away."

"They were yours," she said, "and I liked to come up here and find them. They reminded me of you."

"Keep them for Thomas's children."

"They're all girls. The marbles belong to you."

"Some of them were Pooty's."

"They're all yours now. You can play with them."

I realized her mind wasn't all there, so I took the sack from her trembling hand. She cried and hugged me.

The next night, my last at home, Thomas brought DeeAnne and his girls over. Momma and Harriet had cooked all day. It was a fine meal of baked ham, scalloped potatoes, boiled onions, fresh-baked bread, cherry and apple cobbler, and cookies that Thomas's daughters had baked.

When the meal was finished, us men went out on the porch while the women did the dishes. We visited a little bit, but Harriet's husband wasn't real friendly with me, and I could tell Thomas was tired from plowing.

After the dishes were done, DeeAnne came out, all smiles, and grabbed my arm. "Come on, Henry, let's go for a walk."

I looked at Thomas, who shrugged, so I accompanied her to the creek.

"We're glad you came home, Henry, and we'd love for you to stay. You could make a decent living here, though there's hard work involved. Lord knows Thomas could use the help, what with us having no boys."

"Nothing against any of you, DeeAnne, but it's just not in my constitution to farm."

"That's what your momma said, so I'm not surprised, but I want to ask you to do one thing for me before you leave." She began to cry.

I felt helpless. "What is it?"

"See LouAnne before you go, please. She knows you're here and wants to talk with you."

"She could've come out here."

DeeAnne shook her head. "She didn't think you wanted to see her."

"That's not it, DeeAnne. Now that she's married and such, I just don't know what to say."

DeeAnne stepped to me and kissed me on the cheek. " 'I'm sorry' would be a start."

Chapter Thirty-four

Before I left home the next morning, I bathed and shaved, then put on my good clothes and accompanied Momma out to the burial plot to pay my final respects to Pa, Van, and John. Momma cried all the way.

"Pa had a long life. I just wish your brothers could've lived, married, and had children. Maybe they'd've stayed around here and helped," she said as we stood outside the stone wall. "I don't know what I would've done without Harriet's husband. He's a fine man, he's just not a son."

I hugged Momma, trying to shut off her tears, but I couldn't.

Harriet's husband came out of the barn leading my borrowed gray, and Harriet carried my carpetbag out of the house. They joined us at the stone wall. I took the carpetbag from Harriet, who gave me a halfhearted hug.

"You shouldn't have waited so long to see your momma," she said.

I nodded and turned to my horse, tying the carpetbag behind the saddle. I shook Harriet's husband's hand and thanked him.

"Who the hell are you?" he asked, with only a hint of a smile.

"Just someone who once lived here." I turned

around and took a final look at the place. "It's sure changed."

"Everything's changed, Henry, but you," Harriet said.

Nodding, I stepped to Momma, hugged her a final time, and kissed her on the cheek.

"You got your marbles, didn't you?"

I patted my pants pocket. "Right here."

She smiled, stroked my cheek a couple times, then let me go.

Harriet cleared her throat. "You can find LouAnne at Johnson Mercantile, just off the square in Fayetteville."

I nodded. She'd already told me a dozen times where to find LouAnne. I mounted the gray and headed toward the creek, waving good-bye without turning around.

I had to return the horse to Fayetteville. After that I didn't know where I'd go except that I'd leave Washington County.

As I rode though Cane Hill, I tried not to look at the town or the people, but it was Saturday morning and the street was active. A couple men pointed at me, and I heard one of them identify me as the man who had killed Beryl Fudge. I nudged the gray's flank with my heel and sent him to trotting away from the town.

Shortly after noon I reached Fayetteville and re-turned the horse to the house the conductor had pointed out to me. A man I took to be in his sixties came out and stared at me as I dismounted and tied the gray to a hitch-ing post. He eyed me hard as he ambled my direction. "You Henry Lomax?"

I nodded.

"I pictured a meaner, older man as the one who killed Beryl Fudge." He extended his hand, and I took it. "I always wanted to shake the hand that killed Beryl Fudge. He killed an uncle of mine, Beryl Fudge did."

"Obliged for the use of the horse," I said. "Do I owe you anything?"

He shook his head. "You paid me and a lot of Washington County years ago when you beat that bushwhacker to death."

"Thanks," I said as I untied my carpetbag from behind the saddle. "I best be going on." I walked away, but when I turned the corner I glanced back and saw the old man still staring at me, a look of awe upon his face.

I passed the train depot, then started toward the square, trying to screw up the courage to go to Johnson Mercantile. More than anyone else I wanted to see LouAnne, but I was scared I wouldn't know what to say. I walked by a saloon and was tempted to go in and calm my nerves, but I feared I'd wind up drunk before I eased my worries.

When I saw Johnson Mercantile, I had to admit I was impressed. It was a tall redbrick building with a pyramid of canned foods in one window and leather goods in the other. Judging by the horses and buggies tied outside, the store seemed to be doing a good business. When I walked in, the store was crowded with folks tending to their Saturday business.

I wandered among the tables piled with goods, dodging the young kids who were darting back and forth chasing each other. Nobody paid me any mind except a female clerk my age or a little older who motioned for another clerk to finish up.

The woman patted her hair, which was tied in a bun, straightened her apron down her front, and walked toward me, smiling slightly. She was a pretty woman in a wholesome sort of way.

"Can I help you?" she asked.

I nodded. "I'm looking for LouAnne Burke."

"No one here by that name," she replied.

I sighed and bit my lip. "I guess somebody told me wrong."

She stared at me a moment, laughed, then drew back her hand and slapped me across the cheek. No female had slapped me like that since I was a kid.

"LouAnne?" I cried.

She nodded, her eyes filling with tears. "It's Lou-Anne Johnson now."

I grabbed her and hugged her, laughing like I was crazy. The store suddenly quieted as everybody stared. A couple aproned boys no more than twelve years old walked up and eyed me suspiciously.

LouAnne kissed me on the cheek, then broke free. "Listen, everyone," she said, "this is Henry Lomax. We grew up together." When she announced that, a man I took for the storekeeper came across the room, wiping his hands on his apron. He was tall and had a good, decent look about him as well.

"Henry," said LouAnne, taking the storekeeper by the arm, "I'd like you to meet my husband, Phillip Johnson."

Then she motioned to the two aproned boys, who moved shyly toward me, the younger one hiding behind the other. "These are my boys, Henry." She pointed to the older one. "That's Joe Don, but we call him Jodie."

He was the spitting image of Pooty. Grinning, I extended my hand. "Pleased to meet you." He shook it shyly, and I glanced up at his momma. "He looks just like Pooty."

Her lips turned downward, and a tear fell down her cheek. "I know. Sometimes I forget and call him Pooty."

"And who's his brother?" I asked, turning to the little boy.

LouAnne's voice broke when she introduced, "Henry Harrison Johnson."

I felt a lump in my throat and saw Phil Johnson step to his wife and pat her on the shoulder. I extended my free hand to little Henry, but he cowered behind his brother.

"You won't kill me, will you?"

"Henry," scolded his father, "that's not a question to ask someone."

"He killed Beryl Fudge for killing Uncle Joe Don."

"That was a long time ago, son."

Little Henry offered me his hand, and I shook it.

"Okay, boys, get back to work and help folks," Johnson said, his voice soothing.

"Just a minute," I said, standing up and shoving my hand in my pocket. "I've got a sack of marbles for you two. Your uncle Joe Don and I played with them as kids." I extracted the pouch of marbles and handed them to little Henry. "Now share them with your brother."

Johnson smiled at his sons. "What do you say?"

"Thank you," they said in unison.

Then Johnson turned to his wife. "Why don't you take a walk with Henry? I'm sure you've much to talk about."

I stood up, and the two boys walked away, little Henry glancing back over his shoulder at me.

LouAnne untied her apron, tossed it behind a counter, and snatched her bonnet from a nearby peg. After tying the bonnet, she grabbed my arm and steered me toward the door. I was glad to be out from under the gaze of all the customers. I peeked at LouAnne and thought I saw more tears, but the brim of the bonnet kept me from getting a good look. If they were indeed tears, I didn't know if they were tears of joy or sorrow.

"Your husband seems a decent sort."

The bonnet bobbed with agreement. "He's a good, dependable man. Works hard, loves our boys."

"I'm surprised he let you leave with me."

"He knows what you've meant to me all these years."

I didn't know what to say, but I recalled what DeeAnne had suggested the night before. "I'm sorry, LouAnne. Sorry I left you, sorry I never wrote back, but I feared you might get hurt if you went with me, and I didn't want that. I'm still known around here as the man who killed Beryl Fudge. Folks just don't forget some things."

LouAnne took my arm in hers. "My mind always told me it would never work with you, but my heart always wanted to try. I waited five years."

I was flattered that any woman thought that highly of me.

"And then Phil finally persuaded me to marry him."

"I think it turned out fine, LouAnne. You got a fine husband, two cute boys, and what looks like a fine business."

She nodded. "But something's been bothering me all these years, something I've never told anyone."

I didn't know what it could be.

"I always felt responsible for Pooty's death."

Shaking my head, I patted her arm. "No, you couldn't've been. It was one of those things."

She bit her lip. "But I am, Henry, and that, not just your leaving, has weighed on me all these years."

"I don't understand."

"You had hidden a sack of gold in the limestone ledge over Jordan Creek."

Stopping in my tracks, I turned around, grabbing both her arms and staring at her tear-streaked face.

"I took it," she said, "and hid it. If it had been there when the Kansans came, they'd've left and Pooty'd still be alive."

All these years I'd blamed myself for Pooty's death, and she was blaming herself.

"I wasn't stealing the gold, Henry. I was keeping it for us, when you wrote me or returned home. I waited five years and never touched the gold, not a coin of it."

I could only shake my head. All the years I'd spent roaming the West, trying to make a fortune, and LouAnne had been holding one for me, waiting for my return.

"What happened to the gold?"

"Phil and I used it to buy and stock the store."

I hugged her. "Good. I'd probably just've squandered it. Don't blame yourself for Pooty. What's to say he might not've been killed another way? Those of us that survived can't change a thing about what happened."

LouAnne looked up, then stood on her tiptoes and kissed me.

"I'm glad you came by, Henry. This's been a heavy burden to carry in my heart all these years about Pooty, and I feared you'd blame me for stealing the money."

"I stole it, too, LouAnne. Only difference is, you put it to more decent work than I would have."

She smiled, then kissed me again. "Thank you, Henry. I always loved you and always will, like I loved Pooty."

"Then why were you always slapping me?"

"To get you to look at me. You were always looking west."

"Phillip's better for you than I would've been."

"True, but not as much fun. My heart's always wanted you."

I smiled. "No one's ever said anything nicer to me."

She patted my hand. "I guess you best escort me back to the store before people start talking."

"We wouldn't want that."

Arm in arm we walked to the mercantile. I wondered if I could've been a decent husband for her and decided probably not. It was best that it had turned out this way, though my heart was heavy that it had. I let go of her outside the mercantile.

"Take care of yourself, Henry, and please visit if you ever come back."

"Sure, LouAnne, and take care of those two boys. Nobody's ever done anything as nice for me as naming a son after me."

She nodded and stepped inside. I lingered a moment until she disappeared in the shadows and the whistle of an arriving train snapped me out of the past into the present.

I shifted the carpetbag in my hands and started back up the street, my step as heavy as my heart. Maybe I'd've been a better person had I stayed in Washington County and married LouAnne. The more I thought about it, the more depressed I got. When I passed the saloon, I decided to go in for a drink or two.

I pushed open the door and stepped inside, my eyes taking a moment to adjust to the dimness. The saloon was crowded, and I had managed no more than two steps before I heard my name being called.

"Henry Lomax, you son of a bitch," came the shrill voice, "I'm gonna cut your marbles off!"

I looked across the room and recognized Amanda Fudge charging through the patrons, scattering them, tables, and chairs left and right. She rumbled across the room like a herd of stampeding buffalo.

After a moment's consideration I decided I wasn't nearly as depressed or thirsty as I had thought. Any ideas I had about lingering fell away when I saw the knife in her hand. I had the carpetbag to use as a shield, but her momentum would've run me over. I spun around and darted back out the door, racing down the walk.

Screaming profanities at me, Amanda burst out of the saloon. But I quickly outdistanced her. I got enough of a lead I figured I was safe, but then she stepped into the street, grabbed the reins of a passing buggy, and tossed the driver out. As she crawled into the wagon, the springs went flat beneath her tremendous weight. She put the knife between her teeth and shook the reins, prompting the terrified horse in my direction.

I turned the corner and ran.

"Come back, you son of a bitch!" she mumbled.

Behind me I heard the galloping horse and the screams and shouts of the people we passed. Glancing over my shoulder, I saw the buggy swaying back and forth.

She was gaining.

I turned another corner and had gone no more than fifty feet when I tripped and my carpetbag flew ahead of me down the street. I rolled over in terror and saw her start into the turn, ready to trample me. But as the wagon slid into the corner, one side lifted off the ground, and the buggy slid along on only two wheels. It teetered, hit a bump, and toppled over, dragging the horse down not fifteen feet from me and sending Amanda Fudge rolling down the street. I hadn't seen that much fat move since a pig race at the fair when I was a kid.

Scrambling to my feet, I grabbed my carpetbag and raced toward the train depot, hoping to catch the train out of town before Amanda quit rolling down the street.

I bounded up the depot steps.

The conductor cried, "All aboard!"

I shoved my way up to the ticket counter and pushed a couple bills to the agent.

"Give me a ticket."

"Where to?" asked the agent.

"As far from here as I can get on the train outside."

The agent counted the money and issued me a ticket. "Have a good trip."

I grabbed the ticket, bolted out the door, and hopped on the train just as it started to move. I didn't know where I was going, but that was nothing new for me.

ABOUT THE AUTHOR

A native West Texan, PRESTON LEWIS is the author of many western novels as well as numerous nonfiction articles on western history. In 1993 Lewis won a Spur Award from the Western Writers of America for his story, *Bluster's Last Stand*. The author currently resides with his family in Lubbock, Texas.